Altering his expr _____ _____ pose, Alistair caught Cassandra's e_____ lowered his voice to a sultry drawl. "Miss Russell, I implore you. Help me. Help Neville. If you have a heart, come with me to Curzon Street, please."

Her eyes flickered, her lashes fluttered. She bit her lower lip and fumbled in her reticule for a skeleton key. "You can explain his problem to me over coffee." She tried to move past him, but Alistair tightened his grip on her arm and held her in the open doorway for just a moment.

"Neville needs you," he whispered at her neck.

Cassandra's eyes filled with water. She faltered. "Coffee, first."

"You are so very kind," the viscount said.

Cassandra's brow furrowed as she wrenched her arm free and swept past Alistair. He followed and waited on the sidewalk while she hovered at the threshold of her tiny shop. She flipped the signboard in the window which announced Russell's Emporium was closed, then briskly turned her key in the lock and tucked it in her reticule. "I am ready."

"Thank you for agreeing to hear me out."

"You are welcome, Lord Catledge," she said, uncertainty in her voice. "At least I think you are welcome. Truth be known, I haven't quite made up my mind about you."

Alistair smiled. Who would have thought mummy-hunting could be such fun?

WILLIAM W. JOHNSTONE
THE BLOOD BOND SERIES

BLOOD BOND   (0-8217-2724-0, $3.95/$4.95)

BLOOD BOND: BROTHERHOOD OF THE GUN (#2)
                              (0-8217-3044-4, $3.95/$4.95)

BLOOD BOND: SAN ANGELO SHOWDOWN (#7)
                              (0-8217-4466-6, $3.99/$4.99)

Available wherever paperbacks are sold, or order direct from the Publisher. Send cover price plus 50¢ per copy for mailing and handling to Penguin USA, P.O. Box 999, c/o Dept. 17109, Bergenfield, NJ 07621. Residents of New York and Tennessee must include sales tax. DO NOT SEND CASH.

THE LADY'S MUMMY

Bess Willingham

Zebra Books
Kensington Publishing Corp.

http://www.zebrabooks.com

ZEBRA BOOKS are published by

Kensington Publishing Corp.
850 Third Avenue
New York, NY 10022

Zebra and the Z logo Reg. U.S. Pat. & TM Off.

First Printing: January, 1997
10 9 8 7 6 5 4 3 2 1

Printed in the United States of America

To my incorrigible and very romantic husband, Frank.

Chapter One

London, 1820

Cassandra sat on the edge of her bed, lacing up her sturdy black half-boots. A teakettle whistled from the rear of the apartment, signaling breakfast and startling her onto her feet. The stiff skirts of her black mourning gown rustled as she crossed to the opposite side of her bedchamber. Stepping behind a japanned screen, she stood with arms akimbo and gazed affectionately at an elaborately decorated Egyptian coffin that rested supine on wooden saw-horses.

"Good morning!" Cassandra called. "Time for breakfast, Tia. Come on, sleepyhead, get out from under there."

She bent forward at her waist and peered beneath the coffin at a nest of old quilts and rags that lay upon the floor. A brisk rapping of her knuckles on the gilded wood of the mummy case caused the entangled blankets to wriggle and writhe. At length, a monkey's head emerged amid the tattered scraps of patchwork. Blinking its nut-brown eyes, the animal threw off its covers and extended its hand to Cassandra's. She lifted the monkey into her arms, surprised as always at the strength in the tiny fingers that gripped her shoulders.

Miss Cassandra Russell was well aware how odd it appeared for a young, unmarried woman to share an apartment with a monkey who slept beneath a mummy's coffin, but she cared not a whit. Her mother's death had left her lonely and depressed. She felt more cut off from the outside world than ever before, so why shouldn't she indulge her eccentricities?

After all, Tia was her only friend. Unless Cassandra included her fellow members of London's Society of Egyptologists—but they were only acquaintances, not real friends.

Then, of course, there was Audrey, her maid.

And Cleo, her mummy.

Audrey's voice came from the small parlor in the front of the apartment. "Yer breakfast is waitin', ma'am, and I've done set a plate of fruit and nuts for Tia as well." Then, under her breath, Audrey muttered, "Bless me, 'ave I sunk so low as to 'ave to set a place fer a monkey at the table?"

Stepping from behind the screen that hid Cleo's coffin from plain view, Cassandra answered her grouchy young maid. "I heard that, Audrey. And might I remind you that Tia is not your mistress; I am. You may not approve of the way I run my household, but I'll thank you to keep your opinions to yourself. If that is not satisfactory, then I shall be forced to let you go," she threatened idly.

With Tia on her hip, Cassandra entered the front parlor and seated herself at the round table where she dined, studied, and often painted imagined scenes of ancient Egypt in vivid watercolors. The gray Spry monkey, a gift to Cassandra from an aging archeologist, scrambled from her lap and sat in the chair opposite her. Tia politely bared her teeth, flapped her hands, and made enthusiastic squeaking noises when Audrey shuffled forth with a pot of hot tea.

"I ain't servin' tea to no monkey," Audrey said. "That is where I draw the line."

"I am quite aware of your limitations in that regard," replied Cassandra, smiling. Audrey was vociferous in her opinion that a monkey was not a proper pet. But recently the young maid had begun to lay out food for the animal, launder its printed neckerchiefs, and sing to it when she thought no one was listening. Cassandra was certain that Audrey adored Tia—deep down.

"That plate of almonds, prunes, and dried apples looks just fine for Tia's breakfast," Cassandra commended her dour servant.

Audrey poured her employer a cup of tea, then gestured toward the platter of hot rolls, toast, and marmalade she'd earlier set on the table. "T'aint much of a breakfast, ma'am, but I warmed them rolls over the fire. They's some sausages in the pantry—"

"No sausages, Audrey." Cassandra patted the high waistline of her black bombazine gown. "I believe I have gained half a stone in the year you have worked for me."

Audrey stood beside the table, her head tilted sideways, her hands on her hips. "Has it been a year, miss?"

"To the day, Audrey."

"Well, then. If you don't mind me saying so . . ."

Cassandra replaced her teacup and reached for a buttered roll. "Speak your mind. You've never been one to hold your tongue before. Are you unhappy in my service?"

Audrey screwed up her face. "Oh, no, ma'am. That ain't it."

"You haven't gotten yourself into . . . trouble, have you?"

"Oh, no!" the maid cried, shaking her head. "No, ma'am!"

Cassandra breathed a sigh of relief. "Well, then, I can only guess what is making you unhappy. I suppose it is this crowded apartment. There isn't much I can do to remedy that situation. I live above my shop because it is convenient, and my quarters are crowded because my collection of antiquities requires so much space." She shrugged, and tore off a bit of her roll. "I suppose I could spare an extra two shillings each month, if that would entice you to stay on with me."

Audrey's tight expression eased, and she wiped her hands on the front of her apron. "That's monstrous kind of ye, ma'am. I don't know what I'd have done after me Tom died if it wasn't fer you."

"I understand," replied Cassandra. "Consider it done, then. Is that all, Audrey?"

"No, ma'am. I mean—" Audrey's face colored, and she stumbled over her words. "What I mean, is. Well, Miss Cassandra, it's been one year since I came to work fer ye. And 'twas one year ago that your dear mother died, God rest her soul."

The hard lump that instantly formed in Cassandra's throat made it difficult for her to swallow. As if sensing her discomfort, Tia quickly appeared in her lap and stared up at her with dark, quizzical eyes. Cassandra sipped her tea and listened stoically while Audrey stammered out her faltering speech.

"It's just that you've been in mourning for a year now. And I was thinking . . ." Audrey twisted the skirt of her apron in her hands and fidgeted in her scuffed, thin-soled boots. "Well, ma'am, I was thinking that one of your lighter-colored gowns might be just the thing to brighten up your spirits. That nice gray frock with the peach-colored satin plaiting at the hem would do for half-mourning, miss. And then we might obtain a reputable mantua-maker to sew up some more fashionable gowns that would show off that lovely figure of yours. What do you say, Miss Cassandra? Oh, please, ma'am, say you'll do it! You're too young to mope about like this!"

Cassandra cleared her throat, pressed her serviette to her lips, then spoke in carefully modulated tones. "I appreciate your concern, Audrey, but I do not wish to end my mourning. Pray, do not speak of it again."

"But, ma'am—"

"That is enough, Audrey!"

Rebuked, the young woman lowered her head, and in a near-whisper replied, "Yes, ma'am." She turned and started toward the pantry, but after a few paces, abruptly pivoted. "Dear me, I almost forgot. I found this over there on the floor this morning, Miss Cassandra. Someone must have slipped it beneath the door last night." From her apron pocket Audrey withdrew a cream-colored envelope sealed with an impressive wax insignia. Returning to the breakfast table, she handed it to Cassandra, then removed Tia's empty plate and started toward the pantry.

"Judging from the seal and paper, the note appears to be from the Society of Egyptologists, Tia." Cassandra took the proffered envelope and unceremoniously ripped it open. Her unstifled cry of surprise stopped Audrey dead in her tracks.

"What is it, ma'am?" the maid gasped, whirling around.

Cassandra's heart thumped wildly against her ribs, and her limbs felt clammy beneath her skirts. Tia moved restlessly in her lap, grabbing at the missive as Cassandra snatched it from her reach.

"Giovanni Belzoni, Audrey! Only the greatest archeologist and Egyptologist in the world. Perhaps you knew him as the Patagonian Samson from his days at Sadler's Wells. But for the past five years he's been in Egypt, reportedly exploring the tombs near Thebes."

"Oh, Lord. He's dead, is he?" Audrey responded, her chinless face smeared in an expression of deep commiseration.

"No, dear, he is not dead. On the contrary," replied Cassandra, recovering from her shock. She pulled Tia upon her shoulders and turned a beaming smile on her confused servant. "He is coming to London! Here, Audrey! The great Belzoni is coming here—to our very own city!"

With Tia's arms entwined around her neck, she jumped to her feet and waved the thick sheet of vellum writing paper in the air. "Oh, he's bound to have brought back all sorts of treasures, mummies as well as ancient statuary and relics. Why, of all the people in the world, Giovanni Belzoni is the one person I'd like most to meet. And now he is going to attend a special meeting of the society," Cassandra whispered in awe, clutching both Tia and the sacred letter to her heart. "Oh, at last!" she cried, tears flooding her eyes. "I shall meet my hero at last!"

Under her breath, Audrey said, "Now, why ain't I surprised to learn my mistress's hero is an Italian circus performer turned grave-robber?" Turning toward the pantry, she said over her shoulder, "'Tis wonderful to see you happy, ma'am. Leastways, you might consider gettin' some new dresses made up to meet this bone-diggin' swell."

"New dresses?" Cassandra repeated, her pulse still racing. "Oh, yes. That is a capital idea, Audrey. Send for Madame Racine at once, will you?" Then, planting a kiss on Tia's head, she whispered breathlessly, "Oh, Tia. For the first time in a year, I'm happy. Truly happy! Surely, Signor Belzoni is the only person in the world who can tell me how to escape the pharaoh's curse. Then he will help me find a proper home for Cleo and my other antiquities. You and I—and Audrey, too, if she cares to accompany us—shall move to proper quarters, where we won't be stumbling over Coptic jars and coffins all the time."

Tia answered by baring her teeth, then clattering them in a noisy show of approval.

Alistair Gordon, Viscount Catledge, sat in the gloom of his brother's oak-paneled study and peered across a massive mahogany desk. Neville, the Earl of Hedgeworth, stared back, a slight adjustment of his black eye-patch underscoring the physical disparities between the two brothers. Though the March sun had been shining brightly when Alistair arrived, it felt to him like the dead of winter inside his brother's town house. Despite the fire that crackled in the hearth, he felt a coldness in his bones as he watched his brother's good eye twitch.

Alistair was angry. An urgent post from his brother had demanded his immediate return from Catledge Hall, Leicestershire, to London. Alistair was sure that Neville considered it a great joke to summon his younger half brother from the country during the last month of fox hunting season. The more he thought of it, the angrier Alistair became.

He shifted in his chair, recalling Suzette Duval's petulant expression when he'd shaken her awake and told her to pack her portmanteau. "Ah, *bijou,*" she had said, lifting the counterpane invitingly. "Since you have come sneaking into my bedchamber, why don't you join me . . . for just a little while, no?"

Alistair had chuckled bleakly. "My brother has summoned me to London."

"So there is to be a reconciliation?" Suzette gasped. "Oh, Ali, you have finally taken my advice!"

"On the contrary. It was Neville who initiated this correspondence. It seems he requires my services, though for what purpose I have no notion. Come now, you must get dressed!"

Mlle. Duval had struggled to her elbows, allowing her scanty negligeé to slide off her bare shoulder. "You are not about to become a bore, are you, *chéri?*"

Alistair's struggle to ignore Suzette's dishabille manifested itself in a burst of frustration. "Damme, would that I were the carefree dilettante everyone perceives me to be! Then I might toss this letter on the hearth and ride out with the hounds, forgetting all about Neville's cryptic summons!"

"Ride out with the hounds, Ali? But, what about *me?*"

Alistair turned his back on her. "I do not need to tell you how much I detest this hurried departure from

Catledge Hall, Suzette," he said tightly. "But this may be the opportunity I have been waiting for, a chance to redeem myself in my brother's eyes. Come now, my carriage is waiting. We must leave immediately."

Sitting in Neville's study, Alistair now wondered why he had been so hasty. What difference would a half-hour delay have made in a journey that lasted two days? Why, the hateful Earl of Hedgeworth was probably biting back his laughter, thinking that Alistair behaved more like a recalcitrant schoolboy hauled in by a reproving headmaster than an out-and-out Corinthian roué.

Alistair cleared his throat, attempting to suppress the irritation rising in his chest. "Your note mentioned something about a life or death situation," he reminded his brother.

"I would not have summoned you to my home unless it were vitally important," said the Earl of Hedgeworth. "Not after such a long time. And certainly not after our last unfortunate encounter, when you acted as if you wished never to see me again." After a stretch of silence, the earl added quietly, "No, Ali, I would not have sent for you on a whim."

Alistair let out a derisive snort. Having been offered a drink when he first entered his brother's study, he now cupped the bowl of a crystal snifter in his upturned palm. Drawing a deep breath through flared nostrils, he twirled the glass gently, watching with feigned interest as the topaz liquid spun like gleaming threads at the tips of his fingers. "God knows, you have never done anything on a whim, Neville," he murmured.

"No, I have always placed business before pleasure, and you have always done the opposite."

"Well, I came when you summoned me, didn't I?" Alistair said, wondering whether he had been unwise to do so. Perhaps the rift between him and his brother was irreparable after all. "And I might have come before now if you weren't always pointing out how much we dislike each other, how Father set us up to be natural-born enemies, and all that other folderol. If you were not so determined to fulfill Father's bitter prophecy, Neville, I might come around more often. Have you ever thought of that?''

Neville scoffed. ''Bloody poppycock, that's what that is. But I see that you've developed some backbone, and that's good. You needed some!''

''Why did you want to see me?'' demanded Alistair.

''Because my Egyptian collection has been stolen,'' the earl said bluntly. ''Not all of it, of course. But the most important pieces, including my mummy.''

Alistair was incredulous. ''Do you mean to tell me that note of yours was a ruse to get me back to London at top speed—just so you could tell me you've lost your *mummy?*''

After a long pause the earl said hoarsely, ''You have a soft heart deep down, Ali. Everybody knows that. Otherwise you'd have put a bullet in my back years ago and taken the title you rightly deserve.''

''Nonsense,'' Alistair said, swallowing.

''Not a soul in London would've blamed you for it,'' continued the earl. ''They'd have slapped you on the back and said you should've done it ten years ago, when I first returned from Egypt.''

''You were ill when you returned,'' Alistair replied softly. ''I've never blamed you for anything you said, or did . . . then.''

For several moments the dark study reverberated with a silence broken only by the muted sounds of coaches rumbling down Curzon Street. Neville rubbed the ridge beneath his thick lower lip with a hand that was surprisingly young and strong. Reminded that his brother was just past the age of forty-two, Alistair caught his breath in disgust and horror at the gaunt cheeks, slack jowls, and lined forehead that made the earl's face appear a hundred years old.

''I truly regret that your Egyptian collection has been vandalized, Neville,'' he said, rising to freshen his drink at the sideboard. Returning to his chair, he glanced admiringly at the curiosities that decorated his brother's study. Interspersed among low-slung Empire chairs and book-laden satinwood refectory tables were myriad Egyptian antiquities. Earth-colored Coptic jars were grouped on tabletops, red granite lions with gilded wings flanked the marble mantelpiece, and on a pedestal in a shadowy corner, a limestone bust of an Egyptian queen presided, her aquiline nose tilted proudly, her almond-shaped eyes staring straight ahead.

"But I fail to understand why you sent me that misleading note in order to get me here," Alistair resumed. "What is so urgent about the loss of a few antiquities?" He slouched in his chair, legs crossed languidly, his mood softened both by drink and the heady realization that for once, his brother needed *him.* The reversal in their roles was simply too incredible to fathom. But what in the world did Neville expect Alistair to do?

"I want you to find my mummy and apprehend the thief who stole it," the earl announced flatly.

Alistair nearly fell out of his chair. "You can't be serious," he exploded, a fine spray of brandy misting his trousers. "Surely you don't expect me to go skulking about London looking for a missing mummy!"

"Why not?" countered Neville. "I'm prepared to make it worth your while. Even if you are not deep in dun territory—which I trust you are not—you can't be so wealthy that you wouldn't want to be *even wealthier.* I'm prepared to give you everything I own if you can find my mummy, my most prized possession, and return it to me."

The earl leaned forward, his skeletal fingers gripping the edge of his desk. "Please, Ali. Don't dare to refuse me. Even if you hate me, you must think of the harm that will come if that mummy is not found."

"I've no doubt you're greatly upset, Neville," said Alistair, "especially considering the hardships you endured transporting those antiquities to England. One of your servants has apparently developed sticky fingers. Call in a Bow Street runner, why don't you? That's my advice."

Neville's face darkened. "Even an irresponsible rakehell such as you should be able to comprehend the enormity of my loss. You haven't forgotten the mummy's curse. Have you?"

"I resent that remark," Alistair said. "In fact, I resent every hateful remark you have ever made to me, Neville. You might have been able to intimidate me once with your cutting sarcasm and your superior attitude, but I am a grown man now, with a title and income of my own. I no longer require your financial assistance. I will not tolerate your insults."

Neville's lips curled in a snarl, and he adjusted his black eye-patch as if to scrutinize his little brother more closely. "So you've decided to give me a piece of your mind, have you? After all these years? Independence is an exhilarating thing, is it not, little brother?"

Alistair cringed as his brother's harsh laughter turned into a dry, choking cough. "Good God," he said. "Are you all right?" The earl's face was a shade grayer than it had been a year before at Alistair's uncle's funeral.

"As well as a half-blind cripple can be, I suppose." The monogrammed square of linen the earl held to his lips muffled his voice. "Lucky for you that your uncle Woodfin turned up his toes when he did, wasn't it, Ali?"

"Do not pursue this," Alistair warned.

Neville winked his bulging eye. "And you are luckier still that your mother's uncle died without issue, leaving you everything he possessed, such as it is."

Alistair stretched his fingers, then coiled them into a fist. "I suppose you are going to tell me next that I am *lucky* your mother died during childbirth, leaving Father a young widower and obliging him to marry *my mother*."

"Better to be lucky than wise in this world," remarked Neville. "You were always luckier than I, Ali. Even as a child. Do you think I truly wanted the burden of Father's title, with all its incumbent responsibilities? Do you, Ali?''

"Every man wants a title, Neville. I suspect you realize the benefits that yours entitles you to."

Neville pressed the steepled points of his fingertips to his lips. "That is what the common people think, is it not? But, oh! To be a younger brother, Ali! Just think! You have had the best of both worlds. Even before Woodfin died, you received a handsome allowance from the Gordon coffers, and for doing what in return? Why, absolutely nothing!''

"Enough!" thundered Alistair.

The earl cocked his head appraisingly. "But Woodfin came through for his young nephew after all, and now you've got your own fortune and title. You were right to tell me to go to hell at Woodfin's funeral. You are much too young to tolerate my melancholy. I wager you are quite an eligible bachelor these days, with your handsome face and strong legs.''

"The ladies are rather fond of me," Alistair shot back, aware that his vast understatement was salt in the wounds to a man whose scarred, ravaged face once made an Almack's patroness swoon in fear. The earl had gone into seclusion shortly after that incident, and for the past eight years had stepped outside his elegant town house for nothing more festive than the occasional funeral.

"Ah, Ali! My little Ali-Cat! I'm sure you are quite the ladies' man. But that does not signify," Neville croaked. "You reacted violently to my insult, but you ignored my mention of the mummy's curse. That should not surprise me; you've always preferred the trivial over the profound. Still, you must realize the danger that exists to the unwitting fool who buys that mummy, and to the public at large if it is ever put on display without proper precautions being taken.''

Alistair laughed harshly. "So that is what has you in such a pother! Your mummy is lost, and you fear its curse will infect all of London! Egads, you really do believe that there is a curse attached to that mummy! Oh, come now, Neville, I'd have thought you were more sensible than that. *There are no such things as mummies' curses!*"

"Oh, no?" Neville jeered, jerking off his eye patch. "Then how do you explain this?"

Alistair's laughter ceased abruptly. His glass clinked against his teeth when he shakily raised it to his lips, but he managed not to look away. "Many of Napoleon's men went blind while they were in Egypt. Your status as an English spy would not have given you any sort of immunity from that dreadful disease."

"But Boney left Egypt in '99, and the rest of his army pulled out in 1801," argued Neville. "My eyes were still clear then, when I was abandoned by the French scoundrels and betrayed by my cowardly British brethren. And I didn't lose my eye until *after 1810,* when I removed my collection—and my mummy—from its tomb in the Valley of the Kings."

Alistair inhaled deeply, as much to regain his composure as to show his impatience. "That does not prove the existence of a mummy's curse, brother."

"I was a healthy man before I removed that mummy from its tomb, Ali! Now my lungs work harder than a whore on payday, my legs don't work at all, and my stomach is in constant revolt. If this hellish existence is not a curse, then you tell me, Ali! What is?"

"But your physical ailments have nothing to do with the mummy," Alistair said doggedly. "You are a man of science, Neville. How can you allow yourself to be taken in by such superstitious nonsense?"

The Earl of Hedgeworth's chin dropped to his chest, and he cradled his shaggy head in his hands. Alistair could barely make out the words he spoke, so thick was the emotion in the earl's voice. "Sir Anthony died before we even finished loading the antiquities on the boat." He rambled on, his monologue disjointed and often incoherent. "And that rabid Mameluke who attacked us must have been a victim of the curse as well," Neville finally articulated.

Gripping one of the golden sphinx-heads that ornamented the arms of his chair, Alistair curled the fingers of his other hand more tightly around the base of his brandy snifter. "Collect your wits, Neville. You're slopping over, you know. It just isn't done."

After a few moments the older man raised his head. He had clutched and pulled at his hair, so that now it stood straight on end, going in all directions. His uncovered eyes bulged, the bad one veiled in milky whiteness, the good one gleaming with inspiration. "I've got a plan, Ali."

Alistair's heart leapt. "I have heard enough, Neville. This fustian about mummies' curses is making my skin crawl. I am leaving." But he remained seated, pinned to his chair by Neville's oddly hypnotic stare. Repulsed and saddened by his brother's present condition, yet mindful of his filial responsibilities, Alistair was simply unable to leave. Somehow he knew if he did, his relationship with his brother would be severed forever. And though he did not understand why, given his brother's antipathy toward him, that thought disturbed him terribly.

"What kind of plan?" Alistair finally eked out. He ran his tongue along his upper lip and tasted sweat.

"I have been thinking of ways to help you locate my stolen mummy. Here, I have made a complete list of all the items stolen." Neville reached into a drawer and extracted a sheet of thick vellum.

Placing his brandy glass on the edge of Neville's desk, Alistair reached for the list. "Retrieving stolen goods is hardly within my bailiwick," he commented.

"Not as exciting as hunting foxes, perhaps," remarked Neville, replacing his eye patch. As if Alistair's acquiescence invigorated him, the earl's voice grew stronger. "But think of all the good you will be doing your brother—and your country too, of course."

"My country?" Alistair asked absently, scanning the list.

"Yes, your country," answered Neville. "I have bequeathed my collection to the British Museum, and it is most eager to receive these precious artifacts upon my death. You see, the curse will end only when I die."

Alistair rolled his eyes. "Who told you that, Neville? Was it some crazy Arab bugger offering to sell you *fermin* from the local potentate? How much did you pay them for the right to dig up their national treasures anyway? Christ on a raft! Hasn't it occurred to you that they made up all that nonsense about curses just so they could take your money, then scare you out of the country?"

"I did not know of the curse until I began removing the mummified pharaoh from its tomb," Neville said. "With a dozen workmen's torches illuminating the burial chamber, I could not miss seeing the ancient warnings. And even though I could not decipher the Egyptian hieroglyphs, the vivid pictures painted on the wall told the story clearly."

"But it was too late, then," said Alistair sarcastically.

"Yes. Anthony had already removed the other mummy, the pharaoh's mate—his queen. Those mummies were meant to spend eternity together, Ali. The desecration of their shared tomb—their eternal separation!—has brought the pharaoh's wrath upon my head."

"Fustian!" retorted Alistair. "Every unfortunate event that has occurred in your life, Neville, has a perfectly logical explanation."

Neville continued his explanation, seemingly oblivious of his brother's jibe. "Once the individual responsible for separating the royal mummies is dead, the curse is extinguished. That is why I would never allow the British Museum to take possession of my collection while I am still living. Of course if the treasures are not recovered, the bequest is meaningless. Alistair, if you can find the evil person who has committed this crime and recover the collection, you will be a national hero."

"I have no interest in becoming a national hero," replied Alistair.

"At least the bluestocking crowd will think you are all the crack," the earl said with a smirk. "And the ton, also, for that matter. Egyptology is all the rage today, according to Fleet Street."

"I have houseguests who are expecting me to return to the country within a sennight," Alistair said, shaking his head.

"She can wait," said Neville.

"Yes, but the foxes cannot. And I have invited well over a hundred people to attend a costume party at Catledge Hall at the end of the season. Which,by the way, will be in about a week. Bloody hell, I must have been an idiot to drop everything and rush to London. I thought you were dying, Neville!"

Belatedly, Alistair realized he had made that point. Several times over.

A grin split the earl's cadaverous face. "So you really do care. Oh, how very nice."

"No, as a matter of fact, I do *not* care!" Alistair rose to his feet, still clutching the list in one hand. "You are the outside of enough, Neville. I might have helped you if you condescended to speak to me like an adult. But you insist on taunting me, goading me, treating me as if I were some bacon-brained imbecile, just as you always have—even before you went to Egypt!" He leaned forward and slammed his open palm on Neville's desk, his body thrumming with barely suppressed rage, blood roaring in his ears.

"You really shouldn't take it so personally, little brother," said Neville smoothly. "When you were a child, I resented your existence. Father saw to that. By the time I had returned from Egypt, I had simply developed a strong distaste for my fellow man." He touched his eye patch and lifted his brows knowingly. "I suspect you would have too, Ali, if you'd wasted your youth and ruined you health for your country, only to be cut off from government like a gangrenous toe after you had served your purpose."

"What did you expect, Neville? You were a spy! Surely you knew it was a thankless task when you took it on. Did you think you would be made some kind of war hero when you returned to London after wandering around in the desert for ten years?"

Neville's brows snapped together, and his voice rumbled ominously. "I did not *wander* around in the desert. I was gathering intelligence—"

"All right, all right," Alistair interrupted, shutting his eyes and pinching the bridge of his nose in exasperation. "This is ancient history," he said after a tense silence. "I do not want to discuss it."

"Nor do I," agreed Neville, gesturing for Alistair to sit.

With a heavy sigh of resignation, Alistair slumped in his chair and turned his eyes from Neville's deeply creased visage.

For several moments they sat quietly, then Neville spoke, his voice a harsh, guttural sound. "Do you really hate me so much, Alistair, that you refuse to honor my last—indeed, my only—request of you?"

Alistair stared at his brother through a misty veil of hot tears. He felt like a puppet on a string, and for that he hated his brother more than he ever had. But he knew if he refused to help Neville, he'd hate himself more when the wretched man died. Blinking back his emotion— because he'd sooner slit his throat than shed tears in front of the Earl of Hedgeworth—Alistair answered at length. "All right, Neville. I will help you find whoever stole your antiquities. But I cannot spend the rest of the fox-hunting season in town. I intend to return home in order to host my theme party, no matter what."

"Might I ask what the theme of this exclusive crush is?"

Alistair tasted bile in the back of his throat. "The title is *A Long Egyptian Night*, Neville."

"Ah! How fashionable." Neville nodded, victorious and

smug. "Well, then, little brother," said he, clapping his palms together. "My plan begins with finding Sir Anthony Russell's widow."

"Sir Anthony? The man who assisted you in removing the artifacts from the tomb?"

"He tried, poor bastard," replied the earl. "His wife has lived in London these past ten years, though I have not communicated with her in some time. Her name is Rhoda, Lady Russell. She is an expert in Egyptian artifacts and her own extensive collection is very similar to mine. She is also active in the Society of Egyptologists, a group of erudite individuals who meet to study and discuss Egyptian culture and antiquities. She may have some knowledge that will be useful to us in apprehending our thief."

Alistair puzzled over his brother's words, then tucked the folded list of stolen goods beneath his vest. Standing again, he asked incredulously, "Are you suggesting that this robbery was committed by someone other than an ordinary thief?"

"Someone entered my home in the dead of night, picked the lock on the door leading to the rooms that house my collection, then selected certain objects and absconded with them. This person or persons chose those items for a specific reason, though I am unsure why. All I can tell you is that the items stolen were taken from the pyramid I entered near Thebes, in the Valley of the Kings, in the year 1810. Lady Russell was present when I entered that magnificent tomb, along with her husband and their young daughter. She is aware of the mummy's curse, and believes in it. Surely her insight into this matter would be most useful."

Foreboding slivered up Alistair's spine like an asp, and he couldn't help blurting out, "Bloody hell, Neville. It makes my blood run cold to think of you sneaking into some long-forgotten sacred tomb and plundering it like some greedy Arab grave robber! And now you want me to creep around London and get your precious mummy back!"

"So that the curse will not spread to innocent people," intoned Neville. "God knows I don't care what happens to the idiot who stole my mummy, but whoever else opens that coffin will suffer the mummy's curse—just as I have. Don't you see what that means Ali? The lives of many innocent persons are at stake. We must retrieve that mummy! Quickly!"

"I don't know who is more insane—you, for believing in a mummy's curse, or me, for allowing myself to be talked into searching for a stolen corpse!"

"I am not crazy, Ali. And I would plant a fiver in your face for saying that—if I could get up out of this wretched Merlin chair."

Alistair tugged at his shirt cuffs and squared his shoulders. "If you could leave that chair, I suppose you would find Lady Russell yourself," he said. "By the way, where is she?"

"She has a shop on Pickett Place, the Strand," answered Neville.

"What sort of shop?"

A crooked smile contorted Neville's face. "It's called a *magazin de deuil* in French. Lady Russell's shop, in particular, bears her husband's name. At any rate, Russell's Emporium specializes in funerary paraphernalia, fancy coffins, hired mutes and weepers, black accoutrements, and somber attire for every gradation of mourning imaginable."

Alistair could only shake his head. For a man who'd dedicated his life to pleasure, the thought of spending an afternoon with Lady Russell of Russell's Emporium struck him as the most cruel sort of punishment. "Wonderful," he replied, moving toward the study doors. "Can't think of any place I'd rather be."

"The foxes will wait, Ali," said Neville. But his brother had already slammed the door shut behind him when he added, "And so will the minx."

Chapter Two

Cassandra tied a ribbon around a stack of paid invoices, then tucked the neat bundle into one of the compartments of her rosewood writing desk. There had been little traffic in Russell's Emporium that morning, and the rumblings of her stomach were just beginning to remind her of nuncheon, when she heard the bells of the shop door tinkle.

Rising, Cassandra glanced at Tia. The monkey was squatting on its haunches next to the heavy brass wax-jack, idly fiddling with a dry quill, scraping and jabbing the pen's nib on scrap paper discarded after Cassandra's morning communications. Tia's eyes followed her mistress across the room, but the monkey remained on the desk, one tiny hand spread flat on the paper, the other clutching the quill above the writing surface.

Quietly weaving her way through a maze of coffins, bolts of dull black fabric, and other funereal inventory, Cassandra crossed the back room and paused before a curtain of multicolored beads. Pivoting, she raised her finger to her lips and smiled when Tia mimicked her command for silence.

In the front of the shop, before a row of glistening coffins, stood a man. His back was to Cassandra, and though she couldn't see his face, she judged him young and handsome by the broad expanse of his shoulders, the sinewy length of his elegantly booted legs, and the rich luster of his dark hair. Or was it simply his *attitude* that told her he was good-looking?

Cassandra spied him raking his fingers through his thick, wavy hair. The way he studied his own reflection in the shiny surface of the polished coffin, obviously admiring the face that peered back at him, reminded her of Tia sitting before a mirror, entranced and totally unselfconscious. But the way his hair coiled at the back of his neck, and the way his shoulders squared beneath his coat, piqued something in Cassandra's interest other than amusement, mockery, or maternalism. This man—even from the back—sent a frisson of anticipation through Cassandra's body. This man was more masculine, more unabashedly at ease in his own skin than any man who had ever entered Cassandra's shop.

Not that Russell's Emporium was the greatest place in the world to meet men, Cassandra reminded herself. Especially if a girl liked live ones—under eighty.

The man obviously thought he was alone in the small emporium. Puffing out his chest, flicking a piece of lint from his sleeve, he preened like a peacock. He shrugged his shoulders to adjust the fit of his bottle-green cutaway jacket, then tugged at his shirtsleeves and pulled on the ends of his simply tied cravat.

Suddenly, as if he felt Cassandra's appraising stare, he glanced over his shoulder and called out, "Hello? Hello, is anyone in here?" But Cassandra quickly stepped to the side of the curtain and peeked around the door frame, staying out of his sight while surreptitiously continuing her observation of his interesting behavior. With a firm pat to Tia's backside, she sent the monkey scampering up the steps to her apartment. She was in no hurry to reveal herself; in fact, she intended to watch her customer a bit longer before emerging from the inventory room. Spying on him while he preened gave her a delicious sense of mischief.

But there was something more compelling about the man than his good looks and vanity, Cassandra sensed. There was an air of impatience about him, an edginess— as if he worried that his reflection would not always assure him of his youth and vitality. His self-absorption betrayed his unhappiness with his inner self, as well as his determination to perfect his outer appearance. Projecting the right image to the public was important to this man, Cassandra thought, but why? His discontent was puzzling, and rather poignant. Cassandra wondered what kind of handsome gentleman had wandered into her shop. She studied him a while longer as he studied himself.

Alistair's loud announcement of his presence had failed to scare up any sign of life. After a leisurely examination of several prominent displays of black-feathered headdresses, the viscount returned to the polished coffin that now reflected his darting gaze. While his eyes scanned a room chock full of curiosities, his nimble fingers adjusted an elegantly tied cravat.

Doffing his beaver hat, Alistair appraised his reflection in the polished mahogany of an upright coffin. Frowning, his eyes glanced off an entire row of gleaming caskets that lined one wall of the tiny shop's interior. Mirrored in their glossy patinas was a vast array of funeral paraphernalia, black armbands and hatbands, black buttons and mourning scarves and an immense selection of dark-colored silks, crepes, cashmeres, and other fine fabrics.

Everything one needs to throw a good funeral, the viscount thought, his eyes returning to his own slightly amused and admittedly handsome reflection. How very ghastly this place was! No wonder it was empty—and as quiet as a tomb. This was hardly an establishment likely to attract a throng of passing pedestrians.

Outside, the boisterous chimes of St. Clement Dane's Church mocked this most solemn place of commerce. *Oranges and lemons say the bells of St. Clement's!* The little shop remained eerily unattended.

Not that Alistair was easily spooked. An admiring once-over in the coffin's shiny surface drew an elegant shrug of his broad shoulders. His brother's request that he come to this West End address to secure Lady Russell was odd, true, but not nearly so odd as Neville himself. Certainly not odd enough to risk forfeiting the fortune Neville had promised if he succeeded in finding the missing mummy. Or the chance at being recognized as a national hero—an honor not without its appeal despite Alistair's earlier derision of the notion.

Poor brother. Poor, wretched Neville. Alistair bared his teeth and examined two perfect rows of impeccable enamel. No two brothers had ever been less similar, he assured himself not for the first time. How was it that his elder brother could be so unrelentingly morbid when there were horses in this life yet to race, foxes still to corner, wagers to win, and women waiting—just waiting—to be seduced?

Perhaps it was because he could enjoy none of those things, Alistair remembered guiltily.

Bloody hell! Where was that blasted Lady Russell anyway? Alistair did not intend to loiter forever in these depressing quarters. And besides, he'd promised his brother to return the old woman to Curzon Street by the end of the day. Enough preening. More pressing matters demanded the viscount's attention. Alistair heard a movement behind him.

He pivoted on the heels of his shiny top-boots. And came face-to-face with one of the most exotic-looking women he had ever seen. Her olive skin was flawless. Her eyes tipped up at the corners and sparkled with feline curiosity. Streaks

of fiery red highlighted her thick dark hair, swept back
and cinched in a neat bun at the nape of her neck.

"Good heavens, do you always sneak up on your customers?"

"I did not sneak up on you, sir," the woman replied,
lifting her chin a notch. Looking down her nose, she bore
an amazing similarity to Neville's limestone Egyptian
queen. "You were so engrossed with your own reflection
that you failed to notice my presence."

"You could have announced yourself," said Alistair.
"'Twould have been the polite thing to do."

"Why? I have been in the shop since early this morning,"
the young woman countered. "I was at my desk in the rear,
behind the curtains there, going over some numbers."

"But I called out rather loudly," said the viscount. Having been caught in the act of admiring himself was irksome
indeed. "'Twas more likely you were having a spot of tea
back there, and did not wish to be disturbed. Come on
now, gel, 'fess up. Nothing worse than a stalwart dissembler, that's what I always say."

"I was not taking tea, sir," the young woman retorted.
"I simply did not hear you enter the shop. I admit to
being rather oblivious when I am in deep concentration,
particularly when I am engrossed in my bookkeeping
chores, but I am not ordinarily deaf to my customers'
entreaties. Perhaps the church bells drowned out your
voice." She squared her shoulders and leveled the viscount
a vanquishing stare, apparently having rendered all the
explanation she felt she owed.

"Is that all you have to say for yourself?"

"Have you been here long, sir?" she inquired frostily.

"I have been here far too long!" Alistair drew himself
up to his full height also, and peered down his nose at the
compact bit of baggage who so brazenly defied him. "I've
a good mind to report your dereliction to Lady Russell,
the owner of this establishment. She will not be pleased

to hear that you neglect her customers' needs in favor of sipping tea in the rear of the shop."

"I was not shirking my responsibilities," the woman said, her patience plainly slipping away. "And I resent your assumption that my customers are ignored while I loaf about. That is simply not true."

The viscount's grin was all out of proportion to the sparse relief he truly felt. Still, he was gratified to think he had put this saucy chit on the defensive.

"Is it not true, madam, that the customer is always correct? Should you not be exercising a bit more diplomacy in the handling of my complaint? I should think that in a business of this nature, you might have acquired a sort of *delicacy* in dealing with your clients, a gentleness of manner you might employ in assuaging the tender feelings of those whose loved ones have just passed on to other side. Humph! But you have treated my lament with the scarcest of sympathy!"

The woman's lips, full and ruby-colored, curved upward. "I assure you, sir, there are none so disenchanted with false civility as those who are dead, buried, or left behind to grieve."

"Dead, buried, or left behind? That includes all of us, does it not?"

"All except those who refuse to face reality."

The woman's placid poise was unsettling, all the more so because it belied the tiny flecks of gold that flashed in her eyes as she returned Alistair's stare. She seemed to be in total control of the cool, calm, and collected image she was projecting. How did a simple shop girl ever come to possess such sang-froid, such disdainful elegance? Or was she merely a bluestocking chit feigning superiority to cover up her lack of breeding? Whatever the answer, Alistair thought she was most intriguing. Sparring with her just might turn out to be fun.

"Ah, a philosopher," he said. "You and every other bluestocking in London. How predictable. Although, I suppose if one is surrounded by death on a daily basis, one might be inclined to ponder excessively the meaning of life."

"Perhaps. Might I ask your name, sir?"

With a flourish the viscount produced a small, engraved calling card that bore his name and title. "Permit me to introduce myself. I have no philosophical inclinations, no aspirations toward sainthood, and, most important, no pretensions toward civility. Truth be known, I am totally undeserving of my title."

"Ah, a ne'er-do-well dandy. How predictable," parried the young woman. She plucked the embossed card from Alistair's fingers and glanced at it. Looking up, she said, "My name is Miss Cassandra Russell."

"How very pleased I am to make your acquaint—Russell, you say?" Alistair paused in mid-bow, but his eyes continued to travel the entire length of a black bombazine dress, from its unadorned hem to its high-necked bodice.

When he slowly straightened, he felt the intensity of Cassandra's topaz gaze. "Well, then. It seems I owe you an apology. I am afraid I mistook you for a shop girl."

"Your apology is accepted," Cassandra replied regally. "On the condition, of course, that you behave as a gentleman from here on out, and state your business. Please."

Thinking to rattle her a bit, the viscount turned his most heated gaze on her. In the past, that seductive look had always yielded great success with the ladies. He had no doubt it would now unnerve this minx, leaving her wobbly-kneed and nervous. Somehow her serene self-confidence challenged him to gain the upper hand. "Truly, Miss Russell," he drawled, "all work and no play makes for an exceedingly dull time."

Cassandra's black-lined eyes snapped like leather whips, and her sculpted cheeks became darker, more prominent against her olive skin. "May I help you, my lord?" she asked icily.

Comprehending that Cassandra was not interested in

flirtatious banter, Alistair supposed he should explain his business. "I am looking for Lady Rhoda Russell, the proprietress of this establishment. Would that be your mother, by any chance?"

"It would, sir. Might I ask your business with her?"

"'Tis my brother, Neville, Earl of Hedgeworth, who has business with your mother. Not I, certainly. Despite my title, you see, I fear I am blessed with a high degree of irresponsibility, a trait so very common it is practically endemic among younger brothers. But since my brother is . . . ah, indisposed at the moment, I am acting as his emissary."

"Does your brother wish to arrange a funeral?"

"That does sound like his idea of fun, but no. It's a trifle premature to start picking out shrouds, I do believe."

"It is never too early, my lord. One mustn't neglect such matters. It only adds to the burdens of the bereaved when the inevitable occurs. Which it must, you know."

Alistair frowned. "You sound like my brother. I get the mother-grubs when I hear all this talk of dying. Make hay while the sun shines, that's my motto!"

Cassandra's lips twitched as if she were fighting the urge to laugh. "I thought you said you were not a philosopher, my lord."

"Touché!" cried Alistair. He really liked a good set-to with an impertinent woman.

Cassandra stared at him, her eyes flashing incongruently behind a mask of sobriety.

"So, where is Lady Russell?" Alistair inquired.

"Passed on, sir."

"Passed on—" For a split second the viscount forgot himself and gave full vent to his shock. "You mean, she is . . . dead?"

"That is what I mean, my lord." The ruby-colored lips that Alistair had been admiring so ardently were now compressed to a single straight line. Cassandra's nostrils flared and her amber eyes narrowed in defiance to the viscount's nosy questions.

Alistair was forced to concede that his opening gambit had perhaps been less than artful.

"Good Lord! What an unfortunate turn of events."

"To say the least," Cassandra acknowledged primly.

"But you see, Neville insisted that I bring your mama to him," the viscount continued after a lengthy silence made all the more prickly by Cassandra's scornful expression and serene reticence. This was clearly a woman of few words—a woman who hid herself behind stony silence or elliptical retorts. In much the same way that Alistair hid himself behind good looks and rakish grins.

"I am sure your brother will understand the inconvenience of his request when you explain why my mother is indisposed." Cassandra's unflinching stare was beginning to cause the skin beneath the viscount's necktie to chafe.

"You do not understand, Miss Russell. My brother's reason for seeing your mother is really quite urgent." In a fit of pique, he wrung his beaver hat like a wet rag. "Bloody hell, I did not wish to disappoint my brother."

"There is no need for profanity, my lord. And besides, I thought you said you were irresponsible," observed Cassandra. "In light of your general good-for-nothing nature, I am sure he will understand that you are not up to bringing a dead woman back to life in order to satisfy his request."

"Listen, Miss Russell," Alistair said, recouping his composure. "May I call you Cassandra?"

"No."

"Oh. Um, well. My filial obligations are the only duties in life I take seriously."

"How very commendable, my lord." The faintest hint of a smile played across her lips.

Cassandra's inscrutable equanimity was becoming to Alistair an unnerving and alarmingly attractive characteristic. Most fashionable ladies would have been giggling, blushing, or babbling by now.

Or running a slender hand up his shirt-front.

That thought brought to mind his *chère amie*, Mlle. Suzette Duval, who was undoubtedly waiting for him to return to her town house, and provide a full explanation of Neville's urgent post.

This young woman, on the other hand, was a true original—self-assured, cultivated, and totally unruffled. Alistair couldn't take his eyes off her, and his body was positively thrumming with nervous energy. What had gotten into him? Well, it was something he would have to figure out—but only after he figured out what to do about the untimely demise of Lady Russell.

"Might I ask, when did your mother die?" he inquired.

"A year ago, Lord Catledge. I am surprised your brother did not know, if he was indeed my mama's friend, as you say."

"I am afraid Neville has been holed up in his study for about eight years. Ever since some cup-sprung, stiff-rumped prune at Almack's dared to peek under his eye patch. She swooned, and Neville lost whatever sense of humor he had remaining, right then and there. Now he is a musty old curmudgeon—never jolly at all, if you know what I mean."

"What a pity," Cassandra said. "I gather that you are an all-round party boy if ever there was one."

"Now, that is too impertinent by half, young lady—"

"You all but admitted you are spoiled and rich," she reminded him, eyes flashing.

Alistair snorted derisively. "In polite society, one is customarily permitted to criticize one's self without fear of unanimous agreement from one's peers."

"I have no peers among the aristocracy," rejoined Cassandra. "Perhaps that explains my ignorance of the rules applicable to modern discourse and polite conversation—in your set, that is. Still, I should think you might find it refreshing to talk with someone willing to tell you the truth. A man of your elevated status is undoubtedly accustomed to hearing only what you wish to hear."

"I admit, I have had my fill of sycophants this season." Alistair cocked his head and slanted Cassandra an appraising look. "But you, Miss Russell, are most unusual. Might I ask where you are from?"

"I was born in England, my lord," she replied stiffly. "Just as you were, I suppose."

"Yes, yes. But you are clearly of foreign stock—"

"Now it is you who insult me, my lord! I am not of foreign stock any more than you are! I am a citizen of England, and I have lived in London my entire life." She lowered her eyes and clasped her hands, as if debating whether to continue. "Excepting the periods of my childhood in which I accompanied Father on his Egyptian expeditions," she finally added softly. "Mother and I always went along on those adventures."

"How very sporting of you," commented Alistair. A measure of envy crept into his voice. "It must have been a very exciting childhood, trekking down the Nile and gazing at some of man's most mind-boggling architectural achievements."

Cassandra's eyes grew misty. "Yes, it was."

Alistair toyed with his necktie and swallowed the sudden lump in his throat. "To have shared all that with your father must have been . . . well, I admit I cannot quite comprehend it."

"My father was quite an amazing man, my lord. His death when I was ten years old came as quite a nasty shock."

"I suppose so," commiserated Alistair. Even as he spoke, however, his mind swirled with questions evoked by Cassandra's reminiscing. Inclining his head politely, Alistair inched closer to Cassandra. "You are Egyptian," he said.

"My mother was Egyptian," Cassandra corrected him. "My father, Sir Anthony Russell, was every bit as English as you. And so am I."

"Well, my dear, despite your hybrid heritage, I know

that my brother would consider you the most exquisite female in the world. He loves anything Egyptian. And your Egyptian mother contributed far more to your looks than did your English father."

"I am sure that is very flattering," Cassandra said. "I must admit that I am also an enthusiastic Egyptologist. However, I cannot recall my mother ever mentioning your brother. What did you say is his name?"

"Neville Gordon, Earl of Hedgeworth," replied Alistair. He leaned toward Cassandra and injected a certain intimacy into his voice. "Perhaps you know him by a different name. Tell me, were you present when Sir Anthony entered a hidden tomb in the Valley of Kings in 1810?"

"Why do you ask?"

"My brother was the Englishman who came up with the bright idea of removing all those wondrous treasures from that tomb and returning them to England. Surely you remember him."

Cassandra's expression altered drastically. Pressing one hand to her throat, she stared at him wide-eyed, her question wrenched from her throat in a strangle. "Pray, what does your brother look like?"

"Like a dead man, frankly. But I suppose he was healthy when you met him. And though he is seven years my senior, he probably looked a bit like me at the time, only fair-haired . . . and taller. In his youth he was a handsome buck, rugged through the jaw, with piercing blue eyes and a smile that could charm a snake." Somewhat acerbically, Alistair added, "But of course that was in his youth. I daresay, Neville does not smile much anymore."

Cassandra's voice quavered. "You look nothing like him. . . ."

"I am pleased to say I inherited my mother's dark hair and eyes, while Neville got Father's Nordic looks and icy temperament." After an awkward pause, Alistair added, "I am afraid we are only half brothers, you see. Neville's mother died, and father remarried." Memories of child-

hood slights brought a counterfeit flippancy to Alistair's
mannerisms. "Lucky for me, I suppose."

Cassandra reacted archly. "Your attitude is nothing like
your brother's either," she observed.

"My brother and I are as different as night and day,"
the viscount began. His speech was interrupted by an osten-
tatious readjustment of his shirt-cuffs so that they just
peeked from beneath his coat sleeves. "But that is not
what I came here to discuss. Have we established that you
know my brother?"

"Yes, my lord. I know exactly who your brother is."

"Good. Then you must help me. Since your mother is
deceased, God rest her soul, you must accompany me to
Curzon Street, where my brother will most likely interrogate you concerning your knowledge of—"

"Never!"

"Excuse me?" Incredulous, Alistair stared as Cassandra
trembled with emotion. "Why, whatever is the matter with
you? If you are worried about leaving your shop unattended, then I assure you I will personally compensate you
for a reasonable loss of business." He scanned the empty
shop. "Though it does not appear business is booming at
the moment."

"I wouldn't throw your brother a rope if he were drowning!" Cassandra spat out. "I hate him! He is the reason
my father is dead!"

Alistair's attraction toward Cassandra quickly waned
while his irritation toward his elder brother waxed. Surely
Neville must have anticipated this hostility from Lady Russell, if not from the deceased woman's daughter. Yet the
earl had chosen not to forewarn his unwitting half sibling.
Damn his eyes! The earl was probably sitting at his desk,
laughing, even now.

"Miss Russell, I understand how you must feel toward
my brother, but I do *not* understand why you believe Neville
is responsible for the death of your father. I shall give you

the benefit of the doubt, and assume you have good reason
to feel that way."

"You are too kind by half," replied Cassandra, her voice
dripping with sarcasm. "But I would much prefer that you
depart these premises, my lord."

"Not until you agree to come to Curzon Street and speak
with my brother." It was a matter of pride now, thought
Alistair. He did not care if the little hussy came to Curzon
Street or not; but he couldn't let her think she could bully
him about as if he were an errant child. Alistair Gordon,
Viscount Catledge, was not about to leave Russell's Emporium with his tail tucked between his legs.

"I wouldn't go to Buckingham Palace with you, not if
King George invited me himself!"

"You will go, and that is final!"

"I shan't!"

Alistair drew in a harsh breath. This woman's stubborn
defiance was becoming a bore. And besides, he realized
with a shock, it truly irritated him that she hated his brother
so deeply. Who did she think she was, after all? She didn't
know a thing about Neville Gordon, and had no business
hating him—that privilege was distinctly reserved for the
earl's mistreated younger brother.

"Miss Russell, I shall not argue with you any longer. If
you do not accompany me at once, I shall—"

"You shall what?" Cassandra's posture was ramrod
straight, her eyes as hard as diamonds. *"You shall do what?"*

The viscount laughed. "I shall direct my solicitor to
instruct the law court to order you to appear before my
brother."

His empty threat drew nothing but scorn. Oh, what a
pother this entire business had become. Miss Cassandra
Russell was exceedingly vexatious, all the more so when
she threw back her head and taunted him. "Try it!"

The viscount studied the tips of his gloved fingers. "If
you toss me out now, I shall only return on the morrow.
I suggest you prepare to accompany me to Curzon Street.

You will need something warm to throw about your shoulders. It is quite chilly out there, despite the bright sunlight."

Cassandra's eyes narrowed. "I suggest you not waste any more of your time attempting to persuade me to meet your brother. Whatever business he might have wished to conduct with my mother, I can assure you she would not have cared a whit about it. There are other shops in London that will be more than happy to cater to your brother's funerary needs. You might suggest he consult one of them."

With a grim foreboding, Alistair realized Cassandra was the first person he had ever met who was totally unaffected by his wit and good looks. She regarded him coldly as he studied her, the two of them eyeballing each other in as brazen and heartless a display of mutual scrutiny as had ever taken place in London.

Well, Alistair Gordon was not one to be trampled by a cheeky upstart like Cassandra Russell. "If you would pipe down, you might be made to understand that Neville did not summon your mother for assistance in picking out his burial clothes. On the contrary, his purpose is far more urgent than that." He raised his hand to forestall her continued denials of cooperation. "Come now, just put a sign on your door that you are closed—"

"My lord, you do not seem to be hearing me—"

"Oh, I hear you all right," Alistair replied, smiling. "I am simply not in agreement with what you are saying."

"You are the most harassing scoundrel I have ever met!" Cassandra even went so far as to shake a delicate fist in his face, a gesture the viscount found exceedingly amusing, if not quite so threatening as it was intended. "Really, Lord Catledge, I believe it is high time you took your leave. I have had my fill of you, and I wish you to be gone."

"But you have not heard all that I have to say. I am sure I can convince you to accompany me to Curzon Street, Miss Russell, if you will only listen to logic—"

"You are a rude man, my lord!" Cassandra stamped her half-boot and pointed her forefinger toward the door. "I asked you to leave. Now, must I summon a charley to have you removed?"

"And you are as immovable as an Egyptian pyramid, miss!"

Cassandra exhaled sharply, her eyes flashing. When she spoke, her voice was whisper-soft. "You are most uncharitable, Lord Catledge."

"'Tis you who are uncharitable, Miss Russell. You could help my brother if you would. And perhaps your country as well," Alistair added with sudden inspiration.

"My country?" Cassandra repeated.

"Yes. Surely you realize that Neville would not have dared to impose upon your mother—knowing how she feels about him—if this matter were purely a selfish one. No, dear girl, this matter is one of national importance."

"What are you talking about?" Cassandra frowned, but she was no longer pointing toward the door.

She was wavering, weakening, crumbling. Good!

"Well, Miss Russell, it may take a moment or two to explain. Is there a place where we can sit down?"

The question seemed to fluster her. "No, there are only my inventory rooms in the back of the shop, and my private quarters upstairs. It would be most inappropriate . . . my country, you say?"

"Yes, yes, it would be inappropriate to entertain me here. Then perhaps you will accompany me to that new little coffee shop just down the street. A walk in the brisk air will do us good." Alistair gestured toward the door. "My driver will follow, and return us in my carriage. I believe you will find the outing enjoyable."

Cassandra took a hesitant step forward, then two tiny steps backward. The shop suddenly shrank—or so it seemed to Alistair, whose senses swelled to near bursting with Cassandra's expanding aura. She had blossomed beneath his eyes as he bandied words with her, and now she exuded a feminine allure that enveloped him. Perhaps it was the intensity of her anger, but he could have sworn her presence intensified ... filling the room with her essence, displacing everything else, including the row of shining coffins behind him.

She was looking up at him, biting her lower lip, studying him intensely. "A matter of national importance, you say?"

"You are an English citizen, are you not?" He leaned closer. "You would help your country if you were able, would you not?"

She closed her eyes for a moment, and when she opened them, her lips were pressed tightly together, her eyes bright with decision. "Let me get my pelisse," she said, disappearing behind a curtain of colored beads into the nether regions of her morbid inventory rooms.

A restless shuffle of papers and a high-pitched squawk caused Alistair to cautiously venture toward the back of the shop. He could have sworn he heard Cassandra whispering to someone in the back room, but before he got a chance to part the beads and poke his head into the rear section of the emporium, she reappeared with a black woolen cloak draped over her arm.

"Did I hear you talking to someone?" Alistair asked, holding Cassandra's proffered outer garment while she stepped behind a glass-topped display case and produced a reticule and bonnet from underneath. He craned his neck to see into the room behind her, but the beads swinging in the doorway obscured his view.

Cassandra slipped her slender arm through the drawstrings of her reticule and carefully positioned the black bonnet over her sleek coiffure. Hastily tying the ribbons beneath her lifted chin, her sparkling, golden-flecked eyes met Alistair's gaze for an instant, then glanced away.

"Who is back there?" Alistair demanded, perplexed by Cassandra's curiously evasive tactics.

Skirts swished as she ushered him to the front of the shop. "My pet monkey does not want to go upstairs. You heard me telling her to behave herself," Cassandra replied. She pulled up short, faced him, and stared up expectantly.

"You act as if you expect me to disbelieve you," Alistair said. "Of course, I hardly know you, but you do not strike me as the sort of girl who would weave clankers or play jokes on strangers. If you say you have a monkey, I believe you."

"And what do you think about my having a pet monkey?" she asked him.

"It's prime and bang-up to the mark!" he exclaimed, somewhat surprised that she would even care what he thought. Had she really expected him to disapprove of her keeping the animal? If she had, where did such insecurities stem from?

"Why, I hear that such animals are all the crack this year among the ton, but I've never actually seen one," Alistair commented, intrigued that Cassandra would indulge such a whimsical fancy. Her affection for a monkey lent an entirely new dimension to her character. Perhaps Cassandra Russell was not as somber as a Westminster judge after all. "What is its name, pray tell?"

"The monkey's name is Tia, my lord. She was given to me by a member of the Society of Egyptologists." Cassandra looked at him expectantly, and added, "I assume you share your brother's passion for Egyptology. You do, don't you?"

"Tia, eh? Good heavens, my brother would really be besotted with a girl like you. Even *he* hasn't starting naming household pets after ancient Egyptian deities. Not that Neville has any pets. I'm afraid he's too much of a misanthrope to go in for that sort of thing."

"A misanthrope is a person who hates mankind, my lord," said Cassandra. "That does not necessarily condemn him to hating animals, as well." She reached for her pelisse and Alistair placed the lightweight black woolen mantle on her shoulders. Nervously, she edged away, but not before he got a whiff of the incense aroma that surrounded her.

"You haven't answered my question," she said. "Do you share your brother's passion for the study of Egyptian history and for that country's antiquities?"

Breathing in the blended smells of cinnamon, tea leaves, and clean skin, Alistair felt invigorated, acutely aware of every inch, every fiber of the woman who stood before him. "I am becoming increasingly intrigued with all things Egyptian," he answered. "But I have much to learn."

"Undoubtedly," Cassandra agreed, her skirts brushing the viscount's boots as they walked slowly toward the door.

Staring at Cassandra's sculpted profile, the viscount reveled in the dramatically altered atmosphere he felt. Every particle of air in the crowded room suddenly buzzed with energy. Every inch of his body thrummed with arousal.

But it was not just his physical appetite that was aroused; he felt a burgeoning revival of all his senses, a revitalization of his jaded soul.

And all because he had met a woman who dared to pick a fight with him, who dared to resist his charms? Preposterous, he thought, swallowing a hearty laugh. Absolutely impossible!

Still, he had to admit he'd never encountered anyone like Cassandra Russell. Never before had he met a woman so antagonistic toward him, so diametrically opposed to him, so immune to his charm and play-acting. When his smile evaporated, he did not even trouble himself to replace it with his perfect, gleaming grin or his sly, seductive smirk. He simply stared in amazement at the strange little termagant who'd tweaked his nose. He wasn't sure whether he was going to hate her or love her once he got to know her—but he was eager as hell to find out!

"I am sure my brother will compensate you generously for the time you expend in troubling yourself with this, er, national crisis." Alistair tapped the brim of his beaver hat and bowed slightly as he reached for the door.

"I have not yet agreed to meet your brother," Cassandra said.

"Stubborn wench," Alistair allowed in a rasp of admiration.

"Spoiled aristocrat," Cassandra responded, a grudging smirk upon her lips.

"Perhaps you are right," the viscount said. "Though I would like the opportunity to change your opinion of me." The sounds of people bustling along the sidewalk pervaded the small shop when Alistair opened the door. He paused, wondering at the meaning of his own words. This woman was right—he did talk nonsense!

To think he had met a woman capable of putting up a good fight aroused him. But to think he had met a woman who could look into his heart and read his most private thoughts—well, that frightened the living daylights out of him.

Altering his expression to a debonair repose, he caught Cassandra's elbow. "Miss Russell, I implore you. Help me. Help Neville. If you have a heart, come with me to Curzon Street, please."

Her eyes flickered, her lashes fluttered. She bit her lower lip and fumbled in her reticule for a key. "You can explain his problem to me over coffee." She tried to move past him, but Alistair tightened his grip on her arm and held her in the open doorway for just a moment.

"Neville needs you," he whispered at her neck.

Cassandra's eyes filled with water. She faltered. "Coffee, first," she replied breathlessly, but staunchly.

"You are so very kind," the viscount said.

Cassandra's brow furrowed, and she shook her head in painful deliberation as she wrenched her arm free and swept past Alistair. He followed and waited on the sidewalk while she hovered at the threshold of her tiny shop. She flipped a signboard that announced Russell's Emporium was closed, then briskly turned her key in the lock and tucked it in her reticule. "I am ready."

"Thank you for agreeing to hear me out."

"You are welcome, Lord Catledge," she replied, a note

of uncertainty in her voice. "At least, I think you are welcome. Truth be known, I haven't quite made up my mind about you."

Alistair smiled. Who would have thought mummy-hunting could be such fun?

Chapter Three

Cassandra stared across the tiny café table, half certain that she'd lost her mind. By now Audrey was probably crazed with worry, wondering where she'd gone. Especially if the fussy maid had shuffled down the steps to announce nuncheon and found Tia alone in the inventory room. For all Cassandra knew, the monkey might already have shred every invoice on her desk, unraveled the bombazine off the bolts, and plucked clean every black plume in the place. She couldn't worry about that now.

The viscount's cryptic reference to a matter of national importance had intrigued her. Cassandra realized that Lord Catledge might be nothing more than a fast-talking four-flusher, but he could weave a good yarn. Having decided not to cut him off, Cassandra now felt like a child eagerly awaiting the end of a bedtime story.

Surely she was entitled to a bit of harmless fun after a year of mourning. And that was precisely what Cassandra considered this rare outing—a fluke, a respite, an *interlude*. She had not truly believed Alistair's gammon about a national crisis. She accompanied the viscount to the coffee house because she found him vastly amusing and entertaining, not because she thought she owed it to her country to hear him out.

National crisis, indeed! Cassandra was not a worldly girl, but she recognized a Banbury tale when she heard one. The longer Lord Catledge prattled on about everything *except* a national crisis, the more thoroughly Cassandra was convinced that he had induced her to leave her shop on false pretenses. But that idea bothered her even less than the notion of Tia tearing up the storeroom. Today's outing was merely a diversion, Cassandra told herself—on the level with viewing the dancing bear at Astley's Royal Amphitheatre.

Suddenly Cassandra felt a chill, as if a ghost had passed through her. Circumspection returned in a sobering flash, and hugged her like a jealous wraith. She had no business being alone in a coffee house with Viscount Catledge, she chided herself.

She really should leave.

"Is your coffee all right?" the viscount was asking her. And he was incredibly pleasant to look at, and charming in that odd, quirky way of his. He was not at all what she would have expected from a rip-roaring rakehell aristocrat.

Cassandra murmured her approval of the coffee and watched Lord Catledge doctor his with drops of brandy from a bottle furnished by the waiter. She smiled faintly.

"Perhaps you are not a coffee drinker," the viscount said. "Shall I instruct the waiter to bring a pot of tea?"

"Oh, no. The coffee is fine. It is just that I have noticed I am the only woman in this place." She scanned the noisy crowd of men, all of whom seemed to be talking at once.

"Are you concerned for your reputation?"

"I should have a chaperon," Cassandra replied evasively. "'Tis improper that I should be here alone with you." A renewed surge of anxiety rattled her nerves. Was she safe?

"Aren't you being a trifle prudish? You cannot truly be concerned that some harm might befall you," Lord

Catledge said. When she didn't answer, he sighed. "Would you like to leave now? My carriage is parked nearby, you know. I can spirit you back to Russell's Emporium in no time, if that is what you wish."

Cassandra hesitated. She opened her mouth, but no words came out.

"Are you feeling faint or something?" Alistair asked quizzically, his dark eyes trained on her, his forehead creased with concern. "Because if you are, I will escort you home immediately." He gave her a lopsided grin and added, "It has been my experience that women often faint when they want to go home."

Cassandra struggled to frame a suitable answer to an inquiry made all the more reasonable by her strange, sudden reticence. She almost lost her train of thought, staring at the thick lock of black hair that fell over Alistair's brow no matter how often he combed it back with his fingers.

It was a thick, black wavy cowlick that fell haphazardly over his right eye and required him to toss his head, or thread his fingers through it, in order to see. That one defiant lock of hair totally undermined Alistair Gordon's affected vanity, making the elegant viscount more real, more masculine, less perfect. And infinitely attractive.

Cassandra's demitasse cup clattered when she replaced it on the china saucer. "Forgive me, my lord. Yes, I am quite all right. It's just that I have not been about much lately. I am still in mourning for my mother, you see."

"Yes, I can see that," Alistair said.

Audrey's advice to go into half-mourning echoed in Cassandra's ears. "It has been a year and a day since my mother passed away," she remarked, self-consciously fingering the black silk bow of her wide-brimmed bonnet. "I realize it would not be inappropriate to go into a period of half-mourning, but truly I have not felt compelled to do so."

"Why not dispense with mourning clothes altogether?" suggested Alistair.

"Dispense with them . . . altogether?" Cassandra considered it scandalous for a gentleman in the company of a lady to refer, however obliquely, to the act of undressing. "Why, sir, you should be ashamed of yourself!"

Alistair's brows arched devilishly. He started to speak, perhaps to lodge a protest against Cassandra's inference, but then he clamped his lips shut. A wave of color highlighted a rakish grin, but Viscount Catledge made no attempt to explain his rude intimation.

Instead, he simply stared at Cassandra as if she'd actually given him an idea he hadn't thought of. "Miss Russell, surely you cannot believe that I meant to offend you. Your response to my suggestion, I admit, baffles me." He frowned in a moue of innocent bewilderment, obviously false. "Unless, of course, you have been rereading *Pamela*, and have cast me as a dastardly rakehell." He pushed his coffee cup aside.

"Certainly not," snapped Cassandra. "The last book I read was *A Voyage to Abyssinia*. Melodramas hold not a smidgeon of interest for me. And besides," she added, "*Pamela*'s persecutor repents in the end, and marries the serving-girl he tried so desperately to corrupt; I doubt you are susceptible to such a redemption."

"You are probably correct," admitted Alistair. "But I know a great many ladies who consider *Pamela*'s story titillating, and their constant perusal of it colors their perception of mankind, causing them to accuse many well-meaning gentlemen of the most lewd inferences."

Cassandra scoffed. "That, kind sir, is a reflection on the sort of women you are accustomed to keeping company with." But she was no longer entirely certain that Alistair intended his proposal as a double entendre. The possibility she had misconstrued his commentary was appallingly real. As a matter of pride, however, Cassandra deemed it necessary to treat his remark as premeditated effrontery. To act otherwise would be to admit an atrocious faux pas.

Alistair frowned. "Now you have insulted my friends."

"I suppose I have," Cassandra said with a top-lofty air.

"And I am not sorry. I am not accustomed to such gutter-talk from a gentleman."

"I am sure I did not—" The viscount shrugged, and began again. "What I mean is, I am sure I do not know what you are talking about. Gutter talk? Surely, you did not really think that I meant you should dispense with—Oh, fustian!" He took a long drink of his coffee and brandy, his face darkening with emotion. "What do you mean, exactly, Miss Russell?"

"Take care not to crush your cup in your hand, my lord. Good heavens, you are red in the face, and as tightly wound as a steel spring. You seem terribly out of sorts. I suggest we forget this matter," Cassandra added after a brief hesitation.

"I think that is a capital idea," the viscount concurred through clenched teeth.

Thank heavens, thought Cassandra. After all, she wasn't sure what she had meant. "You brought me here to convince me I should meet your brother, my lord. In fact, you induced me here with some ridiculous nonsense about a national crisis. As of yet I have heard nothing that might advance your cause in my eyes. Wouldn't you care to argue your case?"

"Must you be so serious, Miss Russell?"

Cassandra rankled at the viscount's teasing criticism. If there was anything that annoyed her, it was being told she was too serious. "I agreed to accompany you to this scandalous establishment in order to hear you out on the subject of your brother's request," she replied. "Pray, do get on with it."

Grinning, Alistair pushed his hair out of his eye. "You don't get about much, do you, Miss Russell?"

"That is none of your business, my lord," Cassandra said indignantly, hooking a finger beneath the black bow tied under her chin. She twisted her neck, and wondered if those bonnet strings were any less comfortable than the tight swaddling mummies wore.

Alistair was undaunted. "You are much too young to be wearing those widow's weeds, and proper decorum does not require you to drape yourself in black shrouds forever. Pardon my boldness, but a year of mourning is considered quite respectful."

"Pardon *my* boldness, my lord, but I feel it is not your place to tell me when I should come out of mourning."

"You don't like it when someone tells you what to do. That's it, isn't it?" Alistair sipped his coffee, winking at Cassandra over the rim of his cup. "Can't say as I blame you. I've always had a rather stubborn streak myself."

"I am not stubborn," Cassandra said. "But I am capable of making my own decisions, thank you very much."

"That is obvious," agreed Alistair, glancing about the room. "Otherwise you would never have accompanied me here. Not that there is any reason why you shouldn't have. This is a respectable establishment, frequented by merchants and businessmen, and ladies out for a day of shopping."

Despite the chill that which wrapped around her ankles every time someone entered the café, Cassandra felt uncomfortably warm beneath her pelisse. Irritated as much by the viscount's impertinence as she was by her own odd, visceral reaction to his brazen charm, she shivered with disquietude. Prudence, discretion, and proper breeding implored her to stand up, hail a hackney cab, and beat a hasty retreat home. But she did not.

She was too intrigued by Alistair Gordon to flee for safety.

The viscount grinned crookedly. "Ah, well. I suppose we should get on to more serious matters after all. I wanted to explain to you about my brother."

"Oh, yes, the Earl of Hedgeworth. How could I forget?" With a jolt, she remembered why Alistair had invited her to join him for a cup of coffee. Scolding herself for forgetting why she was there, Cassandra suddenly felt silly and vulnerable. The viscount was a plump-in-the-pocket hell-born buck who wouldn't waste a minute of his precious time on a bluestocking chit like her, absent some nefarious, ulterior motive.

Why should he, Cassandra thought, when diamonds of the first water sparkled all around him, at elegant balls and assemblies, at fancy house parties in the country, and in every drawing room in Mayfair?

Her confidence melted. For a moment, staring into Alistair's delightful, deceptively playful eyes, she had forgotten herself, but now Cassandra remembered who she was. She was the serious, somber daughter of Sir Anthony Russell, an English adventurer, and his wife, Rhoda, an Egyptian shop mistress. She was a lonely woman who planned funerals for a living. She lived with a monkey, a mummy, and a surly servant named Audrey who slipped out at night to rendezvous with every man who winked at her. And she was safe and secure in her own ordered little corner of the world.

From the tragic death of her father, Cassandra had learned enough about adventure—its seductive nature, its sly quicksand-pull, and its inevitable horrific dangers—to know better than to court it, encourage it, or even flirt with it. The viscount was devastatingly attractive, that was true. But his mischievous good looks, his quick smile, and mercurial nature spelled sheer adventure to Cassandra's cautious eyes. He was alluring, but he was as dangerous as a scorpion in the Egyptian desert. The easiest way to avoid his sting was to stay as far away as possible.

The waiter had produced two fresh cups of coffee, and Cassandra watched Alistair sweeten his with a healthy dollop of brandy. "Isn't it a bit early in the day to be imbibing alcohol?" she asked.

A grimace froze on Alistair's face, and when he spoke, his voice was as brittle as ice. "What was that you said?" Slowly lowering the bottle to the table, Viscount Catledge pinned his frigid gaze on Cassandra.

"I said," she replied, "is it not a trifle early in the day to begin partaking of alcoholic beverages?"

Alistair stared at her as if she'd grown another head. "I thought that was what you said." He picked up the bottle again and emptied it into his coffee cup. Cassandra watched him drain the mixture, which she estimated to be at least four parts brandy to one part coffee, inasmuch as the cup was almost empty when he refilled it. Then he slammed the cup down on the table, stared at her, and exhaled a sigh redolent with alcoholic fumes.

"Ahhh!" He ran his tongue along his upper lip and gazed at Cassandra through lowered lids. "You should try a bit of brandy in your coffee, Miss Russell. Truly, I believe it would do you good."

Cassandra felt the sting of indignation in her eyes. "Lord Catledge, are you implying that my personality is so lacking in charisma that it *requires* enhancement by means of alcohol?"

Alistair's lids drooped seductively, but whether that was the result of intoxication or sheer impudence, Cassandra didn't know. "I did not say that, Miss Russell. But I assure you, a little snort would do you a world of good." He lifted his brows and grinned wickedly. "For pity's sake, loosen up!"

"Ooh!" Cassandra shook her head in disbelief. "What kind of tippling scoundrel would get himself foxed over coffee in the middle of the day with a lady he has just met?"

"Why, a merry-pin like me, I suppose," said Alistair, laughing. "But I am not drunk, dear, not by a long shot." After a brief hesitation Alistair leaned forward and said soberly, "Really, Miss Russell. I am not drunk. Shall we cease tormenting each other for the moment and get on to discussing the purpose of this meeting?"

"Yes," agreed Cassandra, tapping her fingertips on the tabletop. "Let's."

"My brother wanted desperately to speak with your mother about his recent loss."

"His recent loss? Do you mean a loved one of his died?"

"The earl is not *bereaved*, Miss Russell." Combing that thick shock of hair off his forehead, Alistair said, "On second thought, perhaps that is the most apt description of his current state of mind. You see, my brother's mummy has been stolen."

Cassandra gasped. Her skin rippled with goose bumps as she thought of how devastated she would be if Cleo were to be stolen from her. "His mummy? That is tragic! Tell me what happened, as much as you know, that is," she said.

"Neville's collection of Egyptian antiquities is quite extensive, as you have probably guessed. Some might consider his cache the spoils of war, given the manner in which he came into possession of them."

"Pray tell, how did he acquire them?"

"That is rather a long story, miss. Suffice to say that shortly after Napoleon's army left Egypt, my brother hid a great many objects in a tomb near Thebes. In addition, there were hundreds, perhaps thousands of artifacts already in that tomb. Then he wandered around the desert like a crazed Bedouin for almost ten years, always returning to the tomb to stash away any treasures that he found."

"Why didn't your brother return to England?"

Alistair shook his head. "He went a wee bit mad, if you ask me. When the British finally recaptured Cairo, effectively ending the French occupation of Egypt, French troops were allowed unhindered passage home on the condition that all antiquities in their possession would immediately be given up. General Menou threatened to destroy the lot rather than turn them over to the British. Neville prevented that from happening, and compromised his cover into the bargain."

"I did not know that, of course," murmured Cassandra. "How very admirable."

"The British recovered a vast store of treasures, but the really good stuff was now secreted in Neville's hiding place. Of course, it was necessary then for Neville to flee Napoleon's henchmen. Neville presented himself to a British officer and told his story, exempting the exact location of his hiding place, I'm afraid. Good thing. Seems there was some misunderstanding at that point. Sir Abercromby was the only chap who knew Neville was a British subject, spying for the Crown. But he had taken a cannonball in his leg at Alexandria and died just a few months earlier."

"So the earl was abandoned." Cassandra was saddened by the injustice, and sighed pensively.

"Quite so," agreed the viscount, leaning back in his chair to cross his legs. "And I daresay, he was most overset by the ungentlemanly treatment he received from his own countrymen."

"It drove him mad," Cassandra whispered.

At length, the viscount said, "And then my brother met your father."

Cassandra nodded, her mind flashing back ten years to the day when her father met the strange Englishman on the banks of the Nile River. "Yes, your brother had located a well-hidden tomb in the Valley of the Kings. We went there, my parents and I, to see the magnificent burial chamber of a long-dead king and his queen." She closed her eyes, remembering. "Father said he'd never seen so much gold in his life. 'Struth, the place gleamed with gold so that my eyes were nearly blinded!"

Alistair cleared his throat, and Cassandra realized she'd drifted far into her imagination, into the past. She blinked her eyes and stared at him. "Go on," she said.

"Neville apparently agreed to divide the antiquities with your father if he would help in getting the loot back to London."

"Yes. But something went dreadfully wrong."

"Neville said Sir Anthony was murdered as the ship

was being loaded," continued Alistair softly. "Something about a raving lunatic who attacked them?"

Cassandra shivered and hugged her arms. "Oh, 'twas horrible!" She shook her head, attempting to quell the hideous images that loomed in her memory. "From nowhere, the madman emerged, his white *dishdash* swirling around him so that he looked like a terrible tornado. He ran onto the deck of the ship, his scimitar held high above his head. He attacked Father, and Mama grabbed me, turning my face away. I could not see what happened next. I do not even know how Mama and I got out of harm's way. But we did, and then . . . Father was dead."

"And what became of the murderous Mameluke?" whispered Alistair.

"He got away, unfortunately. At least that is what Mama told me. She said he was probably some Arab traitor who'd been promised a commission by Napoleon, then left behind when the French Army returned to Paris. Perhaps he was bitter toward your brother, perhaps toward Napoleon. But he got his revenge by killing Father, an innocent man."

Alistair fell quiet, toying with the handle of his coffee cup.

Cassandra's breathing returned to normal, but her heart still ached with the memory of her father's death. "Had Father not listened to your brother, he would be alive today," she finally reminded the viscount bitterly.

"Surely, you don't blame your father's death on Neville!"

"Yes," said Cassandra staunchly. "I do. And for that reason I do not care to offer my assistance. The story of your brother's betrayal is tragic indeed, but that is no concern of mine." She made to rise, but Alistair reached across the table and laid his hand atop hers.

Stunned, Cassandra's body went stiff. Alistair's kidskin glove covered her lace mitten, his fingers tightening around her hand like a vise.

"Aren't you interested in the mummy's curse?" he asked.

Cassandra's stomach plummeted to her feet, and she felt the room tip from side to side as if she were viewing it through the porthole of a tempest-tossed ship. "Mummy's curse?" she repeated, lowering herself to the edge of her chair. "What do you know of that?"

"So you do believe in the curse," Alistair stated smugly. "Then you must hear me out."

Recalling the tragedies heaped on her family by the mummy king's evil spell, Cassandra's blood ran cold. The horror of her father's death, and the pain of her mother's final days, were certainly manifestations of the curse. The mummy king had wreaked his havoc on both her parents, then doomed Cassandra to a life of unmarried solitude. Cassandra knew full well the price she and her parents had paid for disturbing the mummy's resting place, but she'd never heard another person speak of it. And she'd never given any thought as to how the strange Englishman had been affected by the curse. She only hoped that the great Belzoni could instruct her on how to escape the curse.

"I am listening," Cassandra managed. "Pray, do go on."

Alistair took a deep breath before he spoke. "Shortly after my brother loaded his artifacts on the boat, he became very ill. He lost his sight in one eye, as well as the use of his legs. He wheels himself around in a Merlin chair now, coughing and blaspheming, and, in general, being bloody disagreeable."

Cassandra swallowed hard and reached for her coffee cup. She was too upset to remind the viscount to mind his language.

"At any rate," said Alistair, "Neville feels his physical deformities are the result of the mummy's curse."

"I fear your brother may be correct," said Cassandra. "Forgive me if I do not show a great deal of sympathy for the Earl of Hedgeworth. If not for his avarice, my father—"

"Nonsense! Neville never meant to hurt anyone, least of all himself!"

"Perhaps he did not intend to invoke the wrath of the pharaoh, but he did," countered Cassandra. "And I have nought but resentment toward him."

Alistair scowled and folded his arms across his chest. "Then I suppose you do not want to hear the rest of the story?"

"The part that involves a national crisis?" Cassandra retorted.

"It involves much more than that," said Alistair. "It involves the welfare of thousands of innocent people. The mummy has been stolen from Neville, you see—"

Cassandra gasped. "Good heavens! Do you mean to say that it was the pharaoh's mummy that was stolen?"

"Just so," snapped Alistair. "I suppose that you are aware of the longevity of the mummy's curse."

"It will expire when the people who disturbed his burial place are dead." She propped one elbow on the table and rested her forehead against her open palm. "That includes me, of course."

Alistair unfolded his arms and leaned forward. "Yes, that is exactly right. So you see, Miss Russell, you are in grave danger."

"Danger?" Cassandra heard her voice tremble, and she felt her legs go numb beneath her mourning gown.

"Yes, grave danger. Perhaps the mummy will seek revenge on you, as the last living soul who was present when he was removed from his final resting place."

"But I am not the last living person who was present then. There was your brother," argued Cassandra feebly. "He is still alive."

"He is half dead," answered Alistair, digging into his vest pocket for some coins, which he tossed onto the table.

"The mummy can do nothing more to punish him. I fear you will be the monster's next victim, Miss Russell."

"You are not suggesting the mummy climbed out of its coffin and ambled away from your brother's custody on its own?" asked Cassandra, her pulse fluttering.

Alistair chuckled. "Of course not. The old fellow was stolen by someone who knew precisely what he was doing. I am leaning toward a conspiracy theory, if you really want to know. 'Twould be near impossible for one man acting alone to break into Neville's town house, find the rooms that house his collection, pick the lock, and then remove a nest of coffins weighing more than two horses. And all in the dead of night without so much as a floorboard creaking? No, I think the crime was masterminded by someone very knowledgeable in Egyptology, and carried off by a band of expert hirelings."

"I think your logic is well-founded. What do you propose doing?" Cassandra asked.

"I propose we form a partnership of sorts."

Grasping the edge of the table for support, Cassandra echoed the viscount's astounding words. "A partnership?"

He smiled. "My brother is unfit to launch an investigation into the missing mummy, yet he has convinced me it is vital to the public's interest that the mummy be found."

"I quite agree with him on that score," murmured Cassandra. She didn't have to be told that if the mummy were removed from its nest of coffins, the curse that had already ruined her parents' life, Neville's, and perhaps her own, would spread unchecked. Like the plague, the curse would infect anyone who tampered with the king's coffins, unwrapped the corpse's linens, or even treated the remains with less than utter reverence. Until both she and Neville were dead, that mummy had to be left in its coffin, undisturbed. Otherwise, a disaster of apocalyptic proportions was certain to occur.

"I must therefore find the mummy and apprehend the villain who stole it," explained Alistair. "The pharaoh's

remains must not be defiled further. You are a member
of the esteemed Society of Egyptologists, are you not?"

"I am."

"I must infiltrate that group in order to learn *who* in
London might be interested in the buying and selling of
stolen Egyptian antiquities."

"That is a logical starting place," Cassandra conceded.

"And you must help me." Alistair reached for her hand.

"I must?" Cassandra gulped. For a moment she sat in
stunned silence, unsure of her obligations, confused by
her mingling emotions. She did not wish the mummy's
curse on any other living soul, but she did not relish the
thought of forming a partnership with Alistair either. The
complications seemed enormous. "I must think on this,
my lord," she finally said.

"Think on it, my dear lady," suggested the viscount.
"But do not allow your trepidations to stand in the way of
your conscience. Human lives are at stake, you know. I
truly need your assistance."

"I understand," Cassandra lied, then added vaguely, "I
want to go home now." No longer acutely aware of her
surroundings, she rose shakily to her feet and grabbed her
tiny reticule. Now the coffee house and its patrons seemed
a blur, and Alistair a warm, masculine presence hovering
at her side. He tucked her arm in his, and she leaned on
him for support.

She felt faint and cotton-headed as they left the coffee
shop. "You must help me. . . ." Alistair's entreaty reverberated in her brain, repeating itself in a thick singsong tone,
like some monstrous chant. Was he toying with her? she
wondered as he made a flourishing gesture toward a black,
gleaming carriage parked conveniently at the curbside.

A liveried footman bedecked in a smart uniform of gold
and green quickly positioned a wooden step beneath the
carriage door so that Cassandra could ascend. The viscount
gently held her elbow, assisting her into the compartment.

Cassandra leaned back against the squabs, relieved that

she would soon be home, safe and snug in her own apartment, where she could sort out her feelings and decide whether she should encourage the viscount's attentions or refuse to help him. The danger of the mummy's curse was so terrifying to her that she could not know for certain whether its danger was real or part of her lurid imagination. She desperately craved solitude, and a respite from the unsettling effect Alistair was having on her.

She watched him duck his head as he entered the compartment. He settled himself across from her, rapped on the trapdoor above his head, then met her eyes and smiled.

The carriage gave a bounce when the coachman jumped on the box. Then Cassandra heard the footman scramble up the rungs at the rear of the carriage and shout excitedly, "Whoa! Watch yerself, ye fool!"

Lord Catledge lifted his brows quizzically and slid across the leather-upholstered bench seat. Raising the shade, he peered out toward the coffee shop just as the footman yelled again.

"I said, watch it, ye idiotic madman!"

A snap of the reins and a jolt of the equipage followed. Then, above the sound of wheels rumbling slowly over cobblestone, Cassandra heard the heavy clatter of horse's hooves galloping alongside. The footman was screeching now, yelling obscenities Cassandra had never heard before, but which clearly expressed the man's outrage and fear.

"Good Lord, whatever is going on out there?" Cassandra asked.

"I see nothing unusual on this side," Lord Catledge answered.

"Perhaps the commotion is on this side of the carriage," Cassandra suggested. She was nearest the door adjacent to the street, so she leaned over and raised the shade, then squinted against the glare of the sun beating on the thin windowpane.

The footman's voice rang out. "What are ye doin', ye bloody arse!"

A black-caped horseman swept alongside the carriage, and Cassandra started. She recoiled, but not before a deafening crash brought the windowpane in on her. Something whizzed past her head, leaving her bonnet askew and her ear scraped and burning. Clapping her hand to her injury, Cassandra reeled backward, more frightened than hurt.

The next few moments were a scrambling confusion of shouts and horses' whinnies and pounding hooves.

Dazed, Cassandra felt Lord Catledge grasp her shoulders and lower her on to the carriage seat. The tip of one half-boot remained on the floor. The viscount covered her shoulders with a lap blanket, and Cassandra stared up at him, shocked and disoriented. At the sound of his harsh invective, she widened her eyes. He had picked up the offending projectile in his hand and was studying it with a look of consternation on his face.

"What is it?" Cassandra asked weakly.

"A rock," answered the viscount. He banged on the trapdoor, and when it opened, he instructed his driver to return to Russell's Emporium posthaste.

"Don't ye want us to pursue that scum whot attacked us?" the beleaguered coachman asked.

"No!" bellowed Lord Catledge. "I want to get the lady home to safety. Afterward we can set about finding the rotten scoundrel responsible for this joke."

"Joke?" Cassandra whispered thickly, holding her ear. The trapdoor slammed shut and the carriage increased its speed.

"Someone must think it terribly amusing," muttered the viscount grimly as he knelt beside Cassandra and examined her ear. Removing her bonnet, he smoothed back her hair and gazed down at her as if she were some sort of rare treasure, or priceless antiquity. His expression confused Cassandra, but she struggled mightily to remain lucid.

"I don't think you have any injuries though. The top of your ear is scraped, but there is no blood to speak of. We should be grateful for that. I suppose you are a trifle shaken up, that's all."

"What kind of joke?" Cassandra managed to ask. The edges of her vision were growing ragged. "What is that you are holding in your hand?"

"'Tis a rock," answered Alistair. "There is a piece of paper tied round the rock with a string. Here, you can see for yourself." He held the crumpled piece of cheap foolscap before her nose, and Cassandra narrowed her eyes, attempting to focus her blurred vision. The letters seemed to vibrate upon the paper, and she was forced to ask the viscount to read it aloud.

He heaved a grim sigh. "The note says, 'Beware of the mummy's curse.'"

"Beware of the mummy's curse?" Cassandra repeated, incredulous. No! she protested silently. It could not be!

Pressing her palm to her forehead, Cassandra felt her breathing quicken and her pulse pound as the light in the carriage compartment faded. Struggling to maintain her tenuous hold on reality, she turned her head and saw the viscount's sympathetic face become two, then three identical images.

She held up her tiny purse. "Pray, hand me my *sal volatile*. I fear I am going to faint."

Alistair reached into the reticule and quickly produced the smelling salts. Waving the tiny bottle of ammonia beneath her nose, he said softly, "There, there. I am sure it is some cruel joke, not to be taken seriously. Do not overset yourself, Cassan—Miss Russell. Compose yourself. Everything will be all right."

"No," Cassandra said as the compartment blurred. "I do not believe it will," she whispered just before everything went black.

When she awoke, she was still in the viscount's carriage, but it was not moving. She opened her eyes to see his concerned smile. He knelt beside her, gently stroking her hair.

* * *

Cassandra stepped from the viscount's carriage into his waiting arms. Had she been thinking clearly, she would have opposed his carrying her into her shop, but she was still dazed from fainting and too weak to resist the strong embrace that lifted her off her feet. Besides, she had never been held by a man, and to her surprise, she discovered she liked it. Wrapping her arms about the viscount's neck, Cassandra laid her head on the soft superfine of his coat, crossed her ankles, and wondered what Audrey would think of this unexpected drama.

The viscount's liveried footman jumped down from the boot, rushed to the shop door, and pulled it open. Entering, Alistair turned sideways to avoid scraping Cassandra's boots against the door frame. The tinkling bells that announced the arrival of customers brought Audrey flying from the back room of the shop.

"Oh, miss! Whatever in the world has happened to ye?" the rough-complected girl cried, wringing her hands. "I was worried outta me mind, I was!"

"I am quite all right, Audrey. You can put me down now, Lord Catledge."

"I shall do no such thing," replied the viscount. "I presume your living quarters are on the first floor, and I have no intention of allowing you to climb those stairs. Not in your condition." He smiled at Audrey, whose gaping stare was difficult to ignore and much harder not to laugh at. "Would you be so kind as to show me to Miss Russell's apartment, gel?"

"Oh, yes, my lordship!"

Cassandra kicked her feet. "Oh, put me down!"

"No!" Alistair turned a beaming grin on Audrey, as if enlisting her aid in the conspiracy to restrain Cassandra. His charming smile apparently had the desired effect, for Audrey bobbed a curtsy and jerked her head toward the beaded curtain.

"By the bye, me name's Audrey," the girl said coquett-ishly, beckoning Alistair toward the inventory room.

"This is Lord Catledge, Audrey," Cassandra said sourly.

Audrey weaved her way through the maze of inventory in the back room, Alistair following close behind.

Cassandra clutched at the walls as they slid by, but her efforts to force Lord Catledge to release her were futile. "Good heavens! Let me down, my lord! I demand it. Audrey, what are you doing? I forbid you to show this man my private living quarters! It just is not seemly, do you hear?"

Over her shoulder Audrey flashed a coy smile. "'Tis this way, my lord," she said, gesturing toward the stairwell.

Alistair was careful to avoid brushing Cassandra's head against the plastered walls as he climbed the stairs and entered her apartment. Cassandra noticed that his eyes scanned her small sitting room with interest, lighting for a moment on a painted wooden box filled with miniature statuettes of ancient Egyptian servants. He paused and perused the rooms with avid eyes.

"This is not an opportune time for you to study my antiquities," Cassandra pointed out.

Alistair tightened his grip on her body. "I cannot help but notice the expert craftsmanship in those pieces," he said, looking down at her. "It does not require an Egyptologist to see that you possess many fine pieces. Why that box of ushabti alone is probably worth a small fortune."

Cassandra nodded. "The ancient Egyptians believed that those figurines would do their work after death," she said. Quoting from the *Book of the Dead*, she intoned, "'O shabti, if the deceased is called upon to do any of the work required there . . . you shall say, Here I am, I will do it.'"

Audrey stopped short and whirled around with her hands on her hips. "I hope you ain't gettin' no ideas, miss. 'Tis bad enough I got to wait on ye hand and foot in this lifetime. I ain't about to do yer dirty work for ye in the next!"

All three shared a laugh as Alistair crossed into Cassandra's bedchamber and laid her on her bed atop a patchwork coverlet. Tia scampered up beside her and grimaced threateningly at the viscount. When Cassandra removed her bonnet, the monkey took it and crouched beside her, toying absently with the satin ribbons.

"I wouldn't worry none about that little creature," Audrey advised the viscount. "She's perfectly harmless, that one."

Cassandra quickly grabbed a bolster and arranged herself in a half-sitting position against the plain wooden headboard. Primly smoothing down her rumpled skirts, she averted her eyes from the viscount, painfully aware that he was the first man who'd ever stepped foot inside her bedroom, and acutely embarrassed by the warmth she felt rising to her cheeks.

From the corner of her eye she saw Lord Catledge bow stiffly. "Well, I suppose I shall be on my way," he said hesitantly.

Cassandra bade him good-bye and thanked him for assisting her home, but when he made no move to leave, she slanted her eyes upward. At length she said, "Was there something you were waiting for, my lord?"

Audrey made a pretense of busying herself at the tripod washstand, but the curious maid was clearly hanging on every word the others uttered. Cassandra shot her employee a quelling gaze, then faced the viscount and sighed impatiently. "Do not let me keep you from your business, Lord Catledge. I am sure that you are a very busy man."

"Didn't I tell you I was an irresponsible ne'er-do-well?" he countered.

Cassandra scoffed. "And if I recall correctly, I told you I didn't believe a word you said. 'Struth, my lord, your actions contradict your words." She cradled Tia against her bosom and affectionately stroked the animal's furry head.

Now that his arms were empty, the viscount crumpled
his beaver hat in his hands. "I should like the privilege of
calling upon you again, Miss Russell." After a brief hesitation he added, "To discuss the urgent matter of the stolen
mummy. And, of course, the significance of today's incident." He cut his eyes in Audrey's direction, indicating
he did not want the servant to know what happened.

"Really, Lord Catledge, your brother's stolen mummy
is none of my affair. And as for today's incident, it would
appear to me that you have a few enemies around town
who wish to play a joke upon you. That message was clearly
intended for you, not me."

"Was it?" the viscount murmured.

Cassandra studiously avoided looking at the japanned
screen that shielded Cleo from view. "I have no interest
in mummies, aside from a purely academic one."

Audrey, however, pointed toward the lacquered panel
and blurted out, "But, ma'am, you ain't forgettin'—"

"Audrey, hush! That will be quite enough of your saucy
lip!"

Audrey whined, "But, ma'am!" Then, taking note of
Cassandra's vanquishing stare, she meekly returned her
attention to the washbasin, where she was wringing out a
cool rag.

Lord Catledge stepped forward, perched himself on the
edge of Cassandra's bed, and reached for her hand. Clasping it in his, he said, "How can you say the stolen mummy
is none of your concern? You went pale as powder at the
threatening reminder of the pharaoh's curse, and I daresay
you do not strike me as a fainthearted, simpering miss! You
of all people must recognize the dreadful consequences of
allowing that mummy to fall into the wrong hands. I need
your help, Miss Russell. I *must* see you again!"

"I am sure you are quite capable of apprehending the
thief of your brother's mummy. You do not need my assistance, my lord."

Lord Catledge tightened his grip on Cassandra's hand

and leaned toward her. "Miss Russell, you must reconsider."

Tia bared her teeth and gave the viscount's glove a smart slap. Cassandra quickly withdrew her hand.

"Why, you little—" The viscount began, frowning at the monkey, but his voice faded to a murmur.

Gently removing the monkey from her lap, Cassandra suppressed a smile and said, "Run along now, Tia." When her pet disappeared behind the screen, she faced her visitor and continued. "However, if you are determined to infiltrate the Society of Egyptologists, you may attend the next meeting at my invitation. It is a special event scheduled for next Thursday evening at Lord Tifton's home. The great Signor Giovanni Belzoni will be the guest of honor." She couldn't suppress the exultant tone that suddenly filled her voice.

"Belzoni?" the viscount said, frowning. He seemed to puzzle over the name for a moment, then his eyes lit up, as if he'd remembered something of vital importance. "Are you an admirer of his?"

"Oh, yes," gushed Cassandra, and fell back on her pillow, clasping her hands at her breasts. Belatedly realizing the indecorum of her supine posture, she straightened like a ramrod and smoothed her skirts again. To cover her embarrassment at having displayed such girlish rapture and silly hero worship, she added brusquely, "The great Belzoni is admired by every Egyptologist in London, perhaps the world. What a foolish question, Lord Catledge."

"Yes, I suppose it was," replied the viscount, smiling. "Well, at any rate, I shall escort you to Lord Tifton's home next Thursday. What time should my carriage arrive, miss?"

"I did not mean—" Cassandra stammered, flustered by the viscount's assumption that she was to accompany him to the meeting. "What I meant to say was—"

Audrey appeared at Cassandra's bedside with a wet washcloth, and interjected. "I'll have the miss ready to go by eight o'clock, my lord."

"I do not think . . . I did not agree . . ." Audrey slapped a frigid, sopping-wet rag on Cassandra's face, covering her mouth and nose, cutting off any further protest.

Chuckling, Lord Catledge stood. "I am looking forward to seeing you, Miss Russell." He pivoted on his shiny boots and left the room.

When the door slammed behind him, Cassandra pulled the washcloth off her face and demanded angrily, "How dare you?" Staring at Audrey, she practically shouted with fury, "I've never been so angry in my life! I should fire you on the spot, you cheeky ingrate!"

Audrey rolled her eyes and batted her lashes, feigning an innocence she'd surely lost a decade earlier. "Oh, sorry, miss. I thought you wanted to attend the meetin' with the gentleman. Really, miss. Didn't mean to cause you no trouble."

"I am sure of it," grumbled Cassandra. She rose shakily, allowed her maid to extricate her from her mourning gown, then fell back onto her hard bed in a wilted heap of lawn pantaloons and sheer chemise. Audrey deftly unlaced her boots and laid them by the nightstand.

"Just leave me be, will you? I am going to sleep, and I do not want to be disturbed until the morrow."

"Wouldn't you like some supper, ma'am?"

"Take the night off, Audrey," Cassandra said, her eyes growing heavy already. She felt Audrey throw a warm blanket over her, then heard the girl steal lightly from the room. A deep sleep overtook her, and she dreamed of sandy dunes, waving palm trees, and serene, majestic pyramids.

From somewhere in the darkness came the sound of slow, shuffling footsteps.

Cassandra drifted in the murky blackness of her dream-state, vaguely aware of another presence in her bed-chamber.

She tried to wake, but sleep tugged hard.

At last, she roused. Her lids flew open.

Black, vacant eyes met hers. A bandaged hand reached out to touch her face. Against the blackness of the darkened bedchamber, the mummy's stark white swaddling shone luminously.

Cassandra tried to scream, but terror stole her voice. Then a cold, damp cloth covered her nose, a strong, unpleasant odor filled her nostrils, and her mind succumbed to deep, drugged sleep.

She dreamed again.

But, as always, her mother turned her face away just as Father was stabbed.

Chapter Four

Audrey crept up the stairs, careful to avoid the steps that creaked. Praying that her employer had not noticed her empty bed, she ran her hands along the walls through pitch blackness, and when she reached the top landing, produced a key from her pocket. Before she inserted it into the lock, however, the door yawed open.

That was odd. Puzzled, Audrey shook her head. It was not unusual for her employer to get out of bed and return to the stockroom to look over some newly arrived goods, or to peruse account books. But it was not like the efficient Miss Russell to forget to relock her apartment door when she retired for the night. Audrey's senses snapped to full alertness as she stepped across the threshold and hesitated in the darkened sitting room.

Frigid vapors twined themselves around her thin-stockinged ankles, and Audrey shivered. Moving into the room, she saw the casement windows flung open. Thin lace curtains flapped in the night breeze, framing a wedge of London's moonlit skyscape. Audrey knew that the surface of the neighboring rooftop was a drop of approximately

ten feet from that window. She also knew the window had
been shut when she sneaked out earlier.

She started toward the window to close it, laying her key
on Cassandra's round table as she passed.

A muffled sound—footsteps perhaps?—came from the
rear of the apartment. Audrey pulled up short and froze,
her pulse pounding. She pricked her ears and held her
breath. Bathed in shadows, the drawing room was as eerie
as a haunted crypt, and while Audrey's eyes adjusted to
the lack of light, fear stippled her flesh with goose pimples.
Seized with the notion of fleeing down the steps and into
the street to seek assistance from a passing charley, she
slowly turned on her heel.

She took a step, then went rigid again. The shuffling
sound repeated. Cocking her head, Audrey listened to the
bumps, creaks, and footsteps emanating from Cassandra's
bedchamber.

She was near panic, but she could not leave her mistress
alone in the apartment with an intruder. Wildly, Audrey's
eyes searched the room for a weapon. Silently mouthing
curses, she vowed to make order out of Cassandra's chaotic
Egyptian collection if she lived to see another day. Antiquities were strewn around the room, interspersed with dusty
Greek translations, drawing pads, pots of watercolors,
paintbrushes, and rolled-up maps of ancient civilizations.
Limestone slabs inscribed with inexplicable hieroglyphs
leaned against walls, alabaster jars were stacked in corners,
and statues flanked the fireplace. Audrey hefted a basalt
goddess sporting an antler of upraised arms on the top of
her head, then crossed the room in silent, catlike strides.

Her thin-soled boots glided soundlessly across the well-
worn carpet of the drawing room. Audrey traversed the
corridor, then stood before the half-open door of Cassandra's bedchamber, cold sweat trickling down her bosom.
She steeled herself, and with both hands on the base of
the statue, lifted it above her head.

Through the crack in the doorway she spied Miss Russell's bed, and recognized the inert form of her employer beneath the quilted comforter. Miss Russell appeared to be sleeping, but how could anyone sleep while an intruder rifled through her room? Perhaps her employer had been knocked unconscious, Audrey thought. Or worse . . .

And then she heard slow, heavy footsteps making their way around the room. Unless Tia had taken to wearing Wellington boots, Audrey knew those footsteps were not made by an eight-pound monkey. Behind the door, a flickering circle of light moved in an arc, as if someone held aloft a branch of candles. The rear portion of the bedchamber was obscured by the door, but Audrey recognized the sounds of objects being picked up and replaced. Someone was nosing around, picking through Miss Russell's possessions like a mudlark sifts through trash. A thief! And he was searching for jewels, money, and other valuables.

Where in the world was Tia? Why wasn't the monkey screeching at the top of her lungs, like she did when Audrey accidentally stepped on her tail, or forgot to bring her a banana from the fruit market?

The wind keened mournfully, and somewhere a dog wailed at the moon. A shutter banged rudely against the side of the building, and Audrey started. Miss Russell hadn't stirred a bit, and Audrey feared her employer's motionless form was evidence of serious injury. Audrey couldn't hesitate much longer, not without endangering her employer's life.

She drew in a deep breath and said a silent prayer. A newfound courage energized her. She tightened her grip around the base of the goddess statue.

With the toe of her boot she pushed the door open wide. It gave a warning squeak, leaving Audrey no choice but to rush in like a frontline infantryman. She reached the center of the room and pivoted frantically, her gaze scanning the room like a searchlight. She saw her enemy almost instantly.

Audrey gasped in horror.

The mummy heard her. Its bandaged hand jerked away from the japanned screen, and it wheeled around to face her. Audrey planted herself in the center of the room while the creature, its head tilted inquisitively, stared at her.

Her voice finally erupted in a scream.

The mummy reared back, its hooded eyes widening beneath layers of linen wrappings. A stifled cry escaped its lips, and the branch of candles in its grasp flickered wildly. The beribboned beast's free arm clawed the air in a gesture that Audrey interpreted as some sort of evil warning or threat. Awful gurgling sounds bubbled out of the hideous thing that advanced on her, and Audrey screamed again.

"You stay away from me, ye monstrous son of the devil!" She held her ground as the mummy shortened the distance between them, one arm reaching out for her, one arm holding the candles aloft. "I said, ye best keep away from me, ye godforsaken creature! I'll knock yer head off if ye come any closer, I swear I will."

A guttural snarl rumbled up from the mummy's swaddled throat, and its black eyes gleamed maliciously. Audrey crouched lower, and the mummy advanced.

She waited. With every fiber of her being, Audrey tensed for action and allowed the monster to advance nearer . . . and nearer still. As the space between them closed, she saw the being's eyes darken, black pupils constricting. The mummy's gaze was wild, frantic beneath the vivid glow of the candlelight. With the black stone statue in her grasp, Audrey reached high behind her head.

Her spine curved like a drawn bow, her torso stretched, and her neck muscles strained as Audrey's weight shifted to her back foot. Then, with a primordial grunting sound, she rocked forward and let go the statue. Fear imbued her with a superhuman strength, and the momentum made possible by Audrey's forward press sent the cylindrically shaped goddess hurtling through the air like a missile fired from a cannon.

Dropping the candlestick, the mummy threw up its bandaged hands in a defensive gesture and managed to deflect the major impact of the statue. Still, the ancient goddess struck the creature's shoulder with considerable force, causing the mummy to stumble backward with a loud exclamation of anger and pain. It shielded its face with its hands in an unexpected display of pacifism.

Glancing furtively toward the door, the mummy whimpered like a wounded dog. Audrey stepped back, allowing the creature a wide berth. But the interloper's retreat filled her with grandiose courage, and she could not resist heckling the cowardly monster as he made his escape.

"Why if that ain't a French turn, I ain't never seen one!" crowed Audrey, quickly scooping up the fallen candelabrum. One of its tapers was snuffed, but the other still burned bright. With one hand she wielded the heavy silver ornament above her head. With the other she beckoned the monster to approach, challenging it the way a boxer might lure his opponent into the ring.

"Come on, ye big ball a' cobwebs! Let's see whot yer really made of!" Backing its way out of the bedchamber, the mummy suddenly pivoted on the threshold and loped across the corridor with surprising agility. Audrey followed at a safe distance and brightened the small drawing room with her candle just in time to see the mummy hoist its weight through the open window. She rushed forward and leaned over the sill, watching as the creature fled across the neighboring rooftop, clutching its injured shoulder and moaning in agony.

Through the early morning mist she saw the mummy traverse the flat roof with startling alacrity.

The mummy vanished in a cloud of fog. Shivering more from relief than from the bracing air, Audrey pulled the windows shut and latched the cockspur fastening.

A soft, high-pitched wail emerged from Miss Russell's bedchamber. Rushing to her employer's side, Audrey cried, "I'm comin', miss! Don't fret! The monster is gone!"

* * *

Though her head ached terribly, Cassandra applied her-self diligently to the menial task of polishing the coffins on display in Russell's Emporium. Nausea and unaccountable weariness had beset her throughout the morning, symptoms she attributed to the stress of last night's incident. Every time she thought of the hideous mummy hovering over her, its evil face leering, its hand outstretched, she shivered with fright. Unable to think of anything but the danger she had so narrowly escaped, the monotony of dusting and waxing coffin lids was a welcome relief.

Catching sight of her reflection, she paused. Did she see a flicker of deception in her own eyes? Rubbing her chamois cloth along the slick mahogany surface, Cassandra grinned ruefully. The mummy was not the only thing on her mind, she admitted silently. Lord Catledge had been in her thoughts constantly ever since he carried her into the shop in his arms.

She started at the sound of the tinkling bells above the shop door.

"Good day, Miss Russell," said Lord Catledge. He saun-tered into the shop, a crooked grin on his handsome face. Standing before her, he bowed slightly and doffed his hat. "I hope I am not disturbing you."

A wave of queasiness washed over Cassandra, and she swallowed hard. "I have much work to do this day, my lord," she replied, strangely happy to see Lord Catledge and yet desperately hopeful that he would not prolong his stay. She feared she would be sick any moment, and it would simply not do for the viscount to witness her violent illness.

The viscount's brows knit together. "Are you all right? You look a little . . . green."

Cassandra touched her dust rag to her perspiring face before she realized what she was doing. "Oh, my!" Flinching at the strong odor of the polish, she tossed the chamois aside.

"I fear I am not well today," she confessed, confounded by her mixed emotions. She did not want to banish the viscount from her shop, yet she did not want him to see her looking so puny.

Lord Catledge reached toward her, a white linen handkerchief in his hand. The gesture was oddly disturbing to Cassandra, and roused unpleasant sensations, but she smiled her thanks and pressed the cloth to her clammy skin.

"I had thought the scrape on your temple was insignificant," said the viscount. "But I am grieved to see that your injury is more serious than I thought. Well, 'tis a good thing I stopped by to pay a visit. You must allow me to send my doctor around."

"Oh, no," cried Cassandra. "That is really quite unnecessary." Her head throbbed, and her knees were weak beneath her gown, but the expression of pity on the viscount's face galvanized her determination to look well.

"Posh! It is necessary! I am fully responsible for your injury. Though that rock—and the warning—were directed at me, you would not have been in the line of fire had I not insisted you accompany me to the coffee house."

Cassandra lifted her chin to meet the viscount's gaze. "I was not going to trouble you with this matter," she said evenly, "but since you are convinced that the warning tied around the rock was meant exclusively for you, I think you should know about last night."

"What about last night?" Lord Catledge ran his fingers through his hair and stared at Cassandra with deep concern in his eyes.

Her nausea subsided, leaving Cassandra with an inexplicable tingling that could be blamed only on the viscount's presence. Returning his gaze, she realized that she had formed a precipitous first impression that now seemed entirely false. She had based her initial attitude solely on the viscount's self-deprecating words, his arrogant appraisal of his reputation, his prideful irresponsibility, his flippant behavior.

But perhaps Alistair Gordon was not the dilettante he proclaimed himself to be. He was, after all, clearly concerned about her head injury. And Cassandra could not forget the feelings that his warm embrace had inspired in her. She had struggled to be released from his arms, but while she was there, she felt protected, needed—desired. Could a man whose eyes were so soulful, whose embrace was so tender and protective, be entirely bad?

"What is it you want to tell me about last night?" repeated the viscount, stepping nearer. Cassandra wasn't sure if he meant to shake the information from her, or whether he was preparing to catch her if she suddenly fainted. Her pulse was racing and she found it difficult to breathe with him so close to her. His masculine scent, a mixture of starch, soap, and tobacco, wafted toward her. Her feet moved backward, but the viscount inched forward until Cassandra's back arched and she looked up into dark, demanding eyes.

She should have pressed her hands against his chest and pushed him from her. But she dared not touch him, for she did not trust herself to break away.

Her throat constricted as she tried to speak. "Last night, a mummy broke into my apartment—"

"A mummy?" Lord Catledge interjected. "Did I hear you correctly? Are you sure that your head injury was not the cause of this . . . this *apparition*?"

The viscount's cynicism broke the spell. Cassandra recoiled, and said tightly, "I am quite positive that a mummy, or someone dressed as a mummy, was here last night. I caught a glimpse of the monster as he loomed over my bed, but then everything went black, almost as if I had been knocked unconscious. I suppose I would have thought I was dreaming, but Audrey saw the creature also, and managed to chase him away."

The viscount bid her to continue, his expression changing from astonishment to acceptance to quiet anger as Cassandra told her story. Several times he interrupted with murmured protestations, such as, "I cannot comprehend . . ." or "Who would do such a thing?" But by the time Cassandra finished, it was evident that Lord Catledge believed her.

She explained how Tia appeared at the window shortly after the mummy's departure. "We were quite frightened ourselves, you know, and worried about Tia's whereabouts. We were having tea in the drawing room, mulling over the evening's events and trying to make sense of it all. Then we heard the scratching at the window, and saw Tia's face pressed against the glass. Audrey had secured the latch. Tia would have spent the night outside had we not heard her and let her in. She was freezing, poor thing."

"Lucky monkey," said Lord Catledge. "I suppose she was scared out of her wits when she saw a mummy in her apartment. Where is the little scamp?"

"Upstairs, hiding under Audrey's skirts, most likely. That was where she was when I came down this morning. Oh, perhaps this is of some importance! Tia was clutching this when she scrambled across the windowsill," said Cassandra, producing a small scrap of white nainsook.

With a puzzled look the viscount turned it over in his hand and noted, "'Tis a fine piece of goods for a mummy to be wrapped in."

"Just so," agreed Cassandra, tucking the fabric back into her pocket. An uncomfortable silence fell in the small shop. Lord Catledge appeared deep in thought, perhaps perplexed by the mystery of the mummy and the warning he had received. He rubbed his lower lip and tossed his thick black hair off his forehead, affectations Cassandra had noticed in the coffee shop. She watched him, and suddenly realized how close to the surface his emotions truly were.

Was that why he hid so often behind a rakehell's disguise? she wondered. Or was she wrong to think she saw beneath his arrogant façade? Perhaps he was exactly what he professed to be, and it was she—the overanalytical intellectual who thought too much—who was deluding herself.

"Miss Russell," he started haltingly, "I am distressed."

Impulsively, Cassandra laid her hand upon his sleeve. The intimacy of her gesture seemed to startle both of them, and she quickly withdrew.

"What is distressing you?" she asked.

"I am concerned for your safety, dear lady. Yesterday I was quite convinced that the rock that was thrown through my carriage window was meant for me. I thought it was a warning, an attempt to scare me off my investigation."

Cassandra had spent a restless night analyzing the events that had occurred. "I disagree," she told Lord Catledge. "I think the warning was meant for me as well. The note said, 'Beware of the mummy's curse.' Do not forget, I was present when the pharaoh mummy was removed from the Valley of the Kings."

"You were a child!" cried Lord Catledge.

"That would not matter to an angry mummy bent on avenging the desecration of his royal tomb."

The viscount crushed his hat in his hands and grinned crookedly. "Do you really believe in the mummy's curse? Come now, be truthful. Do you *truly* believe it?"

"Do you believe it?" returned Cassandra. She stared at Lord Catledge until she saw his cheeks darken and the muscles in his jaw flinch.

Through tight lips he answered. "It matters not whether I believe in this curse. My brother does. What I am most concerned with is finding my brother's missing mummy, and ridding London of that fearful creature who dresses up like one and terrorizes innocent women such as yourself!"

"How very noble and gallant of you, my lordship." Cas-

sandra regretted her sarcasm the instant those words
escaped her lips. Why was it so irresistible to challenge the
viscount's motives and test his integrity? Why did Cassandra
find it so difficult to believe that he was, in fact, genuinely
concerned about her?

"I see that you suspect my intentions are dishonorable."
Under his breath Lord Catledge added, "That does not
surprise me. I am rarely thought well of."

She had wounded him, and she hated herself for it. "No,
no. I merely meant to say . . . oh, forgive me!" Cassandra
shivered with cold, but her face and neck felt sticky and
warm. "I am not feeling well today, and I am a trifle on
edge."

"That is understandable," said Lord Catledge gently.
"All the more reason why I must insist on removing you
to my quarters for your own safety."

"No!" Cassandra nearly jumped out of her skin. "Are
you insane?"

Undaunted, the viscount continued. "Then you must
allow me to stay here."

"No!" She stamped her foot for emphasis, and to her
chagrin he smiled as if her stubbornness amused him.

"Will you permit me to hire a Bow Street runner to
provide security for your premises and your person?" he
asked politely.

"I am perfectly capable of taking care of myself, Lord
Catledge. You have no need to worry. And besides, Audrey
is quite a worthy adversary."

"Ah, yes. I remember Audrey," he said, nodding. "She
does appear quite a bit more, er, stalwart than you—in
the physical sense, at least. But I doubt she could offer
you any real protection against that mummified brute if
he shows up here again."

"She attacked the mummy with a basalt statue," Cassandra pointed out. "And she drove him out of my bedroom
and through an open window."

"If your maid had not returned home precisely when

she did, however, there is no telling what could have happened to you."

Cassandra had already considered that, and the notion terrified her. Throughout the day she had wondered what the mummy had in store for her, absent Audrey's timely appearance. She trembled, partly from fright and partly from the alternatingly hot and cold sweat that covered her skin.

Perhaps it was anxiety that suddenly caused her stomach to roil. Or perhaps she was coming down with some dire illness. She knew only that she had never experienced such debilitating symptoms, not even when, as a child, she had sailed through turbulent seas with her intrepid parents. Her queasiness returned with a vengeance, prompting an end to her interview with the handsome viscount.

"Are you all right?" Lord Catledge asked. He grasped her elbow and bent toward her. "Would you allow me to assist you upstairs?"

Cassandra felt a violence in her stomach that required her immediate exodus. Shaking her head, she pushed the viscount from her. "Go, please! I beg of you! I am not feeling well!"

A bewildered look crossed his face, but when Cassandra clapped her hands over her mouth, he seemed to understand. He said quickly, "Can you get upstairs safely? Is Audrey there to assist you?"

"Yes, yes! Now, go!" she demanded.

"I shall return tomorrow," he promised, backing away. "The night after that I shall accompany you to Lord Tifton's salon. Pray, do not forget!"

The door slammed shut, the bells above it tinkling their indignation. Cassandra lurched up the stairs and made it to her small washstand in the bedroom. Audrey held her head as she bent over the porcelain bowl. Afterward, the sturdy maid tucked her into bed and pulled the curtains. Tia abandoned the safety of Audrey's skirts to curl up beside her mistress, and Cassandra slept soundly the rest of the afternoon.

Mlle. Suzette Duval lowered her gaze from the colossal head of Memnon. "Ali, sweetheart, do not fret so! You will make this quaint Original your *amie*, and she will tell you everything you need to know." Beneath the green-silk-covered brim of her plumed bonnet, the Frenchwoman's eyes sparkled like emeralds. "Use your charms if necessary, love. I know that you can do it."

Alistair's mistress was grating on his nerves. "I am quite weary of this subject, Suzette. 'Struth, I wish I had never told you about my brother's missing mummy."

"But, *chéri*, that is what friends are for. *Mais, oui?*"

"Friends do not strip naked and threaten to run into the street unless they are made privy to a man's innermost secrets!"

Shrugging the epaulets of her green corded-silk spencer, Suzette laid a finger on her chin and assumed a look of nymphlike innocence. "Love, I was only trying to amuse you. You looked so sullen, so out of sorts!"

"'Twas not a fair method by which to extract confidences from me," the viscount returned, his expression as stony as the two-story sculpture looming above his head. Now that Suzette was no longer nestled in his lap, *sans culottes*, it nettled him that he had broken his tradition of keeping his troubles to himself.

"I beg your forgiveness, my lord," replied Suzette, but her eyes still glittered with amusement. "I wished only that you would tell me your problems, so that I might bear the burden of them with you. Did I not offer some very prudent advice?"

"Surely, you do not believe that Cassandra Russell knows anything about the theft of Neville's mummy?"

"You believe in her innocence so strongly, and you have met her only twice?" Suzette asked, a hint of feminine

accusation creeping into her voice. "Perhaps there was
more to those meetings than you first disclosed to your
faithful mistress, no?"

"Balderdash! Are you quite out of your mind?"

Suzette lowered her eyes and pressed her lips together.
She turned from Alistair, and her hurt reaction stabbed
him with guilt. "Forgive me for being peevish," he said.
"I really did not want to attend the museum today. Perhaps
that is why I am so out of sorts." He grimaced at the
thought of missing yet another day of fox-hunting season.
"I would rather be at Catledge Hall than Montagu House,
you understand."

"Oui, bijou," the green-eyed woman said softly. "I understand." She moved closer, and Alistair caught the scent of
French perfume. Too floral, he thought, remembering
Cassandra's spicy smell. Suzette continued. "But you need
a diversion, love, after what you have been through these
last few days."

"I should not have burdened you with my troubles,"
the viscount said. Always before, he had found Suzette's
nearness wildly exhilarating; now her presence was cloying,
agitating. Folding his arms across his chest, he gazed high
above his head at Memnon's implacable expression. "I
wish to change the subject."

"Do you wish to leave?" Suzette laid her hand on Alistair's arm. She lifted her heart-shaped face to him, her lips
curved invitingly.

Uneasily, Alistair returned her smile. "Good heavens,
no. I am here at your request, Mademoiselle. I do not wish
to disappoint you. On the contrary, I intend that we view
every object in this museum before nightfall!"

Suzette's laughter was deep-throated, sultry.

Alistair felt a peculiar disquiet, as if the fox he'd been
chasing had suddenly popped underground. "Come, there
is much to see." He gave the gigantic Memnon one last
perusal, then moved away at a leisurely pace with Suzette
at his side.

"But it would take days to see everything in the British Museum," Suzette pointed out. "I wanted to visit only the Egyptian Saloon, and obtain some ideas for my costume. *A Long Egyptian Night* is less than a sennight away, you know."

"You need not remind me," said Alistair.

"I must confess I also thought this was an appropriate forum for the airing of your troubles, Ali." Suzette paused before a magnificent seated pharaoh carved from black granite. "Is he not a magnificent man, that ancient king? I understand that the ancient Egyptians thought their rulers were gods."

"I did not know you were so well informed on the subject of ancient Egyptian beliefs," said Alistair.

"I must read to keep myself amused while you are away from me," said Suzette, giving the pharaoh a backward glance as she took Alistair's arm again. The two walked a few paces to another statue, this one the painted limestone figure of a priest. "See how he steps forward with his left foot? He is stepping forward to receive the offerings left for him in his tomb, and he is preparing to experience the afterlife."

Peering at the placard beside the statue, Alistair said, "According to his calling card, this chap is from the Old Kingdom, during the Fifth Dynasty. That makes the fellow about twenty-five hundred years older than Christ."

"He is holding up very nicely," commented Suzette, her eyes scanning the statue's short kilt and well-proportioned legs.

Alistair watched Suzette's profile with mild curiosity. A great admirer of women, he had made it a practice never to compare one to the other. Truth be known, he liked all sorts of women—tall, short, thin, voluptuous, blondes, brunettes, and redheads. So why did it occur to him now that Cassandra's burnt copper hair reflected the sun's rays like a glinting prism, while Suzette's jet-black curls did nought but absorb the light, giving none of it back. Compared to Cassandra's olive skin, Suzette's creamy complexion looked wan.

Even Suzette's coquettish manners seemed missish in contrast to Cassandra's stark candor. And for a moment, Alistair wished he were anywhere in the world but the British Museum, strolling down the Egyptian Gallery with his beautiful French mistress on his arm. He wondered how Cassandra Russell was spending her day, and whether her stomachache was better. He was surprised to discover that he was worried about her.

"Would you care to visit the mummy room?" he asked, gently pulling Suzette away from the statuesque priest's carved muscles.

"Oui, bijou," she murmured, her green silk parasol tapping the floor as she strolled beside him.

Entering the gallery of the mummies, even Alistair could not suppress a gasp of astonishment as he viewed a huge sarcophagus intricately carved with feather decorations, geometric figures, and hieroglyphs.

"A small curricle would fit inside there," he remarked. Stepping closer, he touched the unusual stone with his fingers. "I wonder what this is—"

"It is calcite, my dear boy," came a low, sonorous voice from behind. "Or alabaster, if you prefer."

Alistair pivoted, his line of vision level with the man's barrel chest. Looking up, his gaze met two twinkling eyes set deep beneath bushy brows. A well-tanned face, framed in a thick beard and mustache, set off the man's gleaming white teeth. Instinctively, the viscount thrust his hand forward and introduced himself.

"I am Giovanni Belzoni," returned the man, nodding inquisitively toward Suzette.

Mlle. Duval smiled and extended her green-gloved hand as Alistair introduced her. Hooking the curve of his polished cane over one arm, Signor Belzoni inclined his head politely and took Suzette's fingers. Holding them to his lips, he studied her face for a moment longer than was strictly necessary. "Have we met, mademoiselle?"

"No, signor. We have not," Suzette said demurely.

Alistair arched a brow, but he was accustomed to contending with that sort of masculine attention. Suzette's appearance was, after all, designed to inflame the male passions. She was French, was she not?

"What an honor, signor," Alistair cut in. "And a fortuitous coincidence. I am attending the meeting of the Society of Egyptologists on Thursday evening, and was actually looking forward to meeting you there."

"I intend to be there, for I need to raise some blunt for my next expedition. 'Tis public record, or I would not admit it, but I am experiencing the most vexatious set of circumstances associated with my recently acquired collection of antiquities. Disposing of them for a sum sufficient to cover my expenses is proving difficult. Bad enough that while in Egypt I had to contend with that conniving French consul Drovetti, who undermined my efforts at every turn! But now that duplicitous Henry Salt is driving me mad! Do you know that the British Museum refuses to offer me a fair price for Sethy's alabaster sarcophagus, yet the cheeseparing trustees will not release it to me either?"

Bewildered by that speech, Alistair smiled blandly. He looked questioningly at Suzette, but she appeared equally at a loss for words. "I am distressed to hear that, signor," the viscount replied after a length.

Ignoring Alistair's awkward commiseration, the tall Italian, as if seized by inspiration, suddenly snapped his fingers. "Did you say your name was Gordon, man?"

"I did," answered Alistair warily.

"Are you related to Neville Gordon by any chance?"

"He is my brother," said Alistair.

Belzoni grinned from ear to ear. "Well, what do you know! I consider Neville a dear friend of mine, though I have never laid eyes on him. We have been corresponding for years, you see. Lord Hedgeworth's advice was of the greatest assistance to me when I was digging in the Valley of the Kings. Your brother knows that area like the back of his hand. No other living soul can boast of such a knowledge."

Alistair stared in amazement. "You and Neville have been corresponding?" he asked. "By letter?"

Belzoni's laughter echoed in the cavernous hall. "Of course, by letter. How else did you think, my boy? By carrier pigeon? I dare say, Neville's letters sometimes took months to reach the British consulate in Alexandria, but Colonel Misset was not opposed to acting as our intermediary. His successor, that moody Mr. Salt, was even more eager to pass along Neville's intelligence, though for his own aggrandizement. Ah, well. Pity that your brother's letters have been stolen from me."

Suzette interposed a delicate inquiry. "Did you say that you have never actually met Lord Hedgeworth, signor?"

"Never. I am looking forward to meeting him while I am here in London. In fact, we are having dinner on Friday evening. He is doing well, I presume?"

Suzette demurred, her silence forcing Alistair to answer the difficult question. "You do not know of Neville's, ah, condition?" he began.

"In all the letters your brother wrote to me, he never spoke of himself. Lord Hedgeworth is a stranger to me, though I would say a rather intimate stranger. I feel as if he has been with me, cheering me on as it were, during those trying moments in Egypt, when I thought I never would get out of the country alive, much less with my hard-won collection of antiquities. As for the man himself, I know only that Lord Hedgeworth is a genius in the realm of Egyptology. His willingness to guide me toward the great treasures of the pharaoh's tombs has been exceedingly generous, and providential."

"You might as well know, sir, that my brother's health is very bad. Over the years Neville has become a recluse because of his disfigured face. Trachoma left him blind in one eye, and he wears a patch to cover the diseased socket."

Belzoni frowned. "I am sorry to hear that." Pensively, he added, "Do you know that in all our correspondence I never thought to ask Neville Gordon his age? Pray, tell me a little about Lord Hedgeworth before I meet him."

"Neville is forty-two, sir."

"Ah, the same age as I."

Struck by the fact that Neville was the same age as this robust giant of a man, Alistair was subdued. "My brother is very difficult to describe, signor. I would prefer you see for yourself what shape your ink-and-pen friend is in, then form your own opinions regarding his character."

Belzoni lifted his shaggy brows and let out an exclamation of understanding. "Ah! I think there is much here that does not meet the eye! And will you be at dinner next Friday evening, young fellow, when I am to sup with your brother?"

For the second time in as many days, Alistair accepted an invitation that was not actually extended to him. "Yes, I will be in Curzon Street on Friday evening," he said.

"I also," injected Suzette. "I am looking forward to seeing you Thursday night as well, signor."

Alistair stared at her in surprise as Belzoni bent over her fingers once more. "You are an enchanting creature," the big man said, peering at her intently. "And there is something very familiar about that lovely face of yours. . . ."

Suzette smiled, but her cheeks remained pale. Was the woman so accustomed to being adored that blushing was beyond her? Before Alistair could ponder his mistress's brazen behavior, Belzoni gripped his hand again, this time pumping it enthusiastically until Alistair almost gasped with pain.

"Good-bye, signor. I am glad we had this opportunity to acquaint ourselves prior to Thursday's meeting, and Friday's dinner party."

"Good-bye," said Giovanni Belzoni, bowing politely.

Her voice full of promise, Suzette trilled, *"Au revoir."*

And while a fuzzy sense of dread enveloped Alistair, the great Belzoni ambled from the mummy gallery, whistling a jaunty tune and tapping his whitethorn cane on the floor.

Tinkling bells announced the arrival of Alistair and Suzette. For a moment, Russell's Emporium appeared untended, as it had when Alistair made his first visit there just a few days before. Giving the place a quick once-over, he sighed with relief.

"Good," he said softly. "No one is here. Let us go. I told you this was a terrible idea. 'Tis wrong to insinuate myself into this girl's life merely to learn what she knows about the members of the Society of Egyptologists." Alistair's voice was strained, his expression taut. "I do not like it. Let us go."

Suzette rearranged her ermine muff and laid a restraining green-gloved hand on the viscount's arm. "I am not leaving," she said.

"Suzette, this type of trickery is . . . pure fraud. I will not be a part of it, I tell you. Now, let us go!"

"You are as squeamish as an old woman, love," Suzette replied laughingly.

Alistair glanced at the still curtain of beads before bending to peer into Suzette's face. The white feather plumes that swayed above her green leghorn bonnet and tickled his eyebrows only fanned his irritation. "I came here because you threatened to come without me if I did not," he reminded his lover in a hushed, menacing voice.

Suzette turned a determined look on him. "You did not want me to come alone, did you? You know that I would have," she added, batting her lashes.

Alistair cringed. "But why? Why is my brother's business any concern of yours?"

Suzette clucked her tongue as if Alistair's question were completely illogical. "Love, *you* are my business! It is you that I am concerned about. You have let this macabre mummy-theft depress your spirits to the point that you are no longer even interested in making love to me. Now, Ali," she went on, clearly exasperated. "I know you well enough to realize that when you do not want to make love to me, something is terribly wrong! Is it not natural that I should want to help?"

"By thrusting me at the feet of another woman?" Alistair said in a stage whisper. "By insisting that I make friends with a strange Egyptian woman who runs a funeral shop?"

"I know it is a sacrifice, dear. But your brother has asked a favor of you, and I can see with my own eyes that you will not be happy until you have complied with his request. And I agree with the earl that making friends with Cassandra Russell will introduce you to the most likely group of suspects." She laid her green kid glove on the side of Alistair's face. "There, now. I am sure she is an odious bluestocking with the complexion of an aborigine, but you must suffer for your happiness, darling. *N'est-ce pas?*"

Alistair gritted his teeth and crushed his beaver hat in his hands. "Then, I should have come alone, Suzette."

"No. You would not have come had I not accompanied you. Then, when your poor brother died, you would have always regretted not coming to his aid when he called upon you. Come, *bijou*. Relax your nerves. I think I hear the dowdy hoyden coming."

Chapter Five

Descending the stairs to her inventory room, Cassandra heard whispered voices in the shop. Thinking that customers had called while she was upstairs refreshing herself, she quickened her pace. With a fixed smile upon her lips, she crossed the inventory room and entered the shop, the swinging curtain of beads clacking behind her.

A well-dressed couple turned. At first glance, Cassandra recognized Alistair Gordon, and a dormant bud of unwarranted happiness burst inside her. Then she saw that his face was flushed and anxious, his eyes flickering with uncertainty. The woman next to him was smiling and staring curiously, as if she were surprised by Cassandra's appearance. Something was not altogether amiable about the way in which the viscount's companion appraised Cassandra.

And now Lord Catledge, watching first one woman and then the other, wrung his beaver hat and fidgeted.

Cassandra drew up short.

An awkward silence momentarily engulfed the tiny shop, then Alistair Gordon's faltering smile widened, and the woman next to him became thin-lipped and rigid.

Cassandra stepped forward, murmuring a muted salutation.

"Hello, Miss Russell," returned the viscount, bending low over her lace mitten. "I trust that you are feeling better today."

"Much better," said Cassandra, her eyes darting from Lord Catledge to the beautiful woman next to him.

"I would like to introduce you to Mademoiselle Suzette Duval," he said.

"Bonjour, Miss Russell. What a pleasure it is to meet you. Ali has not ceased chattering about you since he met you. I confess, I was beginning to be alarmed that my sweetheart was becoming infatuated with another. I simply could not wait until Thursday to meet you at the Society of Egyptologists' meeting."

"Thursday? The meeting?" Cassandra repeated, startled. "Oh, yes. Dear me, there is something I must explain." Her mind racing, Cassandra searched for a plausible excuse to exclude this saucy Incomparable from the Thursday salon. Honoring her agreement to accompany the viscount was one thing; attending with what appeared to be his brazen mistress in tow was quite another! "You see, there has been a misunderstanding," she stalled.

"Misunderstanding?" Suzette questioned, fluttering her thick eyelashes ominously.

Cassandra stammered, but her lie began to coalesce. "Yes. The Society of Egyptologists does not allow nonmembers to attend, I am afraid. It was rather precipitous of me, in fact, to extend an invitation to Lord Catledge." Cassandra felt her cheeks burning, and she averted her eyes. "But when his lordship expressed an interest in attending, I impulsively offered to sponsor him at Thursday's meeting."

Alistair's tone was waggish when he interjected. "What you are saying is that you can sponsor me, but not Mlle. Duval. Is that correct?"

"I fear I have already superseded the rules of our close-knit society by insisting that an outsider be allowed to accompany me," said Cassandra. "This week's meeting is particularly exclusive inasmuch as an honored guest is going to enlighten us as to his recent exploits in Egypt."

Suzette brightened. "Would that be Giovanni? But, my dear, Giovanni is expecting me! You needn't worry that your fellow Egyptologists will turn me away from the door. Not when Giovanni Belzoni is the honored speaker. Why, I just spoke with him yesterday morning, and I assured him that I would be in attendance." She pressed a finger to her cheek and added demurely, "Of course, I might make arrangements to attend with my brother, Pierre, if the two of you wish to be left alone—unchaperoned."

"That is perfectly acceptable to me," said the viscount, grinning decadently. "I am of the firm opinion that when one no longer requires a governess, one no longer requires a chaperon either."

"Oh, no!" cried Cassandra. "That is not acceptable." She frowned at Lord Catledge, and was slightly shocked at the sly wink he gave her.

"Delightful," purred Suzette, her narrowed eyes sliding from the viscount to Cassandra. "Then we shall all go together. My dear brother, Pierre, will absolutely adore Miss Russell, do you not agree, Ali?" Clucking her tongue, she slanted Cassandra a sly look then cut her eyes at Alistair. "Why did you not tell me she was so beautiful, *bijou*? Why, she has the chiseled features of an Egyptian queen!"

Cassandra stared at Alistair, wishing she could read his thoughts. He returned her gaze with an air of gaiety, but said nothing to alleviate her bewildered state. Then, abruptly, as if jerked from a deep reverie, he shook his head and exclaimed, "Suzette, did I hear you correctly? Your brother, Pierre, cannot attend the meeting of the Society of Egyptologists!"

"And why not?" demanded Mlle. Duval. "He is as good a friend of Signor Belzoni as I!"

"Just so!" The viscount clamped his jaws shut and turned a threatening gaze on his cheeky mistress.

The couple seemed on the verge of a squabble. The air in Russell's Emporium thickened with tension.

Watching Mlle. Duval suggestively walk her fingers up Alistair's waistcoat, Cassandra wondered how such an ill-mannered woman could command the attentions of such an independently minded man as Alistair Gordon. Then she chided herself for indulging such prurient curiosities. She would probably never see Lord Catledge after Thursday evening—he was an aristocrat and she was a chit—so his personal affairs were really none of her concern, no matter how titillating a mystery they might present.

Still, when the viscount turned his dark, brooding gaze on her, Cassandra could not deny the shiver of apprehension that rippled through her. "I trust the presence of Mlle. Duval's brother will not inconvenience you, Miss Russell," he said, apparently as discomfited as she that the Frenchwoman's brother had been insinuated into Thursday's meeting.

Cassandra shook her head slightly. "As long as Signor Belzoni is in attendance, I haven't a care who else is present."

Mlle. Duval purred her approbation. "Oh, how handsome the four of us shall be! I can barely contain my excitement. Pierre has been so disconsolate, moping about in London, so far away from his Parisian friends. He will fall at your feet, my dear girl, I am sure. By the way, *chère*, what do you intend to wear?"

"As you can see, mademoiselle, I am in mourning," Cassandra answered. "I shall be wearing black."

"I quite think I am partial to black bombazine," the viscount said, his dark stare fixed on Cassandra's warm face.

Suzette's sultry laugh was derisive, provocative. "Oh, come now, *bijou*. You *abhor* black, and you well know it! Haven't you always said that black depresses you, and sends you into a state of melancholy? Black is for widows, love . . . and for undertakers.''

"Black crepe is not very chic, I admit," said the viscount. "But Miss Russell turns out quite nicely in her drab bombazine. My former friend, the exiled Brummell, could not have held a candle to her understated elegance."

Cassandra added in a prickly tone, "Besides that, I am not an undertaker, mademoiselle. I am in mourning for my mother, who died a year ago."

"A year ago? Then your mourning should be over," said Mlle. Duval, squaring the shoulders of her green capote cape. Cassandra felt the scrutiny of the Frenchwoman's bright eyes, and knew that a rivalry of sorts had commenced. How ridiculous! To be sure, Lord Catledge had been flirting with her. But Cassandra had no doubt that his interest in her did not extend to any serious consideration of courtship. He was merely trying to make his mistress jealous.

Thinking to dispel the charged atmosphere of tension that had descended, Cassandra abruptly inquired, "My lord, have you had any success in your investigation into the theft of your brother's mummy?"

"Ah!" The viscount smiled. "That I have not, I am afraid. I was hoping to make some progress at the meeting on Thursday. I trust you will introduce me to the esteemed members of the society?"

"I will do my best, my lord," assured Cassandra.

"Have you heard of anyone seeking to buy or sell mummies?" Suzette queried.

"No," Cassandra replied elliptically, having no interest in conversing with Mlle. Duval on any subject, let alone the commerce of mummies, a trafficking she found morally reprehensible.

Lord Catledge interpolated. "I have heard that mummies are often traded in certain quarters for their medicinal values. Is that true, Miss Russell?"

Cassandra nodded ruefully. "I am afraid so, my lord."

Suzette spoke up quickly, as if she were determined not
to be excluded from the conversation. "If you accept the
fact that bitumen, or pitch, has any healing properties,"
she argued, "then you must assume that a mummy pos-
sesses some value as a medicinal compound."

"I find the notion utterly insupportable," said Cassandra. "Though I have heard doctors once thought ground-
up mummies produced a powder with enormous healing
properties. I daresay, I would not stir a teaspoon full of
mummy powder into my tea if I were suffering from a
stomach ailment, would you, my lord?"

Lord Catledge chuckled. "No, I think not. I have even
heard that some scientists are experimenting with mummies to determine whether they can be made into a superior writing paper. And that certain industrialists are
investing exorbitant sums of money into developing a sort
of mummy fuel, on the theory that mummies burn enormously well. What do you think of that, Miss Russell?"

"I think a sheet of foolscap would be less troublesome
to produce, my lord," answered Cassandra. "And as for
mummy fuel, I for one prefer to throw logs on the fires
rather than dead Egyptian fellows."

Lord Catledge and Cassandra shared a laugh while
Suzette smiled tightly and rammed her hands deep into her
ermine muff. A touch of color tinged the Frenchwoman's
cheeks as she stared down the tip of her upturned nose. "Is
your interest in mummies purely academic, Miss Russell, or
do you by any chance own one?"

The bells of St. Clement's pealed in the background,
their clamorous chimes an eerie tocsin. An ear-popping
pressure suddenly permeated the shop, causing Cassandra
to cut her eyes at Lord Catledge. He grinned back happily,
seemingly immune to the altered ambience of the room.

Suzette Duval's darkening gaze, however, betrayed the
Frenchwoman's heightened awareness.

Cassandra shook her head. "No, mademoiselle, I do not
harbor a mummy in my midst."

The viscount chuckled. "I can't say as I blame you for that. Blasted nuisance, they are! Ungrateful chaps too. Always running off, or disappearing without so much as a fare-thee-well. Ask Neville, my brother, if you don't believe me!"

Mlle. Duval's mouth formed a little "O." *"Bijou!"* she exclaimed. "You really are a card! Now we must be running along, for you promised that we should visit that dear little shoemaker on Fish Street Hill. You remember, don't you, love? The one who makes those exquisite satin slippers with bugle beads that cap the toes?"

"Egads! That odious little man?"

Suzette nodded, all sweetness and femininity. Whether the viscount recognized his courtesan's smile for what it was—a fictitious display of good-natured amusement— Cassandra could not know. Even her limited experience with men had taught her they could be extremely slow-witted creatures, blind to the duplicities of women and deaf to their sarcasms. Men interpreted words at face value, while women detected texture and nuance in every syllable uttered. Cassandra had learned that lesson well from her years as a funerary consultant.

"I am forced to retreat, then," Alistair conceded, his eyes twinkling. "It seems my friend is eager to be shod. Besides, we have taken up enough of Miss Russell's time."

"Good-bye," said Cassandra, offering her hand. Lord Catledge gently grasped her fingers, his lips brushing the delicate lace of her crocheted mittens. The warmth of his breath penetrated the fine netting of black that overlaid her skin, but Cassandra's shivery response was eloquently concealed by the serene expression plastered on her face.

"Au revoir," said Mlle. Duval in a clipped tone. Turning, she exited the shop in a swish of green skirts and flouncy scalloped hems. Lord Catledge followed his mistress, pausing in the doorway to don his beaver hat and flash Cassandra a rakish grin.

Then the door slammed shut and the bells above it

tinkled rudely. Cassandra stood in the middle of the shop for a long while, thinking that there was something very odd and potentially dangerous about the viscount's interest in her. His behavior, as well as Mlle. Duval's, was inexplicable.

For starters, why did the possessive Frenchwoman ask Cassandra if she owned a mummy? Cassandra was baffled, and full of dread. Something horrifically exciting was going to happen; she could feel it in her bones.

And as she pondered her predicament, Cassandra thought of the mummy's curse. Isolated in her strange little world, she had always found the curse a convenient excuse for her lonely existence. The disgruntled pharaoh had cursed her to a life as lonely as the one he was spending in eternity—that was what her mother told her and that was what Cassandra had allowed herself to believe. But did she really believe it?

Was it the mummy's curse she was so afraid of—or was she simply terrified by the possibility that the curse might one day be removed?

Now that Alistair Gordon had held her in his arms, Cassandra knew she could never be happy in her solitude again. She smiled at the irony of her situation. She was happy until Lord Catledge came along. Perhaps the wretched Egyptian monarch realized that his curse was meaningless to a bluestocking intellectual who had never been kissed. Perhaps in his infinite wisdom the ancient king knew that a woman would not miss what she had never known.

But now that she knew what it felt like to be held by Alistair Gordon, the mummy's curse of solitude was unbearable.

Alistair leapt aside, yelping indignantly. "Good God, man, hasn't that contraption any brakes?"

Neville's Merlin chair whirred past, stirring a draft that

ruffled the tails of Alistair's cutaway coat. "Sorry, little brother," the Earl of Hedgeworth said over his shoulder. "I suppose I am like one of those wretched chaps rumbling off to my execution in a creaky old tumbrel. I might not like my destination, but I had much rather pelt to the scaffold like the devil was behind me than crawl to it like a defeated snail."

Alistair examined his clothing with an air of exasperation, then turned to Suzette and rolled his eyes. "What was it you wanted me to show me, Neville? I have not the leisure to pick through broken pottery shards all day," he said, pausing to examine an exquisite teapot shaped vessel of blue-green faience.

"Pottery shards, *ma foi!*" Suzette breathed.

"In case you have forgotten," Alistair said, "I am hot on the heels of a mummy. I can ill afford to tarry."

"You are on the trail of a stolen *pharaoh* mummy," corrected Neville severely. "And you can spare me a few moments of your precious time, I am sure. As I said, the foxes will wait."

"Perhaps, but my masquerade party will most certainly not wait," Alistair retorted, following his brother's rolling chair past rows of shelves containing mummified cats, miniature ushabti figures, amulets, papyrus writings, statues, and other Egyptian antiquities. The walls of Neville's storeroom, taking up the entire rear part of his town house, were covered with ancient artwork and hieroglyphs. Several times, as Suzette brought up the rear of the column, Alistair heard her gasp with astonishment, but that was not surprising. Neville's cache was stunning not only for its vastness, but also for the amount of gold it contained.

At last the brothers came to a clearing. Halting abruptly, Alistair drew in his breath. Though he had seen this particular antiquity many years earlier, the sight of it still filled him with awe. The hollow block of gleaming yellow quartzite that loomed from the shadowy corner dwarfed the hunched figure of Neville, who sat before it in his chair.

The rectangular box, almost five feet high, was a magnificent testament to the sanctity accorded ancient kings. "'Tis
truly beautiful," Alistair murmured unthinkingly.

Suzette rushed past, sinking down beside the sarcophagus, unabashedly examining its intricately carved hieroglyphs with her fingertips.

Situated on a slightly raised platform beneath an oil
lamp's shimmering arc of artificial light, the sarcophagus
clearly assumed the highest place of honor in Neville's
collection. The rest of his antiquities palled in comparison
to this majestic treasure, seeming as trinkets or cheap bau-
bles that merely gathered dust on the shelves. But though
Alistair had long ago feigned disinterest in Neville's ram-
bling orations, he recalled that the smaller statues and
amulets had once been crammed inside the pharaoh's
burial chamber to provide comfort in the afterlife. Surely,
the Egyptian monarch who had inspired these artistic
labors had been much loved and highly revered, if the
massive size of his yellow sarcophagus was any measure.

For several moments Suzette, Alistair, and Neville shared
a reverent silence, each drinking in the dazzling, awesome
sight of a centuries-old work of sacred art. Suzette was on
her knees, caressing the sculpted corners of the box, feeling the raised relief of the deities with all the reverence
of a blind woman touching her lover's face.

After a time she looked questioningly at Neville, and he
identified the figures who stood with their arms outstretched, enveloping the sarcophagus in a loving, protective embrace. "Isis, Nephthys, Selkis, and Neith," he
answered, his good eye lambent, his fingers chafing as if
they itched.

Alistair strolled casually toward the huge sarcophagus,
his boots crunching on the sandy floor. Running his hand
along the cool stone of the upper rim, he whistled appreciatively, then turned a grudging smile on Neville. "It has
been quite a while since I was here. I had forgotten how
impressive your mummy's coffin is."

"Was," said Neville. "As you can see, all that is left is the outer case, or the sarcophagus. Twenty men could not have removed that hollowed-out slab of stone from my house. Not without a complicated system of pulleys and levers, that is. Why, the lid itself weighs more than a ton."

Alistair peeked over the side. "I see that the burglars made away with the inner coffins. That was no small task."

Suzette rose to her feet. "How many coffins were there?" she questioned, peering into the empty bathtub-shaped shell.

"There are three coffins, mademoiselle. One fits within the other, of course, and the smallest one contains the mummy's body."

"Along with the mummy's golden funeral mask," added Alistair.

"Yes, and a horde of amulets and sundry items that were snatched from my shelves."

"At random?" Suzette queried.

Neville wheeled himself to a better-illumined area of the clearing and cocked his head. He seemed to be appraising Suzette from another angle, studying her intensely. Suzette must have been aware of his scrutiny, for she turned from Neville and went round to the other side of the sarcophagus, where she effectively hid herself from view.

"No, there was nothing thoughtless about the manner in which this burglar—or these burglars—operated." Neville squinted up at Alistair and abruptly asked, "By the bye, did you find the Russell woman?"

The change of subject took Alistair by surprise. "Yes! Well, no. Not exactly."

"Yes, no, not exactly? What the devil does that mean? And where have you been these past two days anyway? I thought I told you to bring Mrs. Russell back to me at once! If you intend to depart for Catledge Hall within the next three days, you had better get this investigation under way." His sour look glanced off Suzette. "And quit monkeying around!"

Over the empty sarcophagus, Alistair cast a beleaguered glance in his mistress's direction. Then he stared down into his brother's contorted face and summoned his restraint. "In answer to your question, I did find Russell's Emporium. 'Twas exactly where you said it should be. But Lady Rhoda Russell is deceased, I'm afraid."

"Damme! Dead, is she?" In his agitation, Neville combed his fingers through his hair. "Then, we shall have to alter our battle plan—"

"But her daughter was there," said Alistair. "A quite attractive young woman, I might add. Egyptian stock, and all that."

Neville's jaw slackened. "Her daughter? Sir Anthony's chit? Good God! I had forgotten . . . but yes, of course! The girl must be a young woman now. How old did you say, Ali?"

"My guess would be about twenty, Neville, though I daresay, I did not question the girl to that extent. She has been a most reluctant participant in my investigation." Alistair smiled at Suzette, but she had bent to study a line of text incised along the length of the quartzite box, and was not looking at him.

Neville's beefy lips glistened, as if he were drooling with anticipation. "Tell me everything, Ali. Do not spare a single detail. What did she say? *What did the Egyptian girl say?*"

"For heaven's sake, Neville. Calm down." Alistair related the gist of his first meeting with Cassandra Russell, adding at the end of his story that the woman seemed rather disinclined to assist the Earl of Hedgeworth in any manner.

"She does not understand," said Neville bluntly. "If I could but talk with her, I am certain I could make her understand."

"She does not want to come here, Neville." Alistair leaned heavily against the stone sarcophagus and folded his arms across his chest. "She was most adamant in her refusal to do so."

"So she thinks I am responsible for Anthony's death, eh? Aye, in a sense I suppose I am."

Alistair's boots scraped the floor in an abrasive show of exasperation. "Must you carry the weight of the world on your shoulders? I have been made to understand that a crazed Mameluke dashed upon board the ship as it was being loaded and murdered poor Sir Anthony before anyone had a chance to stop him. Surely, you are not to blame for that unfortunate happenstance."

Suzette's head popped up on the other side of the sarcophagus. "Was the rabid Turk apprehended?" she asked.

Neville's head jerked around to study her. "No. He escaped, and the boat departed Egypt, and that was that."

"Surely the tale does not end there," Suzette said. "Did the widow Lady Russell not return to London with Anthony's share of the treasures?"

Neville's good eye narrowed to a slit. "I see my little brother has indulged in some pillow talk. I suppose there is no harm in telling you that Lady Russell did return to London with half the loot. 'Twas payment owed to Sir Anthony. I would not have cheated the lady."

"No, I would not have thought so," inserted Alistair.

Suzette asked, "Was there another mummy in the cache removed from that same tomb?"

"There were thousands of artifacts removed, too many to enumerate. I cannot answer your question," replied Neville quickly. Too quickly, thought Alistair. He sensed his brother was lying; hadn't Neville already mentioned a *pair* of mummies that were removed from the well-concealed tomb in the Valley of the Kings?

Before Alistair could demand further elaboration, Neville forestalled his question with an uplifted palm.

"I do not know what antiquities Lady Russell owned at the time she died," Neville mumbled, turning his back and propelling himself from the clearing. He wheeled his chair to a cluttered refectory desk, its legs shortened to accommodate his seated stature. There he rummaged through a pile of sketchbooks, crumbling maps, and manuscripts, at last producing a well-worn black leather binder.

Neville turned over the yellowed pages carefully but with an air of impatience. At last he froze, his eye bulging. "Here she is!" he exclaimed breathlessly. Placing the open scrapbook across his lap, Neville pivoted and shoved off from the desk, then coasted back into the arc of light that shimmered over the pharaoh's sarcophagus.

He lifted the book for Alistair's inspection.

"Good God! The resemblance is remarkable. Come around here and look, Suzette!"

The Frenchwoman peered over Alistair's arm. "Who is it?"

"You do not recognize her?" Alistair asked, incredulous.

Suzette frowned. "All I see is a crude drawing of an Egyptian woman. She wears the traditional Egyptian veil covering her face, but a European walking dress. Her ensemble is a bizarre montage of continental fashion and ancient Egyptian costume. All I can see are her eyes—very strange eyes too."

"Strange eyes," agreed Alistair, transfixed by the charcoal portraiture. "Is it her mother, Neville? Is it Lady Rhoda Russell as she appeared when you met her in the Valley of the Kings ten years ago?"

Neville nodded. "She was quite beautiful then, poor thing. Even that veil could not conceal her enchanting eyes. Men were inexorably attracted to Rhoda. Anthony simply accepted that fact, I suppose. Surely, she gave him no reason to suspect—Ah, well. 'Twas her eyes that betrayed what that provincial costume sought to hide. Her eyes were—"

"—exquisite," Alistair finished. "Exotic." Just like her daughter's eyes, Alistair thought. He stared at the picture, and in his reverie the delicate pencil strokes blurred and wavered until, at last, Cassandra's face was superimposed upon the drawing. The pensive expression Alistair imagined evoked a certain melancholy in his soul. He felt an unrecognizable longing, a deprivation that his senses registered but his logic defied. Why did Cassandra's image keep popping into his mind? What could a bluestocking eccentric offer a jaded buck?

"Yes, but see the sandals on her feet," Suzette pointed out.

"So incongruent with the muslin gown and woolen cloak." Alistair laughed at the strange attire that Lady Rhoda Russell wore, but he felt a pang of sadness for her also. She had been caught between her native Egyptian world and the culture of her English husband. "I wonder why she came to London after her husband died," Alistair mused. "Why not remain in Egypt?"

"Do not think too much on it, brother. Your purpose is to unravel more perplexing mysteries."

"Like who stole your mummy?" Alistair said.

"Precisely. You had best get on it. Off with you now."

"Do you mean you summoned me here to show me this?" Alistair asked, tossing the sketchbook into Neville's shriveled lap. "And this?" He waved his hand at the golden box behind him. "I am beginning to wonder why I jump every time you snap your fingers."

Neville snorted his disgust. "What twaddle is that! I have been sending notes to your town house requesting your appearance for the past two days."

"I have been busy," snapped Alistair. "For one, I went to the museum and inspected much of the Egyptian galleries. You will never guess whom I met."

Neville cocked an eyebrow.

"Your letter-writing crony, the great Belzoni."

"How poetic of you," snarled Neville. "Did you introduce your charming self?"

"Why, of course," said Alistair, propping his arm along the top edge of the empty sarcophagus. The need to regain control of his emotions tightened his expression to one of smugness. He willed his body to relax, his mind to release the image of Cassandra's face. "He allowed that he was coming here Friday night to dine with you."

"Yes, we have much to talk about."

"Suzette and I are looking forward to being here."

Neville's chin shot up, and he glowered at his brother. "You and Suzette? You what? What did you say?"

"I think you heard me. Surely you do not intend to entertain your guest alone, do you? For shame, Neville. Such a distinguished traveler craves stimulating discourse."

"—titillating *on dits,* you mean," injected Neville. "Mind you, I am not interested in presiding over some pretentious salon for fashionable Egyptmongers."

"Mlle. Duval made quite an impression on Signor Belzoni, from what I could see. You would not want to disappoint him, would you?" Alistair smiled at his brother's obvious chagrin.

Suzette leaned forward, touching the sleeve of Neville's well-cut but old-fashioned dark blue coat. "My lord, my brother and I would be honored to dine with you and your guest."

"Your brother?" Neville sputtered.

Alistair cut his mistress a quelling gaze. "Now, really, Suzette. I have agreed to allow Pierre to accompany us to Thursday's meeting of the Society of Egyptologists, but do you have to tow him along Friday night?"

Suzette's eyes flashed. "Do not be cruel, *bijou!* Little brother knows no one in London, and he mopes incessantly in our dismal little town house. What harm would it do to include him in Friday night's affair?"

"What harm indeed?" cut in Neville, a sinister smirk twisting his lips. "How moving it is to see a sister so concerned over her brother's welfare. Take heed, Ali. The Society of Egyptologists' meeting is Thursday night, you say? Well, well. Thank you for inviting me, dear brother. I shall be more than happy to attend with you."

"What? Attend with me? And Suzette? And Miss Russell?"

"And Pierre," reminded his mistress.

"Are you cra—" Alistair checked his impulsive outburst, but in his anger he had thrust off from the slab of stone against which he leaned. Now, standing straight and taut, he towered over the craggy figure of his brother. "Good God, Neville. I am sorry, man, but that is quite impossible."

"Why?" Neville croaked. The escarpment of his rugged face crumbled like an avalanche.

"Because I am already imposing on Miss Russell," Alistair tried to explain.

"One more person will not matter, then," said Suzette sweetly.

Neville's good eye skipped across the lighted clearing. "I understand your reluctance to be seen with me in public, Ali," he said thickly. "God knows, can't say as I blame you."

"Bloody hell!" Alistair threw Suzette an apologetic glance, but reckoned she'd heard much worse. "Oh, all right, Neville. You may go. Miss Russell will be terribly angry, and she will have every right to be."

"You can charm her, chéri," cooed Suzette. "Go and see her at her droll little shop and tell her that your brother— who is Giovanni's good friend—would like to attend Thursday's meeting. I am sure you can persuade her."

Alistair grumbled. "You have tremendous faith in my ability to be charming, Suzette."

"But of course, love! You charmed me, didn't you?"

Neville chuckled, and wheeled himself away.

Cassandra frowned when Alistair Gordon entered her shop. "You are at least two hours early, my lord," she said. Beside her, Tia sat on the glass countertop and played with a handful of black buttons.

Cassandra suppressed a smile as Tia's watchful gaze

traced Alistair's movement across the shop. Clutching a fistful of buttons, the monkey moved closer to Cassandra and crouched protectively.

Doffing his beaver hat and inclining his head, the viscount's eyes were pinned to Tia. When he straightened, he said rather apologetically, "I have come to, er, warn you off."

Cassandra sighed with relief. "I thought for a moment that you had arrived early to collect me for tonight's meeting." She laid aside a stack of black kid gloves she'd been sorting, and smiled at the viscount. "Warn me off, you say? If you are referring to the fact that your friend, Mlle. Duval, has invited herself—and her brother—to tonight's meeting, I accept your apology," Cassandra replied graciously.

"Then you are not furious with me?"

"Only a little," Cassandra replied. She itched to ask him what he saw in that French romp of his, but her strong sense of propriety condemned such boldness.

The viscount's grin broadened. "How lenient you are! I am not sure I could practice such cordiality were I in your position. After all, you made it quite clear you were straining the protocol of your society by inviting me to Belzoni's presentation. And on top of that, you were put upon to indulge the presence of Mlle. Duval."

"And her brother," reminded Cassandra. She was pleased to see the viscount smiling.

"Yes, and I am about to test your indulgence even further." Alistair stepped forward, leaning across the countertop so that Tia recoiled in instinctive territorial apprehension. "I pray you will not think ill of me," Lord Catledge drawled.

Already Cassandra recognized this tone of voice as the viscount's most persuasive, seductive one. His entreaty rolled off his tongue like pure molasses. "I hate to impose upon you—" he began.

Cassandra thought him devilishly irresistible. "Go on," she urged him.

"When my brother understood that Giovanni Belzoni was to be in attendance at tonight's salon, he was practically green with envy. You see, he is as much enthralled with the illustrious traveler as you are. So, when he asked me if he could accompany us to tonight's gathering, what was I to say?"

Mesmerized by the viscount's soulful expression, Cassandra almost blurted out her unqualified assent before she even realized what he was asking. Belatedly, she grasped the gist of his plea, and the liquid warmth she had felt beneath his smile vanished.

"You are asking me to allow the Earl of Hedgeworth to attend the Society of Egyptologists as my guest?" she asked, stricken.

Lord Catledge drew in a deep breath. "Yes, I am."

The anger and outrage Cassandra felt could not be expressed in words. "No!" she said. "I am sorry, my lord, but I have already told you how I feel about your brother. He was responsible for my father's death!"

"An allegation that Neville disputes," Lord Catledge said through tight lips.

"Clearly, you do not take kindly to my remarks regarding your brother." Aware of Tia's restlessness, Cassandra stroked her pet's sleek head reassuringly. "Perhaps even you do not realize the extent of your devotion to him. Indeed, you heap insults on the man yourself but brook no criticism of him from others. Blood is thicker than water, I suppose."

The viscount's face darkened ominously.

Cassandra practically bit her tongue, attempting to staunch the flow of invectives streaming from her lips. Pressing her hands to her hot cheeks, she shut her eyes and said, "La! I do not practice this sort of incivility. My natural bent toward diplomacy abjures such impolitic boldness, but oh! . . . you do provoke me so, my lord! And I am no dissembler. I will speak my mind, on that you can be sure."

"I am well convinced of your truthfulness," said the viscount. A cord of muscles in his jaw twitched, and if his hat did not soon disintegrate in his fists, it would be a miracle. "But I take issue with your conclusions. Come, take this opportunity to meet my brother, and perhaps he can explain to you what happened on that fateful day some ten years ago. It might put your mind at ease."

Gathering Tia up in her arms, Cassandra struggled to speak above the lump in her throat. "I should never have agreed to accompany you to tonight's meeting. First you insinuate yourself into an exclusive salon, then you invite your . . . your *courtesan* and her mopish brother. Now you expect me to entertain the monster whose actions brought about my father's murder? I think not, my lord!" She hugged her pet monkey close to her breast.

The viscount accepted that barb like a hot dagger in his heart. "Monster?" he croaked. "You dare to call my brother a mons—"

Horrified, Cassandra wished she could snatch her words from the air and eat them. "I did not mean—" Had a swarm of bees invaded that tiny shop, the air could not have held more sting. "Oh, my lord, I am so very sorry!"

For a long while the viscount merely stared at her. Suddenly, his malignant expression faded. "I forgive you," he said softly. "You do not seem a cruel person."

Tia hooted nervously, shaking her hands in the air as if she'd burned them on a hot stove. "She senses that I am overset, my lord."

"We are quite even, Miss Russell. Perhaps you will now allow me to sweeten the pot a bit?"

"What are you talking about?" With annoyance, Cassandra realized she had broken out in a cold sweat.

"You are a great admirer of Belzoni's, as is my brother." She nodded cautiously.

"Would you like to meet Signor Belzoni? In a more

intimate setting than the one I imagine will be staged at tonight's gathering?''

Cassandra stared. What did this charming, arrogant aristocrat have up his sleeve now? Was there no limit to the measures he would take to get his way?

When she didn't answer, he continued. "My brother has invited Signor Belzoni to dinner Friday night. It is to be a small gathering, just Neville, the Italian, and myself.''

"And Mlle. Duval?''

The viscount smiled.

Of course the piquant doxy would be there, Cassandra thought resentfully; that female Frog was more tenacious than a barnacle.

"Would you please honor us with your presence, ma'am? I shall send my carriage for you.'' Lord Catledge's eyes were warm again, and full of earnestness.

Cassandra loathed the notion of accepting the viscount's generosity, for the price was high. But the opportunity to spend an evening in Signor Belzoni's company was too great to pass up. Tonight's salon would be a miniature crush, what with all the avid Egyptologists in London showing up to get a peek at the famous Belzoni. She would be lucky if she were introduced to the man, much less allowed a few moments of private conversation. "Friday night . . .'' she said, turning the idea over in her mind.

"My carriage shall collect you at eight o'clock,'' said the viscount. "'Tis the least I can do, since you have been so kind to allow my brother to accompany us to the society's meeting tonight.''

"See here! I did not agree—'' Cassandra started to object, but her voice trailed in exasperation. She glared at the viscount and spoke in clipped tones. "I do not know how you manage to get your way so often, my lord.''

He grinned crookedly and donned his crumpled hat. "A man does not get anywhere in life by being timorous, Miss Russell. I am sure the great Signor Belzoni would agree to that.''

Tia scrambled from Cassandra's arms and onto the glass countertop. Without warning she flung a barrage of buttons at the viscount and bared her teeth, not in a smile, but in a grimace of warning. Throwing up his hands, Lord Catledge feigned great injury, and laughingly retreated, buttons crunching beneath his boots like eggshells. "Your pet is none too subtle," he observed wryly beneath the shop door's tinkling bells.

"It is my belief that a lady gets nowhere in life by being subtle," replied Cassandra, allowing herself a grudging smirk.

"Touché!" the viscount crowed, bowing magnanimously before he exited and pulled the door shut behind him.

Through the shop window Cassandra watched wistfully as he crossed the sidewalk and leapt into his gleaming black carriage.

She was beginning to fear Alistair Gordon's uncanny charm, and the frightful way he bent her will to his.

Chapter Six

With a row of straight pins clamped between her lips, Audrey mumbled, "Ye ain't sayin' ye don't wanna go with him, are ye? Um?"

Cassandra looked down at her maid's kneeling figure and shrugged. "Oh, I do not know what I want," she said, sighing. "There is something terribly disturbing about this arrogant viscount, and yet I cannot bring myself to cut him."

"Turn, please, miss."

Cassandra obligingly rotated atop the small stool, her black and gray pinstripe skirts rustling as she did so. Tia, watching from the floor in front of her, did the same, the monkey's pirouette a primitive parody of Cassandra's uncharacteristic conceit.

"Tia's right to mock me," Cassandra observed wryly. "I feel like an undeserving prima donna. Plain black suits me better, don't you agree, Tia?"

Audrey shot the grinning monkey a stern, disapproving look.

"Still, I do appreciate your taking the trouble to repair

my torn hem, Audrey. 'Twas unnecessary, though, to add that row of puffed satin roses." After a length, during which Audrey's needle darted in and out of her festooned hemline, Cassandra added gratefully, "But I must admit your roses transform this somber outfit into a thing of fashion."

Audrey deftly knotted her thread, snapped it off, then groaned as she straightened. Backing away to admire her handiwork, she plucked the pins from her lips and stuck them on her sleeve. "Ye can step down now, miss," she said with a glimmer of pride in her eyes. "But mind ye, don't sit down before his lordship arrives. No sense in mashing that pretty Nelson bustle."

Daintily lifting her skirts between thumb and forefinger, Cassandra twirled her rose-studded skirts. Studying her reflection in the cheval glass that stood beside the japanned screen, she allowed herself a guarded nod of approval. Audrey had indeed done wonders with that bolt of flawed Venetian satin. The tiny black flowers she had formed from the underside of the remnant provided a feminine touch to an otherwise staid mourning gown. Cassandra could not help but admire the effect.

Why, then, was she as nervous as a cat? Smoothing her hair, she turned sideways and studied her trim figure. Would the viscount compare her appearance to Mlle. Duval's? If so, how would Cassandra fare? Why on earth did she even care?

"Now, if it was me," advised Audrey, "I'd rid myself of that prickly white collar round me neck. Ye got a nice bosom, miss. Ye ought not be ashamed to show it."

Cassandra cast her maid a reproving look. "An Elizabethan ruff is quite fashionable, and besides, I would feel naked without it."

"Harrumph! Ye wait and see, miss. That brazen Frenchwoman ye told me about is gonna have her bosom pushed up so high above the low, scooped neckline of her gown . . . why, the gents'll think she's got a cleft chin."

"What an impertinent remark!" Cassandra exclaimed, laughing just the same.

Audrey's chuckle abruptly ended when a knock sounded at the door. "Oh, miss, he's 'ere! He's 'ere!"

Cassandra snatched her bonnet and woolen cloak from the foot of the bed. Audrey leapt before the mirror and gave her own bosom a good heave-ho. Then, in a blur of black and gray satin, both women bolted from the room. Attempting to pass through the bedchamber door at the same time, they were momentarily stuck, and it was only with a unison of groaning that they managed to break free and burst into the drawing room. There they jostled one another like racehorses, and dashed toward the summoning knock. Tia scampered along on their heels, alternately treading her knuckles and flapping her hands in the air.

Reaching for the latch, Cassandra felt a band of iron clamp her wrist.

"Ouch!" Startled, she jumped back.

Audrey jerked Cassandra gently around and stood nose to nose with her. The harried maid widened her eyes and pressed her forefinger to her lips, compelling silence.

Cassandra realized then that her heart was beating wildly. Seconds stretched like pulled taffy while she attempted to steady her pulse and compose her wits. Duly admonished by Audrey's unheard-of display of decorum, and acutely aware of the viscount's presence on the opposite side of her door, Cassandra finally whispered, "You're hurting me!"

Dropping Cassandra's wrist, Audrey's voice was barely audible. "Aye, but 'tis the maid who will open the door, not you. Stand aside now, miss, and don't act so anxious. Calm yerself. 'Twouldn't be proper to appear too pleased to greet his lordship."

Grateful for Audrey's intercession, for otherwise Cassandra would have flung open the door with flushed cheeks and a tellingly eager countenance, she backed into her small drawing room and clasped her hands in front of her. Audrey cast her a backward glance and mouthed, "Yer reticule! Don't forget it!"

Good Lord, had the excitement of this evening's salon totally robbed her of all good sense? Cassandra swiped her beaded purse off her littered round table. Then she took a deep breath and stood poised and outwardly calm. Inside, her stomach turned flips.

Audrey gave her a tight-lipped smile, then turned to open the door. "Oh! 'Tis you, my lord," she crowed, ushering the viscount inside. "Well, if this ain't a pleasant surprise."

Lord Catledge lifted his brows. "Oh, is it? A surprise, I mean?" he asked, looking a question at Cassandra.

"Well, I knew me miss was goin' out," Audrey explained. "Aye, and now that I think on it, I remember yer askin' her to accompany ye to that Egyptian gathering. But I'm such a simpleton, I'd forgot it was you comin' 'ere this very night. And me mistress nary mentioned a thing about who was pickin' her up." Audrey's coquettish smile widened to reveal a mouthful of dental problems.

The viscount bowed politely, first in Cassandra's direction, then in Audrey's. "Am I to feel slighted?" he asked. Cassandra felt the warmth of his gaze as he unabashedly took in her full appearance. The pleasure his scrutiny gave her was all out of proportion to the hint of masculine admiration his curving lips betrayed. "It appears, Miss Russell—might I call you Cassandra?"

"No."

"Ah." He gave Audrey a lopsided grin. "Well, it appears that you neglected to tell your devoted servant it was I who was coming to escort you tonight."

Audrey quickly inserted, "Miss Cassandra don't sit home every night, mind ye. She's sought after by scores of handsome dandies."

"Beating your door down, are they?" Lord Catledge asked, his lips twisting.

Cassandra felt her throat constrict. "For heaven's sake, Audrey. We must not give his lordship a mistaken impression."

The viscount's eyes twinkled merrily. "Well? Is it not true that you have legions of suitors?"

"I am sure his lordship is quite aware that I remain in mourning," Cassandra said coolly. "'Struth, I have not been about much lately."

"I believe we have established that," said the viscount, holding out his arm in a gesture of chivalry. "Come now, Miss Russell, we must not be late."

Audrey gave a huff of dismay as she pulled a fidgety Tia up into her arms. "I'll make ye some tea when ye return, miss," she said as Cassandra swept through the door and started down the stairs.

Behind Cassandra's back, the viscount frowned at the maid's puckered face. "Good try, Audrey, old girl," he said, winking. "But you mustn't feel the need to puff up your mistress's virtues. I am quite aware of her lovely attributes, competition or no."

Audrey shifted the monkey to her hip and shook her finger. "I know men," she countered through squinty eyes. "They don't fancy a woman lest some other man 'as his eye on her to boot."

"Ah! What a shrewd woman you are," answered the viscount, retreating across the threshold. "But consider this. How often has a bold man been disheartened when, thinking he was about to set foot in territory unexplored, he learned another had preceded him?"

Cassandra's voice lilted up the stairwell. "What in the world are the two of you chattering about?"

Alistair Gordon smiled at Audrey. "Why, we are talking about the great explorers of the world, Miss Russell," he called over his shoulder. In a whispered drawl he added, "I confess, dear Audrey. I would like to be the man who puts your mistress on the map."

*   *   *

It was a short ride from Pickett Street to Lord Tifton's Craven Street town house. Therefore, the viscount saw no need to arrange for two carriages to transport his entire party from Russell's Emporium to the Egyptian salon. He had collected Neville and the Duval siblings before he picked up Cassandra at her shop in the Strand. This obliged him to ride on the bench beside his coachman so that his guests could enjoy the relative spaciousness of the carriage compartment.

The brief period of his separation from Miss Russell filled him with trepidation.

"Are you all right?" he asked her when she emerged from the carriage.

"Yes, of course. Why wouldn't I be?" Cassandra asked, accepting a footman's hand as she stepped to the ground. Brushing past Alistair, she continued toward Tifton's front door.

Staring after her, Alistair was startled by a whisper-soft coolness at his neck. *"Are you all right?"* Suzette mimicked him, her voice low and sultry. "What is the matter, *bijou?* Did you think that I would be unkind to your precious little stray pet?"

The jealousy in Suzette's throaty voice raised the hair on Alistair's neck. Turning slowly, he answered, "How very odd that you should suddenly develop a dislike for Miss Russell."

"I do not dislike the *jolie laide.* She has a certain exotic appeal, I grant her that. But she is not your type, love."

Alistair could not resist a chuckle at Suzette's expense. "'Twas you who encouraged me to nurture a friendship with the woman. You said it was my duty as a brother to carry out Neville's wishes. Are you sorry that you said that?"

"Family obligations are paramount to selfish whims, that is true," Suzette said petulantly, linking her arm with the viscount's.

Alistair peeked over his shoulder to see Neville assisted from the carriage and into his Merlin chair. Pierre, who had emerged lastly, bounded ahead—his many-caped coat flying behind him—and grasped Cassandra's elbow as the front door opened for her. "Why, that impudent rapscallion!" Alistair said through gritted teeth.

It was Suzette's turn to chuckle. "What is the matter now? Are you jealous that Pierre has taken an instant attraction to your little Egyptian?"

"I should have known," grumbled Alistair, resentful that he'd been excluded from the interior of the carriage on the short trip to Tifton's home. Contemptuously, he warned Suzette, "I care not that he's your brother. I will not countenance that *parvenu rakehell* ill-treating Miss Russell. Mark my words!"

Suzette shrugged and hugged Alistair's arm tighter to her bosom.

Having entrusted their coats and hats to a phalanx of unctuous servants, the party was ushered up the stairs to the main floor. There paused the viscount's group, which was in reality Miss Russell's coterie, despite Alistair's usurpation of responsibility. They gave a collective gasp of astonishment.

Pierre grunted. "Standing room only," he muttered in an English far less continental than his sister's. Alistair noted with disdain the Frenchman's pinched-in waist, puffy trousers, and huge stand-up lapels. With his sharp stinger-shaped nose, the overall effect of Pierre's figure was rather beelike, Alistair thought. Amused, he had to think quickly when Pierre turned and arched a perfectly shaped brow.

"Something the matter, my lord?"

"Deuce it all!" Alistair exclaimed, breaking his stare from Pierre. "Where is Neville?" Realizing that his brother had been abandoned in the marble foyer, Alistair hesitated. He could not but feel a certain anxiety in leaving Miss Russell to the devices of the Duvals. Suzette was liable

to provoke all manner of dissension in her jealous mood.
Pierre's hands were chafing in lascivious anticipation.

Recognition of fellow society members illumined Cassandra's face, and before Alistair could detain her, she forged
into the throng of the drawing room.

"Not to worry, old man," said Pierre easily. "I'll look
after the ladies. Go and see about your brother."

Ten minutes later, Alistair entered the drawing room,
pushing Neville's Merlin chair before him. A sea of unfamiliar faces swilled about, and a passing footman deposited
a flute of champagne in Neville's hand. Unable to imbibe
and negotiate a wheelchair contemporaneously, Alistair
waved off the offer of drink. His thoughts were on finding
Miss Russell.

"I am getting seasick, Ali," Neville complained after
Alistair had circled the crowd a third time. "What is the
matter? Lost your girl?"

"I would have thought she might spare me a few
moments of her time," admitted Alistair ruefully.

Neville pointed. "There, Ali. Your girl is over there. Now
you can quit promenading me around the room."

Alistair halted and zeroed in on Cassandra. Neville lifted
his wineglass in the air.

Smiling, Alistair took it from him absently. He sipped,
cocked his head, then stared down at his brother. With
surprise, he noted, "You called her my girl. Thank you,
old man."

Neville squirmed, clearly uncomfortable with the thawing relations between him and his brother.

Alistair said, "I hadn't thought you would notice my
attraction for Cassandra so quickly. In fact, I don't believe
I realized the full extent of my feelings for her till just
now."

Something between a cough and a guffaw emerged from
Neville's throat. "I had only to take one look at her and
I knew. Good God, I'd have you committed to Bedlam if
you told me you were not falling in love with the likes of

her. She puts that French pussycat of yours to shame, I swear it."

"Um." In the back of his mind Alistair had already ended his affair with Suzette. Now he had only to plan the logistics of shucking her off. He reckoned that Wellington's disengagement from Napoleon had been no less complex and daunting. "And Suzette appears to be jealous," he remarked absently. "Most uncharacteristic."

Alistair replaced the wineglass in his brother's hand.

Neville said, "I wouldn't give you a farthing for that continental tart, little brother. Get rid of her."

"Would that it were that simple. I have asked her to be hostess at my upcoming masquerade. She has been planning it for ages."

At that, Neville craned his neck and squinted at his younger brother. "Then do it after the ball. Immediately after. Need some help, Ali? Turnabout's fair play. Quid pro quo and all that."

Alistair grinned and squeezed his brother's shoulder. "Will you be all right here a moment? I would like to go and fetch Cassandra."

Neville dispatched his brother with a curt nod, and Alistair made his way across the crowded room. He found Cassandra, flanked by the Duval siblings, in earnest conversation with an elderly gentleman wearing the dark blue uniform of the Royal Navy. At Alistair's appearance she broke off and introduced him to their host, Lord Tifton.

"Another gate-crasher?" Lord Tifton inquired, winking at Cassandra. "Or is this man a friend of yours?"

"I invited him, my lord," Cassandra said evasively.

"That is all the endorsement he needs, then," said Tifton, his watery eyes twinkling. "Having known you as long as I have, dear girl, I can say without hesitation that you are an astute judge of character as well as a true scholar of Egyptian antiquities."

Alistair took an instant liking to the man. "My lordship, Miss Russell was quite explicit in stating that the Society

of Egyptologists wished to limit the size of this gathering.
Please understand it was at my insistence she agreed to
sponsor my attendance tonight. I apologize for any inconvenience—''

"Dear boy, that is quite enough groveling! I fear that
many of the society fell prey to the supplications of their
friends. Miss Russell is not the only member who has
brought along a retinue of curious antiquarians. After all,
Belzoni is the toast of London. Everyone wants to catch a
glimpse of him.''

"Where is the great Belzoni?" Suzette asked pointedly.

"The hour of nine is approaching," Pierre added.

"Ah, the French are always so impatient," Lord Tifton
remarked jovially. "You might bide the time by examining
the little exhibition I have arranged on the table next to
the podium, eh?''

Cassandra gestured toward the other side of the room.
"Go and look," she urged Suzette and Pierre. "Lord Tifton
has put many of his antiquities on display. I have seen
them before, of course, but one never tires of examining
those curious ushabti. Have you put out your jewelry also,
my lord?''

Deep creases bracketed the man's smile. "Yes, dear. And
a fine array of cosmetic objects, amulets, and weaponry.
Go, Monsieur Duval, and have a look! Now, what is this?''
A footman bearing a silver tray had appeared at his side.
Lord Tifton took the proffered note from the salver and
scanned it. "Will you excuse me, please? Our guest of
honor has arrived, and is prepared to address our assembly.
Cassandra, do take your friends to that side of the room,
won't you? There you shall have the greatest vantage point,
my dear." He bowed. "Have a good evening, all," he bade
them, then retreated.

Alistair retrieved Neville and wheeled him to the area
indicated by Lord Tifton. All the chairs and settees in Lord
Tifton's drawing room had long since been occupied, so
that Alistair's group was obliged to stand. Having been

alerted to Belzoni's imminent arrival, however, they positioned themselves in front of the podium and the table heavily laden with Lord Tifton's antiquities. Alistair took his place next to Cassandra, and Suzette quickly appeared on his other side.

A hush fell, and Alistair looked around to see Giovanni Belzoni's turban-wrapped head and swarthy face cutting a swath through the crowd. Gawking people stepped aside, allowing the huge Italian and Lord Tifton to proceed toward the podium. As the guest of honor passed, his flowing white robes billowed against Alistair's leg.

Lord Tifton first addressed the murmuring assemblage. Little introduction was required, and less was called for, inasmuch as everyone in that room was fidgeting with anticipation. Lord Tifton quickly turned the meeting over to the great Belzoni.

He seemed larger than life with his thick black beard and mustache. He spoke for some time about the wonders of ancient Egypt, the indecipherable hieroglyphs of the Rosetta Stone (which he believed would soon be interpreted by a French prodigy named François Champollion), and the unwarranted frugality of the British Museum's trustees. After an impassioned plea for donations needed to finance his next expedition, Signor Belzoni agreed to take questions from the audience.

A bespectacled gentleman standing on his tiptoes posed a question from the rear of the room. "Signor Belzoni, much has been said of late concerning the medicinal and industrial values of mummies. Would you care to comment on that?"

Cassandra whispered, "That is Lord Killibrew, my lord. Perhaps the question he has raised marks him as a suspect in your investigation."

Noting her sarcasm, Alistair replied sotto voce, "Thank you. I shall interrogate the man thoroughly before the night is through."

Belzoni chuckled. "Mummies have no special healing

power, I assure you. It is a shame that so many of them are being ground into medicinal powders, or being used to stoke the fires of noxious manufactories. I tell you, mummies should be revered, not used up like compost."

Belzoni's answer drew a buzz from the nodding crowd, but soon Pierre Duval's voice rose above the din. "Do you believe in the mummy's curse?"

Cassandra flinched, and turned to stare wide-eyed at the impudent Frenchman. Noticing her disbelief and shock, Alistair suppressed the urge to wrap a protective arm about her. Instead, he edged closer to her—close enough to see the wispy baby hairs that curled against the nape of her neck, and smell the fragrance of her skin. The pressure of his fingertips upon her arm drew a quick sideways glance from her flashing topaz eyes, but Alistair did not retreat. Leaning down, he whispered next to Cassandra's delicately shaped ear, "Pray, do not let on you know anything about the mummy's curse. I have told no one of our incident outside the coffee shop."

Whether the shudder he felt beneath his touch was one of revulsion, fear, or excitement, Alistair could not know. But when his eyes looked a question at Cassandra, her answering stare, ambivalent though it was, excited his senses. Self-consciously, he tore his eyes from her in order that his physical discomfort might naturally abate.

Instantly, he met Suzette's narrowed eyes. She looked as if her cheeks had been pinched hard, but her rising color seemed a result not of her brother's provocative question, but of Alistair's sudden adjacency to Cassandra. With arched brows and tilted nose, Suzette wordlessly accused her protector.

"The mummy's curse?" echoed the big Italian. His brow lowered beneath his turban; his eyes darkened. "Can you be more specific, sir? Dying wishes—or curses, if you care to call them such—are as unique to each man as the print of his hand. Not every mummified Egyptian cursed his would-be tomb violators. Some did. Each curse is different," he said, stroking his beard and frowning. "Are you referring to a particular mummy, and a particular curse?"

Pierre shrugged. "I was of the opinion, signor, that modern grave robbers, such as yourself, had encountered many such curses. Did you not fall desperately ill after entering the sacred tombs at Kurneh, near Thebes?"

Belzoni squared his magnificent shoulders, and his voice boomed. "I take great umbrage at being called a grave robber, sir. Who are you?"

Rolling his weight to the tip of his toes, Pierre crossed his arms across his chest. "My name is Pierre Duval, sir."

"Have we met before?"

"No, signor," replied Pierre, lowering his head in a gesture of humility that Alistair would never have believed was earnest. "Forgive me for using the term grave robber. I meant no disrespect."

Even from where he stood, Alistair could see the slight tilt of Pierre Duval's lips, the sly sparkle in his lying eyes. What sort of game was the canny Frenchman up to? he wondered, gripping the handles of Neville's wheelchair.

Neville had turned to gawk at Pierre also. "What do you know of the mummy's curse?" he suddenly demanded of the young foreigner.

Pierre smiled unctuously at Alistair's brother, as if he were humoring a person of diminished mental capacity. "I know nothing, my lord," he answered, his tone so condescending, Alistair would have liked to strangle him with his impeccable white cravat. "I have only heard rumors."

"What rumors?" persisted Belzoni, much to the murmuring delight of a curious audience.

Pierre inhaled deeply. "I have heard that tragic fates await those men who dare to enter Egypt's sacred tombs. I have heard that the hidden crypts carved in the hillsides near Thebes are cursed by ancient monarchs whose eternal rest has been disturbed. After all, their tombs were carefully sealed many thousands of years ago so that their kingly souls might one day reunite with their bodies. Treasure seekers who plunder their burial vaults disturb their peaceful afterlife. Surely, the wrath of the gods is terrible."

Belzoni appeared thoughtful. "You speak as if you believe the ancient kings were gods."

Pierre drew himself up. "I do not believe in the diety of kings, sir. Indeed, I have risked my neck for my belief."

"*Scusami.* If you have survived the revolution in your country, you must understand the destructive power of rumor. Therefore, I answer your question with a simple no. I do not believe in any curse of the mummy. Does anyone else have a question?"

Neville grumbled audibly and shifted in his chair. Soon Belzoni's question and answer period was over, and Lord Tifton stepped forward again to make some final remarks and to remind everyone that refreshments were laid out in the dining room. Polite applause followed, and then the crowd became a sea of buzzing conversation once again, though gradually it broke up and began to dissipate.

After shaking the hands of several lingering guests, Signor Belzoni appeared at Neville's chair. "*Buona sera,* old friend! I apologize for being waylaid, but one must expect that sort of thing when one is the guest of honor. Good heavens, how are you?" he asked, bending to grasp the earl's hands in his own oversized ones.

Neville managed a sort of smiling grimace. "I won't ask how you recognized me, signor."

"Lord Tifton pointed you out to me," answered Belzoni smoothly. "I am so looking forward to dining with you tomorrow evening. And I have a great surprise in store."

A guttural chuckle sounded in Neville's throat before he waved a hand at Alistair. "I wager I know what it is, you shameless showoff. But here, meet my younger brother's friend."

Alistair introduced Miss Russell. Belzoni's eyes lit as he took her hand in his. "My dear, are you related to Sir Anthony Russell?"

"Yes," answered Cassandra, her chin lifting with pride. "He was my father."

"Dear God!" the Italian exclaimed. He held Cassandra's hand and gazed at her, apparently awestruck. "Yes, yes, you look like your mother! She was a beautiful woman, and exceptionally courageous. Tell me, child, how is my dear Rhoda?"

Cassandra's expression tightened. "She is . . . passed on, signor. My mother died a little over a year ago."

Belzoni's limpid eyes grew watery, and his voice thickened with emotion as he poured out effusive condolences. For a moment Alistair thought the huge Italian meant to embrace the girl in a great bear hug, but then Suzette Duval's trilling voice interrupted, and everyone turned.

"Why, Miss Russell, that is the most beautiful ornament I have ever seen," she declared exultantly. Her compliment, so ill timed and inappropriate, drew startled stares from both Cassandra and Signor Belzoni.

"Why, thank you," replied Cassandra, her hand automatically touching her throat, her fingers toying with the oval-shaped brooch ornamenting her frilled Elizabethan collar. Alistair had admired the unusual piece at her throat, but now he noticed the black center of it was actually a carved beetle. He nodded admiringly at Cassandra's exotic ensemble, and she returned his smile with a slight, hesitant one.

Suzette moved closer to Cassandra, denying Signor Belzoni the intended embrace Alistair had anticipated. "You must have inherited that unique piece of jewelry from your mother. Did you?"

"Why, yes," answered Cassandra. Her eyes cut to Belzoni. "Mother did not own anything of any great value, but her jewelry has a certain sentimental appeal—to me at least."

Belzoni was staring shrewdly at her. "The scarab amulet is the most powerful of all talismans, as I am sure you know."

Cassandra nodded, her eyes bright. Alistair recognized the hero worship in her expression, the reverence in her carefully modulated voice. Strangely, he felt prideful of Cassandra's beauty, her sensible manner of speaking, and her uniqueness. Signor Belzoni was clearly affected by her also, and Alistair was gratified to see that Cassandra had captured his attention.

She replied: "The scarab symbolizes life, of course."

"Immortality, to be more precise," interjected Neville.

Belzoni smiled benignly. "That is a rather optimistic view of the beetle's power, but ancient Egyptians apparently set great store in such magic. At any rate, I am intrigued by your parents' adventures, Miss Russell."

"As I am by yours, sir."

"I regret that I never met your esteemed father. I was fortunate enough to have been befriended by your mother, however. She came to see me at the Blue Boar Tavern, St. Aldate's Oxford, in 1813. She had heard of my interest in Egypt, and was curious, I suppose." He frowned. "Perhaps she meant to warn me . . ." His voice trailed off.

"Warn you of what, signor?" inquired Pierre Duval.

Belzoni shrugged. "I do not remember precisely what we discussed. Do you remember meeting me then, Miss Russell? You were a skinny little thing, not the beauty you are now."

Cassandra's topaz eyes sparkled. "Of course I remember. You were the Roman Hercules, and you balanced twenty men on your shoulders."

"Or so they said," inserted Neville gruffly.

Belzoni threw back his head and laughed. "Yes, or so they said. Actually, I employed a very sophisticated set of pulleys, levers, and ropes in my act. I must say my experience with balancing techniques served me well when I was attempting to devise a water pump for the pasha."

"Yes, and when you went about exploring hidden tombs also," remarked Suzette.

Signor Belzoni stroked his luxurious beard and nodded.

"Yes. And even more so when I transported the great statue of Memnon's head from Thebes down the River Nile. Ah, Neville, you should have seen that sight!"

"I would have liked to, Giovanni," replied the earl in as warm and sincere a tone as Alistair had ever heard his brother utter. "I hope you will tell us how you accomplished that great feat when you dine with us tomorrow evening. It seems that my younger brother has turned our dinner into somewhat of a party."

Pierre and Suzette spoke in unison. "We are looking forward to it," they chimed. Laughing, Pierre excused himself and went off in search of more champagne.

Alistair felt another presence at his shoulder, and admitted Lord Killibrew into the huddle surrounding Signor Belzoni. The bald, bespectacled man shook Belzoni's hand and was politely introduced to everyone else by Cassandra. "I waited until the salon had emptied before I dared introduce myself," he said with a quavering half-laugh. Lord Killibrew appeared full of trepidation, as if he had waited to approach the great Belzoni for fear of a violent rebuke that would leave him totally humiliated in front of a throng of his peers.

"I am afraid I offended you when I asked whether you believe in the medicinal values of mummies," he said, beads of sweat queuing on his upper lip.

"No, indeed," replied Belzoni affably. "Though I am concerned that many fine specimens will be destroyed for such purposes."

Behind his thick glasses, Lord Killibrew blinked. "But you do not disapprove of this latest trend, that of unwrapping mummies for the entertainment of lay people?"

"Not as long as there is a steady supply of them, and the unwrapping is performed carefully with as little damage to the corpse as possible. However, I would not care to disturb the wrappings of a *royal* mummy."

"For fear of retribution?" piped Suzette.

"Sì!" replied Belzoni.

Returning to the conversation, Pierre Duval handed his sister a flute of champagne. They put their heads together and whispered, then he straightened and offered to Cassandra the other glass of champagne he'd been holding. When she shook her head, he turned to Belzoni and said, "Did I hear correctly? Did you admit that you do fear the curse of the mummies?"

"No, monsieur, I admitted no such thing."

Pierre shrugged his shoulders and adopted a bland, disinterested expression, dismissing Belzoni's protestation.

Frowning, the Italian lectured, "The retribution I fear is from future scientists, archaeologists, and Egyptologists who might one day develop the means by which a mummy can be examined *without* the removal of his burial wrappings. 'Twould be a horror to violate all the mummies now in existence when such a possibility exists."

"I quite agree!" exclaimed Lord Killibrew. "You are a forward-thinking man, sir, and I shall be honored to contribute to your expedition fund."

"Grazie," said Signor Belzoni, bowing. "And now I must say my good-byes. It is getting rather late."

Cassandra bobbed a demure, old-fashioned curtsy that struck Alistair as quaint and very charming. Signor Belzoni took her hand and kissed her fingertips while Suzette smirked and Pierre frowned in obvious consternation. Was the young Frog jealous? Alistair wondered peevishly. But his introspection was brief. Lord Tifton's voice suddenly cracked the silence of the near-empty drawing room.

"Dear God in heaven, I have been robbed!" the man cried.

Alistair whirled around to see the elderly gentleman standing aghast before the refectory table on which his antiquities were displayed. At first glance Alistair saw nothing missing, but when he rushed over to the carefully arranged exhibition, the absence of many ushabti figures was evident. With stricken expressions, Cassandra, Belzoni, the Duvals, Killibrew, and even Neville in his Merlin chair crowded round the table. Alistair's eyes locked with Cassandra's, and for an instant their mutual apprehension crackled overhead like summer lightning.

"What is missing?" demanded Neville.

Lord Tifton's trembling, age-spotted hands hovered over his precious artifacts. His face was ashen, his cheeks more hollow than they had seemed before. "The small bronze speculum and the ivory cosmetic box are gone," he stammered. "And a half dozen ushabti figures, at least. Waxen warriors and carved beasts and . . . Oh! dear God . . . the dagger with the golden blade!" He wrung his hands and swayed on his feet, moaning repeatedly that he had been robbed.

Cassandra pulled a bell cord, and when a servant responded, she quickly called for the production of fortifying spirits. "Bring whatever his lordship drinks, and a damp towel . . . and perhaps some hartshorn," she ordered, then efficiently assisted Alistair in getting Lord Tifton over to a velvet-covered sofa.

The small party hastily reconvened around Tifton's reclining form. Had the man been a stage actor, Alistair thought, his prostration would have been considered maudlin. As it was, the suspense of the moment somehow justified the manner in which Lord Tifton pressed the back of his hand against his forehead and wailed pitifully.

"Call in a runner," Alistair advised him, watching Cassandra kneel and pat his bony hands. "Someone who is qualified to conduct an investigation of this sort should be employed right away."

"*Oui,*" said Suzette. "Everyone is a suspect!"

"Suspect?" echoed Lord Killibrew, his balding pate turning pink with excitement. "Oh, dear."

Neville scoffed. "Bloody hell! I am not a suspect! Do you think I have all that loot hidden somewhere on my person? Perhaps you think that I sitting on it. Now, there would be a real magic trick, Giovanni!"

The big Italian was pacing, his white robes swirling round his ankles, his eyes black with fury. "Tifton, is anything else missing—anything at all?"

Lord Tifton managed a weak reply. "I do not believe so."

"Perhaps you misplaced these items, my lord," suggested Suzette. "You may have thought you set them out for display—"

Her brother continued her thought. "But you were mistaken, obviously. I wager that if you check your storeroom now, you will find your missing artifacts intact."

Neville added, "Is it possible that a servant moved these particular items? Or that someone rearranged them during the exhibition, took them across the room perhaps to obtain better light in which to view them?"

"Might they have fallen beneath the table . . . perhaps rolled into a corner where they are hidden from view?" proposed Lord Killibrew tremulously.

Lord Tifton practically spat out the ruby port Cassandra was pressing upon him. Tossing a damp towel aside, he sat abruptly, waving Cassandra away so that she retreated nervously, the half-empty glass in her hands. "Look around!" the retired naval officer commanded shrilly. "Do you see the missing ushabti anywhere else in this room? Eh? Are you fools, all of you? I tell you, I have been robbed, damme! Someone has made off with an armload of antiquities . . . right beneath my very nose."

"Calm yourself," urged Signor Belzoni.

"Have another drink," said Neville.

"Oh, dear," muttered Lord Killibrew repeatedly, until at last Cassandra handed him the glass of port and settled him into a plush armchair, where he sank dejectedly and looked as if he might faint.

Pierre Duval stepped forward. "My lord, was there anyone in this room tonight that you did not recognize?"

"Did you notice anyone behaving queerly?" questioned Suzette.

Lord Tifton wearily shook his head. "Everyone here was accompanied by a member of the society. All guests were vouched for, as it were. No one behaved suspiciously as far as I could detect. But then, I was not spying on my guests, or anticipating being robbed. I was entertaining my guests and seeing to it everyone was well taken care of. Ha! I thought the party was a great success!"

"I am afraid we were all preoccupied," noted Alistair glumly. "Which gave the robber ample opportunity to commit a theft."

"Poppycock!" exclaimed Neville. "We hardly turned our backs to that table. If someone stole anything from it, he would have to be a crack criminal, a master thief!" As if realizing the import of what he had said, Neville shot Alistair a knowing glance.

"Where would a thief have put such a cache of antiquities?" asked Lord Killibrew mildly, reminding everyone of his presence.

"The items were all small ones," remarked Cassandra. "'Twould not be difficult to hide them."

"Even so," said Pierre, "where would a man hide such precious loot as that? Certainly not on his person. Lord Hedgeworth has already pointed out the unlikelihood of that. And I do not notice anyone's pockets or vests bulging unnaturally."

Signor Belzoni made a grand, flourishing gesture with his arms. "I beg to differ," he said, lifting the skirts of his voluminous *dishdash* to expose the vamps of his high-topped boots. "As you can see, there is plenty room in my costume to conceal a gaggle of stolen goods."

"You are the only gentleman present, however, who is wearing robes." Even as Alistair's remark tumbled glibly from his lips, he felt a chilling presentiment that the conversation was veering into dangerous territory. The obvious implication of his statement struck him like a tidal wave, but he knew someone would verbalize the awful insinuation he had hinted.

Waiting, dreading the inevitable accusation, Alistair noticed that everyone in the room looked guilt-ridden, their eyes shifting in suspicious sidelong glances, their bodies tensed for confrontation or poised for flight. Everyone, even Lord Tifton, seemed terrified as the seconds ticked by, so that when Neville Gordon did at last break the glassy silence with a harsh peremptory cough, the group flinched unanimously, then chuckled nervously, and finally sighed with startled relief.

"Good God! Are you afraid to say it, Ali?" the earl challenged, wheeling himself around to face Alistair. "Well, I shall, then. The Italian is not the only person in this room wearing clothes roomy enough to conceal an armload of stolen treasure."

"Oh, no," protested Lord Tifton gallantly. "You couldn't possibly suspect a *lady.*"

Cassandra gasped. "Lord Hedgeworth, are you implying—"

"*Oui!*" Suzette answered quickly, jumping to Miss Russell's side and linking arms with her. "That is precisely what his lordship is implying. He is accusing us of thievery."

Neville shrugged and grinned haplessly, as if amused by the ladies' extreme reactions. "I did not accuse anyone of anything," he pointed out.

Pierre Duval suddenly laughed uproariously. "Why, I think that is the funniest thing I have ever heard!" Tears streamed down his face as he threw his arm around his sister's shoulder in a casual embrace. "What say you, ladies? Either one of you got a dagger hidden in your petticoats?"

The look Suzette turned on her brother was so fierce that Alistair reasoned if she had a dagger hidden on her person, she would surely have unsheathed it and run him through. "Hush, you idiot!" But Pierre merely hugged her tighter as his laughter faded from raucous guffaw to muffled giggles and finally to sniffles of irrepressible amusement.

Cassandra removed her arm from Suzette's and

staunchly announced, "I would like to go home, Lord Catledge. If it is inconvenient for you to return me to Pickett Street, I am sure that one of Lord Tifton's servants will hail me a hackney cab."

Alistair looked from Pierre to Cassandra. "Do not be ridiculous, Miss Russell. I have every intention of returning you to your home. But I do not feel we should leave Lord Tifton at this very moment. . . ."

"I shall stay with him," offered Belzoni. "I think the rest of you should go home. There is nothing more that can be done tonight."

"I shall stay also," declared Lord Killibrew. "I shan't be able to sleep a wink this night; I might as well stay."

Lord Tifton made a feeble protest, but was quickly overruled by everyone. Cassandra took the old man's hands in hers and fervently wished him good luck in retrieving his missing artifacts. "I shall be in touch with you," she promised him, and exited the drawing room.

Suzette and Pierre politely bid Lord Tifton good night, but wasted no time in following Cassandra from the room. Alistair and Neville remained behind only to pledge his lordship their asssistance in recovering his valuables, shake hands with Signor Belzoni, and admonish Lord Killibrew not to overexcite himself. Having gathered their coats and hats, Alistair's wards silently filed out of Tifton's front door. Watching somberly as his footmen lifted Neville into the carriage and strapped his Merlin chair onto the roof, Alistair felt a deep perturbation that far exceeded his sense of loss over a dozen or so Egyptian antiquities.

His emotions were further agitated by the necessity of riding next to his driver rather than accompanying his guests in the carriage. Knowing that his mistress would remonstrate against such ill treatment, he directed his driver to deliver Suzette and Pierre to their homes before journeying toward the Strand.

"How rude, *bijou!*" Suzette said vociferously when he accompanied her to her door.

"Most ungentlemanlike, if you ask me," added Pierre petulantly. Turning stiffly, he goose-stepped into the darkness of the Cleveland Street town home he shared with his sister.

"Whatever is the matter with him?" Alistair had asked. "He's as puffed up as a toad, that one. 'Tis not as if I insulted his honor."

"Perhaps he feels that you have insulted mine, *chéri*. It is the same thing, you know. We are family."

"Yes, you keep reminding me, Suzette," answered Alistair grimly.

Alistair climbed into his carriage, then, and made prickly small talk with Cassandra while Neville snoozed against the squabs. To the viscount's chagrin, the Egyptian beauty seemed as put out with him as Suzette was. When the coach pulled to a stop before Russell's Emporium, Alistair leapt to the ground and accepted Miss Russell's slender hand as she set foot on the cobbled stones, now wet and slippery from the night's intermittent drizzle. He did not want to let her go; he did not want the evening to end before he had an opportunity to talk with her, look at her, be with her.

She withdrew her key from her reticule, unlocked the door, and stepped across the threshold of the shop front. Several branches of candles, no doubt lit by Audrey, burned within, illuminating the steep staircase that led to Miss Russell's private apartment. The streetlights' hazy glow insinuated itself into the thick fog, splitting into strands of golden mist that reached into the open shop door like fingers of fire seeking fresh air. Cassandra turned, and though her nose was pinkened from the cold, her eyes reflected invisible flames.

Alistair wanted to reach out for her, draw her into his arms and kiss away the chill that strained her features. "Cassan—" he started, then began again at the sound of his own voice, so throaty and vulnerable. "Miss Russell, that is," he said after clearing his throat of his thick, unwanted emotion. "I should like to see you to your door."

"You have, sir," replied Cassandra, barring the entrance to her shop with her slight, compact body. "There is no need for you to come in, my lord. I am quite safe."

"I suppose so," agreed Alistair, shivering against the raw draft that seeped up his pants legs. "But what of me? My legs are turning to pillars of ice. Surely you might find it in your heart to offer me a cup of hot tea, or chocolate, if you prefer."

Cassandra smiled at Alistair's attempt to wheedle his way into her shop. "I am too tired for your tomfoolery, my lord. Now, remove your foot from my threshold and allow me to retire." Once again she attempted to close the door, but Alistair remained steadfast.

"Not until you invite me in," he said, his tone playful.

"You cannot be serious," Cassandra protested. "Even were I so careless of my reputation, 'twould be cruel not to heed your brother's fate. He awaits in your carriage, or have you forgotten? Surely you would not abandon him to the elements while you warm yourself before my fire and take a leisurely cup of tea. He would catch his death of cold!"

"Neville is of hardy stock, and tougher than he looks."

"Is that why you got rid of your *chère amie* and her exquisite brother? So that their discomfort in a freezing carriage would not inhibit your attempts to dillydally here with me?"

"Between the two of them, they were wearing enough fancy clothes to keep an army warm. No, 'twas not their comforts that concerned me. I merely wanted them out of the way so that I could be with you alone. Do you understand?" Alistair turned sideways, and attempted to squeeze his body through the opening which Cassandra sought to shut.

Laughing, she pressed her weight against the opposite side of the door. "Yes, my lord. I think I am beginning to understand. You mean to compromise my virtue, sir. You mean to seduce me!''

"Oomph! I might as easily question *your* intent, miss. Do you mean to crush my ribs?''

"If necessary," retorted Cassandra. She leaned heavily on the door from inside.

Alistair grimaced at the first impact of the heavy wooden door propelled by the feather-light weight of Cassandra's body. Though she was slight in stature, she was taut and muscular. As she pushed the door against him, Alistair could hear her puffs of exertion, interspersed with her suppressed laughter.

For several moments the two struggled on opposite sides of the door, and although Alistair grimaced theatrically and muttered the mildest oaths he could think of, he did not intend, nor had he any need, to force his way into Russell's Emporium. He could have easily overpowered Cassandra, but to a fair-minded sportsman, a true gentleman and a committed Corinthian, that would have been conduct unbecoming. Peeking around the door, he grinned and said, "You win, Miss Russell."

She scowled, her golden eyes flashing.

Alistair's body relaxed, and Cassandra took the opportunity to throw herself against the door again. The impact nearly stole his breath.

"Are you all right?" Cassandra asked, mischief and concern mingling in her voice. She stepped onto the threshold and stared at Alistair. In the flickering candlelight, glints of red and gold shone in her sleek coiffure.

Alistair nodded stoically.

"Would you like to come in?" asked Cassandra softly.

Alistair's eyes lit, and searched her face for trickery. Sensing her sincerity, he said, "Yes," and advanced as she inched backward into her shop. With his boot he kicked the door shut, noting that the faded linen shade that heralded Sir Anthony Russell's name to London's pedestrians had long since been pulled to signal the shop's closing hour.

The viscount drew Cassandra to him and closed his arms about her. Hesitating, he allowed her the opportunity to resist, the chance to change her mind, but when Cassandra reached around his neck and pulled him closer, Alistair's breathing quickened, and his heart thudded with anticipation. He lowered his head and pressed his lips to hers.

He did not hear any commotion outside, nor did he hear his brother's muffled cry of outrage. The door behind him burst in, and before he could turn, he was hit on the head from behind. His eyes flew open, and the last thing he saw before he lost consciousness was Cassandra's ghostly pale expression of horror.

Chapter Seven

The door exploded inward with a splintering crash. Cold air whooshed into the room, gulping the sputtering candlelight and drenching the shop with shadows. Instinctively, Cassandra leapt backward, out of Alistair's arms. She saw stunned incomprehension reflected in his eyes, and then she saw the creature behind him. It loomed in the shattered threshold, a hulking silhouette of gauze and bandages blotting the light from the streetlamps.

The creature moved quickly—too quickly for a monster of such huge and awkward dimensions. It raised its arms, a thick mallet poised over Alistair's head.

"Alistair! Behind you!" Cassandra's voice trailed, and her warning faded into wordless shock. Alistair made a half-turn, but it was too late. The mallet crashed down on his head, and as his eyes rolled to the ceiling, his knees buckled and he fell to the floor.

Towering over him like some gloating beast beside its fallen prey, the mummy's hooded eyes glinted, its fingers tensed around the base of its cudgel. Cassandra's heart pounded against her ribs as the creature stared hungrily at her, grunted, then stepped over Alistair's body and advanced.

Limned by the glow of the streetlamps, the menacing mummy shone in luminous white relief against the semidarkness of the small shop. A wave of shock and revulsion swept through Cassandra. Backing away, her eyes glanced from Alistair's crumpled body to the mummy's bandaged face. What sort of monster was this? Where did it come from? Retreating, she found herself against the glass-topped counter in the rear of her store. She could go no farther, for the mummy's cumbersome appearance was deceptive; this was clearly an agile creature, light on its feet, stealthy and quick. After all, had it not jumped from her upper window onto a rooftop ten feet below in order to escape Audrey's brave attack?

Her spine arced backward as she recoiled. Desperately, she grasped the smooth glass behind her, searching for a weapon . . . a pair of fabric shears, a hat pin, anything at all to defend herself.

The monster planted its frayed feet and stood before her, its heavy breathing audible in the stillness of the darkened shop. It slapped the mallet in his open palm several times, a gesture that seemed to Cassandra sadistically playful, as if it wanted her to anticipate the pain its punishing blow would inflict.

"Who are you? What are you?" she managed to eke out hoarsely.

She thought she saw a slight curvature of lips beneath the mask of swaddling cloth. She now realized with utter certainty that Alistair's attacker was a man disguised as a mummy. She had never thought an actual revivified Egyptian mummy was stalking London. The carefully wrapped bandages were an elaborate disguise to be sure, but she hadn't given any previous thought to the criminal's gender. The slow, salacious appraisal he subjected her to now was definitely masculine—and predatory. His eyes glimmered even in the shadows, and he seemed to weigh his options as he stared at her.

"Are you afraid to speak, is that it? Afraid that I might recognize your voice?" Cassandra prodded, growing bolder. If she could only buy some time, then perhaps Alistair would rouse. Yes, that was it! She would stall the creature, and Alistair would awaken and attack the mummy from behind. Then, when the mummy was out cold, they would rip the bandages off its face and discover the true identity of their mutual aggressor.

"What do you want from me? You are after me, aren't you?" Cassandra straightened her shoulders, and while she slid her hands along the countertop behind her, looked her captor straight in the eyes. "At first I thought it was Lord Catledge you were after, but I was wrong, wasn't I? You broke into my apartment while I was sleeping . . . why?"

The mummy shrugged his massive shoulders in a peculiarly familiar gesture. A sliver of subconscious recognition pricked Cassandra's brain but would not take hold. She had to goad the horrid thug into speaking, trick him into revealing himself!

"Are you so timid that you cannot show your face? Or are you covering some dreadful countenance that needs be disguised by a mummy's shroud?" Cassandra taunted her foe, all the while searching behind her, sliding down the length of the countertop, reaching for something to defend herself with when the time came.

"Perhaps your face is pitted, pockmarked, or scarred by disease," suggested Cassandra.

The mummy shook his head vehemently.

"Vain, eh?" Cassandra forced a chuckle, her eyes darting to Alistair's inert body. He hadn't moved a muscle since he'd fallen to the floor, and she didn't know how much longer she could keep their masquerading enemy at bay.

The mummy matched her stealthy side steps, his eyes riveted on hers, his feet trailing ribbons of linen. Having recaptured her breath, Cassandra's senses sharpened. As she studied her stalker's curious gait, she thought his litheness contrasted sharply with his ponderous figure. Sticking out from his unraveling mitts were slender tapered fingertips. This strangely nimble behemoth was not the average London thief. On the contrary, he was a thin, almost delicate man apparently struggling beneath a veritable mountain of rags and padding.

At last Cassandra's fingers closed around the base of a silver candelabrum. Gripping it tightly, she braced herself against the countertop. The mummy halted, cocked his head, lazily slapped the mallet on his open palm.

"Get out," Cassandra said, her voice low and full of warning. "Get out, and leave me alone."

The mummy shook his head no and took a small step forward.

Cassandra repeated her command, but the mummy moved closer. She had no choice. Alistair wasn't coming to her rescue; he couldn't! She would have to fend for herself. She gritted her teeth and—using all her strength—swung the candelabrum at the mummy's head.

Throwing up his linen-padded arm, the criminal deflected Cassandra's blow. The silver candlestick clattered across the floor, and after it the wooden mallet. Having flung aside his weapon, the mummy lunged at Cassandra, his bare hands outstretched. Just as she felt his icy fingertips clutch at her throat, she screamed.

A shot rang out, clapping Cassandra's eardrums like a crack of thunder. The mummy whirled around and crouched low to the ground, then barreled toward the broken doorway. As quickly as he'd crashed into the shop, the villain sprinted out, disappearing into the darkness, the sound of his cushioned footsteps padding over the cobblestones before vanishing into the stillness of the night.

At first Cassandra could not fathom that the mummy had retreated. She half expected him to return, yet she was too frightened to move. The calm, collected countenance she'd mustered during her encounter with the masquerading mummy transformed into abject fright. She trembled with delayed shock. Where had that gunshot come from? Where had the mummy gone?

Then her eyes fell on Alistair, and her concern for her own safety vanished. Cassandra rushed to him, knelt down, and cradled his face between her hands. "Oh, Alistair! Are you all right? Please, open your eyes . . . oh, please!"

Her ears pricked. She heard a muffled voice calling Alistair's name from outside. Neville! She realized that the earl was still trapped inside the carriage compartment, unable to walk, unable to come to his brother's aid. Carefully, she lowered Alistair's head to the floor and ran to the carriage.

Neville was half in and half out of the compartment, his useless legs splayed across the carriage floor, his feeble arms supporting his weight. "Did I get him?" he asked, brandishing a pistol in one hand. "Did I at least wing the bloody demon?"

Cassandra plucked the revolver from the earl's grasp and tossed it on the cushioned bench behind him. The earl was not as light as he appeared, and she struggled to get his frail body back into the carriage compartment. When he was finally leaning back against the squabs, she said, "Lord Hedgeworth, I am afraid that Alistair needs medical assistance. We must go at once and summon a surgeon!"

"If Alistair is injured, I shall murder that infernal brute!" Neville cried.

"Yes, yes, my lordship." Cassandra patted the man's arm and suppressed her own growing panic. "I quite share your sentiments, I assure you. But we must stay calm to help Alistair . . . we must—"

"Well, how delightful," came a low drawl at Cassandra's elbow. She whirled around to stare at Alistair's lopsided grin and the rivulet of blood streaming down his cheek. "The two of you truly do care after all. Fancy that!"

"Alistair!" exclaimed Cassandra. "Are you all right? Good heavens, I feared the worst!"

The viscount pulled himself into the compartment and slumped on the seat, leaning heavily against his brother's shoulder. He took Neville's proffered handkerchief, pressed it to his bleeding temple. "What happened? Are the two of you all right?"

Cassandra pulled the carriage door shut against the invasive chill and listened in amazement while Neville related his story.

"I nodded off, thinking you might spend some time in Miss Russell's company. Wouldn't blame you," the earl added, his tone both gruff and affectionate. Without thinking, Cassandra reached for his hand and squeezed it. The gesture seemed to unnerve him, however, and she quickly withdrew. Neville cleared his throat convulsively before continuing. "I was quite comfortable, you see, with my lap blanket and my heavy coat. I wouldn't have minded waiting."

Alistair shot Cassandra a sly look. "Perhaps you did not mind waiting, but Miss Russell minded my intrusion. In fact, I had just succeeded in getting my foot in the door, when the mummy broke in."

Hoping that the dim gaslight that filtered through the carriage window disguised her burning cheeks, Cassandra turned to Lord Hedgeworth. "What happened after that?"

"I heard a scuffle outside, and then footsteps pounding off into the night."

Alistair snorted. "Our faithful driver deserted us, eh?"

"It takes more than wages to win a man's loyalty," answered Neville. "After that, a mummy appeared at the door."

"A mummy?" repeated Alistair, incredulous.

"'Twas someone *dressed* as a mummy, of course," said Neville. "I am sure it was a man, given his height. But the shock of seeing such a creature temporarily rendered me speechless. For a moment I thought I was dreaming. When he clubbed me on the head, the pain I felt assured me I was fully awake."

"Are you all right?" Alistair and Cassandra asked in unison.

"A lump on my noggin, perhaps," replied Neville. "But I am told I have an extraordinarily hard head."

"Quite true," agreed Alistair, inspecting his brother's hairline just the same.

"The same mummy entered my apartment and searched through my belongings," said Cassandra, watching as the viscount gingerly examined his brother's bruise. "Just a few nights ago."

Neville flinched. "Ali, quit poking at me! Why in heaven's name wasn't I aware that this mummy had been stalking Miss Russell?"

"The opportunity to inform you never arose," he murmured.

Cassandra quickly said, "'Struth, I preferred that Lord Catledge not mention it to you, my lord. But you might as well know it all now. The incident outside the coffee house too."

"What incident?" asked Neville, and was quickly informed of the rock with the warning note tied round it that had been thrown through the carriage window. "Good heavens, a fellow isn't even safe in his own carriage anymore, is he?"

"What happened after the mummy clubbed you over the head?" asked Alistair.

"I passed out, I suppose. When I came to, I managed to open the carriage door. I saw the damage done to the front of Russell's Emporium, and realized that the mummy had trapped the two of you in there. I dare not say what horrible thoughts flew through my mind. I thought it providential that a pistol was tucked inside my boot, and after some industry I was able to produce it. I fired off a rather wild shot, I'm afraid. Damme, I wish I had killed the bas—" Alistair nudged his brother, who abruptly broke off and looked away.

"Forgive my brother's language," said Alistair.

Cassandra nodded, but could find no words to convey her mixed emotions. Even if she had, a lump had formed in her throat, robbing her of her speech. Neville had turned his face toward the window, and Alistair was staring intently at her. The carriage compartment seemed more cramped than ever, the atmosphere more dense and prickly. Despite the cold moisture of the night, Cassandra suddenly felt the need to fill her lungs with fresh air. Tearing her eyes from Alistair's, she reached for the door handle.

He moved quickly, clamping his hand around her wrist. "Pray do not leave, Cassandra."

"I must," she replied firmly. "Can you drive your rig home in your condition? Or should you hail a hackney cab?"

"I am perfectly capable of getting my brother and myself home safely. My wound is not severe," said Alistair, releasing her wrist and assisting her from the carriage. "I shan't be long this time, Neville," he assured his brother, then took Cassandra's elbow and walked beside her toward the storefront.

Cassandra paused at the threshold and glumly surveyed the wreckage of the mummy's break-in. Alistair insisted on going inside to make whatever reparations he could. The broken door lay on its hinges, but with Cassandra's help was soon put upright and into place. A gentle push from Alistair betrayed the door's weakness, however, so he contrived a temporary barricade constructed from shiny caskets culled from Cassandra's inventory. Stepping back, he deemed the added fortifications suitable against all but the most insistent intruders.

"If the mummy comes back, a rampart of coffins will not hold him out," said Alistair. He grimaced as he inspected his handiwork, then heaved a sigh. "Perhaps I should stay here tonight."

"No!" The thought of Alistair spending the night in her apartment was almost as frightening as the mummy's return. "Do not worry, Lord Catledge. I shall push a table against my upstairs door and latch my bedroom door as well. If Audrey is upstairs, I shall insist she sleep with me. She is a worthy adversary, even for the mummy. I assure you, I will be safe."

"I would never forgive myself if something happened—"

Cassandra held up her hand, forestalling any further argument. "You must see to your brother, and also to yourself. Go now."

Alistair hesitated, staring. A cord of muscles tightened in his jaw; he started to speak, but then shook his head. He reached out and gently touched the back of his hand to Cassandra's cheek. His lips curved upward, but his eyes were sad and weary.

Then he squeezed himself through the tiny opening he had left, and from outside instructed Cassandra to push the coffin rampart against it. She could hear his muffled voice on the other side of the door, and she leaned toward it, her cheek pressed against the hard wood, her heart pounding in her chest.

"Good night, Cassandra. Do not forget that we are dining at my brother's home with Signor Belzoni tomorrow night. I will send my carriage round for you. Until then . . . stay safe."

"Good night, Alistair," she whispered. Her fingers stroked the cold door, and her tears wet her face and lips.

The sound of leather ribbons slapping horseflesh was followed by carriage wheels rumbling over cobblestones. Loneliness like Cassandra had never felt suddenly overwhelmed her. If only she had never met the viscount . . . if only she had never talked to him . . . Then she would never have wanted him so badly, and never have suffered through the disappointment of knowing she could not have him.

He was an aristocrat, an arrogant rakehell viscount who trifled with French mistresses and lauded himself for his lack of responsibility. Those were his words, and if they were not true, then he was a liar to boot!

Cassandra's reservoir of tears burst like a broken dam, and with her forehead against the door, she stood and cried until her throat was hoarse and her ribs ached. She indulged herself a heaping portion of self-pity, and reasoned that her life had been one long series of tragic happenings. She sobbed and hugged herself, and poured out her grief in a catharsis of recriminations and regret.

If only her father had never offered to help Neville Gordon, he would not have been murdered by a lunatic! Her mother would not have been forced to eke out a living as a funeral boutique proprietress. Alistair Gordon would not have come looking for Lady Rhoda Russell when Neville's mummy went missing. And, most important, Cassandra would never have fallen in love.

And her heart would never have been broken.

From behind his desk Neville Gordon watched his brother grab another bottle from the liquor cabinet. Head tilted, Alistair drank greedily, and when the liquor trickled down his chin, he removed the bottle from his lips, hiccupped, and wiped the back of his shirtsleeve across his mouth. Wincing at his brother's immoderation, Neville clucked his tongue. "If your head is throbbing now, I shudder to think what it shall feel like in the morning," he said.

Alistair had been tipping the bottle ever since the application of a poultice to his temple by one of Neville's servants, a Welshwoman who believed ardently in the healing properties of sage and white wine. Snatching the bandage from his head, Alistair now slumped into the chair opposite his brother's desk, legs akimbo, liquor bottle clutched in his hand.

"I intend to get rip-roaring drunk tonight, brother. Do not try to stop me."

"Pity. I had thought we might discuss a few things."

"Such as?"

"Your intentions toward Miss Russell, for one," said Neville, nursing a glass of the liquor that his brother guzzled. "To put it mildly, you are fond of her."

Alistair shrugged eloquently. "What of it?"

"Oh, Ali, do not use that belligerent tone with me. I know we have had our difference in the past—"

"Differences? Differences, you call them? God's sacred blood, Neville, you have hated me for years, despised me, ridiculed me, and made me feel as if I were a good-for-nothing!"

Quick, hot anger coursed through Neville's veins, but he tempered his reply. "You are foxed, and so I forgive you for speaking rashly. Still, Ali, no man can make another disrespect himself. If you believe you are a good-for-nothing, do not blame me. You have been blessed with good looks and intelligence as well as wealth and influence. If you have made nothing of yourself, then it is you who are to blame, not I."

"You hated me because you hated my mother," Alistair ground out, his fingers tight around the bottle's neck.

Neville's heart squeezed, but his anger dissipated. He was weary, and Alistair's words were all too true. What was the point in protesting otherwise? After some length he said, "Yes, Ali, I hated your mother. I was a child when she came into our household, and I thought that your mother caused my mother's death. I realized years later that I was wrong; Mother died of disease, and was long dead before Father even knew your mother. But don't you see? I was a *child!*"

Alistair blinked at him in drunken astonishment.

Neville continued. "Father seemed so in love with his new wife. 'Twas very painful, for I had adored my mother and pined desperately for her. Then you came along, and Father held you up to me, as if in comparison. 'Is he not the most beautiful child you have ever seen, Nevie?' he asked me. 'Dark-haired and dark-eyed like his mother!' God, I thought you were the most revolting little brat I'd ever seen! So handsome and witty. So full of energy and jollity. Later on Father laughed when you told jokes. As for me, he only wanted to know what high marks I made at school or how many languages I had mastered."

Alistair pushed a thick shock of black hair off his forehead in a gesture Neville recognized as part of his charm, his unaffected elegance. He watched a crooked smile twist on Alistair's lips.

"Do you find my confession amusing?" Neville demanded.

Alistair grinned. "What is amusing is that we despised each other for such stupid reasons. I thought you were the favored one, the brilliant one who could do no wrong. So I set out to distinguish myself from you by showing just how mischievous I could be. No one seemed to take me terribly seriously, so I adopted the role of prankster, rakehell, and later *roué.*"

"You do yourself a disservice, brother. You could be so much more."

Alistair turned up the bottle but didn't drink. He lowered it slowly and stared at Neville. "Did you really call me away from the country just to tell me that your mummy had been stolen?"

"It provided an excuse for me to see you," admitted Neville. "I do not think I have very long to live, Ali. I wanted to see you before I bequeathed all my worldly goods to you."

"Don't need 'em," said Alistair. "I am rich now, you know."

"Then why come here?" returned Neville. "Why not say 'Brother, go to hell' when you got my post? Why dash all the way to London to find out what my trouble was?"

Alistair sank deeper into his chair. "I do not know."

Minutes passed before either man spoke. "Ali, pull that bell cord, and we will have Digby bring us some coffee."

Alistair complied, then placed the half-empty liquor bottle on the edge of Neville's desk. "I should like to change the subject," he said, falling back into his chair.

"What is it you wish to speak of?" asked Neville. "Or should I ask *whom?*"

"It is Miss Russell," replied Alistair, hands clenching the golden sphinx's heads on the arms of his chair. "I should like your advice. You are my brother, after all, and I need your assistance. Will you help me, Neville—as I am pledged to helping you?"

Neville felt his chest ache with a tender affection, a warm, gratifying sense of belonging that he had not felt in many years. "Oh, yes, little brother! Yes, yes. Ah, here is Digby. Bring us a pot of coffee, man! Or would you care for chocolate, Ali? And see that the guest room is made ready for my brother in case he desires to stay the night. We cannot have him driving the streets of London in his condition, now, can we?" Neville chortled with delight. "No, we must keep him with us tonight and see that his head mends properly, and—"

Alistair exploded. "Christ on a raft! What a mother hen you are!"

Neville broke off and stared at his brother in amazement. Digby looked on the scene with equal disbelief, until Alistair broke the silence with a raucous guffaw. Then the brothers Gordon laughed loudly together, and the gloomy town house on Curzon Street suddenly seemed less an Egyptian museum than an honest-to-goodness home.

*   *   *

"Have you lost your senses, Pierre?" Suzette jerked tight the sash of her robe and sat down at the table in her sparsely furnished drawing room.

Her brother, clad in a crimson velvet smoking jacket, pushed a cup and saucer toward her. "Have some tea, sister. It will calm your nerves. Or would you like something stronger? My medical chest is just in the other room."

"It is little wonder that you were kicked out of the medical academy, Pierre. You take far too many risks," chided Suzette. She sipped her tea, her anger subsiding.

"Are you referring to my impromptu robbery?" asked Pierre, grinning slyly. "Or my midnight masquerade at Russell's Emporium?"

Recalling Lord Tifton's distress, Suzette was forced to smile. "He will never figure out what happened to his precious ushabti," she said. "And the look on Killibrew's face was priceless! Was it not?"

Pierre's laugh tinkled. "I was afraid I would clink and clank all the way to the carriage. Oh, my! And that bronze knife was so terribly cold against my leg, 'twas all I could do to keep from shivering."

"What a clever boy you were to wear your specially pocketed trousers, Pierre. That seamstress who fashioned them in Paris knew how to outfit thieves. What will we ever do if you gain enough weight to fill them out beneath?"

"We shall no longer be able to rob people beneath their very noses, that is certain," gloated Pierre.

"Still, your actions at the emporium were far too risky," said Suzette. The testiness in her voice was gone, but now she frowned, worried that her younger brother might expose them to unnecessary dangers. "Why on earth did you stay inside Cassandra's shop for so long? Why didn't you run away sooner?"

Pierre shrugged in his unique, exaggerated manner. "I hoped to search the premises more thoroughly this time. Had I been able to subdue Miss Russell, I would have gone

Say Yes to 4 Free Books!

looking for our mummy's mate again. That horrid little maid would not have deterred me a second time."

"You were lucky that Lord Hedgeworth did not shoot you."

"That old goat could not have hit the side of a barn!"

Suzette studied her brother, bemused by his flippancy. " 'Twas a *grand coup* that you pulled off in Lord Tifton's home, *mon frère*, but why the encore? Why did you follow Alistair back to Russell's?"

Lifting his shoulders, Pierre slanted his sister a sardonic look. His half-lidded eyes were green, like hers, and his hair every bit as dark. But the siblings' physical resemblance ended there. Suzette's face was heart-shaped, but her brother's features were angular, and his mouth thin-lipped. His gestures were oddly effeminate, reminding Suzette how their papa had berated the boy for his lack of manliness. Nevertheless, Pierre had always been head-strong, and determined to do what brought heaping measures of punishment on his head. It was as if his father's criticisms toughened the boy, making him mean and vindictive. Pierre seemed to hate himself as much as his papa had, and so took risks that guaranteed harsh reprisals.

That was why he'd followed Alistair tonight, Suzette surmised. And that was why he hesitated now to candidly discuss his reasons for doing so. Pierre preferred to cloak his actions in mystery, to force her to guess what he was about. He also had an intensely private side, a dark aspect to his personality that shone now in the gleaming blackness of his eyes. Suzette had never been afraid of her brother, and never would be, but she sometimes shuddered at the thought of what he had done—and was capable of doing.

In the darkness of her bedroom Cassandra listened to the raindrops splatter against her windows. Tia was curled up in her nest beneath Cleo's coffin, and Audrey was snoring loudly in her own tiny room. How could that girl sleep

so soundly after what had happened? Cassandra wondered. Chagrined that her maid had engaged another late-night rendezvous, Cassandra considered it poetic justice that Audrey had been unable to use her key to reenter the shop. A series of frantic knocks had drawn Cassandra reluctantly down the stairs, and it had taken a herculean effort to push aside the caskets to allow Audrey entrance.

Having chastised her maid for such imprudent behavior, Cassandra had shared a cup of tea with her at the small round table in her sitting room. Despite Audrey's promiscuity, Cassandra found her maid's presence comforting, and in relating the night's events discovered a new perspective on her own emotions.

"Oh, ma'am, 'tis like the mummy's curse yer mother used to speak of! The awful creature is trying to kill ye. I never did believe it when dear Lady Russell—God rest her soul—spoke of the curse, but even I seen that monster with me very own eyes. He's after us all, he is!"

"There is no mummy, Audrey. He is a man disguised as a mummy."

"Then what does he want?" Audrey asked, her ruddy complexion darkening with apprehension. "What's 'e after?"

"That I do not know," replied Cassandra truthfully. "I know only that it has something to do with Lord Catledge and the investigation he is conducting into his brother's missing mummy. The trouble started the day I met the viscount, not coincidentally, I am sure!"

Audrey blinked her bloodshot eyes. "Then you don't believe in the mummy's curse, ma'am?"

Cassandra sipped her tea before answering. "I do not say that. Mother surely did. She thought that the pharaoh's curse befell everyone who was present when the great king's resting place was disturbed. Father's violent death convinced her of the curse's potency; her lingering illness convinced me."

"But you were only a child when your father dug up Cleo," protested Audrey.

"Cleo was meant to spend eternity next to her husband, the pharaoh. When their royal graves were desecrated, the curse fell on all who were present, including me."

Audrey reared back. "Do ye really believe that? Can it be true?"

Cassandra stared into her empty cup. "I do not know what I believe, Audrey. If I am cursed, then it is to a life of solitude. 'Twould be an appropriate price for Cleo's husband to exact, do you not agree? I have the pharaoh's precious wife in my possession; Lord Hedgeworth has—or had—the pharaoh in his. What better revenge than to curse me to solitude, so that I shall be as lonely in my life as the royal monarchs are in their eternal repose?"

"'T'aint the mummy's curse that keeps you in them widow's weeds," countered Audrey. She poured herself another cup of tea and laced it liberally with sugar. "If ye don't want to be lonely, change yer attitude. And yer gown. But don't go blamin' yer lack of suitors on some mummy!"

"I know it is foolish to believe in curses, and truth be known, I do not," said Cassandra slowly. "I suppose I have always viewed the world as an Englishwoman—not as an Egyptian, like my mother."

Audrey finished her thought in that uncanny intuitive manner she often had. "But still, the mummy has cursed you in a way. Cleo's a burden, ain't she? She reminds ye of things you'd rather forget. And she's keeping ye from living yer life."

In her frustration, a twinge of bitter remorse tweaked Cassandra's conscience. "If only the mummies could be united! Then I would feel that Cleo is where she should be, next to her husband. And I would no longer be reminded of Father's death and mother's illness every time I enter my bedroom."

"Then do it!" cried Audrey. "If Cleo wants to be leg-

shackled to that dead pharaoh husband of hers for all eternity, then let her be!''

Cassandra looked into Audrey's eyes and dolefully reminded her, "But don't you see? That is no longer possible. Neville's mummy is Cleo's husband. And the pharaoh has been stolen! That is why Alistair came here in the first place, to look for his brother's purloined mummy."

"Ah! Now, here's a neat twist," said Audrey, holding up her forefinger. "You didn't mind the solitude till ye got a gander at that handsome viscount. But he asked too many impertinent questions about Cleo afore ye trusted him, so ye held him off at arm's length. Ye even led him to believe ye ain't got no mummy hidden up here behind a screen."

"I did not trust him because he seemed so arrogant and irresponsible. I did not tell him about Cleo because I did not want his friend, Suzette, to know about my mummy. I am not certain why . . ."

Audrey poked her finger in her mouth, then dipped it into the sugar bowl. "But now ye want to know the viscount a little better, and yer goin' to have to tell him that you've got Cleo up here, waiting to be reunited with her runaway mummy husband."

"I feel it is the proper thing to do," agreed Cassandra.

"But you're afraid, aren't ye?" Audrey leaned forward, her elbow propped on the table, her sugar-coated finger waving in the air. "You ain't never believed in that pharaoh's curse, not really. But it was reason enough to isolate yerself from the world—at least until ye laid yer eyes on Lord Catledge. Now, ye figure that if ye reunite Cleo with her pharaoh, then the curse is gone and ye got no excuse to be sittin' up here all alone. So yer asking yerself whether ye might be willing to risk a heartbreak fer a chance at that viscount!''

Cassandra remembered what it felt like to be in Alistair's arms, and her face flushed with warmth. "No, you do not understand," she argued lamely.

Audrey wrapped her lips around her sugar-coated finger

and slanted a jaded gaze at Cassandra. When she'd licked her finger clean, she pointed it accusingly and waggled her head. "We ain't that different, you and me. You're afraid to let a man get to know ye, afraid he might not like ye when he does. I'm afraid too. I ain't got much to offer, see, like you have. All's I got is my body, and it ain't gettin' no younger. I meet a man, and I figure he won't like me unless I give him what he wants. So I do, and then I never hear from him again."

"I shall not take such risks with my virtue, and you shouldn't either," replied Cassandra staunchly. "Besides, Alistair will never trust me once I tell him I lied."

Audrey waved her hand in front of her face and wrinkled her nose. "Poppycock! Tell him the truth. Ye lied about havin' Cleo because ye didn't know whether ye could trust him. But now ye do."

"Do I?" Cassandra had echoed.

And that was what she lay awake thinking about. Did she really trust Alistair enough to tell him the mummy queen was in her possession?

If she divulged Cleo's existence to Alistair, then she risked losing her precious mummy forever. Whoever stole Neville's mummy seemed intent upon thwarting Alistair's investigation. That same criminal, or gang of criminals, would jump at the chance to steal Cleo. Perhaps Cleo was even the ultimate target of the mummy-swiping caper.

And Alistair must have unwittingly led the thieves to Cassandra's shop. Now Cleo was in danger of being snatched, and Cassandra had to prevent the priceless Egyptian queen mummy from falling into such diabolical hands. If Alistair knew of Cleo's whereabouts, would he unknowingly betray that knowledge to the wrong people?

And if Alistair did find the pharaoh mummy, and Cleo were reunited with her dear, departed royal husband, would the viscount still have any use for Cassandra?

Or would he give her a tight-lipped "thank-you," tip

his hat, and beat a quick retreat to Suzette Duval's warm embrace?

After all, Cassandra was merely a middle-class chit, a bluestocking virgin whose parents bequeathed her neither rank nor wealth. She was hardly a match for the aristocratic viscount.

Rain pelted the windows and the wind keened ominously. A boom of thunder eclipsed Audrey's snoring and sent Cassandra burrowing deeper beneath her covers. A flash of lightning illuminated the room.

Something moved in that instant of brightness. Something on the far side of the room. Cassandra held her breath, her heart pounding furiously, her eyes squinting against the darkness. A shadow scudded across the japanned screen.

Out of nowhere, Tia sprang onto the bed.

"Oh, you silly monkey!" Cassandra whispered, stroking the pet's head as it snuggled beside her, shivering with fright. "You do not like the storms, do you?"

Nor did she. The weather matched Cassandra's inner turmoil, and she wished for nothing more than serenity, peace of mind. She prayed for wisdom and guidance and strength against her enemies.

She prayed to be loved by Alistair Gordon, Viscount Catledge.

Across town, Alistair was finishing a pot of coffee. His brother had asked him many questions during their long conversation, and he had answered all of them as best he could.

All but one, that is.

He had told Neville about the rock thrown through his carriage window, and he'd related every detail of the mummy's attack at Russell's Emporium. The brothers had discussed the significance of the same mummy ransacking

Cassandra's apartment, and the possibility that a gang of thieves had infiltrated London's Egyptologist community.

But dawn's light was peeping through the heavily curtained windows, and still the mystery of the stolen pharaoh mummy had not been solved. Both men felt frustrated by their lack of leads. The mummy—or, rather, the villain dressed as a mummy—would return. Next time his victims might be less lucky than they'd been so far.

"You have yet to answer my most important inquiry," reminded Neville, rubbing his one good eye. He blinked and focused it on his younger brother.

Alistair remembered the question. "I have no answer," he confessed at length.

"Do you not trust your feelings?"

Alistair frowned. "I am more comfortable with women like Suzette."

"Even though her brazen manners grate on your nerves and she is an incorrigible flirt?" asked Neville. "Could you ever trust her?"

"She is not demanding of me," said Alistair.

"You are not demanding of yourself," Neville riposted. "If you believed yourself to be deserving, then you would deserve a more demanding woman."

Alistair cocked his head to one side. "Does it not trouble you that Miss Russell is a chit, a tradeswoman, a *funeral director?*"

Neville's lips twisted in a crooked grin. "Does it trouble *you?* You are the one in love with her, Ali."

Alistair sighed, trying to picture what his life would be like with Cassandra by his side. He could not imagine her in a riding habit, galloping ahead on a spirited mount, leading the chase across open fields. He could not yet see her in an exquisite ball gown, snapping a smart fan and doing the pretty with his fancy friends. Nor could he envision Cassandra tossing dice, and recklessly pushing markers across baize-covered tables.

The thought of her embroidering quietly by the fire,

head bowed over a tambour frame, made him want to laugh out loud.

But he could easily picture Cassandra across the dinner table, raising her glass to him on a cold winter night, her lips curved in an elliptical smile, amber eyes flashing in the candlelight. He imagined himself immersed in long conversations with her, some of them about nothing, others concerning affairs of state, religion, ancient Egypt. He could hear her wise advice, her soft admonitions, and he saw himself—egads!—sober as a judge, with a baby or two bouncing on his knee.

Most disturbing of all these images, however, was the one Alistair could never put into words. He saw his sweet Cassandra staring up at him, her hair splayed wildly across a pillow. She whispered something vague and intimate against his neck. She moved beneath him. Alistair closed his eyes and melted into her.

"Good night, my little Ali-Cat," Neville said, rolling past in his Merlin chair.

Alistair's eyes flew open, and he turned to see his brother pause at the library door.

Neville clutched the doorknob and spoke over his shoulder. "You have answered your own question, brother," he said, his good eye averted. "By the way, have I ever told you how proud I am that you are my brother?"

For a long time after Neville had gone, Alistair remained in the library, staring at the odd assortment of Egyptian antiquities surrounding him. Then he retired to the guest room that had been prepared for him, and slept fitfully for a scant half hour. When he arose, still fully dressed, he bent over a basin on a tripod stand and splashed cold water on his face. He left the house quietly, awakened a stable boy, and rode out on one of Neville's finest mares.

Viscount Catledge had no intention of allowing the marauding mummy to threaten Cassandra again. He meant to stay as close to her as possible, especially at night, when she was most vulnerable to the criminal's evil designs.

He meant to protect her, even if it meant keeping vigil at her Pickett Street establishment, staying safely hidden in the shadows to escape unwanted attention, remaining close enough to see that no harm befell her.

Alistair had never experienced this depth of feeling for a woman. His affection for Cassandra consumed him, and erased his desire for Suzette, and all the other Suzettes he'd ever known. He realized that for years he'd merely been playing at love. Now Alistair knew what true love was, and it made him miserable to think that Cassandra was in danger.

Chapter Eight

Neville Gordon, the Earl of Hedgeworth, was strangely quiet during dinner, yet his good eye swept the room like a Theban eagle's. Cassandra lowered her wineglass and stole a glance at the man she once blamed for her father's death. Her resentment toward him had dissipated. Neville had saved her life, and possibly the viscount's, when he fired off a shot at the mummy in Russell's Emporium. Now when she looked at the earl, she saw a war veteran soured by loneliness and dejection, not a greedy grave robber.

She saw also the unspoken love between the young, handsome brother and the older, misshapen one. It was palpable, if not painfully suppressed. Throughout dinner Cassandra watched the earl's good eye flicker from her to Alistair, then back to her, where it lingered unaccountably. When she confronted the earl's gaze, he guiltily averted his eye and ducked his shaggy head. She knew the foxy old man was aware of every undercurrent that flowed between the four young people at dinner. But she did not understand his surreptitious, almost doting perusal of her when he thought she wasn't looking.

Preempting his brother, Alistair rose from the dinner table and said, "I think the gentlemen shall dispense with port and cigars. Come, let us all retire into Neville's study. I for one do not care to be separated from the ladies, even for a moment."

This unorthodox pronouncement came as a great relief to Cassandra. After enduring Suzette and Pierre Duval's incessant conversation throughout dinner, she was eager for a change of scenery.

Garbed in authentic Arabic costume, Giovanni Belzoni stood and clapped his hands in a gesture of boyish excitement. *"Eccellente!* I hope I do not offend my host and my new acquaintance, Monsieur Duval, but I was not looking forward to being cooped up in this room with you men while our pretty lady friends sat and *thartharred* in the drawing room."

Pierre stood and hovered behind Cassandra's chair, his mouth close to her neck, his breath raising goose bumps of mild revulsion along the sensitive skin of her shoulders. '*"Tharthar*—that is the Arabic word for gossip," he whispered.

"Yes, I know," Cassandra said, her tone clipped. She pushed back her chair and rose abruptly, catching Alistair's eye as she did so. The viscount arched his brow in an ineffable show of sympathy.

The Duval siblings had dominated the conversation at the dinner table, plying Signor Belzoni with sycophantic flattery while peppering him with questions concerning his past expeditions. Cassandra and Alistair had listened with polite forebearance, their eyes meeting across the table, communicating their mutual wish to be alone, where they could whisper their private thoughts, touch each other, study each other's features without restriction.

Several times Cassandra's eyes had met Alistair's gaze, and when she did, his lids had fallen lazily, seductively. His dark eyes had twinkled, eliciting more than one smile

from Cassandra as she feigned polite interest in Suzette's and Pierre's pretentious prattle.

Once, the viscount had even winked at Cassandra, then cast her a lopsided grin before raking his dark hair from his forehead. Pressing her serviette to her lips, she hid her smile and the tingly warmth she'd felt creeping up her neck. At least, she hoped she hid her emotions. As she moved away from the table, Alistair's eyes seemed to penetrate her, reveal her. Had anyone else in the room been paying the slightest attention, he or she might have been privy to Cassandra's innermost thoughts.

Perhaps it was fortuitous that the Duvals were preoccupied with interrogating Signor Belzoni. Had Suzette and Pierre not been so intent on ingratiating themselves to the celebrated strongman, they surely would have caught wind of the growing attraction between the viscount and Cassandra. For, though schooled in hiding her emotions, Cassandra felt tonight that she was as transparent as the aerophane oversleeves of Suzette's low-cut evening dress.

Perhaps she was out of her element, Cassandra thought, stealing a critical glance at Suzette's gown. The flair of a French *modiste* was evident in the daring cut of Suzette's plunging neckline. The Frenchwoman's breasts, peeking out from her snug white satin bodice, were crisscrossed, separated and held high by appliquéd ribbons of green cord. Her skirts were white satin with a pale green stripe running vertically, and beneath her hem peeked delicate green slippers with ribbons that tied about her slender ankles.

Suzette's gay green confection, with its scandalously revealing neckline, frivolous rows of embroidered flowers, and tightly laced bodice bespoke the woman's free-and-easy attitude toward life. Cassandra smoothed the black netting of her own gown and tried to picture herself in such an outfit. The notion was absurd, she chided herself. Bright colors did not suit her. Tiny rows of prim posies and rosettes hardly matched Cassandra's personal outlook

on life. The unambiguous simplicity of black and white was more her style.

But Cassandra had relented to Madame Racine's insistence that she wear a fashionably cut gown, even if it was done up in black and white. Audrey the maid, suddenly an arbiter of high fashion, was somewhat mollified by the graceful, classical lines of Cassandra's black crepe frock and sarcenet slip. Madame Racine's creation was, in fact, much to Cassandra's liking. A simple white satin bodice with deep vandykes of black velvet exposed only the tops of her bosom, while short puffy sleeves accentuated the olive skin of her arms. The effect, Cassandra thought, was understated yet elegant.

"Allow me," cooed the unctuous Frenchman, gripping Cassandra's elbow as he guided her toward the dining room door.

Pierre Duval gripped her arm, but the viscount held her in the grasp of his dark stare. Cassandra lifted her chin a notch, held Alistair's searing gaze for a heart-thudding beat, then turned her head. Her cheeks burned with humiliation as she realized she was flirting outrageously with Alistair Gordon, and he was flirting back.

Stunned by her own brazen behavior, Cassandra clasped her hands in front of her to regain her composure. Marching woodenly at Pierre's side, she realized she had never flirted with a man before. For years Cassandra's aloofness had been a shield against human intimacy, a barrier erected to protect her from the heartache of adventure, from life itself!

But now her defenses were shot through with longing. The thick armor of indifference she'd worn her entire adult life was useless against Alistair Gordon's appeal. She wanted to run her fingers through his thick black forelock. She wanted him to sweep her up in his arms and hold her next to him, the way he had when he'd carried her into her shop. The feel of Alistair's strong embrace lingered

in Cassandra's memory, warming her skin like the hot Egyptian sun.

She knew that he was an aristocrat and she a common chit, and that the chances of his offering marriage were slim to none. But such cold logic could not dispel Cassandra's yearning. Not tonight anyway. She wanted the viscount. She admitted as much to herself. It was as simple as that.

Neville pushed his rolling chair away from the table, and waved his party out the dining room door. "I think my guests will be quite pleased by the little surprise we have in store for them, Giovanni. We can take our port in there, though I must insist that no smoking is allowed. The reason shall be obvious soon enough."

Cassandra wrenched her elbow from Pierre's fingers and briskly followed Giovanni Belzoni to Neville's study. Stepping across the threshold, she saw that the room was more a miniature museum than a private office. In the center was a large refectory table, atop which lay an oblong figure covered by a shroud of black velvet. The unmistakable shape of a human form, prostrate beneath its morbid finery, seized Cassandra's imagination.

Suppressing a gasp of astonishment, she moved quickly to a campaign chair with arms supported by golden sphinx heads. Sinking into it, she practically shivered with anticipation.

Neville deftly maneuvered his Merlin chair between the two Egyptian chairs. "I suppose I shall be able to keep that Frog away from you, young lady," he said in a stage whisper. "At least for a time."

With a sigh of disappointment, Pierre Duval lowered himself into the chair that matched Cassandra's and grinned at her from the other side of Neville. Twisting in his wheelchair, the earl pinned a withering gaze on the young Frenchman. Pierre met the older man's stare with a casual shrug, then tossed his head and haughtily exhibited a chiseled profile.

Alistair, who had entered the room last, was left no other option than to sit next to Suzette on a velvet love seat. When Cassandra cast a glance over her shoulder, he smiled sheepishly and lifted his brows. His look reassured her that he felt nothing but bemusement at the Duvals' machinations. Cassandra smiled easily, and impulsively laid her hand on Neville's sleeve.

Signor Belzoni's voice boomed through the room. "Ladies and gentlemen, please make yourselves comfortable. This procedure has been known to require several hours." He stood behind the refectory table, his raised arms outstretched above the draped figure as if he were delivering a benediction or revealing the Gospel. Cassandra thought the great Italian, with his thick black beard and long, flowing robes, wore the same smug, self-satisfied expression Moses might have had when he descended the mountain, knowing the Ten Commandments by heart before anyone else in the world had even seen them.

When Belzoni's eyes floated heavenward in solemn reverie, he might have been an ancient cleric standing at a sacrificial altar. His head tilted to one side, and he lifted his shaggy brows, as if he heard strains of music inaudible to the others. Moments ticked by, and the fire crackled in the hearth while the huge man stood silently, still as an obelisk, his lips curved in an enigmatic smile.

"What in the devil is he going to do?" piped Pierre, drawing a scowl from the great Belzoni.

"Hush, you soft-brained tadpole!" scolded Neville. "Or I shall insist that you be driven home."

Signor Belzoni waited for complete silence. With hands hovering over the velvet-draped figure, he eyed each spectator, commanding their attention, drawing them into his imagination with his hypnotic charisma. Cassandra, of course, knew there was a mummy beneath the shroud, and she suspected everyone else in the room knew also. But Belzoni's showmanship, his mastery of stage theatrics, his ability to play a crowd, were so acutely honed that knowing

a mummy lay beneath the velvet cloak did not mitigate the excitement of waiting for its unveiling.

Suzette's breathless voice broke the silence. "*S'il vous plaît,* signor! I cannot endure this any longer!" Throwing a glance over her shoulder, Cassandra saw the pretty Frenchwoman clutching Alistair's sleeve, her hand at her throat.

Neville grunted his disdain for Suzette's sudden sensibilities, and Cassandra squeezed the earl's arm in complete agreement.

At last Signor Belzoni snatched the edge of the velvet coverlet, and with a flourish hurled it from the table. A collective gasp of astonishment rose as the black shroud settled on the floor in a heap. Surely everyone had expected a mummy, but the corpse was still an awe-inspiring sight, with its thick layers of dingy bandages and its eerie quietude.

Cassandra turned her head to see Suzette feigning a swoon onto Alistair's shoulder. When the viscount stood abruptly to get a better look at the mummy, the fainting Frenchwoman fell over on the spot he vacated. Cassandra could not resist a snicker when Suzette's eyes flew open in surprise; she looked as startled as if she'd been summarily dumped from Alistair's lap. Reviving rather quickly, however, the girl threw Cassandra a mean look, fanned herself vigorously, and sat straight against the low back of the love seat.

Alistair moved in pantherlike strides. Standing beside Signor Belzoni, he touched the mummy gingerly, expressing his amazement in hushed tones. "What an incredible specimen this is."

Belzoni's chest puffed with pride. "My lord, this mummy is hardly the finest example of Egyptian embalming that I have seen. This individual's body was not treated with the same care accorded to a monarch or high priest. But that is why I do not mind unwrapping it—"

"Unwrapping it?" Cassandra echoed, her hand tight-

ening on Neville's arm. "I have never seen a mummy unwrapped. 'Struth, I am not sure the ancient Egyptians would approve." Further reflection muddled Cassandra's conflicting ethics. In the end, curiosity won out, and she admitted the usefulness of unwrapping the mummy. "In the name of science, I suppose there is no harm," she murmured after a brief internal debate.

"Until men of science invent a method whereby we can see beneath the mummy's bandages," said Alistair, "we must unwrap the shroud to learn the ancient Egyptians' embalming techniques."

"Besides, unwrapping mummies is all the rage in London drawing rooms this season," added Neville dryly.

Pinching the earl in affectionate rebuke, Cassandra settled back into her chair. "I see that I am to be overruled," she said. "Therefore, I shall simply relax and enjoy myself."

"An excellent motto, Miss Russell," said Alistair, his eyes twinkling.

Brandishing a large pair of scissors above his turban, Signor Belzoni cried out, "Let us proceed!" And with that he pressed the tip of his shears against the mummy's breast and began cutting away the bandages.

An hour later, after innumerable layers of linen had been cut through, Belzoni was forced to use hammer and chisel to crack the hard resin that encased the mummy's body. Rivulets of perspiration streamed down his face as he pried the stained and hardened bandages from the corpse. Around the refectory table lay yards of shredded fabric, brittle bits of caramel-colored resin, scraps of dried flowers, dust, dirt, and other unidentifiable ancient debris. A peculiar cloying odor wafted from the increasingly disheveled mummy, causing Cassandra to withdraw a perfumed handkerchief from her reticule and press it to her nose.

"Are you all right?" asked Alistair, his concerned tone as comforting to her nerves as a warming pan to frigid toes.

Cassandra nodded her head. "Could I . . . come closer?" she asked, relieved to see Signor Belzoni casting aside his heavy mallet and hammer. The mummy was completely uncovered now, its shriveled amber-colored body exposed to air for the first time in centuries.

Alistair extended his hand, beckoning Cassandra to come forward. Suzette and Pierre immediately left their seats and stood around the table also, Pierre clutching his sister's arm while she stared in utter fascination at the desiccated corpse that lay before them, its snaggle-toothed jaw gaping, its sunken eyes blind beneath pads of ocher-colored linen.

Gently grasping her elbow, Alistair pulled Cassandra to his side. The knot of people around the refectory table was tight, and she was forced to stand so near him that his strong thighs pressed against her crepe dress, his hips bumped hers, his sleeves brushed her bare skin. Pierre Duval slithered up beside her, his sister on his opposite arm. Edging away from the dandified Frenchman brought Cassandra even closer to Alistair, and for once Cassandra was grateful for Pierre Duval's annoying presence.

The viscount bent his head and whispered huskily, "Has the esteemed Society of Egyptologists never witnessed a mummy unwrapping?" His questioning tone was as airy and ticklish as the tip of a feather tracing circles on her sensitive skin.

"Lords Tifton and Killibrew very much disapprove of the desecration of mummies, my lord," Cassandra answered, her throat parched. She cut her eyes at the viscount and met his black gaze. A seductive smile played across his lips, causing a wave of humid heat to stifle Cassandra's breathing. Gasping, she touched her handkerchief to her throat.

Quickly, Cassandra turned from the viscount and directed her attention toward Signor Belzoni and the remarkable cadaver. With immense relief she saw that her response to the viscount's disturbing physical presence

had gone unnoticed. Signor Belzoni was making a minute examination of the corpse's fingernails, which were capped with golden stalls, and his audience was oohing and aahing appropriately.

All except Suzette, of course, whose green eyes, heretofore riveted on the mummy, flashed like lightning at Alistair's intimate murmurings and gestures. Cassandra met the woman's eyes, and a certain understanding passed between the two rivals. Cassandra meant to fight for the viscount's affections, and Suzette meant to sabotage her efforts. A line was drawn in the sand, and both women steeled themselves for battle.

"What have we here?" Belzoni exclaimed, holding up a small dried-up mouse. Suzette and Cassandra momentarily forgot each other. The Earl of Hedgeworth jostled his way into the huddle and peered up at the tiny rodent that dangled by its tail between Belzoni's thumb and forefinger.

"Catch, Neville!" cried the mischievous Italian, tossing the animal onto the earl's lap.

Without flinching, Neville scooped up the mouse and laid it on the refectory table. Amid friendly laughter he grinned crookedly. "Your theatrical nature is still with you, I see, Giovanni."

For the present, then, the Frenchwoman was mesmerized by the unwrapping of the mummy. Cassandra knew that Suzette would not jeopardize this magical moment by throwing a jealous tantrum; nor would she risk offending her host, Neville, by acting rudely toward one of his guests. A shrewd and calculating woman, Suzette would make her displeasure known to Alistair later. Whether the viscount yielded to his lover's possessive remonstrations remained to be seen.

Alistair Gordon was hardly a passive character. He was not the sort of man to submit meekly to his *chère amie*'s demands. In the end, Cassandra suspected, he was a man who would do precisely as he wished, no matter what his lover, his brother, or his Corinthian pals advised. But she

also knew, too well, that Alistair's infatuation for her would never alter her status as a bluestocking chit, an unpedigreed girl without illustrious lineage or great fortune.

The viscount might develop a *tendre* for Cassandra; he might even offer her carte blanche in return for her exclusive devotion. But would he ever seriously consider marrying her? That was quite another matter.

Alistair's whispers raised goose pimples along Cassandra's neck and back. "This is so fascinating," he said sotto voce. "Look, our mummy is covered with jewels and amulets."

His arm encircled her waist, and she wished for once that she carried one of those silly fans women were always using to banish the vapors. When the viscount's fingertips began to walk lightly up the row of fabric-covered buttons on the back of her satin bodice, Cassandra held her breath and glanced about. Everyone else's eyes were glued to Signor Belzoni and his careful ministrations. No one noticed Alistair's arm behind her back, or the sudden surprise that had set her lashes fluttering.

Cassandra's pulse quickened. Thrilling to the deliciousness of Alistair's breath along her shoulders, the danger of his fingertips dancing up her spine, she shivered with anticipation. Belzoni had built the tension in the room to a roaring crescendo, and as he rummaged through the linen wrappings for precious jewelry, the tiny throng of onlookers hung on his every word, their gazes were zeroed in on him, their attention totally usurped. Indeed, Cassandra felt as if something wonderful and amazing was about to happen.

Signor Belzoni plucked a magnificent lapis lazuli heart scarab from the mummy's breast and held it aloft, his black, feral eyes squinting with glee. "This, surely, is the most important protective amulet a mummy would have worn. Our ancient friend relied upon this sacred beetle to assist him in presenting his heart to the goddess of truth in the hall of judgment."

Alistair took the dusty blue beetle from Belzoni's fingers and turned it over in his hand. "I thought most heart scarabs were made of a dark green stone," he commented. Cassandra offered him her handkerchief, and he began polishing the lapis lazuli to cerulean brightness.

Belzoni spared the viscount a quick grin before he continued patting down the mummy. "You are quite right, Lord Catledge. But our mummy does not seem as ordinary as I thought he was. Look here, tucked beneath the mummy's underarm."

"Another mouse, signor?" sneered Pierre.

"A wedge of cheese, perhaps?" teased Suzette.

Watching the Italian unravel a cone of dingy bandages, Cassandra could hardly contain her curiosity. "Is it not unusual to see these other items packed alongside the mummy's body?" she asked, clutching Alistair's arm.

Alistair answered, his voice thick with anticipation. "Correct me if I am wrong, brother, but lower-class mummies were often haphazardly embalmed and even more sloppily buried. I believe you told me of cases where spare body parts have been found beside a mummy's body."

"You are quite right, little brother. Ancient tomb robbers are partially responsible for the jumble, in my opinion." Neville leaned forward, his good eye narrowed, his hands gripping the arms of his wheelchair. "But what in the devil—er, excuse me. What can this be?"

Impatiently, Belzoni stripped the ball of linen bandages, unwinding it like a skein of knitting yarn. At last the unevenly shaped bundle, originally the size of the big man's fist, dwindled to its core. Tobacco-colored ribbons drifted to the floor in a dingy heap. With a muffled *thunk-thunk,* two objects fell from Belzoni's hands into the debris heaped upon the refectory table. Quickly, the Italian thrust his fingers into the pile of bandages surrounding the mummy. Sifting and digging through the detritus as if he were panning for gold, Belzoni's eyes gleamed like jet

and his black beard glistened with perspiration. Again the atmosphere in the room became charged with suspense.

Belzoni's body tensed. His fingers tightened around something beneath the surface of the linen shavings. His face froze in a rictus of surprise.

"What is it?" demanded Neville and Alistair in unison.

"Non lo so," said Belzoni, breathing rapidly. "I do not know." He lifted his clenched fists and held out them out side by side as if he were playing a shell game. Rolling his forearms, he opened his hands and showed his flattened palms.

Suzette gasped at the sight of the two objects that lay in Belzoni's hands, a small heart-shaped silver locket in one, and in the other, a flat piece of tooled metal. Her brother gave her a little shake, and the Frenchwoman quickly clamped her mouth shut.

Signor Belzoni tilted his head sideways, affecting a quizzical expression. *"Interessante!* But not what I expected. This locket is hardly an ancient artifact."

Cassandra and Alistair exchanged glances. Pierre and Suzette traded worried looks. The Earl of Hedgeworth broke the silence by rasping, "What the hell does it mean, Giovanni?"

Exhaling a loud snort of exasperation, the giant Italian stroked his beard thoughtfully. "Do you remember, Neville, my adventures in Kurneh?"

"Kurneh?" the earl repeated. His tone was one of puzzlement, echoing Cassandra's own bewilderment at this twist in the conversation. "The year was 1817, if I recall," Neville finally replied. "I sent you all the maps and drawings I had of the area. Led you to quite a cache of mummies, did I not?"

"Sí, that you did. That is where this mummy was found," said Belzoni. "That is also where I met that very strange fellow who joined my expedition. Without remuneration, I might add. Did I not write to you of him, Neville? The man became a pest, a threat to the harmonious workings

of my camp, and when we got to the Valley of the Kings,
I finally threatened to shoot him if he did not depart from
my presence at once.''

Neville's wizened features brightened with sudden memory. "Yes, I remember your letters now. What an odd piece
of news that was. I never could make heads or tails of it.
What was the man's name?"

"I do not remember. I suppose I could look it up in my
journals; those that were not stolen anyway. But the man
was present when this mummy was discovered. The sight
of it immediately overset him, even though the coffin was
quite ordinary. It was the Egyptian equivalent of a pauper's
pine box, you understand—quite unprepossessing. Still,
the man's alarm was unmistakable. He did not want my
workmen to remove the coffin, or to open it—under any
circumstances."

"Why?" Cassandra blurted out, her curiosity roused to
fever pitch.

Belzoni shrugged his massive shoulders. "At the time, I
thought he feared the *wadjet* eye that was painted on the
side of the coffin. Many people believe it is an evil eye
rather than the symbol of restored health and rejuvena-
tion, which it is."

Neville's bottom lip protruded as he fidgeted in his chair.
"Did the man recognize this particular coffin, Giovanni?"

Again Belzoni shrugged. "I know only that when he saw
it, he began jumping around like a madman, brandishing
a saber sword and threatening to kill any of my workmen
who dared to disturb this mummy ... this *particular*
mummy. Which was extremely odd, since there were thousands of mummies to be found at Kurneh. So many, in
fact, that when I sought a resting place and contrived
to sit, my weight crushed a number of skulls like flimsy
bandboxes."

"What is it about this mummy that caused such upset?"
questioned Alistair. "I thought it was a rather ordinary
mummy, especially with its sloppily dressed bandages. A

royal mummy would have been more carefully wrapped, and not as heavily coated with that horribly thick resin."

"Quite so," murmured Neville.

"Then why did this strange man object so strenuously to your disturbing this one?" queried Cassandra, noticing for the first time the agitated expression on Suzette Duval's face. Pierre was grasping Suzette's arm so tightly that his knuckles were white; Cassandra wondered that the Frenchwoman was not in pain from her brother's viselike grip.

Belzoni sighed heavily and turned the tarnished metal plate over in his hands. "Perhaps my strange friend did not want me to find these. Perhaps he had placed these items there previously, and wished to retrieve them without my knowing of it." Nodding his head slowly, he continued in a pensive, slightly astonished tone. "I should have known . . . yes, yes . . ."

"Should have know what?" cried Cassandra, unable to contain her excitement. "Pray, signor! Do not prolong this suspense!"

Alistair's arm was around her shoulder now. He leaned forward as she did, his body flush against hers. The rush of pleasure Cassandra felt resulted as much from Alistair's closeness as it did from the enigma of the locket and the metal plate in Belzoni's hands.

At last Belzoni turned his twinkling black gaze on Cassandra. For a moment she felt that the perceptive Italian was appraising her, classifying her like an intriguing artifact he might have dug up from the sand. A twinge of embarrassment tempered her enthusiasm. The great adventurer seemed vastly amused by her excitement. No doubt, he considered her a voluble bluestocking whose passions were limited to cataloguing antiquities. Little did he know that Cassandra would have tossed Belzoni's mummy onto the crackling fire behind her in exchange for one of Alistair's sumptuous kisses.

"I should have known that the strange scoundrel had been inside the caves at Kurneh before!" cried Belzoni,

his face darkening. "And that he recognized this coffin—"

"—and knew what was in it," Neville finished.

"Nonsense," said Pierre Duval. "If he knew where the
Kurneh mummies were hidden, he could have retrieved
his possessions without your assistance."

"Not necessarily," said Belzoni. "In the desert, a single
sandstorm can make familiar landmarks vanish. Perhaps
the man visited the tombs and deposited these items with
the intention of returning, then found himself unable to
locate the Kurneh burial grounds again."

"But what is that metal plate you are holding?" insisted
Alistair.

With the voluminous sleeve of his white robe, Signor
Belzoni rubbed the tarnished bronze vigorously. Then,
wordlessly, he passed the metal plate to Neville.

A moment ticked by as the earl glared at the object in
his trembling hands. Cassandra swallowed hard, willing
herself not to shatter the prickly silence. Alistair's fingers
clutched her arm and she snuggled closer beneath his
protective wing. Suzette and Pierre huddled against each
other, looking down at Neville with a mixture of dread
and hatred in their eyes.

Painfully, as if his shaggy head weighed a hundred stone,
the Earl of Hedgeworth lifted his chin. His good eye glimmered like rain-speckled glass, and his forefinger shook
when he stabbed the air. "This shako plate came from a
Bonapartist's uniform!" Neville sputtered, his agitation
robbing him of coherent speech. "See the bloody eagle,
with its bloody crown?" The earl held the insignia aloft,
his chin quivering in outrage.

Pierre Duval peered at the bronze eagle and clucked
his tongue. "Now, how the devil do you suppose a French
shako plate wound up tucked beneath a mummy's arm?"

"That is precisely what I would like to know," replied
Alistair, removing his arm from Cassandra's shoulder.

"And precisely what we shall discover," added Neville,

dropping the offending item onto his lap and pushing back from the table. The earl's arms worked furiously to roll his chair across the carpeted study. Reaching the door, he halted abruptly and wheeled around to face his guests. "Thank you all for coming this evening. I must retire now. My brother will see you out."

Alistair bolted toward the door, but Neville had already rolled across the threshold and slammed the door shut behind him. The viscount followed his brother into the corridor. The muffled sound of voices filtered through the heavy oaken doors, but Cassandra was unable to make out the gist of the brothers' conversation. Returning to the study, the viscount stood with his back to the door and eyed his guests with undisguised vexation. "I apologize for my brother's behavior," he started to say.

"No need," assured Signor Belzoni. "I feel I know your brother well. I suppose he is entitled to his idiosyncracies now and again."

A knot twisted in Cassandra's stomach as she took in Alistair's frustrated expression as well as Signor Belzoni's weary resignation. "Let me assist you in cleaning up," she offered, stooping. "Here, the floor is strewn with bandages," she stammered.

Belzoni protested, catching her arm as she rose to her full height. "Let your gentleman escort you home, my dear," he told her gently. "I shall remain here and see that our mummy friend is disposed of properly. Who knows? Neville may reappear yet, to offer me a nightcap. The rest of you should go, however. Enjoy what is left of the evening."

Cassandra forced a smile and skittered away. She gathered her reticule from the Egyptian campaign chair while the other guests bade one another good night. Pierre and Suzette suddenly seemed as close knit as twins, hurrying toward the study door and babbling *"Adieu, adieu!"*

"Oh, wait there!" Striding across the thick Aubusson carpet, Signor Belzoni overtook Pierre Duval at the study

door, grasping the younger man's elbow in a bearlike grip. Pierre started, pivoted, recoiled. With the strength of one hand, Belzoni held him captive.

Suzette turned, surveying her brother's entrapment with chary interest.

Cassandra's senses heightened to the tension between Signor Belzoni and Pierre Duval. She stood beside Alistair and watched the flustered expression on Pierre's pallid face.

Nose twitching, as if he were sniffing the air for danger, the Frenchman's pink-rimmed eyes widened in alarm. Belzoni grabbed his pale, slender hand and pumped it furiously. *"Un momento*, monsieur. All evening I have had the strangest sensation." Belzoni narrowed his eyes and rubbed his hirsute chin. "I feel that we have met," he said, drawing Pierre closer as much by force of will as by brute strength.

Pierre's Adam's apple bobbed convulsively. Tremulously, he denied having met Signor Belzoni before. "Perhaps you saw me when I was in the audience of one of your performances," he replied.

Belzoni cocked his head. "I made it a practice to stay out of the path of the terrible Corsican. Were you in London during the wars?"

Pierre blanched and withdrew his hand. "I am proud to say my family remained in Paris, and survived the Terror, though Papa eventually lost everything. I daresay, he threw in his lot with the wrong side, but who was to know that Napoleon would fail so grandly?"

"Have you ever been in Spain by any chance?" Belzoni said. "Perhaps I met you there—"

"No, signor. I have never been to Spain," admitted Pierre stiffly.

Belzoni smiled. "You say you remained in France during Napoleon's reign. *Interessante.* You would not have been able to witness any of my performances. I have not been on the stage, you see, since 1814." Waggling his finger at

Pierre's sharp-tipped nose, the grinning Italian said, "But still, I am sure that I know you from somewhere. Perhaps you are the relative of someone I once knew."

"Impossible!" Suzette snapped. In a softer tone she added, "You are mistaken, signor. My brother and I were born, raised, and educated in Paris. We have only recently journeyed to London." She started to say more, but flushed scarlet instead and plucked her brother's sleeve. "Come, Pierre, we must take our leave. I have a sudden headache, from breathing in all that mummy dust, I am sure."

"Educated in Paris?" Belzoni asked. "Might I ask what is your training, monsieur?"

Pierre lifted his chin. "I attended medical school—"

Suzette cut him off. "Come, Pierre! My head is aching!"

Turning on his heel, the thin man slipped lightly across the threshold and was heard clattering across the marble foyer after his sister. Angry French words hissed back and forth, then both voices lowered to a hushed confidential tone.

Belzoni chuckled and reached for Alistair's hand. "Rather a sensitive fellow, don't you think?"

Alistair laughed. "He is far too sensitive. But I must see him and his sister safely home. I bid you good night, signor."

Smiling easily, Belzoni turned to Cassandra. She offered her hand, and he lifted it to his lips, his dark eyes gleaming with interest. Releasing her fingers, he said, "I regret that I did not have the opportunity to speak with you at length, my dear. It seems our meetings are always spoiled by some unpleasant business. How is Lord Tifton holding up after last night's theft?"

"I sent around a note expressing my condolences, but I have heard nothing, signor," said Cassandra. "I can only imagine his lordship's distress."

Belzoni nodded. "Neville has told me many interesting things about you, and your parents," he remarked at length.

Cassandra felt her throat constrict. Here was her chance to ask the great Belzoni the questions that burned in her mind. Here was her chance to find an appropriate resting place for Cleo, her prized mummy. Surely, this man could tell her how to secure Cleo a safe resting place without invoking the mummy king's curse! But her tongue would not loosen, and her lips would not move! Cassandra stood mutely, staring up at the huge Italian's kind, twinkling eyes.

Alistair touched her arm, jolting her out of her frozen state. "Cat got your tongue, Cassandra?" he teased affectionately.

She rallied instantly. "There are some matters of great importance which I would like to discuss with you, Signor Belzoni, if I might be so bold. Please, sir. I had hoped to speak with you last night, but the chaos that ensued when Lord Tifton was robbed made it quite impossible."

Belzoni patted her arm. "My dear, I should be most pleased to talk with you about any subject you choose. Might I be permitted to call upon you . . . say, one day next week?"

A sigh of relief escaped Cassandra's lips as she nodded vigorously. Alistair told Signor Belzoni her address and explained precisely how to find Russell's Emporium. "There, now," the viscount said, taking Cassandra's arm. "Are we prepared to drive the Duval siblings home?"

"Yes, my lord," said Cassandra, nodding good-bye to Signor Belzoni, who retreated into the drawing room with a sly smile on his bearded face.

But when Alistair and Cassandra entered the foyer a few seconds later, Suzette and Pierre were nowhere to be seen.

A dour-faced butler shuffled forth, his arms laden with coats and hats. "I'm sorry, my lordship. The French pair insisted I fetch their things first. Seems they were in a bit of a hurry."

Alistair's brows knit. "Do you mean to tell me that

Suzette and Pierre Duval have gone off without a carriage
. . . just like that?''

The servant's balding head reddened. "No, my lord.
They didn't go off without a carriage. It was your carriage
they took. 'Twas that bounder Frog—oh, excuse me, my
lord. But he done told your coachman you *wanted* him to
be driven home first. I knew it was a lie, but . . . well. Wasn't
much I could do, ya see."

"You are joking!"

"No, my lord. I never do. Joke, that is. Would you like
me to have Lord Hedgeworth's carriage brought round?"

Alistair threaded his fingers through his thick hair, but
when he shook his head, his raven forelock fell back into
place across his furrowed brow. "Yes, do that. I shall see
Miss Russell home in Neville's gig."

Lord Hedgeworth's impressive chaise and four clattered
to a stop in front of Russell's Emporium. Before Neville's
liveried coachman could alight, much less produce the
small set of stairs he employed to assist his passengers in
disembarking, Alistair Gordon flung open the door. After
jumping nimbly to the cobbled sidewalk, the viscount forestalled the driver's descent with a raised hand. "Stay where
you are, and wait for me here," he called up to the startled
servant. "I shall see Miss Russell inside her establishment."

He hesitated, staring at Cassandra. She stood in the open
doorway of the carriage compartment, her head tilted to
protect her feather-ornamented bonnet. Clutching the
skirts of her black ermine-trimmed coat, she poised one
satin-slippered toe at the edge of the cab. In the dense,
swirling fog, her lamplit face, framed by the curve of her
bonnet brim, was dark and exotic. Alistair's hands reached
up and gently encircled Cassandra's waist.

He lifted her from the carriage, holding her against his
body as her slippers hovered above the cobblestones. Her
topaz eyes widened, betraying her anticipation. Like a man

awakening from a deep sleep, Alistair slowly became aware of his surroundings. He heard carriages rattling along in the darkness, and, in the distance, a bawdy tavern song belted out in drunken duet. Cassandra's spicy aroma, the newness of her gown and coat, soap, and her wine-scented breath filled his nostrils. Her uncorseted body shifted restlessly beneath his fingers. Alistair glanced up at the sky as gray clouds scudded across the blue-black canopy.

The ash-tinted clouds cast Cassandra's face in shadows. Then the dingy puffs slid past the moon to allow swatches of silvery light to play upon her upturned face. The effect was strangely mystical, as if Cassandra held the very moon and stars within her spell, manipulating them to her advantage, calling upon them to do her bidding. A dense longing squeezed Alistair's heart, and he ached to know the secrets of this mysterious woman's allure. Never before had he shared his brother's fervent love for Egyptian artifacts; but now Alistair thought he'd never experienced anything so hypnotic, so mesmerizing, as the charm of Cassandra Russell.

She was as enigmatic and as puzzling as the Pyramids, that was true. Her strict decorum and emotional restraint set her apart, imbuing her with the aloof detachment of an arrogant cat. But her eyes glowed as hot as an Egyptian desert, and Alistair had already felt the scorch of her scrutiny as well as the slow burn of her passion. He held her tightly to his chest, and saw her lips turn up in a sly little smile.

That Cassandra was of a reserved nature could not be denied. That she possessed a strong potential for uninhibited merriment was less obvious, but intriguingly evident. That Alistair loved her was becoming painfully clear—to him, at least. He muttered a silent oath as he felt his body responding beneath Cassandra's weight.

Alistair wanted never to leave Cassandra's side, yet he wondered whether his fantasy was wise. He was reminded of the disparity in their social positions, the difference in

their upbringings. But his doubts were like the clouds
sliding past the moon; behind them glowed the brightness
of his passion.

Cassandra parted her lips and tightened her grip on
Alistair's shoulders. The viscount's body tensed involuntarily, his heart beat faster, and his stomach twisted like a
wet-wrung mop. The cloth coat Cassandra wore did little
to disguise her feminine attributes. Alistair felt the imprint
of her breasts against his chest, the firmness of her thighs
against his skintight breeches. He would have kissed her
then and there had the visor of her bonnet not prevented
him.

She slid down the length of his body, and her slippers
touched the ground. Alistair lowered his head and whispered, "Please allow me to see you to your apartment
door."

Even in the moonlight, Cassandra's henna-colored blush
deepened her olive complexion. "Come in, then," she
replied softly, moving toward the shop door.

He took her shop key, quickly unlocked the door, and
ushered her inside. The eerie stillness of the shop's interior, its rows of coffins and racks of mourning finery, added
a preternatural element to his mood. Glancing up at the
lintel, Alistair realized the shop bells had been removed
when the door was repaired. He felt he'd entered a silent
crypt with Cassandra, a secret place. "I am glad to see the
mummy's damage has been erased," he said, relocking
the door and returning the key to Cassandra.

"'Twas very kind of you to send a man over to repair
my shop door." Cassandra moved into the shop, tossing
off her bonnet and coat in quick, easy movements. One
coy glance over her shoulder was all the prompting Alistair
needed. Like a somnambulist, he followed her through
the curtain of beads and into the rear room of the shop.
There, he stood in darkness, the gas streetlamps unable
to penetrate the gloom of this dark interior.

The effect of being surrounded by such total blackness

was disorienting. For a moment Alistair wondered if Cassandra had deserted him.

A scraping noise pricked his ears. A point of flame appeared. Above it materialized Cassandra's face, her eyebrows arched in exaggerated V's by the strange glow of the sputtering candle. As she lit the remaining tapers in the heavy candelabra, the room faded into view around her. A desk, bolts of fabric, coffins, boxes of merchandise, and several wooden filing cabinets quavered in the melting shadows.

Silently, Cassandra replaced the flint and set the tinderbox beside the candelabra. She smiled inscrutably, then pushed off from her neatly organized desk. Her eyes glowed like embers as she moved toward Alistair, yet she kept her counsel, stealthily approaching him as if she hoped to catch him unawares. His skin prickled at the intensity of her stare. His pulse hammered, and he experienced the odd sensation of being hot and cold at the same time.

She was inches from him now, removing her black kid gloves, plucking the tip of one finger, then the next. A sudden gush of blood through Alistair's veins left him lightheaded for an instant. Just as quickly, he regained his bearings, bracing himself, anticipating further shocks to his system as Cassandra stood closer. He was like a man who'd been knocked down by a ball of fire; only now the fire had rolled over him, and he was standing up, brushing off his clothes, examining himself for damage. Realizing that he was unscathed, Alistair gulped in the fresh, intoxicating breath of life and felt giddily grateful.

But the conflagration was not over. Cassandra's eyes were burning brightly.

Alistair's extraordinary awareness of his surroundings—his heightened sensitivity to the damp air, his sudden consciousness of London's own night music—ceased to exist. Now he existed in a tiny penumbra of flickering light.

There was nowhere else; there was no one else. *This* was all that existed.

His voice cracked. "Cassandra—" And his jaw tightened in chagrin at the sound of it.

She lifted a finger to his lips, rubbed her thumb along the stubble of his beard.

Alistair felt her body move into his embrace, and he instinctively tightened his arms around her. Cassandra tilted her head, allowing him to kiss her. The candles had guttered in their liquid pools of wax before Alistair released Cassandra from his arms.

By the time he scrambled into his waiting coach, there was a pinkish tint to the morning sky. Settling back against the squabs, Alistair sighed wearily, but with deep satisfaction.

He drew his hand across his bristly jaw, grinning. Cassandra's neck, nape, and shoulders were *extremely* sensitive, he reflected drowsily. He closed his eyes and quickly fell asleep.

Alistair dreamed he was an ancient Egyptian king, floating down the River Nile on his beautiful sailing ship. It was a sleek, finely crafted ship, its fore part adorned with paintings of the queen's profile, its stern carved expertly to resemble a huge lotus blossom. The oars of a dozen bronze-skinned slaves slapped the silver water in a steady, hypnotic motion.

Inside a stately cabin supported by gleaming white pillars, Alistair and his queen lounged on mounds of fluffy pillows. A cool breeze fluttered the cotton flaps of this private sanctuary, ruffling Alistair's hair, blowing fluttery kisses across his suntanned skin. His beloved queen stirred, turned her face to him, and smiled. She was so beautiful, this queen named Cassandra.

The viscount prayed to his God that he would spend eternity with her.

Chapter Nine

Inside her shop, Cassandra leaned against the door, fingers clenched tightly around the knob, forehead pressed against the cold glazed glass. The clatter of carriage wheels faded, and the stillness of the early morning rolled in. With a sigh, Cassandra shoved off from the door and moved through the shop on shaky limbs. Pausing in the small inventory room to gather her outerwear, she experienced a deep and sudden longing for Viscount Catledge. He had only just left, and yet she yearned for him to return and kiss her again. The slight abrasion on her jawline would not have dissuaded her from succumbing to him right then and there, no matter that the sky was growing lighter.

His departure had been wrenching, yet in the hours preceding, Cassandra had come to terms with her roiling emotions. That she loved Lord Catledge was undeniable. That he was equally infatuated with her was alarmingly obvious and somewhat of a shock. What Cassandra couldn't figure out was how a Corinthian buck could offer marriage to a bluestocking chit. And if he could not—or would

not—she feared her heart would break. For she would not commit herself to a disastrous, extramarital assignation. She was not of the same ilk as Suzette Duval, and no matter how much she loved Alistair Gordon, she would never sacrifice her honor and virtue for him.

That lofty resolution brought a bitter chuckle to Cassandra's lips. Taking a candle to light the dark staircase, she threw her cloak over her arm and picked up her skirts. Whom was she hoaxing? she asked herself wryly. Had she half the noble virtue and veracity that she silently espoused, would she not have confided to Alistair the existence of her mummy? Wouldn't she have told him that the criminal who stole Lord Hedgeworth's mummy was, almost certainly, after her prized mummy as well?

Surely, the viscount's investigation would be aided by the knowledge that the stolen mummy's mate was resting comfortably behind a screen in Cassandra's bedchamber. By not sharing that information with Alistair, Cassandra was hampering his investigation.

She had been on the verge of divulging her secret when he had embraced her. "Alistair, there is something I must tell you," she had whispered.

His breath against her neck produced a violent shudder that racked her body.

"Ali—" She tried again, her words punctuated by tiny gasps of surprise. "I—must—tell—you—" She felt his lips on her skin. Her thoughts swirled like dry leaves on a windy day, and like parched foliage trampled underfoot, her voice was cracked and brittle. "I want to show you something in my apartment," she had eked out, realizing belatedly that her invitation held myriad unspoken promises.

Alistair's head jerked up. "Good God," he said hoarsely. "By all means, let us retire to your bedchamber."

"Oh, no! I did not mean that," stammered Cassandra. Her explanation came out in a high-pitched staccato. "I mean that I must show you something that is vital to your

investigation . . . which I have omitted from telling you . . . that I think you ought to know."

The viscount touched her cheek and traced her bottom lip with his thumb. Cassandra's nerve endings tingled, and she knew if she allowed Alistair into her bedchamber, she would never have the resolve to deny him her physical self.

"Do you really want to discuss Neville's missing mummy . . . now?" Alistair asked. He held her wrist and slipped her fingers into his mouth. She felt the liquid warmth of his tongue against her skin and forgot all about the musty mummy slumbering peacefully in her apartment.

"We shall talk later, then," she murmured, and a silvery silence fell between them.

Now, with only the dim light of a single taper to guide her, Cassandra tiptoed up the stairs to her apartment. Halfway up, she came to an abrupt halt. At the top of the landing, beneath her door, shone a sliver of light. Wondering why Audrey would be awake at such an ungodly hour, and mindful of the recent bizarre occurrences that had threatened their safety, Cassandra hurriedly ascended the remaining steps and shoved open the unlocked door.

Her sudden entrance drew startled looks from Audrey and Tia. Seated at the round table in the middle of the room, the maid lowered her teacup and perused Cassandra from head to toe.

Hoping to deflect Audrey's attention from the fact that she was *sans* cloak, bare-headed, and distinctly crumpled, Cassandra took the offensive. "What in heaven's name are you doing up this late?" she demanded, dropping her ermine-trimmed wrap, reticule, and headdress on a convenient chair. Tia immediately bounded from Audrey's lap to the hem of Cassandra's gown.

Audrey frowned. "We was waitin' up fer *you*, ma'am."

"I did not instruct you to wait up for me," replied Cassandra tersely. She chafed her palms, then pinched the tip of one of her fingers. Expecting kidskin, Cassandra was surprised to feel her own bare flesh. "What?" She looked

down. "Where are my—oh!" Belatedly, she remembered removing her gloves in order to thread her fingers through Alistair's thick black hair. She'd wanted to feel the texture of his skin, caress his bristly jaw with her palm. The memory brought a flood of warmth to Cassandra's cheeks. Those gloves had been a blasted nuisance.

"Lose yer gloves, did ye?" the maid asked, her lips quirking.

"They are in my reticule," Cassandra muttered, falling into the chair across from Audrey. "Mind pouring me some tea, please?" she asked, stroking Tia's glossy head.

"I was worried," accused Audrey, sliding a Blue Willow cup and saucer across the table. "You can't imagine the sort of things that was flying through my head. For pity's sake, miss, I thought that mummy done captured you—for good this time!"

Cassandra felt the soothing trickle of hot tea flow down her throat. "Do you think that Lord Catledge would not protect me?"

"I suppose he would if he could. But he ain't figured out who broke into your apartment dressed like a mummy, 'as he?"

"No," admitted Cassandra ruefully. He hadn't figured out who threw a warning note wrapped around a rock through his carriage window either. Or who tried to murder him and Cassandra in her shop, just the night before. Or who, for that matter, robbed Lord Tifton of his precious antiquities. "He will though," she insisted dubiously. "I am certain."

Audrey leaned forward and spoke in a hushed voice, as if she were afraid of being overheard. "Are you not frightened, miss, that the mummy will return?"

"So far, the mummy has done no serious harm to anyone."

"It ain't fer lack o'tryin'," argued Audrey.

"But I believe the criminal is after Cleo," said Cassandra. "I do not think he *wants* to commit violence to obtain my

mummy. Though I fear he is becoming more desperate with each passing day."

"What makes ye think 'e's after yer mummy?" Audrey asked suspiciously.

Cassandra decided there was no use in concealing from Audrey any of the facts pertaining to the mysterious events that had occurred in the past week. She told her maid about the hurled rock, Lord Tifton's loss, and the mummy's appearance in the shop the night before.

"It all started when Lord Catledge came onto the scene," noted Audrey.

"It all began when Lord Hedgeworth's mummy was stolen," corrected Cassandra. "His royal mummy is Cleo's mate. The couple meant to spend eternity together, and their separation supposedly carries with it a terrible curse."

"Ye ain't still fretting over that cursed gammon, are ye?"

Cassandra hesitated. Tia's upturned gaze was as round and curious as Audrey's was narrowed and suspicious. Outside, the wind was picking up. Like a mournful hound, it keened and bayed as shutters banged against bricks. Cassandra felt the hair on the back of her neck prickle with apprehension, and she met Audrey's gaze with a strong sense of foreboding. Did she believe in the ancient pharaoh's curse? Her intellect said no, but her intuition argued strongly in favor of the possibility of a mystical retribution, an age-old vendetta executed by a vengeful monarch whose eternal rest had been disturbed.

At length, Cassandra replied, "The pharaoh must have been very much in love with his wife. He would have been enormously angry when Lord Hedgeworth and my father separated him from her. Perhaps he *is* taking his revenge, Audrey."

Audrey's cup clattered to its saucer. "Aargh! Yer so befoolable, lass! I want to show ye something." She pulled a folded handkerchief from her apron pocket and tossed it on the table. Tia quickly snatched the square of linen, then Cassandra plucked it from the monkey's tiny hands.

Cassandra turned the handkerchief over. It appeared an ordinary linen square, well-worn and slightly ragged at the edges, except for the initials J.D., which were embroidered in faded green thread on a tattered corner. "Where did you get this?" Cassandra asked, puzzled.

"I found it today, when I was laundering yer bedclothes. It must 'ave fallen down beneath the counterpane the night the mummy was 'ere."

"What do you make of it, Audrey?"

"The mummy left it," Audrey said impatiently.

"What makes you think this handkerchief has anything to do with the mummy?" Cassandra asked.

Audrey sighed. "'Ave ye been entertaining any gentlemen callers in your boo-dwahr lately, Miss Cassandra?"

"Your French is deplorable, dear. What is worse, however, is your heavy-handed sarcasm. Of course I have not been entertaining gentlemen in my bedchamber."

"I didna' think so," said Audrey smugly. "You was knocked out cold when I stumbled onto the mummy that night. As if you'd been hit over the head—"

"I felt as if I had," inserted Cassandra. "I had the most intense megrim later that night. And all the next day, to boot!"

Audrey reared back, spreading her arms wide in an exhibition of sudden revelation.

Cassandra blinked her stupefaction. "Are you trying to tell me that the mummy—or the intruder in a mummy's costume—bashed my noggin, then hid his hankie in my bedclothes, pretty as you please? All without my knowledge? Why on earth would he have done that?"

"Look at the initials, ma'am. *J.D.!* The creature might just as well 'ave dropped his calling card in the silver salver!"

Cassandra inhaled deeply, her weary mind struggling to follow Audrey's convoluted logic. "The initials J.D. mean nothing to me," she said. "And I think I would remember if the intruder struck me about the head. On the contrary,

all I remember is falling asleep and dreaming about Mama and Father."

"What exactly do you recall about the dream, miss?"

"It is always the same dream," replied Cassandra. She spoke haltingly, struggling to articulate the vivid images that popped into her head. "Mama and Father and I are on the deck of the boat, and the tall Englishman—the Earl of Hedgeworth, I now know—is on the forecastle. The earl is shouting orders to the sailors raising the anchor, and to the stevedores as they lower one last crate of cargo into the hold."

"Go on," urged Audrey. "Tell me what you saw that night in yer dream. You can do it, miss."

Cassandra inhaled deeply, her eyes closed. A wave of sadness washed over her as her recurring nightmare materialized. Along with the weight of fatigue that burdened her shoulders, that sadness hung on Cassandra like a leaden shroud. Even her tongue felt thick and heavy as she relived the worst day of her life.

Had it not been for the insistent tone of Audrey's voice, Cassandra would have shoved the awful pictures from her mind, dragged herself to bed, and prayed in vain for blessedly forgetful sleep. She had little interest in recreating the details of that awful day, that tragic moment immortalized in her hideous repeating dream. Up till then she'd only tried to forget that haunting sequence of blurred events. Like a curse, the dream impinged her wakeful reverie and her nightly slumbers. What she really wanted to do was erase those images forever!

But the streetwise maid was on to something.

Trusting Audrey's instincts if not her judgment, Cassandra forced herself to remember.

"There is a great commotion behind us. I turn to see what is happening. Father rushes off to investigate, leaving Mama to stand behind me, her hands gripping my shoulders. Someone is running up the gangplank, attempting to board the ship. Sailors part to let a man in Turkish dress

run through . . . his bearded face is contorted with hatred and bitterness.''

"Who is the man?" asked Audrey.

"I do not know! I have never seen him before!" Cassandra trembled with fright. Hugging Tia tightly, she pressed her face against the animal's soft fur. The monkey wrapped its arms around her neck and tucked its head beneath Cassandra's chin.

"Come on, remember! Remember!" Audrey insisted.

Cassandra could barely speak above the lump in her throat. "The man raised his arms," she said, then after a few halting starts added, "And the sunlight glinted on the curved blade of his scimitar, blinding me when I stared at it." That flash of white light suddenly struck her mind's eye, jabbing Cassandra with a clarity every bit as painful as the thrust of a dagger. Clapping her hands over her face, she sobbed miserably.

"It's all right," said Audrey. "Sometimes 'tis best to let it all out."

"Mother turned my face away!"

Audrey crouched next to Cassandra and grasped her forearms. "Think back to the night the mummy came! Was yer dream the same that night?"

Cassandra lifted her head and struggled to focus her attention on Audrey. Through a veil of tears she searched the woman's earnest expression. Slowly, her tension eased. The cloying panic that clogged her throat abated. But she was more confused than ever.

"I am sorry," she said, dabbing her eyes with the handkerchief Audrey had given her. "I dreamed that Mama turned my head away. And then I awoke to find the mummy hovering over me, his hand outstretched—" Cassandra stared at the scrap of linen she'd been clutching. A jolt of recognition shot through her. "Audrey, the mummy placed a handkerchief over my face!"

"Aye, miss! 'Twas just as I thought!" Returning to her

seat, Audrey nodded enthusiastically. "'Ave some more tea, miss."

Cassandra sipped the tepid liquid as she pondered the significance of the mummy's handkerchief. "He did knock me out," she said at last, her voice cutting through the meditative silence that had fallen on the room like a chill fog. "My head was aching as if it had been bashed in with a cudgel."

Audrey peered at her. "But he didna' tote a stick, ma'am. I'd a seen it."

"He had no need to," replied Cassandra. "There must have been something on the handkerchief that put me to sleep as soundly as if my senses had been dulled by opium. 'Struth, the man could have performed surgery on my body! I was that immune to my surroundings, that oblivious of any sort of physical sensation."

"Is it some new kind of drug?" whispered Audrey, her face livid with excitement.

Cassandra stood and pulled Tia onto her hip. "I do not know, but for the time being, I shall put this handkerchief into safekeeping."

After explaining to Audrey the events surrounding the mummy unwrapping, Cassandra yawned and nodded toward her bedchamber. "I believe we are on the criminal's trail. He is not so clever as he thinks."

"But far more dangerous than *you* think, miss," Audrey replied tartly. When her mistress threw a reproving glance over her shoulder, the maid added demurely, "If you don't mind me sayin' so, that is."

After Lord Hedgeworth's parlor had emptied, Signor Belzoni dropped to his knees, scooping up bandages that had fallen to the floor. At the sound of Lord Hedgeworth's Merlin chair, he rose quickly from behind the refectory table and dusted off his palms. "Neville! I was hoping you would reappear." Striding toward the center of the room

amid a swirl of white robes, the Italian opened his arms wide. "How very glad I am to see you. I was just sweeping up the dirty linen—"

Neville laughed bitterly. "Speaking of dirty linen, shall we air some, my friend?"

"Only if we can do so over some of your excellent brandy," replied Belzoni.

After a butler had fetched glasses and a decanter, the men convened before the fire. Belzoni brought up one of the sphinx-headed armchairs and settled in it with a satisfied "Ahhh," while Neville hunched in his straight-backed rolling chair.

At length, Neville said, "I apologize for my uncivil behavior earlier. You are far too esteemed and cherished a guest to have received such shabby treatment."

Giovanni Belzoni nodded.

"But there is something very odd going on around here," continued Neville in a thick, rasping voice. "Something terribly sinister is at loose in the city of London, and I feel completely powerless to stop it. Damme, I don't know why I even care. It has been eons since I cared about anything."

"A man cannot live without a passion or two," commented Belzoni.

"Egypt was my passion," said Neville. "For years I had no other love. Oh, do not feel sorry for me! It has been enough, I tell you. At least, it was until my prized mummy was stolen. I should not like to think that my predilection for Egyptian antiquities has caused innocent people to suffer. But the theft of my mummy has caused me to fear just that. Egads, I cannot bear it!"

Stroking his beard, Belzoni's eyes shone eagerly. "You must tell me everything, dear friend. I have spent many years waiting to meet you, and now that I have, imagine what relief I feel to know that I might be of some assistance to you. The guidance you provided me in your letters made me the success I have become."

Neville laughed. "You are the toast of London, are you not? Why do you trouble yourself with a crippled man's conundrum?"

"The fawning public will forget me as soon as someone makes a greater discovery—an intact royal tomb untouched by grave robbers, for example. Fame is not nearly so important to me as your friendship has been. I would not consider leaving London without helping you. And besides, I do so love a mystery."

Neville's good eye shot questioningly toward Belzoni's turban. "You will help me, then?" he asked, a note of wonder in his voice.

Belzoni raised his glass. "I am at your disposal, Lord Hedgeworth."

"That is good," sighed the earl, lifting his glass in return. "I shall need you. For I suspect that Alistair's French mistress and her brother are cunning criminals. But until we solve the mystery of the missing mummy, I have instructed him not to sever his relationship with her. He is hosting an Egyptian theme party at his country manor next week, and I have advised him to allow her and her brother to attend."

Belzoni looked confused. "But unless my eyes deceived me, your younger brother's ardor for the mademoiselle has already fizzled. It appears to me he is now hopelessly enamored with Miss Russell."

"A rare show of good sense on his part," grunted Neville. "For once he is thinking with his head, and not his—"

"Suzette Duval *is* attractive," said Belzoni quickly.

"So is oleander, and it smells sweet too."

"Tell more more about the Duvals," Belzoni murmured, sliding his chair closer to Neville's.

Neville braced himself with a long draft of fortifying brandy. "Unless *my* one good eye has deceived me, you recognized Pierre. I fear the young Duvals are not who they profess to be."

At that, the great Italian leaned back in his chair and

rubbed his lower lip. *"Davvero?* Really?" His turban nodded slowly, sagely, for a length. "Yes, there was something disturbingly familiar about the young man. Your instincts have led me to greatness, Neville, and that is why I am here. So, tell me all that you know, and we will set about to unravel the mystery of the counterfeit siblings."

The purple sky was fading to a fashionable shade of pink when Neville's carriage arrived at South Audley Street. After waving his thanks to the earl's bleary-eyed coachman, Alistair bounded up the marble steps fronting his town house. He had only reached for the heavy brass knob, when the white lacquered door swung open to admit him. Striding across the threshold, the viscount handed his beaver hat and cloak to a butler whose implacable, unquestioning expression belied the fact he'd been awake all night, loyally anticipating Alistair's return like a long-suffering wife keeping vigil for a tardy husband.

Alistair glided across the foyer, then took two steps at a time to his first-floor bedchamber. He shed his clothes on the furniture as he crossed his room, then sank onto the edge of a soft mattress and pulled off his Hessians. As his second boot fell to the floor with a thud, Alistair's head hit the pillow.

Despite his bone-tired condition, sleep eluded Alistair. When the clatter of late-morning traffic entered his reverie, he was still tossing and turning, tangling his limbs in bedclothes dampened by his perspiration. Kissing Cassandra had not only deepened Alistair's affection for her, it had left his mind and body tingling with excitement.

Alistair's excitement contained an element of dread, however. The intensity of his emotions amazed him, even frightened him. Groaning, Alistair kicked at the counterpane and rolled onto his back. Sunlight filtered through the curtains of his bedchamber. He flung his arm across his eyes to block out the offending brightness, but he could

not shield his mind from the vivid image of Cassandra.
The memory of her expression when he had tipped her
chin with his thumb and lowered his head to kiss her
brought with it an acute physical reaction. He groaned
again, and flashed on Cassandra's face.

He had stared at her, standing in the middle of her
tiny inventory room, his heart full of wonder. He'd been
overwhelmed by the profundity of his emotions, and terrified of the power Cassandra had over him. He'd felt his
stomach twist, and the thought of fleeing her strange little
funeral shop and never coming back almost impelled him
out the door.

After all, Alistair Gordon, Viscount Catledge, was a hard-
drinking, smooth-talking, head-turning hell-born babe.
Did his own brother not refer to him as "my little alley
cat?" The thought of waking up next to the same woman,
every morning, for the rest of his life, terrified the daylights
of Alistair. Where women were concerned, his motto had
always been Variety is the spice of life. Falling in love would
cast his former life into disrepute. Conjugal fidelity would
negate his entire philosophy. Marriage would require a
complete reversal and total condemnation of all the liber-
tine ethics he had espoused.

Alistair's fingers had trembled as they caressed Cassandra's cheeks. He came perilously close to bolting.

And then he remembered the mummy. The unwrapping
staged by Signor Belzoni paralleled his own disentan-
glement, his own unraveling. Truth be known, his rakehell
Corinthian disguise was coming undone. Staring at Cassandra, his doubts had disappeared and a newfound clarity
replaced them. Suddenly, he saw things differently. He
realized what the unwrapping of the mummy signified.

A hard, thick coat of resin had encased the mummy's
body. Like petrified amber, the resin shielded the mummy's heart and protected it through the centuries. Signor
Belzoni had taken hammer and mallet to that mummy's
brittle armor and pounded it, cracked it, sending shards

of caramel-tinted resin flying like an explosion of hard candy.

Beneath that shell was a naked corpse. The hard resin, careful embalming, mystical rituals, protective amulets, spells, ushabti, and superstitions of the ancient Egyptians had done nothing to preserve a single man's heart. Immortality had not been achieved by the arts and rituals of self-preservation. If Alistair tried to protect his heart, he would be as the mummy, lulled into eternal sleep by false securities, dead to the world, insensate but hardly impregnable.

Upon reflection, waking up every morning for the rest of his life *without* Cassandra seemed to Alistair a perversion of fate.

But how was he to reconcile his love for a middle-class tradeswoman with his aristocratic status? Viscount Catledge was no green fribble full of unrealistic fantasies. He loved Cassandra, and he thought she loved him. But what would his Corinthian pals say to his marrying a chit? And how would Cassandra fit into his clique? Could a bluestocking intellectual learn to waltz in drop-dead heat at crowded town balls? Could she don a riding habit and follow the hounds at country house parties? Could she do the pretty in Mayfair salons?

Would she even want to try?

Pondering all these thoughts, Alistair had just begun to doze, when his valet shook him awake. "There is a Mlle. Duval here to see you, my lord. She is in the drawing room."

Muttering a sanguine oath, Alistair rose and dressed hastily. He ran his fingers through his hair and merely glanced at his reflection in a cheval mirror. He was in no mood to see Suzette Duval, and therefore had no interest in his own appearance. When he entered the drawing room, and saw her perched on a lime-green love seat, his stomach roiled with displeasure. The sight of Suzette's green muslin dress, matching rice-straw hat, and printed cashmere shawl sickened him.

"Are you ill, *bijou*?" Suzette asked, patting the cushion beside her. She frowned when he leaned against the mantelpiece instead of sitting down. "You have not forgotten that you promised to take me to the dressmaker this morning, have you?"

"I am feeling a trifle green around the gills," confessed Alistair, not at all dishonestly. Suzette's presence was an unsettling reminder of his rakehell past. Now that he'd fallen in love with Cassandra, Alistair wished he could snap his fingers and make Suzette disappear. Unfortunately, his former French mistress was not likely to be such a good sport. "You should go, Suzette. I am ill."

Suzette stood and crossed the room to touch his forehead. "You do not feel feverish."

Alistair refrained from asking how she could gauge his body heat through a kidskin glove. "Nevertheless, I am sick," said he.

Her lips curved. As her eyes slid down Alistair's throat, he realized his mistake in not wearing a cravat and buttoning his shirt to the neck. Her hungry look offended him, and when she touched his bare chest, Alistair snatched her wrist.

"Good God, woman!" In a display of modesty incongruous to the torrid relationship he had shared with the Frenchwoman, he recoiled. "It cannot be past ten in the morning! What are you doing, coming to my home unchaperoned anyway? What will the servants think?"

Suzette drew back and gasped. "The servants, *chéri*?" She batted her lashes, clearly astonished by Alistair's sudden provincialism. "You have never cared a whit what your servants thought," she retorted. "You have never cared what anyone thought, for that matter, including the ton. What has made you so thoughtful of your reputation, Ali? Why are you acting as if I am a perfect stranger? What are you trying to tell me?"

"I am trying to tell you that it is improper for a young lady to be alone with an unmarried gentleman in his home."

Suzette's bottom lip swelled. "You have lost interest in me." She turned her head, as if to hide her hurt expression. "You no longer love me," she pouted.

Alistair sighed. Suzette had summed up his feelings with amazing accuracy, but as a gentleman, as an honorable and respected blood of the beau monde, he felt obliged to launch a nominal protest. "You do not understand," he said, but his voice trailed off.

"You are in love with that haughty, overeducated *jolie laide,*" Suzette accused him. "I saw the way you looked at her last night. Everyone saw, I suppose. Oh, how positively humiliating!"

"You must have known our affair would have to end someday," Alistair said staunchly. "Come now, you didn't expect me to marry you. I never said that I would."

"What a fool I've been!" Suzette clutched her green beaded reticule to her brimming bosom. "I thought you were a dashing man of the world who knew how to protect his heart. I thought you knew how to treat your *chère amie* fairly."

Alistair was stunned not so much by Suzette's outburst, but by her glaring omission. She did not say, *I thought you loved me!*

"You hold yourself out as a buck of the first head," she scolded, her idiomatic jargon and French accent growing more discordant. Alistair would have wagered his entire fortune on the chance that half a dozen servants were huddled against the drawing room door, soaking up this exchange like a sponge slurping dirty dishwater.

He held up his hands in a plaintive gesture. "Please, Suzette. Lower your voice."

"I shall not lower my voice! You have turned out to be nothing more than an unlicked cub, as fickle and romantic as a schoolboy. I should have listened to Pierre's warnings about you! I should never have let you use me in such a vile, wicked manner!"

"Use you?" Alistair echoed incredulously. "Isn't that

the pot calling the kettle black? Have you not used *me*, woman?'' He alluded to the way she insisted on attending Lord Tifton's salon. "I have even played host to your simpering brother,'' he added, reminding her of the debacle at Curzon Street. "By the way, why did the two of you run off so precipitously last evening?''

Suzette tossed her head, and the plumes that towered above her hat waggled precariously. "We waited in the foyer for you and that woman to conclude your conversation with the esteemed Italian Samson. When you did not appear, we took the liberty of borrowing your carriage.''

"Not to mention my driver and footman,'' interpolated Alistair. "Had you waited a scant five minutes, I would have driven you home.''

"You embarrassed me by flirting with that woman,'' answered Suzette. "I wanted to go. Pierre agreed that I was shabbily treated, and he escorted me home immediately.''

Suzette's quick retort smacked of duplicity and defensiveness. Studying her flushed expression, Alistair asked, "Are you sure that is the only reason you fled my brother's town house last night? Or was it because Signor Belzoni's questions were making you and your brother nervous?''

"Do not be ridiculous!''

"Belzoni thought he'd seen your brother before last night. Have they met before, Suzette? Is there something about your past I should know?''

Suzette scoffed at the notion. "Do not be ridiculous!'' she cried, slapping a green fan against her palm. It occurred to Alistair that he hated green. Cassandra Russell wouldn't be caught dead in one of those frothy green concoctions. He almost laughed aloud at his observation, but then he remembered how much he'd paid for Suzette's green gowns, and his sense of humor deserted him.

Alistair nodded toward the door. "I think you had better leave,'' he said quietly.

The menacing undertone in his softened voice seemed to galvanize Suzette's hostility. She arched one perfectly

shaped black brow and lifted her chin. Her cheeks darkened, and when she spoke, her voice was low and throaty, redolent with vitriol. "You cannot do this to me," she said, her eyes snapping.

"Au contraire," replied Alistair. "I can, and I will."

Suzette's eyes widened in surprise, then narrowed in fury. Her jaw worked, and her bottom lip trembled, but not a tear sprang to her emerald eyes. Somewhere in the nether regions of Alistair's town house a pot clattered to the floor and angry voices erupted in argument.

Alistair watched Suzette, and she watched him. They circled each other warily, like big-game cats. He thought she was considering her choices—whether to threaten him, expose him, or stalk him in his London haunts till he relented and resumed his former patronization of her. Perhaps she thought to confide in his tonnish friends, cry on their shoulders, tell them all that Alistair was a fickle, duplicitous bounder. Her eyes brightened. Alistair's narrowed. Clearly, Suzette was ticking off her options one by one.

"I shall tell everyone what you have done to me," she whispered indignantly.

He snorted derisively. The slanderous insults of a former French mistress could do his reputation no serious harm.

Suzette drew herself up. "All right," she conceded. "I see that you do not care what a *fille de joie* such as me says about you." She looked him in the eye. "You are irrevocably lost to me, I see that now."

Alistair felt a twinge of remorse, but nothing more. "I am sorry," he proffered.

"Would you do me one tiny little favor?" she asked diffidently. "Would you allow me to attend your theme party at Catledge Hall next Friday evening? I have already procured my costume, you see." Her voice faltered, and her eyes flickered about the room. She clutched her reti-

cule and shook her head, apparently disoriented, knocked off balance. "It would mean so much to me," she murmured.

By agreement with his brother, the viscount had no intention of revoking his invitation to Suzette Duval and her brother, Pierre. Still, he hesitated, weighing his words carefully. "I was thinking of asking Cassandra to attend," he admitted.

At that, Suzette threw herself into his arms, clutching his open shirt collar, peering up into his face with an expression of pure agony. "Oh, please, *bijou!* Your costume party is sure to be the talk of the season! If you are determined to turn me out, the least you can do is allow me one last chance to salvage my pride."

"You mean one last chance to latch on to someone else," said Alistair, gripping Suzette's forearms and prying her off him. He set her at a respectable distance and held up his hands, forestalling further entreaties. "All right, you shall attend the Egyptian theme party at Catledge Hall. Perhaps if you find another protector, you will acquit yourself of the foolish notion that I have somehow mistreated you."

"And Pierre?" Suzette queried. "He can attend also, can he not?"

Alistair feigned a minor show of protest before he relented. "And, yes, I will hire a carriage to transport the two of you to Melton," he further agreed. At least that would keep the Duval siblings out of his hair, he thought. And it would leave him free to accompany Cassandra to the country in the privacy of his own carriage.

Suzette pressed a handkerchief to her lower eyelid. "Thank you. You are too, too generous," she sniffed sarcastically.

"By half," Alistair agreed.

Suzette swept out of the drawing room, pausing only to glance over her shoulder and blow one final, parting

kiss. As the door closed behind her, Alistair felt a shiver of apprehension. He wished he'd thought to ask Suzette what costume she was planning to wear to *A Long Egyptian Night.* He would like to know precisely what she had up her sleeve.

Chapter Ten

Pensive after an early morning visit from Signor Belzoni, Cassandra did not hear Viscount Catledge enter the emporium. A shadow crossed the floor, and she started. From a pattern book of mourning gowns, she looked up into Alistair's handsome face and sighed with a mixture of relief and heady anticipation. Like the great Italian, Alistair's appearance was unexpected; in contrast, however, the viscount's presence had an unprecedented and unsettling effect on Cassandra.

She pushed her work aside and happily lent her rapt attention to the most attractive lordling in London. The couple seemed flustered and tongue-tied, and several minutes passed before anything of substance was discussed.

Leaning forward, the viscount laid his gloved hands atop the glass countertop. "Please say you will attend my costume ball," he urged intently, his petition underscored by a creased brow and plaintive gaze. "I would not think of staging *A Long Egyptian Night* without the most beautiful Egyptian woman I know in attendance."

"'Struth, I am only half Egyptian," countered Cassandra,

her cheeks warm beneath Alistair Gordon's disarming stare.

Alistair clenched his fists. "Like I am only a half brother," he replied.

"I did forget," Cassandra said softly, instinctively covering Alistair's hand with her own.

His eyes darkened, as if shaded by a passing cloud. "Neville and I share the same father. When his mother died, mine became the second Lady Hedgeworth. We were never very close, unfortunately. My title and wealth are inherited from an uncle, in case you were wondering."

"I had not wondered," admitted Cassandra. "But I suppose that explains the rivalry that exists between you two."

"A rivalry which, it seems, we have resolved," said Alistair. "In large part to you."

"How is that so, my lord?" Cassandra wondered.

"Had I not met you, Neville would not have had the opportunity to save your life—and mine, I am sure—by firing off that shot when the mummy attacked. That incident revealed to me my brother's true nature, his persistent loyalty in the face of my brattish defiance. Since then the man dotes on me as if I am a prodigal of some sort! And to a degree I fear might be regarded as sentimental by many of my boon companions, I have realized how important my brother's love is."

"The earl's intervention was well timed, that is true," said Cassandra. "Even my bitterness toward him has dissolved."

In a blink, Alistair's gaze was bright and sparkling again, his smile easy. He gripped Cassandra's fingers and renewed his entreaty. "Please come to Catledge Hall, then, Miss Russell!"

"I suppose we should be on a first-name basis by now," evaded Cassandra. The bells of St. Clement's tolled in the distance, mocking the pretentious daydreams she had earlier entertained, fantasies that she was the Viscountess Catledge, the much adored wife of Alistair Gordon.

Alistair's taut expression eased. "You may ride with me if you are willing to go as early as tomorrow."

"Tomorrow! For heaven's sake, I could never leave my shop on such short notice," protested Cassandra.

"Then when can you be ready to leave?" asked Alistair. "Can you leave on Tuesday? Would that allow you sufficient time to take care of your business obligations and put together a costume and wardrobe?"

Cassandra's sigh was redolent with indecision. She could not voice the true cause of her reluctance. Doubts and insecurities plagued her. What would she wear to a ball at Catledge Hall? Even if Madame Racine worked day and night for a week, the harried mantua-maker would never have been able to turn out an Egyptian costume as well as a weekend wardrobe suitable for mingling with Polite Society.

And how would Cassandra even know what to wear, what to say, and how to comport herself? The finer points of country balls were unknown to her. The niceties of house-party etiquette were as enigmatic as a Chinese puzzle. She had no idea what the ladies in attendance at a country party were expected to do during the day while the men went fox hunting! She had little conception what women at weekend house parties talked about over needlepoint and tea, and even foggier notions what dancing partners bantered whilst waltzing cheek to cheek.

But she could not turn down an invitation to Catledge Hall! The opportunity to spend a weekend in Alistair's company was far too tantalizing, even if the price of that indulgence was rubbing shoulders with a bunch of stiff-rumped aristocrats. Madame Racine would just have to work fast in sewing up a presentable wardrobe! Audrey would have to tend the store and look after Tia. Cassandra would have to brave the scrutiny of a group of well-bred ladies who, if they scorned and despised her, could ruin her socially—overnight!

But that didn't signify, did it? Without Alistair, she cared

nothing for social standing. And unless she took this chance, embarked on this adventure, accepted this unexpected invitation to Catledge Hall, Cassandra was never going to fit into Alistair's world. If she had hopes of becoming the Viscountess Catledge, she had best overcome her disdain for his peers. If Cassandra intended to convince Alistair he'd be happier married to her than to a frumpy heiress or insipid dandizette, she'd better launch her campaign now. Terrified of the risk she was taking, she nodded her head.

"Yes," she said in a whisper. Then, much louder and more emphatically, "Yes! I would love to attend your costume ball and house party."

Alistair smiled and lifted Cassandra's fingers to his lips. Turning her hand over, he kissed her palm lovingly. The sensation thrilled her, and a delighted laugh bubbled up from deep within her.

"By the way," the viscount said absently, nibbling on the tip of her forefinger. "What is it that you wanted to tell me last night?"

"I should have told you days ago, but—" She drew back her hand, fearful that her confession would anger the viscount. "I was not entirely sure I could trust you, for one thing. For another, I was quite convinced that Cleo's existence should be kept secret for reasons of safety—not only mine, but potentially many other people's as well."

Alistair's grin faded to amused bewilderment. "Who in the devil is Cleo?"

Cassandra explained, and when she was finished, she felt tremendous relief at Alistair's calm demeanor.

"I suppose I cannot blame you for keeping your mummy's existence a secret," he said, rubbing his lower lip as if in deep thought. "And you say that Cleo was the wife of Neville's stolen pharaoh?"

"I am sure of it," replied Cassandra.

"Yes, I believe whoever stole Neville's mummy is trying

to steal yours as well. Damme, perhaps I did lead the criminals to you!"

"But no one knows of Cleo," reminded Cassandra. "Except for you and me. And Audrey, of course. And Tia, the monkey, who often sleeps on the floor beneath the mummy's coffin." She drew a deep breath before adding, "Giovanni Belzoni knows as of this morning."

Alistair's expression was alert. "Signor Belzoni knows? How is that so?"

"He visited me earlier this morning," said Cassandra. "We talked for quite a long time, and he assured me that the legend of the mummy's curse is just that—a legend, grown up around superstition and rumor."

"The Patagonian Samson allayed your fears, then," mused Alistair. "I consider myself fortunate that he did; otherwise you might not have confided in me."

Cassandra smiled. "Oh, I think I would have, Ali. You see, I have thought for many years that the pharaoh's curse was my legacy, and that I was doomed to a life of . . ." She twisted a black muslin swatch in her hand and lowered her eyes. "Well, my lord, I suppose I saw my attachment to Tia as a sign of fate."

Leaning across the countertop, Alistair lifted Cassandra's chin with his thumb. "Did you think that the pharaoh's curse had doomed you to spend eternity as an ape-leader?" he asked softly.

The tear that welled in Cassandra's eye was no longer one of laughter. She blinked it away, but her voice trembled when she spoke. "I suppose it sounds silly to you, my lord."

"It sounds preposterous, dear," he answered. He bent forward and planted a chaste kiss on her dampened cheek. After a moment he said, "I just thought of something!"

"What is it?" Cassandra said, startled at the drastic change in Alistair's tone.

"After your father was murdered, your mother came into possession of all the antiquities Neville had promised him. Neville told me so himself. He even assured me he

would never have cheated your mother out of Sir Anthony's share of the treasures.''

Cassandra's eyes were dry now, and fixed on Alistair's gleaming eyes. "What are you getting at, my lord?"

"Neville is aware that you own the other royal mummy. He must be; he would have no reason to assume otherwise." Alistair's brows rose to twin peaks. "I wonder that he has not emphasized this fact to me."

"Why do you not ask him?" Cassandra suggested logically. "And there is something else." She produced the handkerchief with the mysterious initials J.D. embroidered on it. Alistair examined it minutely before tucking it into his pocket.

His features relaxed. "I finally have something to investigate," he said. "Some notions have come to my mind."

"You haven't much time before you must leave for the country," said Cassandra.

"More than I had before you agreed to attend my costume party, dear. I had planned to depart London the same day as Suzette and Pierre. But since I am not leaving until Tuesday, with you, I shall have plenty of time to do some snooping around here in London. The fact of Cleo's existence has raised some very interesting questions." He rubbed his chin. "*Molto interessante,* as Signor Belzoni would say."

A terrible streak of jealousy shot through Cassandra's body. "Suzette and Pierre are going to attend the costume ball also?" She felt her face grow hot. "Not that I am surprised," she added icily. "I suppose I should have known."

Alistair chuckled and reached for Cassandra's hand, but his flippancy irritated her and she snatched it from him. If Viscount Catledge was as infatuated with Cassandra as he appeared to be, why was he inviting that French trollop and her insipid, wasp-waisted brother to his country house party? Was Alistair playing games after all? Cassandra's fears and insecurities came rushing back. If her chit status

made her ineligible to be the viscount's wife, had he relegated her to the potential role of mistress? Did he now intend to amuse himself with two mistresses instead of one?

Cassandra said coldly, "I do not think I would like to attend your costume party after all, not if Mlle. Duval is going to be there." She rankled at the look of amusement in Alistair's dark eyes.

"My *former* friend was extended an invitation many weeks ago," he explained. "'Twould be most rude were I to rescind that invitation, even if I could. And, besides, she has promised that if I will do her the favor of allowing her to attend, she will not harangue me in public or bother my friends with scandalous details concerning my abrupt dismissal of her."

"But she is your *former* friend?" asked Cassandra tentatively.

"Most assuredly," answered Alistair.

"And you have no intentions of *reasserting* that friendship at any time in the future?"

"Certainly not. After the costume ball, there is no reason ever to see Suzette Duval or her spindly brother again."

Cassandra gave the viscount a half-smile. "All right, then. I shall be ready to leave for Melton on Tuesday at ten o'clock."

Alistair grinned his satisfaction. "One other thing, miss. I believe that Cleo should be removed to safer quarters. Do you have any objection to my making arrangements for the mummy's safekeeping?"

Cassandra bit her lower lip. At length, she said, "You do not think that with Suzette and Pierre on their way to Melton, my mummy is safe?"

"Why take chances?" responded Alistair. "I shall send some men over to remove the mummy to Signor Belzoni's storehouse. Cleo will be quite safe there, I assure you. And in good company, to boot."

Upon Cassandra's assenting to this arrangement, the

viscount bowed. When he straightened, his hair fell over one eye, and he raked his fingers through it as he backed across the floor, departing as if from the presence of royalty. Doffing his hat, he bid Cassandra *adieu* and pulled the shop door closed behind him. Russell's Emporium fell silent.

But only for a moment.

In a flurry of motion, Cassandra raced up the stairs and into the drawing room of her apartment. She hadn't nearly enough time to prepare for her first weekend country house party and her introduction to Alistair's aristocratic friends. Nor was there sufficient time to sew up a spectacular costume for the viscount's theme party. Any rational person would have argued against Cassandra's even attempting such an ambitious foray into the London social scene. Plunging into society precipitously—without the proper gowns or manners—could be ruinous, killing Cassandra's chances at becoming a viscountess even before Alistair Gordon ever thought to propose marriage to her.

But though her pulse raced with trepidation, Cassandra was willing to risk failure. If Alistair ever did entertain the notion of marrying her, she was bound that he would not reject the idea because of her social inferiority. She could hold her own in any setting, even if she didn't quite know the rules. Like her Egyptian mother, she was elegant, composed, and cool-mannered. But like her father, Cassandra Russell's blood boiled with passion. She was not above putting up a fight for her man. She wanted Alistair, and she would have him.

With Audrey and Madame Racine working overtime, Cassandra concluded she could just be ready to leave London by Tuesday morning. She had a hundred things to do, and just as many items to buy on the shopping list that was forming in her head. There was no time to waste. Energized by the thrill of the risk she was courting, she burst into her bedchamber, where Audrey was teaching Tia how to dust.

Turning, the monkey bared her teeth at Cassandra, then waved the feather duster in a manner quite regal albeit totally ineffectual in relation to the layer of dust that coated the table upon which she sat. "Yes, you are a very good girl," approved Cassandra automatically. She turned to address Audrey, who quickly jumped to her feet and grabbed the monkey's feather duster.

Cassandra paused, belatedly stricken by the scene she'd interrupted. After another quizzical glance at Tia, it dawned on her that Audrey was actually teaching the monkey to perform her own housekeeping chores. "Is that why there is dust three inches deep in the drawing room?" Cassandra wondered out loud.

Audrey colored. "She ain't much on dustin', miss. But she's a big help at washin' stockings and such. And she can untangle knots in boot laces better 'n anything ye ever saw."

Cassandra covered the smile that quirked her lips. "I see. Well, we shall discuss the matter later. Right now I have more pressing matters to deal with. I am going to Melton, to attend the viscount's weekend house party and costume ball."

Audrey clapped her hands. "Oh, miss! 'Tis wonderful!"

"Yes, and I shall need your help, Audrey. Can you fetch Madame Racine? I believe it is time to refurbish my wardrobe and dispense with these mourning gowns. And then we must go shopping. I will need new slippers and shawls and—who knows what else?"

A tear sparkled in Audrey's eye as she hugged Cassandra to her breast. "I'm on me way, lass," she said affectionately, then disappeared to her room humming an Irish ditty.

Cassandra gathered Tia in her arms and stood in the middle of her bedchamber. She turned when Audrey poked her head in the door, a bonnet thrust down atop her rust-colored curls, a woolen cloak about her shoulders. "Hadn't ye better purchase some fancy unmentionables, miss?" Batting her eyelashes, the coarse-voiced maid added

slyly, "Ye never know when ye might be wishin' ye had somethin' pretty underneath those stiff-skirted gowns o' yours."

Cassandra felt the heat rise to her cheeks, but she chuckled shyly nonetheless. "Be gone, Audrey!" The woman vanished again, this time slamming shut the apartment door behind her. Cassandra planted a kiss atop Tia's head, rocking the tiny monkey absently while her treason-hearted virtue gave over to ruminations of Audrey's suggestion.

Wearing such garments as gauzy low-cut night rails, frilled pantaloons, and fancy push-up laced corsets would certainly be a novelty to Cassandra. Now that she was free from the fiction of any dreadful bluestocking curse, she thought it rather thrilling to indulge her imaginings. She even wondered what Alistair's reaction would be to seeing her in her unmentionables. Quite unconsciously, she murmured her approbation of Audrey's lascivious notion.

Her thoughts were deliciously wicked; had she not so many errands demanding her attention, she would have taken to her bed and allowed them to run riotously free across her surprisingly vivid imagination. As it was, Cassandra was going to be hard pressed to be ready for her debut into Polite Society.

Undaunted, she summoned her inner strength, closed her eyes, and stood straighter beneath the challenge. Her fear of the mummy's curse was displaced by a steely, meditative resolve. Cassandra now staked her chit heart against all of Alistair's aristocratic prejudices. And despite unflattering odds—after all, what did she know of country house party manners and costume ball decorum?—she wagered she could give those tonnish tabbies and tilt-nosed dandizettes a run for their money. Gambling had never been Cassandra's vice. But by agreeing to accompany Alistair to Catledge Hall in Melton, she was flying as high as any dissolute gamester that ever tossed the dice.

* * *

Returning the brass stare of a leonine knocker, Viscount Catledge stood before the front door of a fashionable Cleveland Street town house. A movement behind him caught his eye. Whistling off-tune and tapping his cane impatiently, he threw a glance over his shoulder. At the curb behind him was parked a black carriage, and in it his older brother's craggy face was pressed against the window. The earl's head popped out of sight when a handsome couple strolled down the sidewalk. Alistair lowered his head so that the brim of his beaver hat concealed his features. He nodded politely, then turned his back in response to the couple's perfunctory salutation.

His aplomb was soon rewarded with the sound of heavy footsteps on the other side of the door. The viscount hooked his cane over his arm, shot a quick look at the ambling couple whose departing backs and bobbing heads bespoke their preoccupation with each other, then scanned the street for busybodies. He breathed a sigh of relief. So far, it seemed, his presence had failed to pique anyone's sustained interest. As long as Suzette and Pierre Duval did not double back on their trip to Melton, he was fairly certain he could get into their town house and search it without their ever being the wiser.

The door swung open, and Giovanni Belzoni stood in the doorway, his bearded face beaming. Dressed in dark trousers and cutaway coat, the gigantic man made a sweeping gesture with his hand. "I have been expecting you, my lord."

Alistair quickly crossed the threshold and pushed the door shut behind him. "What took you so long?" he asked, his gaze taking in the gleaming black and white marble floor of the entrance hall, an ornate Louix XIV commode beside the staircase, and the Chinese-style fretwork of an imposing balustrade. "You claimed you were as expert as

a pickpocket penny-knave when it came to undoing locked doors."

Belzoni lifted his massive shoulders. "Just because I was billed as Jack the Giant Killer does not mean that I am omnipotent, my lord. The lock on the rear door was quite adequate for its intended purpose. In my defense, I point out that no ordinary thief could have picked it without breaking the inner mechanism."

"Are you sure that the Duvals will not be able to detect your handiwork?" asked Alistair, shivering in the chill quietude of the town house. His booted footsteps reported loudly as he strode to a hat rack in the corner and gave temporary lodgings to his cane and hat. Striding back to the center of the foyer, his shadow intersected shafts of sunlight that augured through the narrow side panes of the house's front windows. The ribbed patterns that crisscrossed the checkered floor reminded Alistair of prison bars.

"My work is the result of years of theater training," answered Belzoni. "I assure you, my lord, the Duvals will never know we have been here. Not unless we leave our calling cards in the salver."

Alistair ran his forefinger along the lower edge of a gilded mirror frame. "There is something odd about this place," he said, frowning at the smudged tip of his gray kid glove.

"Perhaps your French mistress and her brother do not enjoy housekeeping," suggested Belzoni dryly.

"I will allow that Suzette is not the domestic sort," replied Alistair, dusting his palms. "Come, signor, let us see what the Duvals have been hiding. We shall begin at the top level and work our way to the basement."

Hours later, the Earl of Hedgeworth started when the door of his waiting carriage was thrown open. "Ali! Giovanni! You two startled me!"

"Did you think another mummy had come to club you over the head, brother?" The viscount threw himself

against the squabs as the compartment door shut behind
Signor Belzoni.

"What did you find?" asked the earl as his equipage
pulled away from the sidewalk.

The viscount tossed his hat on the cushion next to him
and shrugged. "Very little, and practically nothing of any
significance," he said with disgust.

"No antiquities? No mummy wrappings or thievery
tools?" asked Neville. "No evidence that Suzette and Pierre
have secreted stolen artifacts in their rented quarters?"

"No," Alistair replied. "Nor were there clothes in
Suzette's wardrobe."

"Nor food in the cupboard," remarked Belzoni.

"How very odd," grumbled the earl, hunching in the
corner.

In the cramped confines of the carriage compartment,
Signor Belzoni carefully crossed one of his long legs over
the other. "The house has an antiseptic flavor that belies
the fact it has been occupied," he said. "Either Mlle. Duval
packed everything she owns in a portmanteau and carried
it to Melton, or she is not planning to return to her Cleveland Street abode for some time."

Neville's good eye flashed to Alistair. "What do you say
to that, my boy?"

Alistair said, "I think the signor's choice of words is apt.
The house *is* antiseptic. That is a medical term, you know.
And in that vein, I found something I believe may have
some bearing in this case."

"What is it?" Neville and Giovanni lurched forward as
the traveling carriage hit a particularly vicious rut in the
cobbled street.

Alistair withdrew a dog-eared leather volume from
beneath his cloak. "'Tis a medical treatise on the subject
of surgical anaesthesia. I found it wedged between the
pillows of a recliner in Pierre's bedchamber. Apparently
it was forgotten, or left behind in haste when the Duvals
vacated their living quarters." He flipped the book open

and pointed to a particular passage. "Here, you see that young Monsieur Duval was studying a report on the efficacy of a vapor known as ether."

"What in the devil is ether?" sneered Neville.

"According to this treatise, which thankfully is written in English, it is a substance which, when inhaled, reduces the patient to a state of total and senseless unconsciousness. Even the doctor's incision is not felt by a patient under the influence of ether. Imagine, Neville! Sleeping through the most horrific forms of surgery!"

"'Twould be miraculous," allowed Neville.

Belzoni scratched his thick beard. "I am afraid I do not understand the significance you attach to this discovery," he admitted ruefully.

Alistair tossed him the book and reached within the folds of his cloak. Producing the crumpled relics that Cassandra had given him, he quickly explained how Tia retrieved the scrap of linen and Audrey discovered the monogrammed handkerchief. Lord Hedgeworth had already apprised the intrepid Italian of the other details surrounding the ongoing mystery, including the rock thrown through the viscount's carriage window, the burglarization of Cassandra's apartment, and the mummy's attack at Russell's Emporium.

Alistair passed the handkerchief to his brother. "The mummy obviously rendered Cassandra unconscious by saturating this with ether and placing it over her face and nose."

Neville turned the handkerchief, examining the finely stitched green initials, J.D. "So you think that Pierre, dressed as a mummy, broke into Cassandra's apartment—"

"—and drugged her," interjected Belzoni.

"And proceeded to search her premises?" Neville concluded.

"Yes, I believe that is precisely what happened," said Alistair. "He must have been searching for Cassandra's

mummy. Then Audrey, Cassandra's maid, returned from a nocturnal assignation and interrupted Pierre before he found the mummy's coffin."

"Then we have positively identified our culprit," said Signor Belzoni. "Pierre Duval, dressed as a mummy, attacked you and your brother at Russell's Emporium, and would, most likely, have harmed Miss Russell also, had Neville not discharged his pistol."

"I wish to God I had shot the wicked devil through the heart!"

"Pierre Duval is obviously a trained criminal. I suspect that he and a hired squadron of thieves stole Neville's mummy after long and careful planning," said Alistair. "And then he threw a warning rock through my carriage window to scare me off my investigation into the matter." He paused and rubbed his chin. "Or to ensure that I would keep my mind on it. We must remember that all of this criminality was conducted in concert with the beautiful Suzette Duval."

"But how did Mlle. Suzette Duval know that you would lead her to Cassandra's mummy?" asked Belzoni.

"She must have known Neville possessed the pharaoh," answered Alistair. "But a cursory investigation of my reclusive brother would have convinced her of the fruitlessness of attempting to befriend him. She chose to seduce me, his profligate little brother, instead. And then she pestered me relentlessly to reconcile with him. That was passing strange, and I should have known it, but when Neville sent me the urgent post in Leicestershire, I was primed to respond."

Belzoni frowned. "Was your leading the Duvals to Miss Russell an unanticipated bonus to them, then?"

"On the contrary. I believe Suzette knew that Neville would contact the owner of the pharaoh's mate immediately after his went missing. What we must find out now is *how* Suzette knew that."

The Earl of Hedgeworth grunted his impatience. "So,

the Duvals—or whoever they are—stole my mummy as well as Lord Tifton's antiquities. But how did they pilfer Tifton's artifacts beneath the noses of a roomful of people?"

"I am most eager to see my former mistress," said Alistair. "I have a litany of questions for her and her brother."

"You are certain that she and her brother have, in fact, left London for Melton?" queried Neville.

Alistair smiled. "Suzette's social ambitions will require her to attend the party. Moreover, she has absolutely no inkling of our suspicions against her. I would wager my title that she and her brother, Pierre, will be in Melton when we arrive. And while we are on the subject, you are both attending my costume party, are you not?"

Neville nodded. Belzoni crossed his arms and fidgeted in the insufficient space of the carriage compartment. His body was clearly too large to fit comfortably in so tiny a space, and Alistair wondered how the huge man had slithered through the winding subterranean passages of so many crumbling Egyptian pyramids without getting stuck.

"There is one thing that remains a mystery to me, my lords," the big Italian said, frowning. "Why on earth would Suzette and Pierre Duval conspire to steal the Earl of Hedgeworth's mummy? And, having stolen it, why are they now so intent on stealing Cassandra Russell's mummy?"

"Why indeed?" repeated Alistair, turning the monogrammed handkerchief in his hands. As the carriage clattered to a stop in front of the earl's Curzon Street town house, he smoothed the wrinkled square of linen on his knee. "I do not yet understand the intricacies of Suzette's nefarious scheme," he admitted, fingering the green embroidery. "Nor do I know why she and her brother plotted to steal Neville's mummy, and then Cassandra's."

"Thank heavens the dastardly pair did not get Cassandra's mummy," breathed Signor Belzoni.

"But I want my mummy back!" cried Neville. "How the devil are we going to get my mummy back?"

The carriage door opened, and a liveried footman stood back. The occupants of the tiny compartment remained seated, Signor Belzoni leaning forward anxiously, the Earl of Hedgeworth scowling darkly from his corner. Tucking the handkerchief inside his pocket, Alistair answered his brother's question in hushed tones. "When we learn the identity of J.D.," he said, "I am quite certain that we will know why Suzette and Pierre have concocted their devilish plot."

Belzoni clapped his hands. "My sketches!" he cried. "Why did I not remember sooner? When I return to my lodgings, I must examine the folios I filled during my excavations at Kurneh and Thebes. The ones that were not stolen, that is. I believe I know who Pierre Duval is!"

"Who?" Neville and Alistair asked in unison.

But Belzoni waggled his forefinger and grinned. "I want to be certain before I voice my theory, but if Pierre is who I think he is, this mystery will soon be solved."

Alistair took his brother's arm and helped him from the carriage. "If Signor Belzoni is correct, we will recover your stolen mummy, Neville," he whispered.

"I hope that you right, my little Ali-Cat," answered the earl as he was handed into Belzoni's waiting arms. "God's blood, I hope that you are right."

Catledge Hall, Melton, Leicestershire,
Friday, ten o'clock, P.M.

Cassandra closed her eyes and leaned her head against the back of the tole tub. The scent of cinnamon wafted off the surface of the hot water, creating a spicy steam bath that did little to soothe her senses. Already, she could hear the low drone of the costume party, just getting under way in the nether regions of the manor house. She should get out of the water, put on her costume, and make her

entrance to the grand *bal masqué* downstairs. She knew she should. But first she needed to calm her nerves.

Inhaling deeply, Cassandra peeked at a clock on the mantel. Despite the late hour, she slipped deeper into the water, her arms stretched languidly along the sides of the sheet-metal bath. For a moment she wished she could slide below the water's surface and hide until *A Long Egyptian Night* was over. Whatever had possessed her to choose such a provocative costume to wear to the party?

With the hot water lapping at her chin, Cassandra felt her naked arms erupt in goose pimples. Her teeth chattered against an inner chill, but her throat was dry and parched. The humidity in her closed-in bathroom had plastered tendrils of hair against her cheeks and outlined her upper lips with beads of sweat. Lowering her arms, Cassandra sank even deeper into the water, stared at her toes pressed against the opposite end of the tub, and finally confronted her doubts concerning Alistair.

She had thought telling him of Cleo's existence would ease her anxiety, but it hadn't. Despite his magnanimous acceptance of the fact that she'd deceived him, Cassandra feared he was merely stifling a resentment that would reappear once he'd solved the mystery of Neville's stolen mummy.

Though to her it seemed he was no closer to solving that mystery than he had been last week. He had agreed that whoever stole the earl's mummy was also after Cleo. He had also agreed that the same villain was guilty of robbing Lord Tifton and breaking into Cassandra's apartment. After studying the handkerchief Cassandra had given him, a strange glow had kindled behind the viscount's eyes.

He had appeared distracted by his own thoughts, determined yet slightly addled. After backing out of Russell's Emporium, he had turned at the door and leapt into his waiting carriage as if the devil were in behind him. At the

time Cassandra wondered if his strange behavior meant he had a suspicion as to the identity of the rogue mummy.

Now she wondered why he hadn't confided in her when they were alone in the carriage.

Her hand fell into the water with a loud "plop." Sighing miserably, Cassandra wondered if she'd missed some subtle message from Alistair, some hint that he no longer cared for her, some inference that he'd been impulsive to think he ever did. She replayed the carriage ride to Melton in her mind; it was pleasant enough, though Alistair had been tight-lipped on the subject of the mummy.

The conversation had been warm and easy, yet superficial. Alistair had sat across from her during the entire journey, entertaining her with the latest *on dits* concerning Queen Caroline's escapades, and the king's architectural extravagances in Brighton. When he was not soliciting her opinion or asking her polite questions about her work, he had dozed or read a slender novel entitled *Ivanhoe*.

Then two days passed at Catledge Hall, and still Cassandra had not felt the type of intimacy she craved. Alistair had been attentive and kind, but he had not particularly sought her out. He had not attempted to kiss her or hold her in his arms. He had not tapped on the door of her bedchamber at some indecent hour, pleading to be admitted, thrusting his foot across the threshold the way he once had in Cassandra's shop. He had not done any of those things, and Cassandra was left to guess at his secret thoughts.

All he *had* done in the days leading up to the masked ball, or so it seemed to Cassandra, was ride out after the hounds. All he had talked about when his guests convened for informal nuncheons, buffet dinners, and afternoon teas were foxes and dogs and weather and horses.

That left Cassandra with no one to turn to for social intercourse except a gaggle of simpering high-toned chits and dough-faced vixens. The patter at Bedlam would have been more erudite, she told herself several times. The only

thing she had been thankful for was the puzzling absence of Pierre and Suzette Duval. Alistair was mystified by their truancy also, but a letter arrived explaining that Pierre had eaten something that made him ill, and the pair were holed up in an inn along the road between London and Melton.

But the parvenu siblings would arrive at Catledge Hall in time for the costume party, come hell or high water. Anticipating their arrival only added to Cassandra's list of woes.

After two days of learning piquet and whist, watching other women sew or needlepoint, hearing Mozart slaughtered on the pianoforte, and listening to some of the most malicious gossip she'd ever heard, Cassandra's nerves were jangled. At one point, when the temperature outdoors had fallen to an unseasonal low, and a blustery north wind rattled the French doors of the drawing room, a group of tittering women gathered around the marble fireplace.

"Come join us, dear," one of the ladies implored, plucking at Cassandra's sleeve. "We are going to play a game."

"What sort of game?" Cassandra asked skeptically. Looking around her, she saw the other ladies scrambling for seats. Scorning the comfort of an overstuffed wing back, she melted onto a low hassock. The collective look of mischief on the faces surrounding her did not bode well. "What sort of game is this?" she repeated a trifle too loudly.

"You shall see!" trilled the instigator of this folly. "Ladies, pull up your chairs," she instructed, moving about the room. "Oh, shove that sofa over here, dear!" She herded them into a semicircle, then took center stage and clapped her hands. "Is everybody ready?"

Heads nodded, coiffures bobbed, silence fell. All eyes were glued to the woman on the marble hearth.

Out of nowhere, one of the women on the sofa cried, "Ha!"

"Ha-ha," rejoined another woman on the sofa.

"Ha-ha-ha!" trilled the woman at the fireplace.

"Ha-ha-ha-ha!" erupted the next woman in turn, and suddenly a riotous din of unladylike guffaws went up in the drawing room. As the game progressed, the laughter grew more uncontrollable, more raucous, more ear-splitting. Some women clutched their sides and doubled over; some threw back their head and howled while tears rolled down their cheeks. One of them finally wheezed, "Ha-ha-ha-ha-ha-ha!" between painful gasps for air; she barely managed to point her finger at Cassandra before she collapsed in laughter.

At which point, silence descended. And it was a horrible deafening silence that rolled across the tear-stained faces of the startled mob like a biscuit-maker's pin.

For an interminable moment, no one spoke.

Then, finally: "Well!" This from the woman at the fireplace.

"Well, well," replied Cassandra.

And so, despite having achieved the spirit—if not quite the letter—of that peculiar parlor game, Cassandra had to admit that her introduction to the Quality, or at least to the dandizettes with whom she'd been cooped up the last two days, was not an unqualified success. The memory forced her deeper beneath the surface of her now-tepid bathwater.

But she could not complain that Alistair had been a neglectful host—no, she would never say that. After all, she understood his need to entertain his Corinthian pals, and that meant showing them a jolly good time this last weekend of hunting season. Cassandra simply wished that she could spend more time alone with Alistair. If she could, perhaps that niggling insecurity of hers, that odd sensation that she did not fit in, would go away.

But she knew it wouldn't.

Because she *didn't* fit in.

Cassandra was even beginning to fear that Alistair was disenchanted with her because he realized, upon reflec-

tion, that she was a chit and he an aristocrat, and never the two should meet. Had she made some horrible faux pas among his snooty friends, a blunder that she wasn't even aware of? Something other than her celebrated failure at ha-ha? Had she truly embarrassed him?

She did not know. Rising from her bath, Cassandra had no idea what Alistair felt or wanted. She wrapped a luxurious linen towel around her body and shivered. All she knew was that she loved him.

Chapter Eleven

In another part of Catledge Hall, a beleaguered valet backed out of Alistair's dressing room. "Damme, I can dress myself," muttered Alistair, fastening a wide Egyptian collar at the back of his neck.

"Thank God you're wearing the collar," said the Earl of Hedgeworth, a huge animal mask in his lap. "You don't look nearly so naked with it covering half your chest."

"But that short skirt of his should catch the ladies' eyes," the grinning Italian said, standing back to ogle Alistair's costume. "Very authentic," he said approvingly.

Alistair shook his head and tightened the knot of linen at his waist. Snatching up a sheaf of papers from his dressing table, he waved them in the air. "Enough about my costume. What do you make of these reports, eh?"

Signor Belzoni crouched in order to see himself in the mirror atop Alistair's dresser. After straightening his turban, he stretched to full height and replied, "The Bow Street runners did their job, did they not?"

"Not without my constant supervision," Alistair grumbled. "I fear I have neglected my guests, especially Cassan-

dra. But this place has been like a headquarters of war, what with runners going in and out at all times of the night and day. I ordered that they bring me constant updates, however. I am surprised my guests have not noticed."

"Your guests have been entertaining themselves with food, drink, horses, and cards," said the earl. "Most of them have been foxed for the last forty-eight hours. I do not think you need worry about a couple of Bow Street brutes oversetting them."

"Well, at least Suzette and Pierre were located," said Alistair, sighing with relief. "Imagine my shock when I arrived, only to find out they were not here."

"Lucky you had made arrangements for the runners to follow you here," pointed out Belzoni. "You were quite right to hire them to arrest the Duvals and return them to London."

"I did not know the runners would have to double back and search for the filthy Frogs," said Alistair. "Found them hiding out near Northampton, they did. And they were living it up quite nicely too. From all appearances, the two were celebrating."

"I think I know why," spat out the earl bitterly. "Before they left London, they sold their stolen cache of antiquities and cleaned out their lodgings. They must have got a pretty penny for their loot. A small fortune with which to return to the Continent."

Alistair let out a bitter chuckle. "Yes, after that I suppose Suzette and Pierre were no longer interested in attending a quaint country house party complete with parlor games and all-night whist sessions. But, Mlle. Duval—Duvallier, rather—would not miss my costume ball for the world! I was told she and her brother arrived several hours ago."

"Suzette Duvallier," mused Signor Belzoni, tapping his forefinger against his bottom lip. "Took quite a bit of research to come up with that name. If I had not seen her brother at close range at Lord Hedgeworth's party, I might

never have made the connection. It was nothing but a piece of luck that I sketched their father Jean Duvallier at Kurneh.''

Alistair rolled up the sheaf of papers and tucked them in a drawer. "So it was Monsieur Duvallier who interrupted your dig in the valley," he said, "and protested your removing that mummy. The one you unwrapped in Neville's drawing room.''

Belzoni nodded. "He must have recognized it. He must have feared that I would find the shako plate and locket which he had hidden in the mummy's wrappings.''

"But *why* did he hide them there?" Alistair asked not for the first time. "And when?" He slammed a fist into his open palm. So much of the mystery surrounding the Duvalliers was yet unsolved. He knew Suzette's real name, and that her papa met Giovanni Belzoni in Egypt in 1817. He also knew that she and Pierre had stolen Neville's mummy. But he had yet to locate and recover the purloined corpse. And he had yet to figure out why they had committed such a dastardly crime.

Alistair also knew that Pierre had broken into Cassandra's apartment, drugged her, then ransacked the apartment. Only Audrey's timely intervention prevented Pierre from finding Cleo. It stood to reason that Suzette and Pierre had been searching for Cleo all along. Suzette's eagerness to see Alistair reconciled with Neville, and involved in the investigation of the missing mummy, could be viewed only as Machiavellian.

Pierre had stolen Lord Tifton's antiquities, attacked Alistair at Russell's Emporium, and threatened Cassandra. He'd thrown that rock through Alistair's carriage window to deter the viscount from continuing his investigation, or perhaps to goad him further so that Alistair would lead the Duvals to Cassandra's mummy. But as Alistair sat on the edge of his bed and wound the long leather laces of his sandals round his calves, he felt an overwhelming sense of disquiet. There were still so many unanswered questions in this puzzle.

He had to admit Signor Belzoni's assistance had been invaluable. Once Belzoni had made a thorough search of his sketchbooks, he realized why Pierre Duval's face seemed so familiar. Belzoni, who drew constantly and possessed a talent for caricature, had several charcoal renderings of the man who had joined his expedition at Kurneh. Pierre was the spitting image of Jean Duvallier, the madman who'd reacted so strangely to the emptying of the tombs.

Belzoni remembered Jean Duvallier well. He drank too much, roared insults at the natives, and cursed the day Napoleon Bonaparte had been born. He was a malignant presence, and Belzoni's workforce dwindled as disgruntled men returned to the city to seek other employment. Then, when Belzoni literally fell into a hidden vault full of coffins, mummies, and artifacts, Jean went crazy. After throwing himself across a coffin and refusing to leave, or to allow anything in the vault to be removed, Jean was physically restrained. Eventually, he was forcibly transported to Alexandria, given a small amount of money, and deposited in front of the French embassy. Belzoni thought he had washed his hands of Jean Duvallier.

Only later did Belzoni discovered that many of his journals and personal letters had been stolen. Duvallier had stolen much of the written correspondence between Belzoni and Neville, Lord Hedgeworth, letters in which the earl spoke of the pair of royal mummies he and Sir Anthony Russell had recovered near Thebes in 1810. Those letters undoubtedly told the crazed Frenchman where the pharaoh mummy and its mate would one day be found.

Alistair rose to his feet beneath a boulder of doubt. Within the hour Suzette and Pierre Duval would appear at the costume party, and be apprehended by the Bow Street runners.

But still he was worried. Suzette and Pierre had taken great risk to steal Neville's mummy, and it was evident they wanted Cassandra's as well. Had they known the mummy

was hidden behind a screen in Cassandra's bedchamber, they would have stolen it already. Until the viscount understood why the Duvalliers wanted those two particular mummies—out of all the mummies coming out of Egypt—he would never rest. Cassandra's safety might still be jeopardized.

"Egads, I have hardly seen Cassandra these past two days," the viscount blurted out, interrupting a conversation between the earl and Belzoni. Alistair noticed the two men exchange glances as he snapped a thick golden cuff around his biceps, and clenched his fist, grimacing at the tightness of the metal band around his muscle.

"You shall see her tonight," answered Belzoni, winking at the Earl of Hedgeworth.

"Shall we descend to the party, gentlemen?" croaked Neville, wheeling himself toward the door.

At the top of the stairs Alistair lifted his brother into his arms while Signor Belzoni handled the Merlin chair and the huge hyena mask that the earl planned to wear. At the bottom of the stairs, Alistair replaced his brother in the cane-seated contraption, hefted the animal mask onto his shoulders, and adjusted it until the earl's good eye was behind an open slit.

As he rolled the chair into the ballroom, Alistair's hands loosened on the handles. "Bloody hell," he heard his brother mutter, and he silently echoed that sentiment. The glittering ballroom was teeming with people dressed in authentic Egyptian costume, many of them almost nude, dancing and swaying. The muted strains from the orchestra at the far end of the hall seemed paradoxically chaste compared to the gyrations that accompanied it. Champagne flowed freely, and women in transparent muslin tunics or sheaths held ineffectual masks to their faces as they danced lewdly, first with one partner, then another.

For Alistair Gordon to find himself shocked by a display of decadence was unprecedented. But for a breathtaking moment he wondered if staging an Egyptian *bal masqué*—

one that naturally invited near nudity—had been wise, particularly in light of his intentions toward Cassandra.

Cassandra! Alistair scanned the crowd, searching for her. He wondered if she was totally shocked, repulsed, or angered by the tone of the party. Fervently, he hoped her love of Egyptology would override her staunch morality. Having held Cassandra in his arms and felt the passion that radiated from within her, he knew her as an earthy, spirited woman. But the tragedies she had witnessed as a young girl, along with years of living in a stifling funeral bazaar, had instilled in her a fear of adventure and risk-taking. He knew that attending a decadent costume ball was unlike Cassandra, and he was gratified that she trusted him enough to accept his invitation. Knowing that she'd stepped outside the safe, familiar boundaries of her world engendered in Alistair a feeling of protectiveness, intimacy.

He loved her, and it mattered not a whit to him that she was a tradeswoman, and he a scapegrace viscount. If she could transform herself into a lady (something he had no doubt that she could do), then surely he could convert from rakehell buck to dutiful husband. Indeed, he thought with some amusement, his ardor for his French mistress had fizzled at an alarming rate after Cassandra appeared in his life. His Corinthian chums had already expressed astonishment at his unusual lack of ribaldry.

And though he'd been preoccupied the past two days with his Bow Street runners, and busy conferring with Neville and Belzoni regarding the unfolding mystery of Suzette's identity, always, at the back of his mind, had lurked Cassandra's image. Never had he been unaware or indifferent to her presence at Catledge Hall. Just knowing that she was nearby pleased him.

Neville's voice, gruff and muffled behind his mask, jolted Alistair from his thoughts. "You had better see to it that there is plenty of food, Ali. Food to soak up all the champagne that is being guzzled. Damme, the night is young, and this blasted crush already looks like a Roman orgy."

"Egyptian," Alistair corrected him wryly. "And I shall instruct the staff to lay out more cold meats and cheese. Right away." He pushed his brother's chair to the edge of the room, motioned for a footman to bring the man champagne, then vanished in the crowd.

Though his party appeared a grand success, Viscount Catledge looked forward to the moment it was over. More than anything, he wanted to be alone with Cassandra.

An hour later Cassandra stood in the center of her bedchamber, studying her reflection in a cheval glass. The sight of so much bared flesh produced a frightful tremor of uncertainty, a shiver that prickled the back of her neck. Her toes curled in her gold-strapped sandals, and she wondered if Alistair would be as shocked as she was by her sudden transformation from a bluestocking in widow's weeds to a scantily clad Egyptian priestess. Straightening the gold headband that held her thick, braided tresses close to her ears, Cassandra twisted her lips in agitation.

At least, she thought with chagrined amusement, her own gown covered her breasts. The earliest Egyptian gowns, predominant until the eighteenth dynasty, were worn cinched below the bosom, leaving little to a male admirer's imagination. The mere thought of exposing her naked breasts to Alistair's twinkling, obsidian gaze drew warmth to Cassandra's cheeks.

Had she not been so frantic to assemble her wardrobe and complete her costume, Cassandra might have had second thoughts about wearing such a flimsy outfit at a gathering of strangers. Calm reflection might have resulted in her choosing a more circumspect attire, a gown that reflected a lifetime of quiet reserve, an attitude of insularity, serenity. But it was too late to change her costume now. Audrey and Madame Racine had worked feverishly to construct her Egyptian gown, copying many aspects of

Cleo's appearance, but relying more heavily on Cassandra's quick sketches.

Turning from side to side, Cassandra ran her hands down the length of her torso, limning the firm contours of her body, the curvature of her hips, and the indentation of her narrow waist, all of which the narrow ankle-length column did little to conceal. Knotted on her left shoulder, the white linen gown fell across her bosom at a diagonal, leaving her right arm completely bared. Several gold cuffs adorned Cassandra's wrists, accentuating her deep olive coloring and the tautness of her upper arms.

Atop her heart lay her prized scarab pendant. Fingering the ancient ornament, Cassandra felt the warmth from the oils of her own skin emanating from it, and she prayed silently that it would indeed protect her vulnerable heart.

She drew a deep breath, then squared her shoulders and descended regally to the grand Palladian Hall of Lord Catledge's manor house.

Gliding into the ballroom, Cassandra was instantly awestruck. She pulled up short, and gasped. Before her loomed a cavernous rectangular-shaped hall filled with people pulsating with excitement, intoxication, and bacchanalian joviality. Throngs of revelers circulated, stirring the air like anxious bees, some dancing, some mingling, some leering drunkenly at the spectacle of men in short Egyptian kilts, and women in clinging sheaths.

Dazzled by the glitter of bejeweled women, many more scantily clad than she, and the huge chandeliers that glowed beneath the carved coved ceiling of the hall, Cassandra gratefully accepted the flute of champagne placed in her hand. Only after she lifted the glass to her lips did she notice that the servant who handed it to her was barechested and naked except for a white loincloth and a woolly wig of black curls. She gulped, and the champagne seared her throat, then she sputtered delicately as she averted her eyes from the servant's limbs and looked about the room.

Cassandra's second sip of wine trickled down her throat,

spreading a more pleasant warmth throughout her body.
Her nose twitched above pear-scented bubbles, and she
caught the frankly admiring gazes of several men, most of
them dressed in tunics and robes, some wearing elaborate
headdresses and jewelry, a few disguised as animal deities,
their faces half obscured by painted likenesses of falcons,
dogs, and crocodiles.

A man whose face was hidden by a monkey mask met
her stare and deliberately perused her figure, up and down,
his beady eyes black and feral, his tongue flicking thirstily
at his twitching lips. Against an initial jolt of indignation,
Cassandra sipped her champagne and reminded herself
that her costume did, after all, invite attention, and that
she had no cause to be surprised if men were studying her
intensely. Turning from the monkey-man's lascivious stare,
she searched the hall vainly for a glimpse of Alistair, eager
now for him to see her costume.

At the far end of the room, two circular staircases
ascended to a segmental apse in which a small orchestra
was assembled. Conversation buzzed, laughter trilled, and
the occasional rebuke at some intended familiarity erupted
to muffle the incongruous strains of Haydn. The upper tier
of the hall formed a gallery screened by marble columns.
A couple dressed in flowing tunics played hide-and-seek
around the massive columns, then slipped inside a darkened alcove, only to emerge minutes later with naughty
grins on their painted faces.

Cassandra felt a secret smile play across her lips, and
she moved farther into the crowd, joining the rhythm of
the party, smiling at men whose names she didn't know,
nodding at the women she'd been keeping company with
during the past few days while Alistair followed the hounds.

She heard her name called and she pivoted, searching
out the familiar voice. The sight of a jackal's head gave
her a start, but she laughed gaily as it moved toward her,
waist-level, its red tongue glistening, pointed ears erect.
The long black-nosed snout wended its way through a clot

of people, sniffing the air like a hungry scavenger. Lord Hedgeworth stopped his Merlin chair beside Cassandra, his one good eye blinking fiercely behind the lifelike mask.

Taking his hand in hers, Cassandra bent and planted a kiss on the end of Neville's cold jackal-nose. When she straightened, the lower half of the earl's face was split in a grin so wide, she half expected him to throw back his head and howl.

"Egads, I hate to remove my mask if the sight of it engenders such felicity on your part," Neville said, hefting the animal's likeness from his shoulders. "Truly, you are a fearless and devoted Egyptologist if you dare to kiss the jackal's nose."

"The mask is wonderful!" Cassandra cried. "But I would rather see your face, my lord," she added, and was touched by the earl's flustered reaction to that simple sentiment. She gently helped him lower the huge jackal mask to his lap.

Flushed, the earl raked his fingers through his mussed hair and gasped from his exertions. "Faugh! But I could not see very well behind that thing," he croaked. "And it was god-awful hot beneath that stinking carcass too!"

Cassandra smiled. "Pray tell me, Lord Hedgeworth, why did you choose the costume of Anubis, guardian of the dead and opener of the ways?"

Lifting one shoulder, the earl merely replied, "'Tis appropriate, my dear child. Anubis is often depicted as a dog who guards the king. I might appear to you as helpless and decrepit, but I have got some bite left in me yet. Mind you, I'll sink my teeth into anyone who dares to threaten Alistair."

"Such loyalty is commendable," said Cassandra.

"Even if it is lately arrived?" asked Neville, tilting his head so that his good eye scrutinized Cassandra's costume from head to toe. He nodded appreciatively, with no hint of the salacious look she had spied on the monkey-man's face. "I congratulate you on your costume as well. You are

every bit as lovely as Queen Nefertiti, or Cleopatra. Ah, child, you are the image of your mother," the earl said, his voice fading wistfully.

Cassandra murmured her thanks, but the mention of Cleopatra's name reminded her of more serious matters. "Have you seen your brother?" she asked the earl pointedly.

The earl's gaze darted over her shoulder. "He is coming, child. I believe he has been looking for you too."

A strong hand clasped Cassandra's upper arm. Turning, she looked up and gasped. Gazing down at her was the sculpted face of an Egyptian pharaoh.

Cassandra inched backward until she felt her heel strike Neville's Merlin chair. A startled "Oh!" escaped her throat, but modesty did not prevent her from staring at Viscount Catledge. He looked like an ancient granite statue come to life. Nothing but a white linen *shend'ot,* a sort of Egyptian kilt, interrupted the vertical slab of muscle, gleaming flesh, and hard body that loomed over her. Beneath the gold-embroidered hem of that skirt emerged bronze and sinewy legs. Above the knotted waist was a flat, striated belly.

A wide gold collar inset with faience tiles of orange and blue encircled the base of Alistair's throat and covered most of his upper chest. Despite the wide border of the ornament, a vast stretch of skin remained to dazzle Cassandra's eyes. She took another step backward, and almost fell into Neville's lap. "Easy there," she heard the older man say gently. Her knees jammed. Her pulse pounded. She stood ramrod straight and defiantly looked into Alistair's eyes.

But not for long.

In the naked gap between the lower curve of Alistair's collar and the knotted waist of his kilt ran a trail of fine black hair. Cassandra's eyes followed that trail to the top

of his pleated skirt. Then, embarrassed by her thoughts, she tore her eyes off Alistair's kilt.

She sipped champagne. Twin brushfires burned her cheeks, and her stomach ignited. Never had Cassandra been so close to a nearly naked man. When Alistair reached for her free hand and bowed deeply, Cassandra's chest tightened miserably. When she felt his soft lips on the back of her hand, she approached the point of panic. Inhaling deeply, she willed herself to show a modicum of composure. The viscount straightened, and his gleaming eyes mocked her flustered silence. Cassandra merely shook her head, fearful that if she spoke, her voice would betray her addled state.

Lord Catledge frowned. "Is something wrong?"

In Cassandra's wildest imagination she hadn't thought the viscount's body would be so beautiful, so perfectly proportioned, so statuesque. She hadn't anticipated his slender hips and well-shaped knees. The effect his unveiled form was having on her was a shock, not an entirely unpleasant one, but one she would rather not have shared with a ballroom full of strangers. She made a flippant, sweeping gesture with her hand, and finally stammered, "I am afraid I am unaccustomed to so much . . ."

"So much bare flesh?" finished the viscount. Glancing around with raised eyebrows, he said, "I suppose my former rakehell ways are so widely known that my guests assumed this would be a decadent affair. But I hope that you are not offended by the brevity of the Egyptian costumes. After all, you are an avid student of that period of history, are you not?"

His warm smile drew her out. She found her voice and managed a chuckle. "Yes, my lord. I am even shocked at my own costume. How is that for prudishness?"

"As I have said before, you should get about more frequently," Alistair replied, his eyes roving the length of her scantily clad form.

The earl's gravelly voice interrupted. "Then there is nothing for it but to take her out more often, brother."

"In the future I shall do so," the viscount drawled. He shifted his weight, slid one sandaled foot to the side, and propped a fist on one jutting hip. The effect was oddly feral, like the tightly wound pose of a languorous panther.

"Not in that scandalous attire," Cassandra lightly chided.

The viscount grinned. "Your costume is as revealing as mine, miss."

Cassandra was just about to point out that except for the baring of one arm and shoulder, her costume was no less revealing than the current low-necked fashions of the day. At least she had not dampened her linen sheath like some young women did their thin muslin gowns. Smiling, Cassandra held out her arms, inviting Alistair's flagrant scrutiny. Her entire body warmed beneath his admiring gaze.

But before she said another word, she heard the chirring sound of Suzette Duval's voice.

"Oh, Ali! There you are!" Halfway across the room, a hand appeared above someone's head and waved floppily. Suzette's white teeth sparkled as she came up on her tiptoes to show her face above the crowd.

Rankled, Cassandra watched the Duval siblings wend their way around a knot of people. Suzette was heading straight for Alistair with her arms open wide, while Pierre followed, his eyes pinned on Cassandra. The earl's wheelchair rolled back to widen the circle.

"Brace yourself, both of you," muttered Neville uncharitably, and Alistair answered with a muffled snort.

Suzette swooped down. *"Bonsoir, bijou!* I am so happy to see you!" For Lord Catledge, she was all smiles and airy kisses and knowing looks. For Cassandra and the Earl of Hedgeworth, the Frenchwoman had the coldest of expressions, the most mincing of civilities. "Hello," she sniffed to them.

Before Cassandra could stop him, Pierre leaned forward and kissed the air on either side of her face. Taking no note of her wooden response, he then eloquently praised her costume. Suzette immediately asked Alistair whether he liked *her* costume, and she turned on the balls of her feet to model it for him.

Dressed in a white sheath, her ensemble was crowned by a thick black shoulder-length wig with bangs cut straight across her forehead. Her eyes were lined thickly in black paint, and the creases of her lids were contoured with kohl. Turquoise crescents arched beneath her painted brows. Suzette Duval was stunning, and she knew it.

"Very nice," the viscount murmured, casting a shrug at Cassandra.

"Who are you supposed to be?" barked Neville.

"I am Isis, the great mother-goddess," replied Suzette regally.

"And you?" Cassandra asked Pierre, whose costume was a strange blend of Egyptian and English couture. Though he wore the tall White Crown of Upper Egypt, and a white linen tunic, his slender legs were encased in tan buckskin, and a cravat was tied around his neck. As he folded a golden crook and flail across his chest, Monsieur Duval intoned, "I am Osiris, of course."

The earl lifted his mask and waggled the gaping jackal's head in the air. "You would have done better to come as one of the animal deities, like me. Only a man with a perfect physique would dare to wear the costume of an ancient Egyptian." He lowered the mask to his lap and jerked his thumb at Alistair. "See my young brother, here? He can wear the costume without reservation. But the rest of us should cover our bodies as best we can—no sense in scaring the ladies, if you know what I mean."

Flushed, Pierre responded staunchly, "No, I am sure I don't know what you mean, my lord. I prefer not to catch my death of cold, that is all. Hence the tunic, and not the kilt."

A deep male voice announced Giovanni Belzoni's presence. "A reasonable explanation for wearing breeches too, monsieur. I don't doubt that you would be uncomfortable in a costume as minimal as Alistair's." The hirsute Italian, dressed *á la turque*, towered over the huddle as he stood next to Pierre. Peering down, he touched the Frenchman's tunic sleeve, rubbing a sample of the linen between his thumb and forefinger. "Ah, just as I suspected," he exhaled triumphantly. "A fine nainsook, much *too* fine for a mummy's shroud."

Pierre frowned, and sidled sideways toward Cassandra.

"The party is wonderful," Suzette said to no one in particular, her voice brittle. "It will be an immense success, I am sure. I would not have missed it, no matter what. Oh, if only Pierre and I could have arrived before tonight."

"What kept you?" growled the earl.

"Pierre was sick," she answered elliptically.

The earl made a noise that sounded like "Harrumph."

Signor Belzoni slapped Pierre soundly on his back. "Eat something tainted, young man?" he bellowed.

Pierre's head snapped forward, then up. He appeared to be knocked breathless. "Yes—yes, that was it," he said, gulping. He looked at Belzoni with rounded eyes. "We were on the road when I became, er, indisposed. I thought it best we stop and rest a few days. No sense in bringing my illness to someone's house, if you know what I mean. And my sister—Suzette will tell you!—she did not think it advisable that we continue our journey in my weakened condition."

"You don't look sick to me," injected the earl.

"Well, he *was* sick," countered Suzette waspishly. "I made him stop. I made him take to bed and rest. That is why we are late."

Alistair, Signor Belzoni, and the Earl of Hedgeworth exchanged glances. Suzette and Pierre shot each other sidelong looks of mutual distrust. Shifting eyes and wary expressions passed from person to person like a baton in

a relay race. Cassandra found herself mesmerized, and continued to sip her rapidly vanishing champagne while she watched, and listened.

"Where precisely did you lay up?" Alistair questioned Suzette and Pierre.

Suzette's color rose. "We stayed at an inn outside of Northampton, if you must know. I believe the name of it was the Mouse and Mutton. Wasn't that it, Pierre?"

"Not the sort of name one would forget," observed Signor Belzoni, stroking his long black beard.

Pierre snapped, "The Mouse and Mutton it was, yes! I was sick, but I remember the name!"

"And while you were laid up, sir, did you have need for a physician, or an apothecary?" asked Lord Catledge.

"*Moi?*" cried Pierre, clearly incredulous. "Me? Me, call a doctor? Why, that would be preposterous—"

Suzette laid a hand on her brother's arm. "Pierre, that is quite enough. You owe no explanation for your actions."

"I wonder that you did not summon a physician," said Signor Belzoni. "I would have if I were that sick."

"I saw no need to summon assistance," rejoined Pierre in a clipped voice. His concave chest was heaving now with puffs of exasperation, and his pallid countenance was marked with livid patches high on his cheekbones.

"Perhaps because of your own medical training?" suggested Alistair.

Suzette's dark eyes flashed. Pierre's widened in alarm.

"Ah, yes, I forgot that you have had medical training!" cried Signor Belzoni. "Tell me about it, monsieur. I am most fascinated by the latest advances in that particular science. Did you study in Paris?"

Pierre's thin lips, rimmed in bluish-white, barely moved as he hissed at his inquisitors. "I do not care to discuss my past, gentlemen."

Suzette tugged at the sleeve of her brother's tunic and said, "I want to dance. This conversation is beginning to bore me."

"Then perhaps you will find *this* interesting," said Alistair. The threatening tone of his voice arrested Suzette's movement. "I should like to know where you and your brother have hidden the Earl of Hedgeworth's prized mummy."

Suzette froze in her tracks, her hand on Pierre's arm. Her eyes met his, and then she slowly turned from her brother. Her jaded gaze was aimed at Alistair. "How dare you," she whispered.

The viscount gave her a wicked grin. "There is no use in denying your guilt, Suzette. I have spent the last week gathering and analyzing evidence that I believe could hang you and your brother for your dastardly crimes. Not that I would relish such a spectacle, mind you. I merely want Neville's mummy returned. And I know you have it."

"Now, see here!" cried Pierre, but Signor Belzoni clamped a huge paw on the Frenchman's bony shoulder, instantly silencing him.

"Just tell me where the mummy is," said Alistair softly.

Suzette's face hardened. "I do not know what you are talking about, *bijou!* You are mistaken, misled." Suddenly, her glistening eyes turned on Cassandra. "It is that woman! She has seduced you, hasn't she! Bewitched you, even. Yes, yes! That is it. I knew she was a witch the first day I laid eyes on her! What sort of woman, other than a witch, would keep a nasty *marmot* for a pet!"

Taken aback by the vitriol in Suzette's voice, Cassandra quickly riposted, "Mademoiselle, how did you know of my pet monkey?"

At that, Lord Catledge chuckled. "Yes, Suzette, how would you have known of Tia, unless Pierre told you of the animal he encountered when he broke into Cassandra's apartment?"

"I did no such thing!" Pierre blurted out.

Cassandra looked at the tall, thin Frenchman and tried to imagine him as the sinister mummy in Russell's Emporium.

"I am innocent," he protested sullenly, and shrugged his scrawny shoulders.

That shrug! That nervous affectation that seemed so incongruent with the hulking monster who approached her in the darkened shop—now Cassandra recognized it. She remembered, too, that the mummy had been oddly light on his feet, and altogether too supple for his massive shape. She supposed that yards and yards of linen could increase the slender man's bulk. But it would take a tremendous amount of linen swaddling to disguise that thin frame, and someone to help him into the costume, and out of it. Someone like his sister.

Cassandra pointed her finger at Pierre. "You. You threw the rock through Alistair's carriage window. You broke into my apartment, and you attacked Alistair in my shop."

"Ridiculous girl! You have drunk too much champagne," said Pierre.

With lightning swiftness Signor Belzoni's hand shot to the Frenchman's cravat, unknotted it, and snatched the length of linen off the man's chickenlike throat. Beneath the scooped neckline of his tunic, several layers of gauze were clearly visible. Too shocked to fend off the unexpected intrusion, Pierre stood slack-jawed as Belzoni hooked his finger beneath the edge of the tunic and lifted it, exposing the bandaged collarbone.

Cassandra could not help but giggle. "So, Audrey really did let you have it, didn't she?"

"Oh! Pierre, you stupid oaf!" A look of fury darkened Suzette's expression. Grabbing her brother's flail, she lashed at him, striking him about the head several times before Signor Belzoni could relieve her of her weapon. "You stupid, stupid oaf!" she cried, stomping her sandals on the tops of Belzoni's feet.

Two burly men wearing red waistcoats appeared. "What took you so long?" Signor Belzoni greeted them. He handed the struggling Suzette over, then dusted the palms of his hand and said, "Good riddance."

"Cuff them, and take them back to London," Alistair instructed the Bow Street runners, his voice grim. "A couple of days in Newgate, and I am sure they will feel like telling us where Neville's mummy has been stored."

"Aye," said Neville. "And perhaps they will tell us where they've hidden Lord Tifton's loot as well."

"They have quite a bit of explaining to do, if you ask me," said Cassandra, catching Signor Belzoni's twinkling eye.

"Everything will be crystal clear soon enough," the grinning Italian assured her.

Suzette and Pierre were handcuffed without further ado, and unceremoniously escorted toward the door of the ballroom. As the couple and their captors passed through the crowd, several revelers raised their brows and pointed, but most of the Egyptian-clad partygoers were too foxed by that time to give much consideration to the sight. Some of them who did take notice seemed to think the strange procession was some sort of decadent parlor game. A corpulent man in flowing robes fell in behind one of the Bow Street runners, clasped the man about his waist, and urged his friends to form a dancing column across the ballroom.

The runner turned and shoved the drunken man to the floor amid howls of laughter.

"You will never find that mummy!" Suzette screeched over her shoulder, her angry face swallowed by a sea of cobra headdresses, plaited wigs, and tall Egyptian crowns. The last Cassandra saw of her was her upraised fist, clenched in defiance.

"Not a nice lady, that Mlle. Duval," remarked Signor Belzoni.

"She ain't a lady," said the earl. "And her name is not Duval."

Cassandra started to ask the earl what he meant by that intriguing statement. Before she could, Alistair pulled her to his side. Signor Belzoni and the Earl of Hedgeworth discreetly slipped away.

"Has this week been horrid for you, my dear?" Alistair asked, his voice low and husky. He framed her face between his hands, lifting her chin with his thumbs. Staring intently into her eyes, he said, "I was preoccupied. God, how I wanted to be with you. Only you, Cassandra. But I had to piece everything together first. I had to be sure that Suzette and her foolish brother could never threaten us again."

Cassandra allowed her head to tilt, cradled in the strong embrace of Alistair's hands. She felt his breath on her lips and smelled his masculine, woodsy aroma. There were still so many unanswered questions, but her senses were reeling, her mind muddled by emotion *and* champagne. "How did you do it, Ali?" she asked at length. "How did you ascertain Suzette's guilt?"

He smiled, but his eyes held a mysterious look. "In time, my love, I will explain everything to you." He dipped his head and lowered his voice to a sultry drawl. "Tell me, have you been terribly bored these past two days?"

"I am not bored now, my lord." The first brush of Alistair's lips against Cassandra's sent a tremor of anticipation through her body. His taste, a mixture of sweetness and salt and champagne, was intoxicating. Languidly, she drifted into his arms and sighed.

"Would you consider marrying me?" the viscount whispered against her neck. Cassandra ran her palms along his bare skin. A *Long Egyptian Night* was fully under way now, the ballroom undulating with waves of drunken people, the hot, sticky air reverberating with laughter and music. Alistair's skin glowed with a fine sheen of perspiration, as if it had been saturated with a musk-scented oil, and the muscles of his upper arms flexed, straining against thick cuffs of gleaming gold. His body was hot and hard beneath Cassandra's touch.

"Oh, Ali," she murmured, succumbing to his passionate kiss. Her woozy mind hardly registered the fact that he had proposed marriage to her. "I do love you," she breathed earnestly.

"And I love you," Alistair whispered, covering his mouth with hers.

An hour later, Cassandra waited in her bedchamber, a woolen robe wrapped around her instead of Alistair's arms, a cup of coffee at her lips instead of champagne. Hunkered in an oversized chintz armchair, she stared at a point on the wall opposite, her mind methodically analyzing Alistair's proposal of marriage, and her own enigmatic response to it.

Her murmured yes had seemed so natural. Standing in the crowded ballroom amid a sea of half-dressed tipplers whose joie de vivre had been infectious, Cassandra's response had been automatic, ineluctable. Her heart had leapt at the fulfillment of a fantasy she never thought would materialize. Within the protection of Alistair's arms, she had never been happier.

And yet now, alone and stone-cold sober, Cassandra wondered whether she truly wanted to live the dream her heart had wished for. Did she really want to say good-bye to Miss Cassandra Russell, proprietress of a funerary boutique? Did she want to be Viscountess Catledge, nobby wife of the fashionable Gordon scapegrace? Frowning at the dregs in the bottom of her cup, she pondered her dilemma.

Downstairs, Alistair was tending to his guests, dispatching the more inebriated of them to bed, and bidding farewell to those few who lived near enough to be driven home. Afterward, Cassandra knew, he would come to her, whisper those tantalizing words, *I want to marry you*, again, befuddle her with kisses. She had to be ready.

She would not be taken off her guard the way she was earlier in the evening. This time Cassandra would have her wits about her.

Her head had cleared since she ate a small plate of food and washed it down with bitter coffee. She was lucid now.

She knew what she must do and say; she steeled herself for the confrontation.

Setting her coffee cup and saucer aside, Cassandra hugged her knees to her chest. Silently, she rehearsed the words she planned to say to Alistair, the questions she would ask him. She was going to tell him the truth: that she loved him dearly, but the last two days at Catledge Hall had raised questions in her mind concerning their compatibility. She wasn't sure she was cut out to be the wife of an aristocrat. She thought the tonnish ladies she'd been rubbing shoulders with in the drawing room were vapid addle-pates. She was fairly certain they regarded her as an eccentric bluestocking. Did she want to live among people whose conversation bored her, whose estimation of her was equally unflattering?

Fidgeting, tucking her legs beneath her, Cassandra envied those addle-pated women their ability *not* to overanalyze their own lives. She would have liked nothing more than to toss her blasted caution to the wind, rejoice at the unexpected luck of having been proposed to by a viscount, and fall into Alistair's arms like a besotted maiden. But for her that was impossible. Cassandra had to speak her thoughts or be damned. She was not the type of woman to sublimate her most pressing concerns to a stroke of good fortune. Despite her uncharacteristic decision to take a chance by coming to Catledge Hall, Cassandra Russell was still the careful, straightforward woman she'd always been.

And ever since Alistair had whispered that he wanted to marry her—or, rather, ever since those words had sunk in—Cassandra had been beset with worry.

Restless, she got up to light another branch of candles. A faint scratch at her bedchamber door raised goose pimples on her skin. Cassandra crossed the room and turned the lock. Alistair, dressed in riding breeches and a linen shirt left open at the throat, slipped across the threshold like a wraith, his dark eyes twinkling. Without a word he

drew her into his arms and covered her face and neck in kisses.

The sound of scurrying footsteps and giggles startled Cassandra, and she reared back, her eyes flying to the closed door. She pressed her palms flat against the viscount's chest.

"What of your guests?" she asked him breathlessly.

"Most of my guests have drifted to their bedchambers," he said. "Or to someone else's. At any rate, I have done my duty as host, and now I intend to spend the rest of the night with you."

The viscount tightened his embrace, but Cassandra pulled away. "There is something I must discuss with you, my lord." She forced herself to meet his gaze, even though it was difficult to concentrate when he stared at her so hungrily.

Alistair's throaty chuckle contained a hint of impatience. He advanced a step, and she retreated. "Come, Cassandra. Whatever you wish to discuss can wait until morning, can it not?"

"I fear not."

"All right. Speak to me, then," said the viscount. He reached out and brushed the back of his hand along her jaw.

Alistair's touch sent ripples of pleasure through Cassandra's body, making it painfully hard for her to resist him. How she wanted to melt into his arms and let him kiss her troubled thoughts away! But she retreated still, determined to speak her peace.

Clutching her hands at her waist, she said evenly, "You asked me to consider marrying you, my lord." Her even voice belied her quivering insides.

"My name is Alistair, not *my lord*," he reminded her, advancing, grasping her wrist, slipping his hand beneath the sleeve of her robe.

The imprint of his fingers scorched her bare skin. "I cannot marry you," she blurted out.

Alistair's fingers squeezed Cassandra's arm so tightly that she winced, and in a flash he hovered over her. His jaw clenched in reproval, and his black eyes were hard and hooded. "Why not?" he rasped.

"I am afraid, my lord, that I do not . . . belong among your set."

"What the devil—" Alistair stopped himself, released Cassandra's arm, and stepped back with a sigh. Fists on his slender hips, he cast his gaze about the room as if searching for his composure. When at last he spoke, his carefully controlled voice sent shivers of apprehension up Cassandra's spine. "Has someone offended you?" he asked tightly.

"Not exactly," replied Cassandra. "Not intentionally."

"Then what has happened?"

Cassandra cringed at the commanding tone of Alistair's voice. "The other women and I . . . the ladies whom you invited . . . your friends . . ." She was trying to explain, but the viscount's thundering stare disoriented her. At last she managed to say, "I did not make friends with any of them. I had nothing in common with those ladies, my lord. I hardly think I should marry a man whose friends and peers I cannot abide."

Alistair ducked his head and studied his boots for a moment, but he did not, Cassandra observed wryly, attempt to disabuse her of her class awareness.

"You have already considered the disparity in our social positions, my lord," she said. "You must have."

"Of course I have," he said quickly. "And it does not matter to me."

"Perhaps not now," replied Cassandra. "But what will happen when the glow of our infatuation has faded to a dull patina? You will want to continue socializing with your friends, and I will be as useless and awkward as a fifth wheel. Eventually, I will resent you, and you will find me boring."

"You will never bore me."

"I fear that I have these last two days."

Ali held his hands out, palms up. "I concede that I have not been particularly attentive these past two days, but I never thought of you as the clingy, whiny type. I thought you would make do on your own while I attended to important business. Egads, you have always struck me as the most self-sufficient woman I have ever met."

"It does not follow that I enjoy being ignored," retorted Cassandra, unaware till she said those words that she already harbored a measure of resentment toward the viscount for his neglect of her. Surprised at herself, she could not stop the accusation that next flowed from her lips. "Would *you* have enjoyed being cooped up inside this place for two days with a bunch of silly women whose lives revolve around gossip, fashion, and needlepoint?"

The viscount stared at Cassandra as if she had said something odd or vulgar. "You did not care for any of the ladies you met this week?" he queried skeptically. "Well, not to worry. The ladies who attended my costume ball are not necessarily the arbiters of society. I'm afraid my soirees are usually shunned by the Almack's patronesses ... something about my scapegrace reputation and all that."

In the silence that followed that remark, he lifted an eyebrow and grinned impishly. "I may not be a paragon of virtue, but I am fashionable, Cassandra." When he saw she wasn't smiling, he cleared his throat and added sheepishly, "Well, then I shall introduce you to some other ladies when we return to London. Some less, ah, frivolous ladies."

Cassandra's sense of alienation was heightened by his flippant response. His lack of understanding irritated her. Her complaint gained momentum, gathered strength like a tropical storm. "I doubt I will like those ladies any more than I like the ones I met this week," she said through her teeth.

Alistair frowned. "I am surprised by this talk. I had thought you a fair-minded person, Cassandra, and here you have dismissed my entire circle of friends without so

much as a fare-thee-well. You do not know them well
enough to hold them in such low regard. I think your
judgment most unfair."

There was a long stretch of prickly silence before Cassandra cried, "Ha!"

Alistair's eyes widened, then narrowed. His frown deepened.

"What is the matter, dear?" she mocked him. "Have
you never played the famous parlor game called ha-ha?"
Cassandra heard the biting sarcasm in her voice, and, with
a startling flash of inspiration, realized how humiliated she
felt when every cruel, unrelenting female eye in that
blasted drawing room had turned on her. Anger, like a
red-hot arrow, shot through her. "Ha-ha!" she cried, choking back a sob. "Come on, dear, 'tis your turn! La, don't
be such a party pooper!"

She realized how woefully unprepared she'd been for a
week at Alistair's country mansion. With a crushing sense
of defeat, she realized how foolish she had been to fantasize
about being the Viscountess Catledge. She'd been silly to
think she could fit into his world, so far removed from her
own. All she wanted now was to go back to London,
immerse herself in work and black crepe, and forget this
horrid house party ever happened.

"Cassandra, what on earth are you babbling about?"

"Babbling?" she echoed, aghast. Alistair's reaction to
her now was solid proof of their incompatibility. He looked
at her as if she had escaped from Bedlam; he had no
understanding of her isolation. "What am I babbling
about?"

"Poor choice of words," he muttered, raking his fingers
through his hair. He took a step toward her, his arm outstretched.

Cassandra recoiled. "Do not touch me! Please, get out
of my room!"

A look of bewilderment appeared on Alistair's face. He
opened his mouth to speak, but no sound escaped his lips.

Waving his hand helplessly in the air, at last he sputtered, "Cassandra, please be reasonable—"

"Be reasonable?" she cut him off. "I am being reasonable! For the first time in weeks I am thinking very clearly, Alistair. And what I think is that you and I are not suited for each other, not suited at all!"

"But—"

Cassandra forestalled him by turning her back. Tears streamed down her cheeks, but Alistair wouldn't see them. Wringing her hands in front of her waist, she willed herself to sound normal, *reasonable*. When Alistair touched her shoulder, she abruptly moved away. "I would thank you to leave me now, my lord," she finally said stiffly. "Also, I will be leaving first thing in the morning. Please see to it that your carriage is made available."

"I thought we would stay through the weekend," Alistair protested. "I am going to stay, at any rate."

"Stay if you will. I am going home."

Alistair stood behind her for a moment, his frustration palpable. Sighing, he said, "I shall return to London tomorrow as well. I will ride alone though, Miss Russell. You may enjoy the privacy of my carriage without the bother of my company." When she didn't answer, he said, "Good-night," and left her.

Cassandra threw herself across her bed, and when the viscount's heavy footsteps faded, she wept until she fell asleep.

Chapter Twelve

Three days later, Alistair sat in his brother's London study, a dark scowl on his face. Staring back at him, across an uncluttered desk, was the Earl of Hedgeworth. The older man exhaled a blue ring of smoke, tapped a thick cigar on the edge of a silver tray, and wheezed, "Damme, boy, what happened?"

Alistair raked his fingers through his hair. "Hell if I know," he admitted ruefully. "I think she was angry that I did not spend enough time with her at Catledge Hall."

Neville's frown deepened. "You explained to her that you were tied up with Signor Belzoni, myself, and the investigators?"

"I never got the chance, really." Alistair squeezed his eyes shut, trying to recall the exact sequence of events that occurred after the arrest of Suzette and Pierre. He'd been so eager to see Cassandra and hold her in his arms that he wasn't sure at all whether he'd adequately explained the cause for his inattention. Wincing, he conceded, "I am afraid my remarks did little to appease her agitation."

"Umm. She tried to describe her emotions, and you

brushed aside her feelings. Pooh-poohed her fears and insecurities, did you? Couldn't wait to get her in your arms, eh?"

"How is it that you know so much about women?" Alistair countered defensively.

Neville chuckled. "I see many things out of this one eye."

Sighing, the younger brother replied, "All right. So I said some foolish things I truly regret. Can she not realize I am sorry? Can she not at least give me another chance?"

Neville lifted his shaggy eyebrows. "Will she not even answer the door?"

"Her shop is closed! I think that is quite an extreme reaction to my ill-chosen words, don't you?" Alistair pinched the bridge of his nose. His head ached, his eyes felt raw. He'd spent half the night standing in front of Russell's Emporium, pounding on the door, shouting, demanding to be allowed entrance. Cassandra had obviously decided she never wanted to see him again. Even Audrey, with whom the viscount had assiduously curried favor, refused him the courtesy of coming to the door or showing her face.

There was a knock at the study door, and Neville barked, "Enter!"

The double doors swung inward, and Neville's butler appeared on the threshold. Before the stodgy servant could utter a word, two men burst into the room from behind him. Their flushed faces were streaked with dirt, their boots caked with mud. Fear and excitement showed in their round, blinking eyes. Beneath their bedraggled coats, the faded red of their waistcoats was barely visible. Jumping to his feet, Alistair stared in amazement. What on earth had happened to make his hired Bow Street runners look so frightened?

"We lost 'em," the shorter of the men blurted out. "Lost 'em on the road, near Northampton. I think they was waitin' for a place to jump us—"

"How the devil could they have jumped *the two of you?*" Alistair demanded, his body coiled, every muscle taut with rage. He could see that his reaction intimidated the two quivering men, and he clamped his jaw shut, restraining his fury, at least until he understood precisely what had happened. "Did you not have their hands cuffed?" he asked, his voice deadly quiet.

The two men exchanged looks. The taller one crushed his hat in his hands, shifted his weight from one foot to the other, and finally stammered, "The young lady expressed a need to, er ... ah, relieve herself. We had to stop the carriage and allow her that liberty, my lord." He gulped, and elbowed his companion.

"She took a long time behind the rock, and so's I went lookin' for 'er," the other man continued. "I couldn't find 'er at first. Thought she'd disappeared, or runned off, so's I started lookin'. She musta' been hidin' behind a big tree, I 'spose. All of a suddenlike, my head feels like it's been split open. She musta' come up behind me and banged me on me head with a big tree limb! I saw stars, I did! Old Tom 'ere says I was out for nigh an 'our!"

The first man picked up the thread of the story. "I didna' hear a thing, my lord." He looked down at the floor. "While the girl was behind the rock, I took the opportunity to, ah, answer me own call of nature. By the time I had me breeches fastened and come back to the road, I seen that little vixen already on the driver's seat of the carriage. I took off runnin' and yellin' at her to stop, but she was whipping those horses to a frenzy, she was."

"Do you mean to tell me that little termagant and her brother escaped from your custody, stole your carriage, and left you on the road?" Alistair exploded. "God's blood, man! What the devil did I pay you for?"

"We just made it back to town," the shorter man said sheepishly.

"Thought you might want to know what happened," his colleague tacked on.

Neville had wheeled himself from behind his desk. "Bloody hell, Alistair. You know what this means?"

A horrible dread was creeping up the viscount's spine. He knew exactly what it meant. His fists clenched involuntarily, and it took more self-control than he possessed to speak in a barely civil tone. "Suzette and Pierre are loose," he said, his voice raw with tension. "Cassandra's shop is closed. Do you think—Oh, my God!" He bounded for the door, roughly pushing the two Bow Street runners aside.

Neville cried out, "Wait!" and his gnarled hands and stout arms became a blur of motion as he wheeled himself after Alistair.

Shouting orders to have his horse brought round to the front of the town house, Alistair was halfway down the stairs when he halted abruptly and turned. With one white-knuckled hand gripping the railing, he lifted his face and met Neville's eagle eye. "I will not allow those monsters to harm Cassandra." His voice held every promise of cold, malevolent retribution. "I will kill that devil-spawned witch and her lily-livered brother if they so much as touch a hair on Cassandra's head."

"They think she has the mummy," Neville said. He sounded helpless and frightened, and Alistair was moved by his brother's concern. "God help me, I should never have gotten you involved in this mess."

Alistair flashed his brother a bleak smile. "Had you not, I would never have met Cassandra. I owe you a great deal of thanks for that." And then he became all motion again, taking the stairs two and three at a time till he reached the landing, where he halted for just an instant, looked up, and yelled to his brother, whose ravaged face peered at him over the banister, "Tell your servants you expect company this evening, Neville, will you? I should like to bring my fiancée by for dinner, and perhaps a round or two of ha-ha in the drawing room."

"Ha-ha?" echoed Neville, bewildered. The front door of his town house slammed, and the two Bow Street runners

behind him exhaled in relief. "What the devil is he talking
about?" the earl mumbled, returning to his study. He
could only wait for his brother's return. Wait, and watch
the inexorably slow filtering of sand through his Egyptian
hour glass.

With his shoulder flush to the front door of Russell's
Emporium, Alistair shoved with all his might. Behind him,
people continued on their way down Pickett Street.
Though he expected an outraged do-gooder to accost him
any minute, or a vigilant neighbor to summon a charley,
none did. Perhaps it was the early evening chill that put
a briskness in the gait of the passersby. But Alistair still
thought it odd that people hardly gave him a glance when
he backed away from the door a few steps, then lurched
into it, ramming his shoulder against the sturdy wood for
the third time.

The door gave way. Alistair stood in the darkened shop,
mindful that his workmen had not replaced the bells over
the lintel. Pierre could easily have picked the lock and
entered noiselessly. Alistair's forced entry had not been
particularly loud either. From the upper apartment, the
breach of wood and doorframe probably sounded like a
crate of oranges tumbling off the rear of a moving cart.

Alistair crept stealthily up the staircase, feeling his way
along the wall in blackness. There was a sliver of light at
the top of the landing, beneath the door to Cassandra's
apartment. His steps quickened when he heard Cassandra's voice. He froze when an angry male voice answered
her back. The man's voice rose in anger, and Alistair recognized him as Suzette's brother.

Taking the last two steps in a single bound, Alistair
kicked open the door and rushed into the room.

The scene that met his eyes drew horror to the surface
of Alistair's skin. Cassandra sat in a chair at the round
table, her hands and ankles bound. Audrey sat next to her,

slumped over, clearly insensate. In the maid's lap the pet monkey Tia lay curled, her head tucked between her hands, her tail limp. Both Audrey and the monkey appeared to have been drugged, or knocked out.

The room, and all of Cassandra's antiquities, looked as if it had been tossed upside down. Statutes were toppled, boxes of ushabti were scattered on the floor, and papers littered the carpet. At the sight of Alistair, Cassandra's eyes widened in fright, and she struggled futilely against her bonds. "Ali, he has killed them!" she cried. "With some sort of liquid that he forced them to inhale!"

Alistair knew that the effects of the ether would only be temporary, but he had little time to explain. Before he could reach Cassandra's chair to untie her, Pierre Duvallier, wide-eyed and ashen-faced, roared out of the rear bedchamber and into the small sitting room. Alistair moved away from Cassandra's chair, drawing the desperate-looking criminal's attention toward him.

"You fool!" cackled Pierre, brandishing the bronze dagger he'd stolen from Lord Tifton. "Now I shall have to kill you!"

"Better swordsmen than you have not dared challenge me," said Alistair smoothly, his hands held warily at his sides, his feet gliding soundlessly across the carpet.

"But you are unarmed, my lordship," Pierre sneered. "Your skill with blades will do you no good." The thin man lunged. Alistair reared back, and the glinting weapon made a wide arc that missed his nose by three feet.

Beads of sweat popped out along Pierre's upper lip. His movements were jerky, his laughter cracking with false bravado. "You will not escape me, Lord Catledge," he threatened, retreating toward the door that led from the sitting room to the bedchamber.

Out of the corner of his eye Alistair saw Cassandra struggling against the ropes that held her captive.

"What on earth were you looking for?" he asked Pierre, making a sweeping gesture at the antique detritus that

covered the floor. He noticed that his gesture was followed by Pierre's gaze. A fatal mistake, he thought.

"For the mummy, of course," out Pierre spat, blinking perspiration from his eyes. "Unfortunately, I have not been able to persuade the foolish woman to tell me where it is! It is not in this apartment, of that I am sure. I was just about to apply a bit of pressure to Miss Russell, if you know what I mean. Loosen her resolve with a bit of rough treatment. But now that you are here, perhaps you would like to tell me where you've hidden my papa's mummy."

"I think not," replied Alistair. In lightning-quick moves he advanced, his leg whipping out, his boot striking Pierre's hand. The clang of the dagger hitting the floor resounded through the room.

Cassandra gasped. "Oh, Ali—"

But Alistair had Pierre by the lapels of his natty coat. Lifting the man in the air, he roughly pinned him against a wall and leaned into him. The two men were nose to nose, and Alistair could feel the man's shallow pants against his skin. "What do you mean, your *papa's* mummy," the viscount seethed.

Fear constricted the Frenchman's pupils to the size of pinpricks. Stammering, he said, "Those mummies belonged to my papa! He found them in that vault in the Valley of the Kings . . . before your brother or Sir Anthony Russell ever stumbled across them! It was Papa who was the great excavator, not that arrogant Italian. Papa was at Kurneh years before Belzoni got there! And he hid his possessions there, along with other things."

"What things!"

"Treasure! Money! Egyptian artifacts he'd collected himself during his travels!"

"Ha!" Alistair tightened his grip on Pierre's coat and slid him farther up the wall so that the man's pointy-toed boots dangled helplessly. "What makes you think I believe that fantastic story?" he hissed, his heart pounding with

outrage. He would have liked to bang the crookster's head against the wall until his beady eyes popped out.

"Don't! You are hurting me!" Pierre whined.

Alistair's voice was as rough-edged as a metal file. "The royal mummies were found by my brother, Neville Gordon, after the British defeated Napoleon's army. In addition, Neville saved a huge cache of antiquities when Baron Denon, Napoleon's trusted man in Egypt, threatened to destroy them rather than turn them over to the British! The mummies and the treasures belong to Neville, or to the British Museum if he so chooses, not to your father!"

"Not so!" Pierre protested, his eyes flitting around the room wildly. "Papa found them first, and they were his! Now that he is dead, they belong to Suzette and me!"

Alistair snorted with disgust, released his grip on the man's lapels, brought his fist back, and cold-cocked him. Pierre's head lolled to the side, his eyes rolling heavenward until only the whites showed. After flinging his frail body aside, Alistair rushed to Cassandra.

"Oh, Alistair, I was so afraid," she said tremulously. She turned her face up, and he roughly kissed her lips. Then he drew back and studied her expression, watching the tension ease from her face. Relief flooded his body, and his throat clogged with emotion. If anything had happened to that woman . . .

He clasped her shoulders, stared into her wide, trusting eyes, then lowered his head again. This time his kiss was softer, his tongue tracing the outline of her lips, exploring her mouth, mingling with hers. He ran his hands along her shoulders, thrust his fingers in her hair. He whispered, "I love you, Cassandra," against her neck.

"I love you, Ali. And I do want to marry you."

A slow smile widened his mouth.

"Untie me, please," she added dryly, as if amused that he had forgotten that small detail of her present circumstance.

He hurriedly kneeled and reached behind her, his fin-

gers fumbling with the thickly knotted rope that bound her wrists.

Suddenly, Cassandra's body tensed beneath his touch, and she croaked, "Alistair—behind you."

He heard a throaty female voice with a French accent. "Well, well, *bijou.*" His head jerked around, and he saw Suzette standing in the open doorway. "So we meet for one last tryst. Stand up. Step away from the girl." The malice in her sultry voice sent shivers up his spine.

Alistair locked gazes with Cassandra, stood, and faced Suzette. She wore a floor-length forest-green-velvet cloak, hooded, and held a pistol in her slender white hand. Waggling the gun, she motioned Alistair to move farther from Cassandra. He took several long side steps, unsure of the accuracy of Suzette's aim. The last thing he wanted was for her to fire off a shot, miss him, and injure Cassandra.

Stalling for time, Alistair said, "So, you were after Cassandra's mummy the entire time. And to think that I thought you were interested in me." He chuckled.

"You were an entertaining diversion," answered Suzette. "But it was the mummies we were seeking, you see. The one your brother had in his possession, and the one she had in hers. They were Papa's!" Suzette's voice rose in anger. "Before your nasty brother stole them from him." The tip of her gun now pointed at Cassandra. "With her father's help."

Cassandra's eyes flashed, then darkened. "So it was your father who killed mine," she ground out through gritted teeth. Her hands jerked and strained at the ropes that held her. "Your father . . . on that ship . . . with the scimitar . . ."

Suzette's lips curled maliciously. "*Oui*, stupid girl. Papa deserted Puss-in-Boots in 1801, during the long march from Alexandria to Cairo. Many men did. They were dying in the horrid heat, without sufficient food and water. Some of them went crazy, throwing themselves in the Nile and drowning themselves."

"Your papa, however, was not the suicidal type," prompted Alistair. "He deserted Napoleon, and—"

"—joined up with some renegade Mamelukes," Suzette finished. "He had some gold that was taken in Malta."

"Robbed from the Church of St. John, you mean," prodded Alistair.

Predictably, his jibe provoked her, and Suzette swung the gun barrel back toward him. "Napoleon got rich. Why shouldn't his soldiers?" she snapped.

Alistair shrugged. "So your papa used the vault in the Valley of the Kings, and the caves at Kurneh, as storehouses. That is how his shako-plate and locket wound up in the mummy's wrappings."

"*Oui.* He planted them there as a way of staking and identifying his claim. But the greedy grave robbers who came behind him did not pay heed to such a thing."

"Then what happened, Suzette? Did he get lost, forget how to get back to his depositories?"

The Frenchwoman's color heightened, and her grip tightened on the pistol's handle. "Papa was ill."

"He was a murdering fool!" hissed Cassandra, and Suzette's outstretched arm swung again. Alistair's gaze followed the nose of the gun. He stared at Cassandra, then his eyes flicked to Audrey, whose chin rested on her chest. Where was the monkey?

Quickly, Alistair blurted out, "Suzette, what then? Your papa was sick, and when he recovered, he couldn't find the vault or the caves, eh? Understandable," he murmured, staring down the short length of black metal once again. "A windstorm can easily obscure the small winding passages that lead to the tombs. Neville has often described the maze of burial chambers as rabbit warrens."

"After Papa recovered," Suzette said, "he searched and searched. He finally found the burial vault near Thebes, but your brother"—Suzette's eyes cut to Cassandra's— "and her father had already loaded more than half the contents onto their boat!"

"And so your father," breathed Cassandra, her eyes snapping with fury, "dressed as a Turk, rushed onto the boat in a fit of madness and killed mine!" Cassandra's cheekbones jutted and reddened. Her eyes glowed yellow with hatred.

"For the next seven years Papa was so ill he could not work," said Suzette, "and by the time he returned to the Valley of the Kings, he still could not find the tombs where he'd hidden his treasures. In 1817 he joined up with that oafish Italian, Signor Belzoni."

"And then Belzoni reentered the tombs at Kurneh," continued Alistair. "And your papa recognized the mummy case with the *wadjet* eye as the one where he'd hidden his shako plate and locket."

"Yes, and it was at Kurneh that Papa read Belzoni's journals and letters. He discovered the identity of the men who stole his mummies from the tomb at Thebes." She chuckled, as if she were proud of her father's clever deduction. "Your brother confessed all in his letters—quite unwittingly, of course. He described his plunder of the vault near Thebes, detailing every bit of treasure that was stolen, including the pair of royal mummies."

"Neville's letters to Belzoni led you to London," inserted Alistair.

Suzette's eyes took on a glazed, melancholy look. "Poor Papa barely made it home to France before his death. On his deathbed he made Pierre and me promise we would find the royal mummies. It took us many years to save enough money, and during that time Pierre sporadically attended medical school. When the war was finished, we came to London to find the Earl of Hedgeworth. When we learned that Neville was a recluse, I decided to befriend you, Ali. I encouraged you to reconcile with your brother so that I could get closer to him."

"So you have done one good deed, at least," said Alistair.

Suzette jerked her head toward Cassandra, who, Alistair noted, had become amazingly calm. "Once Neville's

mummy went missing, you led us straight to Miss Russell here. So predictable of you, *bijou,*" added the French-woman huskily. "So gallant!"

Alistair ran his fingers through his hair and snorted derisively. Though his movements were casual, his muscles were taut, his senses alert. A quick look at Pierre assured him that the man was out cold and would remain so for some time. "Well, here we are, Suzette. As you can see, your brother has already searched Cassandra's apartment, and the mummy is not here."

Suzette's lips narrowed in irritation as she glanced at her brother, crumpled on the floor. "Where is it?" she demanded. "Where is the queen mummy?"

"Where is Neville's mummy?" Alistair retorted.

"Safely hidden. I thank you for the use of your carriage, by the way. It was useful in transporting our treasures to a safe hiding place." She raised her hand and pointed the gun toward Alistair's head. "Listen to me, girl," she said to Cassandra. "You had better tell me where the mummy is hidden. Or else I shall shoot your future husband, here. And you do so want to be a viscountess, don't you?"

Cassandra stared daggers at the Frenchwoman. Suzette smiled sweetly in return and said, "Tell me, stupid girl!"

Alistair, who stood at right angles to Cassandra's chair, could see tiny brown fingers working at the knots at her wrist. He cleared his throat, drawing Suzette's attention. "Don't shoot," he suggested, his casual tone drawing a confused scowl from her. "Cassandra and I shall be happy to tell you where the mummy is, shall we not, dear?"

Cassandra's expression eased. Behind her back she stretched her fingers, clenched her fists, and rubbed her wrist. A tiny smile curved her lips. "It isn't worth dying over," she agreed.

"Now you are talking like sensible adults," cooed Suzette.

There was a quick flash of gray-brown fur from beneath the round table. A streak of movement—an orange ker-

chief, a coiled tail, four dark hand-shaped paws—shot across the carpet. Tia scampered from Cassandra's chair to the hem of Suzette's long green cloak in the blink of an eye. Suzette gasped. Tia hopped into the air, grabbed the Frenchwoman's wrist, and sank her teeth into soft white flesh. "Ouw! You horrid *marmot!*"

A shot rang out, and a painting on the wall behind Cassandra's head crashed to the floor. Cassandra sprang from her chair and lunged toward Suzette. Alistair leapt between the two women and snatched the gun from Suzette's hand. The Frenchwoman let out a catlike growl and jumped onto his back, her fingers pressing into his eye sockets, blinding him. White-hot pain shot through his body, and he doubled over. The woman clung to him, gouging his eyes, shrieking unintelligible French oaths.

There was a dull thud. Alistair felt Suzette slide from his body. Stunned, he blinked, and black spots danced before his eyes. He felt Cassandra's arms wrapped about his neck and heard her quivering voice. "Are you all right?"

"Yes, yes," he said, his vision slowly returning to normal. He turned his head, and saw Suzette sprawled on the floor, her black coiffure surrounded by a halo of broken pottery. "I hope that was not a rare antiquity you broke over her head." He stared down into Cassandra's limpid eyes and grinned.

"It was a very fine piece, Ali," she said, choking back her emotion. "But you are worth it. You saved my life."

"And you saved mine, Cassandra. In more ways than one." He drew her close to him and kissed her. "Will you marry me now? Will you consent to becoming Viscountess Catledge?"

"Oh, yes," she whispered, her eyes closing as he sprinkled kisses on her cheeks and nose and forehead. He would have liked to kiss every inch of her body, and he fully intended to at his earliest opportunity. "Yes, Ali," she said. "I love you so much."

Epilogue

May 1821, The Egyptian Galleries, Piccadilly

Giovanni Belzoni's white robes swirled about his long legs as he strode confidently from a cavernous room, a wondrous replica of the interior of the tomb of Seti I. He entered a smaller alcove containing only two mummy cases, both of them raised on platforms, their lids removed and propped against a wall.

The towering Italian herded the little crowd of people around the two mummies. The ceiling and walls of the small room were painted dark blue, and were studded with tiny white stars. Egyptian figures and indecipherable hieroglyphs decorated plaster columns, proclaiming as yet some unknown, ancient story. A hushed and reverent silence descended. Gaslight flickered in golden wall sconces, reflecting off the mummies' gilded masks.

"And these," Belzoni said in a booming voice, "are two royal mummies, husband and wife. They were buried together, thousands of years ago. You all know the story

of their temporary separation. Thank God," he said, his voice breaking, "they have been reunited."

Cassandra, Lady Catledge, gasped as she leaned over the edge of the gilded coffin. Cleo's jeweled eyes sparkled back at her, as if to express a profound, eternal contentment.

"Ooh, milady, don't she look 'appy?" gushed Audrey. "'Tis better that she's 'ere, with 'er mate. Know what I mean?"

Alistair linked his arm in his wife's. "Thank heavens Suzette and Pierre confessed where Neville's mummy was hidden *before* they were transported to Australia," he whispered to Cassandra. "Ironic, is it not? The warehouse they rented was not far from the one where Signor Belzoni stashed Cleo for safekeeping."

Cassandra smiled. She glanced at Lord Tifton and saw a tear stream down his deeply creased face. He caught her eye, smiled sheepishly, and said, "I suppose my sentimentality is missish, but I am an old man, and thus you are constrained to forgive me. I cannot help but think how happy I was to have my antiquities restored to me."

Then she turned her attention back to Signor Belzoni.

"Their love for each other was so strong that they intended to spend eternity together," he intoned theatrically.

"Umph," grumbled Lord Hedgeworth. He turned his good eye on Cassandra, and she thought it rather liquid and red-rimmed. "I should think they should tire of each other before another millennium is past."

"Oh, I do not think they shall," murmured Cassandra, snuggling against her husband's shoulder. She felt the movement of something in her belly, and closed her eyes in immense and unutterable gladness.

"Are you all right?" asked Alistair softly, wrapping his arm around her shoulder. Cassandra nodded. She was more than all right. She was happier than she had ever been.

She felt someone staring at her, and met Signor Belzoni's

dark, glittering gaze. "These two royal lovers were meant to be together," he was saying softly, his deep, dramatic baritone thick with emotion. Cassandra heard a collective sigh and noticed that Audrey's face was wet with tears. The sniffling maid leaned heavily against Neville Gordon's Merlin chair. Cassandra held her breath with amazement as the craggy-faced earl wound his fingers around the maid's pinkened, chafed ones. She nudged Alistair's side with her elbow, and his gaze followed hers.

Signor Belzoni said, "It took two lovers to reunite this pharaoh and his queen. Ah, the power of love . . . it is very strong, my friends. *Molto forte!*"

Alistair hugged his wife closer to his body. If the baby was a boy, he wanted to name him Neville. If it was a girl . . . was Cleo too terribly odd?

AUTHOR'S NOTE

The celebrity of Giovanni Battista Belzoni (1778–1823) has been overshadowed by his successors, many of whom relied on his memoirs and notes for guidance. During the Regency period, Belzoni was a famous world-traveller whose exploits fascinated the public. Born in Padua, he spent his early years touring Europe as a circus performer. In 1803, he appeared at Sadler's Wells Theater on the same bill with Grimaldi, the famous clown. As The Patagonian Sampson, Belzoni balanced eleven grown men on his shoulders, amazing the audience.

In 1814, Belzoni went to Egypt. Two years later, he and his workers transported the head of the colossal statute of "Young Memnon" from Luxor to London. Memnon's head became one of the first major antiquities in the Egyptian collection of the British Museum, and inspired Percy Bysshe Shelley to write,

> I met a traveller from an antique land,
> Who said—'Two vast and trunkless legs of stone
> Stand in the desert. . . . near them, on the sand,
> Half sunk a shattered visage lies, whose frown,
> And wrinkled lip, and sneer of cold command,
> Tell that its sculptor well those passions read
> Which yet survive, stamped on these lifeless things,
> The hand that mocked them, and the heart that fed,
> And on the pedestal, these words appear:
> My name is Ozymandias, King of Kings,
> Look on my Works, ye Mighty, and despair!
> Nothing beside remains. Round the decay
> Of that colossal Wreck, boundless and bare
> The lone and level sands stretch far away."

In 1820, Belzoni was in London, where the public adored him. A published account of his travels coincided with an

exhibition in Piccadilly of the replica of the tomb of Seti I, which Belzoni discovered. Though by modern archaeologists' standards, Belzoni would be considered a plunderer, his methods were acceptable to contemporary antiquarians. His name can still be found in the British Museum—where he chiseled it in the bases of statutes he discovered. For information relating to Giovanni Battista Belzoni, I relied heavily on Stanley Mayes, *The Great Belzoni* (London, 1959).

Though ether was not widely used as a generic anesthetic until well into Queen Victoria's reign, it was discovered in the late 1700's. An astute medical student in the 1820's would have been familiar with the drug.

Finally, the term *Egypytology* did not come into general usage until the 1830's, but since Giovanni Belzoni is recognized as a pioneer in that field, I have taken the liberty of using it here.

HORROR FROM HAUTALA

SHADES OF NIGHT   (0-8217-5097-6, $4.99)
Stalked by a madman, Lara DeSalvo is unaware that she is most in danger in the one place she thinks she is safe—home.

TWILIGHT TIME   (0-8217-4713-4, $4.99)
Jeff Wagner comes home for his sister's funeral and uncovers long-buried memories of childhood sexual abuse and murder.

DARK SILENCE   (0-8217-3923-9, $5.99)
Dianne Fraser fights for her family—and her sanity—against the evil forces that haunt an abandoned mill.

COLD WHISPER   (0-8217-3464-4, $5.95)
Tully can make Sarah's wishes come true, but Sarah lives in terror because Tully doesn't understand that some wishes aren't meant to come true.

LITTLE BROTHERS   (0-8217-4020-2, $4.50)
Kip saw the "little brothers" kill his mother five years ago. Now they have returned, and this time there will be no escape.

MOONBOG   (0-8217-3356-7, $4.95)
Someone—or some*thing*—is killing the children in the little town of Holland, Maine.

Available wherever paperbacks are sold, or order direct from the Publisher. Send cover price plus 50¢ per copy for mailing and handling to Penguin USA, P.O. Box 999, c/o Dept. 17109, Bergenfield, NJ 07621. Residents of New York and Tennessee must include sales tax. DO NOT SEND CASH.

WILLIAM W. JOHNSTONE
THE ASHES SERIES